"Epic worldbuilding meets layered characters in this not-to-be-missed debut novel. Hopeful and with lots of heart, pick this up if you love an engrossing read. Can't wait for the next one!"

– Marie Bilodeau, bestselling author of the *Heirs of a Broken Land* series

"Well-crafted characters and deep worldbuilding make *Catalyst* a memorable and moving tale of magic, power, and impossible choices."

– Alex Livingston, author of *The Knave of Secrets*

"Brandon Crilly's debut novel, *Catalyst*, introduces a finely detailed world with an innovative magic system and compelling characters. I enjoyed the novel very much."

– Violette Malan, author of the *Dhulyn and Parno* series

"Layered world-building and taut, troubled relationships are the heart of *Catalyst*, but genre-bending fantasy is its soul. This intriguing novel is one part magic, one part post-apocalypse, one part Getting the Band Back Together, and all of Brandon Crilly's creative spark."

– Tracy Townsend, author of *The Nine*

"Pack your bags: you're going on an adventure. *Catalyst* is an exciting journey into a world of marvels. This book stole my heart."

– Aurora winner Kate Heartfield, author of *The Embroidered Book*

Estelle!
Always good to meet
an avid Fantasy reader.
Hope you enjoy!

CATALYST

BRANDON CRILLY

Detroit, Michigan

Catalyst

Cover Illustration by Olajide Ajayi
Map of Aelda by Sienna Tristen
Interior Design by G.C. Bell

Edited by E.D.E. Bell

Published by Atthis Arts, LLC
Detroit, Michigan
atthisarts.com

ISBN 978-1-945009-90-7

Library of Congress Control Number: 2022941322

To my grandparents, Pat and Claude Martin:

For advice, and compassion

For checking up on me, even in my thirties

For buying every magazine and story, asking about every event

For warmth, and care, and above all, love

I'm where I am because of you.

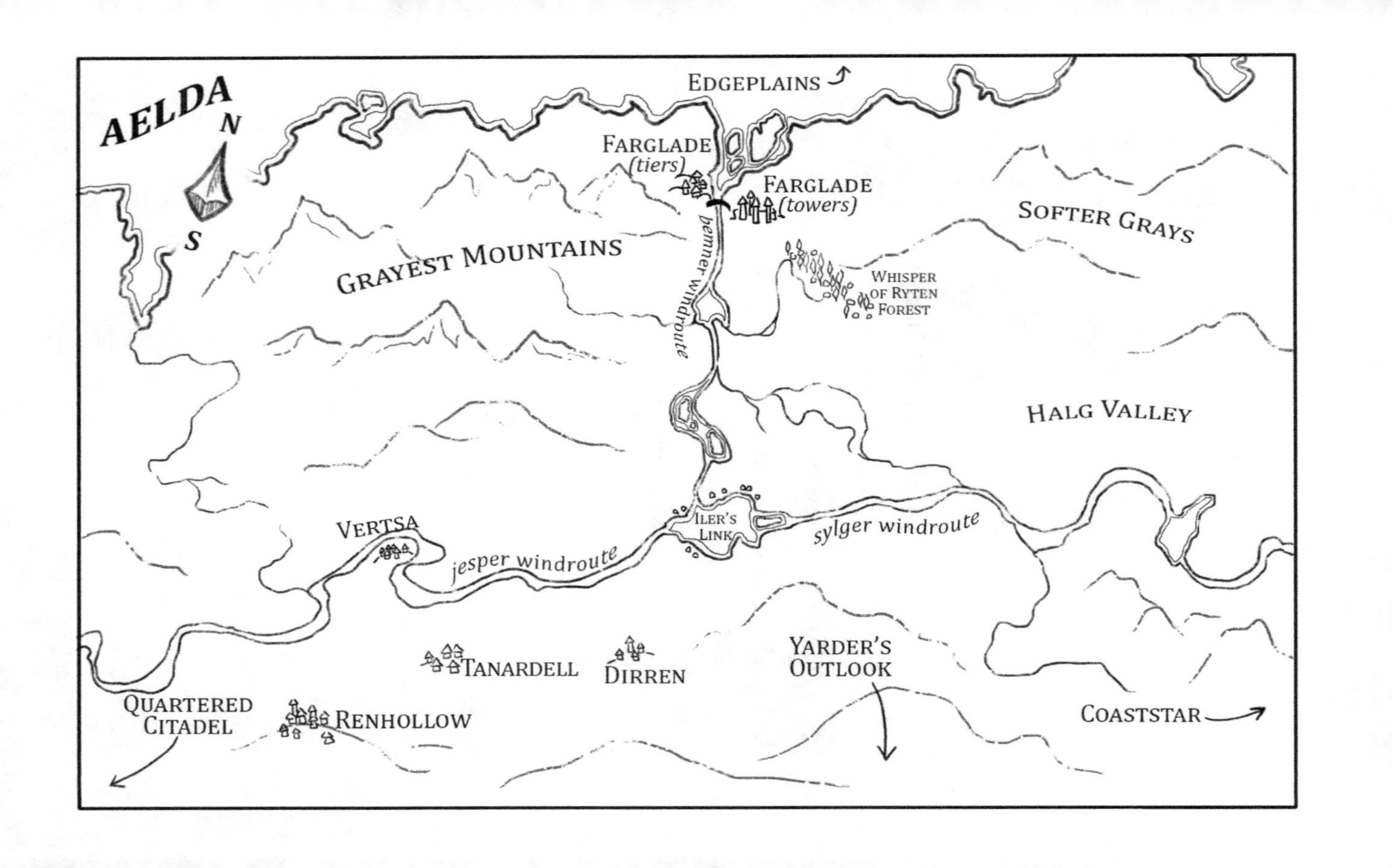
AELDA
N
S
Edgeplains
Farglade
(tiers)
Farglade
(towers)
Softer Grays
Grayest Mountains
bemner windroute
Whisper
of Ryten
Forest
Halg Valley
Vertsa
Iler's
Link
jesper windroute
sylger windroute
Tanardell
Dirren
Yarder's
Outlook
Quartered
Citadel
Renhollow
Coaststar

CATALYST

Chapter One

MAVRIN FELT MORE AND MORE THAT THE ASPECTS didn't smile on magicians.

If they did, he wouldn't have found himself under a battered canvas tent, its patched surface trembling under tonight's heavy Winds. Acting troupes and artisans received enclosures, with actual walls, and windows that could keep out the smells of tanned hide and fermenting berrenfruit. They performed on a stage, instead of a patch of flattened ground set apart from a market square like an afterthought. Magicians never received such treatment.

Or maybe it was simply him.

The audience gathered around his "stage" filled the tent's available space, at least, ignoring the warm breeze and the pungent smells licking under the tent flaps while they watched his first trick, unaware that Mavrin always designed that first one to fail.

When he flourished his violet cloak and snapped his fingers, the patterned bag on the stool didn't so much as fidget. Nor did its hidden wire frame, mimicking the glass orb he'd pretended to slip inside, now stashed in one of his pockets. Murmuring spread through the audience, wondering what was wrong.

The next steps were easy: an exaggerated frown and a lie.

"Apologies. This is a new trick," he said, turning the bag in his hand, pretending to inspect it.

After that, Mavrin would crumple the empty cloth bag and toss it behind him. The children in the front would gasp, the adults would hum in approval, and Mavrin would flash his showman smile before moving on to the real tricks.

"Perhaps I'm coming to the end—"

A heavy tearing sound cut him off as a section of canvas near the entrance ripped free of its clamps. Mavrin's cloak billowed away from his body, almost tugging him across the enclosure. Two audience members hurried to secure the canvas while several others ducked outside, excitedly pointing at the sky.

Mavrin frowned for real. They wouldn't be back.

While the two audience members finished ministering to the canvas, he surveyed his stage. The cloth bag was gone, likely blown under the flaps behind him. Worse, the Winds blew away some of the dirt covering the cable running from the stool to his trunk. Even with the audience's attention broken, there were enough eyes on him that he couldn't fix it, so he needed to hope no one noticed.

Nearby, his garnills fluttered in their cage and pretended they weren't amused. Mavrin waggled his fingers to tsk them.

"Perhaps our Saviors wish to bless this lowly street performer," he said to the audience, faking humility enough to earn some appreciative nods and even one signaled prayer. He would have words with the passing Aspect later. "Right. I require a volunteer. Preferably someone young, or at least small. Who has the courage to join me onstage?"

People glanced at each other, but no one raised a hand. Mavrin's showman smile never wavered, as he imagined larger audiences in proper performing halls. Places with actual walls, to keep the Winds at bay and spare his voice.

"This can't be correct," he said. He pointed vaguely to the west. "Just a week ago, there were dozens of hands in Dirren." Technically correct, if he counted both hands on each audience member. "Do the people of Tanardell lack that same passion?"

For a moment, he worried there wouldn't be a single volunteer.

One more reason to retire, he thought.

A hand shot up to his right, from a child at the edge of the crowd. After the adult behind her nodded permission, she scurried forward.

"Ah, someone willing to assist a poor old man!" Mavrin crouched so they were almost eye-to-eye. "What's your name?"

"Ohanna."

"A pleasure." Mavrin held his hands up, palms out with the first two fingers of each intertwined, combining his pronouns and the universal sign that he didn't worship a specific Aspect. Ohanna enthusiastically did the same, confirming hers with the hand-over-hand sign of the Presence as Passage. She was tiny and willowy, with tawny brown skin and dark hair in a bun that she fiddled with while she faced him, unable to quite bring it under control. "Who is that you're with?"

"My sister. Aulina."

Mavrin looked over the girl's head. "Good evening, Aulina! Thank you for lending your sister. I hope you don't plan on charging a fee."

He winked at the audience, earning some scattered smiles. Aulina dipped her head and tucked her hair behind her ear, a growing smile matching the enthusiasm on her sister's face.

"Ohanna, I'd like to place you on that stool. Would you be all right with that?" When she nodded, he scooped her up gently under the armpits. She was just small enough to fit squarely on the stool, bare toes peeking over the edge. "My dear, your task tonight will be very simple."

As he spoke, Mavrin made a show of wandering the performing area and searching his pockets, passing over the hidden wire twice so he could subtly brush dirt back over it. The top of the enclosure creaked ominously above him as the Winds picked up again outside.

"It should be somewhere . . . aha!" From one of his cloak's inner pockets, he produced a palm-sized crystal, its edges smooth and vaguely teardrop-shaped. "When I traveled the desolate

Edgeplains, I saw many wondrous and awe-inspiring sights. But only one relic of the Time Before Unity crossed my path, and I show it to you now."

Anyone in the audience not paying attention received a hushed whisper or a jab to the ribs, until Mavrin had everyone's focus again. He held the crystal out in his palm, letting their minds do the work better than any scripted dialogue he could provide. People leaned forward to get a better look, to see whether the feeble light from the crackling salt lamps caught the crystal the right way. It wasn't a true Castoff, of course—just a scuffed piece of quartz, several shades lighter and more jagged than a scale from the Aspects—but people were willing to imagine all sorts of things from the Time Before Unity, especially in the hands of a magician.

"This relic, my friends, is unique in all of Aelda. I would be lying if I described its true origins, as I do not know them." He covered the crystal in both hands, not quite like a Requester would with a Castoff, but close. "It's the source of my power, which I share with you tonight. Under the watchful eye of the Aspects," he added, remembering to glance at the tent's ceiling.

He was about to give Ohanna her instructions when he noticed a figure at the back of the crowd, blending in with the darkened canvas. Though a hood masked most of their face, the broad shoulders and the way they clasped their hands over their belt looked familiar.

Mavrin caught himself from stumbling over his hidden wire, and a second later the figure was gone, quick enough that he didn't see anyone ducking out into the market. He put it out of his mind; the last thing this show needed was more distraction.

"When I introduce you properly, Ohanna, I will need you to perform an expert bow to incite the audience into thunderous applause." He glanced at the crowd, so they understood their role. "You know how to bow, of course?"

Ohanna nodded so rapidly she almost fell off the stool.

"Lovely!" He took a breath, letting his scripted lines center him, and called out, "Good people of Tanardell . . . I present to you . . . one of your very own . . . the radiant Ohanna!"

At the exact moment she bowed, Mavrin lifted the crystal in one hand and finally heard the audience gasp as it flickered under the lamps, seeming to generate its own light. At the same time, he tapped the hidden cord with his boot and the compartment on the stool burst open, casting glittering yellow petals into the air. The extra breeze from the Winds made them churn around Ohanna and over the audience's heads, earning more than one astonished cry.

"Thank you!" He crossed back to Ohanna and gently lowered her from the stool. Dropping his voice, he said, "Brilliant. I suppose you'll have quite the story to tell your parents tonight."

The delighted smile on Ohanna's face drooped and she looked at her feet. Mavrin hadn't thought anything of her lack of shoes, but now he noticed the extra stitches on her cotton dress and the discoloration in her cheeks. He glanced at Aulina, spotting premature age lines and dark circles under her eyes.

Mavrin crouched in front of Ohanna. "I'm sorry. Wherever they are, I'm sure they thought your performance was lovely."

"Aulina says the Presence guides them now."

"Of course," Mavrin said, managing to keep any sourness from his voice.

Every second he ignored the audience ticked through his head as he mentally ran through the tools and trinkets stashed in his pockets, determined to win back Ohanna's beaming smile. He would have given her the crystal, if possessing a glass simulacrum of a Castoff wasn't frowned upon in certain circles. His hand settled on his left pants pocket.

"Do you think Aulina would mind if I gave you something?"

Her eyes widened when he showed her the coin. For a moment, he worried she would think it was simply another allotment chit, possibly for something more luxurious than food or water. She'd likely never seen the particular dark blue of dariss before. Mavrin had only ever held three objects made from the crystal, and that was because this coin was part of a set. One always accompanied him when he performed, out of habit, but otherwise they'd never been separated. *And a performance habit doesn't matter if you're retiring, does it?*

"The person who taught me the ways of magic gave me this," Mavrin said, his voice solemn. "For luck. I'd like you to have it."

Mavrin pivoted his shoulder to hide his hands from the audience, not wanting anyone to cause a fuss. Dariss was nothing extraordinary, really, other than it being rare in this part of Aelda. The last thing he wanted was someone pilfering Ohanna because they thought she had something truly valuable. Although maybe the previous owner's good luck would pass to her, even though it skipped him.

To his surprise, she didn't take it right away. "Don't you still need it?"

That question brought the first genuine smile to Mavrin's face that night.

He folded her fingers around the coin. "All I need is the promise you'll take good care of this for me."

Ohanna's eyes lingered on the coin for long enough that he thought she might hand it back to him. Then she shook off whatever had come over her and nodded with the earnestness of a child who understood when to be serious.

Sparse applause led her offstage. Mavrin waited to see the look of shock on Aulina's face before spreading his arms out and facing the audience again.

"Thank you! Now, you may have noticed my feathered friends to the side here . . ."

The rest of the show went as well as Mavrin could have expected. Rope tricks and kaleidoscope projectors were hardly everyday sights, and his not-so-serious attempts at sleight of hand and levitation made the children laugh. After finding and passing around his patterned bag, it jingled with more chits than he expected when he saw the stage he had to work with. Enough for meals, provisions and, depending on the count of luxury tokens in there, possibly a bottle of brandy or cordial. Each was stamped as part of the city of Renhollow's allotment system, which meant they were usable at any town under their authority.

As he towed his trunk and garnill cage down Tanardell's main avenue, the Winds pressed heavily against the back of his cloak and whistled against his ears. Small knots of people clustered in almost every doorway, braving the warmer night air to watch the sky and whisper prayers to each other. A trio of truly brave—or foolish—individuals stood on a flat roof to scream their life stories at the top of their lungs, even though it wasn't the Hidden passing overhead tonight. That Aspect was likely somewhere on the other side of the world, while Their sibling the Catalyst soared above Tanardell.

Mavrin didn't look. He should have double checked the rotational calendar before he booked this performance, even though he had been promised a properly enclosed space. The Aspects passed by at regular intervals, but Their orbit deviated a few kilometers each time; one coasting directly over a community was said to be a blessing, especially when They dipped lower in Aelda's atmosphere. At his age he'd seen every Aspect pass overhead enough times that he could count the spots on the Catalyst's massive underbelly without looking, and he stopped believing in blessings a long time ago.

Between the Catalyst and humanity, the Lifesphere glimmered as always, translucent sheen a constant reminder of how his world depended on the Aspects, and the atmosphere They generated by orbiting Aelda. As long as They kept that intact, Mavrin had no other business with Them.

A large crowd of onlookers stood outside the Wayward Waystop, sharing their liquor allowance in tight metal capsules. A broad-shouldered woman in an engineer's apron held the door open for Mavrin, murmuring, "Success through Salvation," as he passed inside.

Mavrin nodded politely but kept silent.

Like many of Tanardell's buildings, the front staircase led down into a sunken main room, in this case filled with round stone tables and polished stools. Josef, the owner's son, waved at him from a ladder, which he used to secure shutters over the room's narrow windows. He must have started early, since the interior was already toasty from the hearth in the center, its meager smoke curling into the ceiling's pneumatic fan and the vent above. The floral scent of whatever natural oils boiled alongside the hearth's coals soaked the humid air, covering the market stenches Mavrin imagined coating his cloak.

The second-floor hallway was lit only by a candle at each end, so Mavrin collected an averblossom lantern from Josef and descended further underground, carefully balancing his possessions in his hands. His garnill cage bounced against the walls enough times to make the birds tap an angry rhythm with their talons.

"Please, I'm as careful as I can be," he grumbled back. At the end of the hall, he set the lantern down so he could search for the key to his room.

"Quite the performance tonight, my friend."

Mavrin squeaked and jumped, jostling the lantern as he raised his arms in some sort of frantic defense. In its wobbling blue light, Mavrin recognized the broad, hooded figure from his show, and wondered if the ditch his mother predicted as his final resting place was somewhere nearby.

When the figure stepped forward and pushed back the hood,

images of a grisly death stopped flashing through Mavrin's mind—but if anything, he wanted to flee even more.

He almost didn't recognize the wide, ocher face. The wrinkles around the eyes were new but not surprising. The vicious scar on the man's bald scalp was something else, though. It looked like a multi-ended weapon had raked across his skull, but Mavrin couldn't imagine *any* weapon swinging in this person's direction. For all the years they knew each other, Eyasu Temergon had been a non-violent man.

Eyasu bowed at the waist to gently tap a finger against the garnills' cage. They shied away from him, tiny black eyes twinkling in their crimson faces.

"I enjoyed your trick with these little ones. Have you ever done the same with a rabbit?"

His gloves were dark leather, like the ones Mavrin sometimes used, but with rectangular plates sewn into the knuckles and wrist. A heavy cloak covered most of his frame, weighted tassels hanging from the bottom to hold it against the Winds, instead of tied along the front. Mavrin thought he saw armor underneath made of a muted metal he didn't recognize in the dim light.

When he found his voice, he could only come up with, "Rabbits are for amateurs."

Eyasu rumbled a low *hmm* as he straightened. "How have you been, my friend?"

"How have I . . ." Mavrin blinked at him, bemused. After so long—more than ten, but less than twenty years, perhaps—he couldn't imagine being asked a stranger question. "What in the name of the Four are you doing here?"

"I was on the Jesper Windroute near Renhollow and heard your name. Someone from Dirren."

"How convenient for you." Skepticism replaced his confusion. No one whispered his name from town to town anymore. In fact, he doubted anyone ever had.

They stood there in silence, Eyasu still as a granite pillar.

Two heartbeats were all Mavrin could tolerate before he went back to looking for his key. "Well, this was a lovely chat. If you'll excuse me . . ."

"You didn't answer my question."

He hung his head, one hand on the doorframe; that direct manner of speaking was too familiar. "How am I? Older, with less patience for being accosted by strangers on my way to bed. Does that satisfy you?"

Mavrin risked a glance in time to see the light dim in Eyasu's eyes. *That's right, we're strangers now*, he thought, hoping the other man felt it, too.

Except Eyasu stayed in place. "I shouldn't lie to you," he said. "I did hear about you performing, but I came here . . . to speak with you about something specific." He took a breath. "About the Raw."

Mavrin's hand dropped. "You can't be serious." Door and key forgotten, he took a step closer to Eyasu, so he could ignore the sudden cold weight in his diaphragm. "You've materialized out of the sky because of *that*?"

Eyasu straightened a little. "I didn't come here to argue. You need to let me explain . . ."

"I don't *need* to do anything." Mavrin glanced down the corridor and dropped his voice a couple registers. "Please don't tell me you're still trying to prove that theory of yours."

"It was our theory, once."

He shook his head. Eyasu looked different but was still chasing the same demons. "You should've let this go. Let me make something clear: you're wrong about the Time Before. Your beliefs about the Fracture are foolish. And before you ask, I haven't seen anything to convince me otherwise. Thank you and goodnight."

"Age hasn't made you any wiser, then."

"Hidden's fetid breath . . ."

"You shouldn't say things like that."

"I'm sure the Aspects have more important concerns than my language." Mavrin finally found his key and scooped up the lantern. "We're done here. We were done back then, too, but thank you for the reminder of why I was right to leave."

He unlocked the stone dial on his door and opened it wide enough to slide his trunk inside.

"The Raw exist," Eyasu insisted. "I can prove it."

Mavrin schooled his expression as that cold feeling reached into his chest. "We don't need monsters to explain the world. Anything beyond the mundane is the Aspects' doing, whether we like it or not."

He tugged the garnill cage through the door.

Which was when he noticed the two dariss coins floating in the center of his room.

Chapter Two

MAVRIN FELT A HAND ON HIS SHOULDER. "YOU were saying, my friend?"

He brushed the hand off. This was a trick. Someone trying to fool the magician; whoever was responsible had caught him off guard, but it would only take a moment to figure out how.

As he rolled the garnills aside and stepped forward, his eyes never left the coins. He swiped one hand over them, finding no invisible strings. He examined the floorboards beneath them, but none were out of place; no air passed through the cracks from a bellows, which in hindsight would have been difficult two floors underground. It wasn't a trick of the light. The coins weren't rotating or shifting, either, which was odd but not impossible to explain.

Mavrin frowned, running out of ideas. Dariss wasn't magnetic. He might have suspected something involving clockwork except he didn't hear any clicking. Electricity wasn't his area of expertise, but he wondered if some new Renhollow device could use electric current to make something float. There was a more wondrous explanation, too, but he couldn't imagine *that* being used here.

"Mavrin . . ."

"It's a trick," he said, and reached for the nearest coin.

Eyasu grabbed his wrist, holding it in place. "Where did these coins come from?" he asked calmly.

Mavrin cleared his throat and looked pointedly at his wrist. Eyasu considered for a moment and released him. "After I left . . ." Suddenly relating what happened after they parted ways felt strange. "I met a performer, shortly after I decided to pursue magic. He gave me his lucky coins. Said he was retiring."

Eyasu made a thoughtful noise and murmured, "A long time to remain dormant . . . I always worried about one of them finding you, but I didn't expect this." Eyasu looked sidelong at Mavrin, a ghost of a smile returning to his face. "Luckily for you, I can tell you're even more surprised than I am."

"Obviously. Give me time with this and—"

"Are you really so blind that you can't see the most obvious evidence?" Eyasu stopped circling. "You remember what the texts said about dariss?"

"They were exaggerations." Mavrin licked his lips, finding his mouth drier than after his show. "Storybook nonsense fueled by ignorance."

"You only think that because you decided to ignore them."

Mavrin felt his hackles rise, even though he couldn't remember when he stopped thinking about their research. It had been misguided at best, heretical at worst, like the Highest Voices made clear when he was hauled before them. If even half of what he and Eyasu read had been true, what remained of their world would be one more hunk of rock floating through the cosmos. The Aspects would never have saved a species that split open their planet's core.

But Eyasu should have known that.

His former friend stepped into the corridor, returning with a rucksack. Eyasu rummaged through it until he found a rectangular wooden box, about the length of his hand, unremarkable except for the fact that he had it at all. He removed the lid and held the box under the coins, raising it upward centimeters at a time to slowly capture them.

The moment he snapped the lid down, Mavrin heard the clink as they settled into place. "Can you make them disappear for real? I could show you how."

"You shouldn't make light of things you don't understand."

"There you are, pointing out where I've gone wrong." Mavrin dropped onto the edge of the bed, losing the will to argue. Maybe Eyasu would leave now that he had what he thought he needed.

Eyasu held the box away from his face, as though he expected the coins to leap out at him. He placed it gingerly on the low stone block that served as a bedside table. "My fear is a Raw is trapped inside these coins. Wood disrupts their abilities."

Mavrin rubbed at his temple. "I suppose it's perfectly reasonable that you've seen Raw since I left."

"Correct."

Mavrin looked up sharply. "I was being facetious."

Eyasu blinked at him. "I wasn't."

That calm certainty in Eyasu's voice was somehow maddening and disconcerting at the same time.

"Fine. Pretend for a moment I'm willing to go along with this ridiculousness. Are those coins dangerous? Or has this crisis been averted and I can go to bed?"

"The crisis is never-ending," Eyasu said softly. "The important thing is determining what triggered this reaction from your coins, after all this time."

"Well, that's a surprisingly rational frame of . . ." Mavrin froze. His stomach flipped again, like garnills mating in his gullet.

"What is it?"

The floorboards seemed much more interesting than Eyasu's face. "Don't jump to any conclusions, but until this evening, my coins were a set of *three*."

The only change on Eyasu's still form was a sudden widening of his eyes. "What did you give to that girl?"

Mavrin wracked his brain trying to remember how many times he was away from his trunk since arriving in Tanardell. One coin was often in his pocket, so he couldn't imagine it being tampered with.

Eyasu's thoughts, as always, went somewhere else. "Do you know where she is now?"

"Of course not." As Eyasu picked up the box and his rucksack and turned to leave, Mavrin demanded, "Where are you going?"

"She's in danger."

"From what? Being frightened by some floating piece of crystal?" He meant it as a jab, wanted Eyasu to hear the dismissal beneath it, before Mavrin stepped between him and the door.

He had forgotten how much Eyasu dwarfed him.

The front of the other man's cloak billowed open, revealing the armor Mavrin noticed before. It wasn't metal after all, but a chest plate crafted from thick, reddish-brown wood, polished with a lacquer that accentuated the original grain. Matching greaves covered his thighs below a simple leather belt, and Mavrin suspected the same material covered Eyasu's shoulders and arms. The rectangular plates on the gloves were wood, too. He couldn't even imagine the cost of such armor, or how to find a craftsperson with a great enough death wish to use that much lumber for such a ridiculous project.

Sixteen years, he realized. That was how long it had been since they saw each other.

"By the Four, you did go mad," Mavrin breathed.

For a moment, something dark flashed across Eyasu's face. "You know nothing of madness. If you did, you wouldn't sling that word so casually."

He placed a hand on Mavrin's shoulder and steered him gently away from the door.

"Dariss is a natural conduit, as the texts claimed," he said, more calmly. Before Mavrin could protest, he added, "If you think I'm wrong, come along to make sure I don't cause trouble."

Mavrin listened to the sound of booted feet clomping away.

Knowing my luck, he's going to terrorize those poor sisters for something that doesn't exist.

One of his garnills hopped onto the highest rung of their cage with a loud hoot. Her dark eyes fixed on him, as though she knew exactly whose fault that catastrophe would be.

"Damn," he muttered, and stepped out into the corridor, slamming the door behind him.

Eyasu waited at the bottom of the stairs, arms crossed.

"If it helps, I hope I'm mistaken," he said. "But if not, anyone near that coin is likely dead."

Chapter Three

THE CATALYST WAS A DISTANT SPECK ON THE HORI-zon when Mavrin and Eyasu left the Waystop, with the Winds dying down to their usual soft pressure. Most of Tanardell's residents were indoors now; the warmer air drawn from the southern Edgeplains diminished quickly this far north. Even so, Mavrin spent their entire walk nervous about crossing paths with the local lawkeepers, now that he had seen Eyasu's unusual armor.

Like most communities founded in the three centuries since the Fracture and Salvation, Tanardell's squat buildings clustered together to take up as little land as possible, with a stone barrier facing west to deflect some of the Winds. The young person on watch at the wall's gap paid more attention to Mavrin's cloak, waistcoat and high-collared shirt than Eyasu's hood-shrouded form. Mavrin resisted the urge to bow. They went back to scanning the Lifesphere for stars while they leaned on their longstaff.

Heading west forced him and Eyasu to walk directly into the Winds. Mavrin hugged his cloak tighter around his body, thankful for its extra lining. His goggles dimmed the light from the aver-blossom lantern, but not enough that he worried about stumbling or accidentally wandering off into one of the windtowers outside the walls. While they walked, his mind hummed with questions: about Eyasu's wooden armor, dariss and its special properties, and how he could possibly prove anything they studied back in Veristenok. Those questions stayed unspoken, and he couldn't blame not wanting to shout over the Winds.

Past Tanardell's windtowers, they turned down a narrow

path that sloped upward into hillier terrain. Josef had given them directions, thinking Mavrin wanted to return something Ohanna dropped on stage; he said she and Aulina lived in a small growing dome, inherited after their parents passed. Agricultural land like that was carefully monitored by the local magistrate; Aulina must have proven she could manage her inheritance without assistance.

Most growing domes were nestled between cliffs or in low valleys to provide additional cover, but Aulina's sat on top of a hill, where the Winds were more intense. As he tugged his cloak up over his neck, Mavrin stared at the meters-wide gap deliberately built into the thick, iron dome, which curved upward dozens of meters to enclose the orchard inside. Growing domes were supposed to shelter crops from the Winds, but that gap let them flow through unimpeded, with no sign of a gate. A stone sign sat to one side, smudged paint displaying a blob that almost looked like a bright purple berrenfruit.

Eyasu paused in the gap, one hand pushing his cloak away from the scabbard on his belt. Over his shoulder Mavrin saw a simple brick cabin with the sort of gently sloping roof people installed for aesthetics. Its low windows were dark, so he hoped the two sisters were simply asleep. The dark outlines of several rows of trees stood further back, more than he'd ever seen in the relative open like that.

As the Winds picked up again, Mavrin smelled smoke.

Naturally, Eyasu stepped forward instead of running the other way.

Under the Lifesphere's dim midnight glow, Mavrin could make out several missing shingles on the cabin roof and flaking cracks in the brickwork. He imagined Aulina and Ohanna were focused more on maintaining the orchard, and maybe feeding the takka that pulled the small wooden cart near the entrance, if they still had one.

A patch of dirt near the cabin had been scorched and blackened. The burning smell came from a couple half-blackened melli plants; the spiny weed was scattered in patches around the property, like everywhere else in the Moderates.

"Why burn a patch of dirt?" Mavrin wondered.

Eyasu made another thoughtful noise and continued to the cabin. He clambered carefully down the front steps, like he planned to knock on the front door.

When Mavrin was a couple meters away from the burned patch, the world lurched suddenly to the right, then the left. He whirled and saw the brick cabin ablaze, flames shooting from the windows as the heavy reek of ash overwhelmed his nostrils. An eyeblink later, it was half-crumpled under heavy vines and Mavrin could taste soil. Some intact part of his brain willed him backward, and he fell hard onto his backside, the averblossom lantern clattering from his hands. Ten-legged spiders filled the dirt under its blue light, each of their eyes focused squarely on him.

He cried out as a hand grabbed his shoulder. Eyasu crouched beside him, straightening the lamp with his other hand. The cabin stood dark and intact, every imagined danger gone. Mavrin rubbed his arms, feeling tiny legs crisscrossing his flesh.

Channeling. That wondrous thing he dismissed at the Waystop. One more gift from the Aspects, which had apparently been used here. That made as much sense to him as asking whether someone channeled random lucky coins into the air.

Mavrin swallowed bile that tasted like soot and made space for Eyasu to examine the ground. The channeling's lingering effects didn't seem to bother him—unsurprising, since he used to wield that power, back when they were friends.

Something creaked behind the cart. Mavrin struggled to his feet and scooped up the lantern, following Eyasu as he stepped around the back.

Ohanna crouched there, wearing a long, white sleeping gown,

thin hair blowing in the Winds. Her wide eyes looked Eyasu up and down and lit with recognition on Mavrin. To his amazement, she bounded toward him and wrapped her tiny arms around his legs.

She buried her head in his cloak. "Are you here to fix your coin?"

"What do you mean?"

"It didn't protect us," Ohanna sniffed. "The magic is broken. Are you here to fix it?"

"I . . ." He shook off his queasiness. "Of course. I can't very well hand out faulty magic, can I?"

"Where is the coin?" Eyasu asked flatly.

Ohanna shied away from him. "Aulina took it for safekeeping. And then she got angry. She never gets angry. And she broke Father's shed."

Mavrin followed her gaze toward the blackened square of dirt. "Your sister did that?"

When Ohanna nodded, a shiver ran down Mavrin's back. Not an inch of melted stone or brick remained. Only someone with experience channeling could have achieved that precision—a trained Requester, using a true Castoff to ask the Aspects for their aid. But if Aulina could channel, why were she and her sister growing fruit in Tanardell? And why would the Aspects help someone *melt down a shed.*

"They wouldn't," Eyasu murmured, making Mavrin realize he'd verbalized some of his thoughts. If he was slipping back into that old habit between them, this night was truly one of his worst.

Not wanting to dwell on that, he asked Ohanna, "Do you know where your sister went?"

She shook her head, holding back tears.

When Eyasu beckoned at Mavrin, he barely suppressed a grimace. "I need to speak with my . . . colleague. Secret magic discussion. I'll only be a few steps away."

Away from the cart, he lowered his voice. "We need to find Aulina. Something's not right here."

"If only someone told you that sooner." Eyasu didn't so much as look at him. "Can you explain *this* as a trick?"

Mavrin wanted to, desperately. Except the feeling of tiny legs kept creeping up his shoulders, and every rational explanation sounded more unlikely in his head. When he didn't respond, Eyasu snorted and stepped away, to survey their surroundings.

As a distraction, Mavrin fidgeted with his pockets, finding a small coil of rope, some colored handkerchiefs, and a couple mundane copper chips he pulled from behind children's ears. It occurred to him that whoever tampered with his dariss coins might have done something to his other equipment, and he gingerly removed his hands from his pockets.

"Maybe you should look at—"

Eyasu held up a hand. "Find somewhere safe for the girl," he ordered, and stalked toward the orchard.

Mavrin looked around, for shelter and a hiding place, and settled on lifting Ohanna into the cart. He considered crawling in to wait with her, until he caught sight of Eyasu passing between the berrenfruit trees, to whatever he thought was out there. Alone.

"I need you to stay right here. I'll be back once it's safe." He started to pull away, but Ohanna grabbed the sleeve of his cloak. "Everything will be fine."

"How do you know?"

The Winds chose that moment to slide under his collar again. He gently removed her hand and offered his showman smile, hiding his unease. "Because a magician just knows things."

Chapter Four

AT THE EDGE OF THE ORCHARD, EYASU BUNDLED his cloak with its weighted ties and left it at the base of a tree. Violet-flecked berrenfruit filled the branches above, rich in color but without the shriveling that came with leaving them unpicked. Their health likely came in part from the fibrous, mottled tubes connecting the highest branches, giving pollinators a safe route between the trees, unimpeded by the Winds. In time, these trees might grow straight and tall, despite the openness of the growing dome.

Eyasu spared the duration of one footstep to acknowledge this tiny achievement: one more way in which humanity thanked the Aspects, by restoring the natural world that They continued to keep intact.

Three rows in, he spotted movement and slid behind the nearest trunk. Further ahead, side profile visible against the dome's iron wall, was a young woman in a simple cotton gown and no shoes, like she'd been about to go to bed. Aulina's head cocked to one side, brow furrowed in either confusion or concentration as she faced one of the trees.

Aulina raised her hand and the world lurched around him. He braced himself against the disorientation, forcing his eyes to stay locked on the sight of Aulina's hair falling limp against her shoulders, the Winds momentarily blocked by some unseen force. Even though he knew exactly what to look for, he could barely spot the creeping tendrils of energy snaking between Aulina and the tree.

Steam hissed from the bark as the tendrils wrapped around the trunk. With a bright flash that seared Eyasu's vision, the tree collapsed into itself, leaving behind nothing but a scorched patch and the reek of char.

Aulina went back to turning in a slow circle, arms at her sides, her expression serene. The Winds returned to their usual flow, softly rustling the nearby branches.

Something thumped behind him and Eyasu whirled, but it was only Mavrin. He waved at his friend to step lightly. Mavrin grimaced but took the last few steps more delicately, barely making a squelch in the softer soil being fed by the orchard's condensers.

"Did you find her?" he whispered.

Eyasu pointed. As Mavrin peered around their cover, he asked, "How can we tell whether she's—"

Some small animal skittered in the distance and Aulina whipped to her right, hand outstretched. She snarled as a more powerful lurch buffeted Eyasu's senses. He turned away from the channeling this time and clamped a hand onto Mavrin's shoulder to keep him from falling over.

"Hidden's fetid breath!" Mavrin gasped. He blinked a few times and eventually noticed Eyasu's chastising glare. "Please, this isn't the time for -"

His face paled almost to the same color as his hair.

"That isn't possible," he murmured. "They're not real. She must have . . . some sort of alchemical substance . . . maybe her parents experimented . . ."

Before his babbling could get any louder, Eyasu said softly, "Take a deep breath."

Mavrin did, and sixteen years, four months, and twelve days of hoping came to an end, as Eyasu watched the truth settle in his friend's mind.

"Eyasu, what did I just see?"

That was the first time Mavrin used his name that night.

"Aulina is not a Requester," Eyasu said. "She would've been discovered long ago and been invited to Veristenok, yes?" He hated explaining the rest so quickly after so long, but with Aulina still wandering unchecked, he had no choice. "The writings I found suggest the Raw are creatures of energy. They can move through natural conduits. Dariss is the only mineral that functions as one. I believe our bodies can function as another, for the Raw to inhabit."

"For the Raw," Mavrin repeated, and it was unclear whether he believed what he heard or not. "What in the abyss happens now?"

Aulina had wandered past the next row of trees. Each step landed more surely, and her head swiveled back and forth, as the Raw inside became more aware of its surroundings. The dome's curve blanketed most of the orchard in shadow, but she radiated a soft light of her own, like averblossom under a shroud. She stood too straight, as well, as though she didn't need to brace against the Winds.

"If there's any chance of saving her, I need to disable the Raw before it regains its full powers. To do that, I need to get closer. This orchard is too open." He frowned, considering. "I don't want to ask this of you . . ."

Mavrin's eyes went wide. "Then don't? Yes, don't. Whoever's out there can *channel*. Can't you hit her or something?"

Eyasu frowned. That wasn't his plan at all. "With what?"

"Do you have a cabler?"

"No."

"Throwing knives? One of those spheres that spew yoric venom?"

"Where do you see any of those things?" He made a point of gesturing at his absent cloak.

"What kind of terrible warrior doesn't have at least one of those things?" Mavrin demanded, voice rising.

Eyasu held his palm up, barely resisting the urge to shake

Mavrin by the collar. He checked around the tree, but Aulina didn't seem to have heard. By the Aspects' generosity, the Winds' direction worked in their favor, along with the Raw adjusting to a new host. "Seeing one truth must be your limit for the day."

And I'm no warrior.

He fixed Mavrin with a steady stare. "Don't attack. Simply speak. Hold her attention while I get closer, then find cover." Before he could interject, Eyasu added sharply, "Don't pretend that an innocent life doesn't matter to you."

"Damn, unstable, *wobbling* core," Mavrin muttered. "I don't suppose you have something to protect myself with?"

"My bag," Eyasu said. He turned his attention back to Aulina as Mavrin rooted inside.

"Eyasu, these are bits of wood."

"If you'd been listening at the inn . . ."

Mavrin grumbled another curse, dug out what he needed, and darted from their cover.

Meanwhile, Eyasu prayed.

Chapter Five

MAVRIN REACHED A TREE IN THE NEXT ROW unscathed. He fiddled with his pockets, making sure he could easily reach what he took from Eyasu's bag: not one of several squares of wood he apparently carried around, but the box containing the other two coins.

His head pounded, making it difficult to concentrate. An experienced Requester could minimize the side effects of drawing on the Aspects' will, but whatever Aulina was doing felt . . . wild, Mavrin decided, avoiding the first thing that came to mind. The words *study it* broke through the pounding—but that wasn't him anymore. Each step forward came from obligation, not any desire to confirm whether Eyasu had been right all along.

He took a steadying breath and tried to pretend he was a young man again, about to step out for his first major performance. That slowed his heart a little, but it took another few beats before he could force himself out from behind the tree.

"Excuse me! Were you the one who requested an encore?"

When Aulina spun toward him, he almost didn't recognize her. Her tawny skin, darker in complexion than her sister's, was now deathly gray, etched with glistening yellow lines that reminded him of the one time he saw gold. When she leaned forward to examine him, her lips twisted in a way that was at odds with the gracious, loving smile she'd worn as Ohanna approached his stage. Striations of color cut through the whites of her eyes, orange like firelight.

I'm going to die.

Except he'd committed now.

"Do you know the key to a successful show?" He barely kept his voice from wavering. "Give the audience what they want. I'm rather adept at reading people, but I'll admit to being at a loss with you. A joke? Some sleight of hand?"

The strange twist on Aulina's lips grew. It was like she was trying to smile, sneer and grimace all at once, but didn't know how to operate her mouth. For a moment Mavrin thought he saw something transparent and formless moving around her, untouched by the Winds, and hoped it was his eyes playing tricks.

In a harsh, grating voice, she said, "Do not pretend to be unafraid."

"Who's pretending?" He lifted the box in one hand, and Aulina's eyes fixed on it. "This is what you want? Complete the set?"

Aulina extended her hand toward him, and the world tilted sideways before turning black around him. When Mavrin tried to yelp he didn't hear anything. The powerful stench of smoke hit him an instant before the world returned, with the box still in his outstretched hand. A jagged line of burnt ground reached from Aulina to the toes of his boots, but not even a shred of ash touched the leather.

"You hold the rest of me." Besides the grating tone, her voice sounded empty. "We need to be one. Released and open to the world so we may cleanse it."

Mavrin fought the urge to run. "Are you sure you want to do that? My friend . . ." He wasn't supposed to say anything about Eyasu. They had a plan.

"You are destroyers. You must be cleansed."

"That doesn't sound like much of a closing act to me." Mavrin swallowed. "Best to make them disappear."

He twirled his cloak across his body, moving the box behind his back as though to trade it to his other hand, and then spun in a quick circle for good measure. The spin made him dizzier, but he stuck the motion and faced Aulina holding up two empty hands.

"Were you watching carefully?" Mavrin asked. He flashed her a nervous smile. "No?"

Face now expressionless, Aulina raised her hand again.

Eyasu materialized from behind a tree, and as she whirled, he tossed a cloud of powder into her face. She crumpled to the ground, shrieking, and the shapeless form Mavrin glimpsed before thrashed back and forth, as though trying to escape. He staggered away, hands raised against something he had no idea how to protect himself from.

Invisible pressure knocked him onto his back. As he tried to catch his breath, he heard Eyasu shouting, in a language he hadn't heard since their scholarly days: T'var, first used to pray to the Aspects, and later Request assistance from Them.

The world lurched, seeming to pull at Mavrin's skin. He clamped his hands over his ears and squeezed his eyes shut, fighting to hold details in his mind: Eyasu standing over Aulina, Aulina with gold in her veins, he had been holding a box but now he wasn't and he had no idea where it went.

His eyelids flashed with a light brighter than an exploding spark. When it faded, Mavrin opened his eyes expecting the entire world burned to cinders, but instead he saw Eyasu with a closed fist raised toward Aulina. She trembled in place, hissing in rage and pain, as yellow light blazed from between his fingers.

A second light flared across one of Aulina's shoulders and she crumpled to the ground.

The pounding in Mavrin's head faded as he struggled to his feet. He stared at the Castoff in Eyasu's hand, barely believing his eyes, but the mottled surface and gray color were unmistakable. Its light shrunk away, revealing black flecks unique to the Castoff Eyasu had carried before they parted ways.

"Why do you still have that?"

Eyasu ignored him and returned the Castoff to a pouch on his belt. He crouched beside Aulina and turned her carefully onto her back.

Mavrin edged a little closer. "What did you do?"

"Brownblessing ground with reagents." He pointed at the sand-like material still stuck to her face and chest. "Then I asked the Aspects for a holding ward, to cloud the Raw's perceptions and immobilize it."

Mavrin kept his distance while Eyasu carefully and respectfully examined her, looking for the coin. He shook the box hidden in his cloak, confirming the other two still rattled inside. Aulina's face was scrunched tight, chest rising and falling rapidly. The goldish glow remained in her veins, but now they were occasionally criss-crossed with blue that hadn't been there before. That must have been what Eyasu meant by a holding ward. He had spoken to one of the Aspects, probably the Catalyst, and They had Responded to his Request.

"You can still channel."

"Another time," Eyasu said calmly.

There was no immediate sign of the coin; Aulina's hands were open, and there didn't seem to be any pockets on her plain sleeping gown.

Eyasu leaned over her, as if searching for a scent. "Something's wrong."

He shouldn't have sounded so calm, when Mavrin's heart hadn't stopped hammering. "Can you help her?"

"I think I can." Eyasu reached for the longknife on his belt.

Aulina's eyes snapped open, blazing orange.

That same orange light surrounded Eyasu from head to toe, and his entire body went rigid. Mavrin scrambled back, expecting to see Eyasu burned to ashes like that tree, but a moment later whatever energy held him in place melted away. It traveled down the outlines of his wooden armor, lighting up the runes carved into its surface, and as it reached the ground Eyasu stood unharmed, his expression serene and unsurprised.

Aulina raised her hand again, but this time the ground around her burst. A force heavier than a Longwind lifted Mavrin into the air, tossing him into one of the fibrous cables running between the trees. He slipped from it and landed hard on the ground. Eyasu bent over several meters away, trying to catch his breath. Aulina stood with her back to them, attention fixed elsewhere.

Ohanna shivered under the bent trunk of one of her family's trees.

Mavrin tried to yell at her to run but doubled over, the pain from his fall producing a ragged cough.

"Did he fix the coin?" Ohanna asked her sister. And then even softer, "Are you still angry?"

A shudder ran through Aulina's body. Ohanna flinched but didn't run.

When Aulina spoke, the guttural tone was gone, but her voice rasped with soreness. "Can't be angry at you." Her sister stepped forward, but Aulina raised a hand and gasped. "Stay there! Just . . . don't move. Don't move at all."

Breath recaptured, Eyasu looked around wildly. Mavrin realized he'd dropped his Castoff.

"Stay away, stay away," Aulina said breathlessly. She turned in place, not looking at anyone. "I won't mean to do it, but that doesn't mean I won't . . . shield of the Catalyst, strength of the Vital, oh please stay back, just stay back . . ."

Ohanna locked eyes with Mavrin, but he didn't know what to do.

A low moan of pain escaped Aulina's lips. She straightened on the balls of her feet, as though an electric shock coursed through her body. When her body relaxed, an alien voice growled, "Cleanse the child—"

Eyasu leapt forward onto his belly, hands closing around an object.

Aulina spun toward him, snarling as he bellowed in T'var. A bright glow erupted from between his fingers, spawning the same light around Aulina's body. She stiffened. Ohanna screamed.

When Eyasu closed his fist, Aulina crumpled to the ground. He hurried to her side, muttering more words while he tore part of her gown to expose her shoulder.

Mavrin finally willed his body into motion, and the moment he got close Ohanna pressed herself to the side of his leg, weeping. He watched as Eyasu pulled his hand away from Aulina's shoulder, revealing a series of curling characters in T'var's written form, fading from orange to weathered black against her skin, like an old tattoo. Too far away for Mavrin to read and translate. He inched closer, Ohanna practically glued to his side, and saw a dark, circular shape beneath Aulina's skin, in the center of the markings.

"The Aspects granted her protection. She'll be stable for now," Eyasu said when he finished, as though he had been doing nothing more complicated than sewing. "We should return to town. Can you collect my knife, please?"

When he asked a second time, Mavrin shook off his shock and collected it carefully, since Ohanna refused to let go of him. The knife's edge glinted with blue-black crystal, somehow grafted to the common steel blade.

"Dariss." Eyasu scooped Aulina delicately into both arms. "One of our greatest weapons against the darkness, and one of our greatest threats."

Stunned, Mavrin stayed in place. Even with the orchard thrumming from recent channeling and his brain threatening to flee screaming into the darkness, one detail stayed firm: the Castoff tucked into Eyasu's belt pouch. He shouldn't have been carrying that. The last time Mavrin saw that scale, originally shed from the Catalyst, had been when the Highest Voices deemed Eyasu unworthy to carry it.

Somehow, he had it now.

Even stranger, the Aspects saw fit to Respond to his channeling.

Ohanna tugged on his arm, anxious to follow her sister. He let himself be led, too dazed to properly put on a kindly smile for her, even after they left the orchard and the lingering effects of channeling behind. There were too many things wrong tonight, and the coins tucked into his cloak were barely the start.

Chapter Six

EYASU SHIFTED HIS ARMS AGAIN, TRYING TO WORK out another ache. Aulina couldn't have weighed much more than one hundred pounds, but keeping his muscles locked in place for so long wasn't easy, as he paid careful attention to every time she stirred. Occasionally he glanced at the clear sky above, even though the Catalyst had almost completely disappeared into the horizon.

He muttered his thanks anyway.

Ohanna clung to Mavrin the entire way back to Tanardell, falling asleep against his chest sometime before he ran out of calming phrases. Eyasu didn't grow up with siblings in the middling spires of Veristenok, and barely remembered his parents caring for him when he felt scared and alone. Perhaps this was why the Aspects wanted Mavrin with him tonight.

His friend hadn't spoken to him since they left the orchard, even to check if he was unharmed, but Eyasu didn't have the energy to speak first. Mavrin must have had questions. Whether he'd bother to ask them, Eyasu didn't know.

The young person watching the road when they left had been replaced by a tawny-skinned guard with short-cropped curls and the laugh lines of someone Eyasu suspected spent a lot of time with family. They took an instinctive step toward the longstaff propped against the wall beside them, and only waved the hand signal for their pronouns after Mavrin clumsily did with one hand.

"You're the magician," they said to Mavrin. "What happened?"

"An incident at their home," Eyasu said quickly. "Someone attempted to rob them, we believe. We happened to be nearby."

The guard frowned as they stepped closer to examine Aulina. Bandits and robbers were rare in central Aelda, given that the allotment system provided everyone's basic needs. But people were far from perfect, and stories about the Incursions in the north still made heads shake wherever Eyasu went, even though the last one was years ago.

He had wrapped Aulina in sheets, leaving only her face uncovered. The guard spent a long time studying the faint lines visible on her cheeks and forehead. Eyasu shifted Aulina to free one hand and pulled out his Castoff.

The guard's eyes widened. "I'm sorry, Requester. I didn't realize." They stepped back. "Lawkeeper Barris should be in his office by now. I can escort you and summon a healer."

A tiny sound escaped Mavrin's lips, but the guard didn't seem to notice.

"Thank you for your diligence, but we can manage," Eyasu said. "Your post here is important."

He started walking again before they could protest, trusting Mavrin to follow. Only years of practice kept him from glancing back to see if the guard watched them walk away.

This early in the morning, Tanardell's main road was practically empty. Eyasu spotted a line of three shellwagons further up the street, their rounded tops inscribed with the stylized tealeaves and wagon wheels of Renhollow. One had been popped open while laborers loaded sacks of grain and produce onto the back, Tanardell's regular trade to its patron city in exchange for machine parts and other things not manufactured in town. Nearby, a different team examined what looked to be pieces for a new windtower, likely having arrived on the carts. None of them glanced away from their work, but Eyasu steered Mavrin down the first side street they reached.

"You're not a Requester."

Decisive as always, Eyasu thought, and mentally steeled himself. "I beg your pardon?"

Mavrin fixed him with a haggard, bloodshot stare. "I may be a long way from the Quartered Citadel, but I know no one wears armor like that." He flicked his chin at Eyasu's wooden chest plate. "And I know my T'var. Whatever's carved into your armor, it isn't phrases to any Catalyst variation I've seen." Ohanna stirred in his arms, and in a softer voice he added, "You lied to that guard. Or you're lying to yourself."

At the end of the street, Eyasu stopped to check for passersby. "My channeling comes from the Aspects. The Catalyst gives me strength."

"Which variation? Protector? Deathgiver? Who did you choose, after you recovered your Castoff? Something else I'd like an explanation for, by the way."

Eyasu supposed that was the natural and proper question for Mavrin to start with. There were several Aspect-variations of the Catalyst someone might follow, and as far as Mavrin knew, Eyasu was barred from calling on any of them when his Castoff was confiscated. Except figuring out how to finally convince Mavrin about the Raw hadn't left much room to decide how to explain more complicated things.

"Now isn't the time."

Mavrin snorted. "No, of course not. We are in the middle of the street, carrying an injured woman I'm guessing you *don't* intend to bring to the authorities."

"That would be too dangerous," Eyasu said. "The Raw is contained for now, but the coin needs to be removed."

Mavrin swallowed. "It isn't dead?" He stared at Aulina. "This is still madness."

"No, my friend," Eyasu said as he stepped out onto the next street, "this is the world."

They managed to avoid crossing paths with anyone as they made their way to a dead-end road near Tanardell's southern deflection wall. The residence at the end was no different than the others, with its single flat-roofed story and shuttered windows. Two private windtowers twirled to either side, as well as a speed gauge within sight of the front, rings turning slowly in the morning's low Winds. Besides those additions, the only other sign that someone important lived here was the twenty-meter-high stone platform behind the house, braced with iron support posts driven into the ground.

The shallow stone porch was bare except for an old chair covered in takka-skin blankets, supporting a heavyset person in the simple, green tunic of the local Voice. A thin rod of iron held strands of curls into a practical twist over their sleeping face. Bare hands rested against a long sash stitched with diamond patches in varying colors, each sporting a specific phrase in T'var. Eyasu had seen the style before: the sash described the wearer's particular journey of identity, in this case proclaiming the multiple genders she had walked and the pronouns she used now. That sort of proud or celebratory expression wasn't unique to Voices, but was significant as a signal to the community she counseled, that she understood certain paths and experiences.

As Eyasu stopped in front of the porch, the Voice's eyes creaked open and her thick, red eyebrows rose.

"I don't do blessings before eighth hour," she grumbled.

"We would seek the word of the Voice. May we enter and speak with you?"

When he pushed aside enough of the sheets to reveal Aulina's face, the Voice barely reacted. She levered herself out of the chair, grimaced, and beckoned them inside without a word.

"Well," Mavrin muttered, "let's hope this goes smoothly."

The Voice, Jareden Arric, told them to place Aulina on the only bed, in a room no bigger than a closet, and take Ohanna to a sitting area near the entrance that wasn't much larger. It looked to Eyasu like the original residence had been remodeled to make space for a speaking room in the center, where the Voice would receive visitors looking for guidance from the Aspects. The unfurnished speaking room was the most cramped he'd ever seen, but any larger would have made the others around it unusable. Eyasu suspected channeling reworked the interior and wondered why Jareden would choose to remain instead of asking for a new residence when she was appointed.

While they waited for Mavrin to finish settling Ohanna, Jareden led Eyasu to the kitchen, made almost claustrophobic by the large plank table and cupboards lining the walls. The Voice banged around the cupboards, pulling out clay bowls and cups, while Eyasu tried to find somewhere to stand where his armor wouldn't bump the walls. He ran his hands over the old grooves in the table; he'd never seen this much solid wood used in such a way anywhere outside the Quartered Citadel. Jareden lifted the lid from a pot on her convection stove and the smell of spiced amanna joined the bitter tang of dark tea from the carafe beside it. When Eyasu politely shook his head, Jareden grunted and served herself. She finished by pulling a bottle of dark liquor from under the sink and adding some to her mug.

Mavrin stepped inside, and his shoulders drooped further with fatigue. "Please, tell me you're sharing that."

Jareden slid the bottle across the table hard enough to make Mavrin scramble to catch it. While he busied himself with that and the tea, she leaned both fists on the other end of the table and fixed Eyasu with a heavy look. "All right. Make it good."

Eyasu took a deep breath before he began.

"Aulina is inhabited by a Raw."

Mavrin choked on his first sip. "Saviors' tails, don't you know to build up to something like that?"

Under two disapproving glares, he fell silent.

Jareden dropped onto a stool. "Raw don't exist," she said matter-of-factly.

Eyasu felt his chest constrict. "With respect, they do."

"You're really going to tell me these young women were attacked by a metaphor?" Jareden pointed with her spoon, flicking bits of amanna onto the table. "I'm used to people feeding me nonsense before crying their needs to the Aspects, but at least they offer me *believable* nonsense."

"Please," Eyasu said carefully. "Let me explain."

He fully expected the Voice to kick them both out and summon the lawkeepers. Instead, Jareden kept examining him.

"I recognize some of that." Jareden pointed at Eyasu's wooden chest plate. "Those prayers aren't from any direct translation I've read."

"You wouldn't have read them," Eyasu admitted. He had considered hiding them under his cloak, especially after Mavrin's comments. But he needed to be honest and forthright here, if he was going to make any progress. "They belong to the Catalyst as Core."

Mavrin's mug thumped to the table in shock.

Jareden barked a sharp laugh. "A heretic, then? Maybe getting up early wasn't such a bad idea." Her eyes twinkled. "Go on, then. I think I'm awake enough for this one."

Eyasu ignored Mavrin's white-knuckled grip on the table and started recounting what happened, beginning with their meeting at the Waystop. Jareden made the occasional grunt that didn't say whether she believed the story or not. Eyasu tried not to feel optimistic; the fact that her first reaction was to laugh didn't bode well for listening, but not being thrown out on the spot certainly did.

". . . attempt to remove the coin failed, we subdued her. The Raw, I believe, is still inhabiting Aulina's mind and body."

"Is it now?" Jareden's tone was almost disinterested as she

refilled her cup with more whiskey than tea. "Why do that? Why not flee?"

"I believe they can't exist outside dariss without a human host." Eyasu glanced back at the speaking room, wishing he had his rucksack. "I'd be happy to show you my research—"

"Oh, I don't think we need to bother with that yet."

She said it so matter-of-factly that Eyasu almost inched toward the doorway—he'd stayed at this end of the table on purpose, in case this conversation went far worse than expected. No guards burst through her front entrance, though, and Jareden's expression didn't change from its careful neutrality as she added, "Let's see to Aulina."

Eyasu tried to ignore the different depictions of the Aspects studying him from the walls, ceiling, and floor as they re-entered the speaking room. Each of them approved Aspect-variations, unlike his own. Even the four interconnected loops of the Aspects Joined made him momentarily queasy.

Jareden's bedroom stood next to the kitchen; two people could barely fit beside the mattress, so Eyasu let the Voice enter alone, watching what he could through the open door.

Her sardonic smile disappeared as she studied Aulina and the soft gold crisscrossing her veins. She seemed to forget about her mug, almost dribbling its contents onto her sash as she leaned forward. Her other hand delicately pushed aside Aulina's collar to reveal the coin beneath her skin and circled a finger around the tattoo. "What's this?"

"How I contained the Raw," Eyasu said, choosing his words carefully. He hadn't mentioned channeling yet, not sure how Jareden would react. "A binding Request, with the Catalyst's blessing."

The Voice's eyes narrowed.

You can convince her. Hurry, he thought. "The less official accounts of the Unity's collapse," Eyasu added, "say that the Raw weren't like us. Creatures of energy, instead of matter. They could move as energy itself, through our world's natural conduits. Heat and light, for example. Or, in theory, the human brain."

Jareden backed out of the bedroom. A tiny bead of sweat lingered under her red hair.

"If I'm to come anywhere close to believing you," she said, "you're telling me you brought whatever this is *into my home?*"

"The Aspects allowed me to protect—"

Jareden glared past Eyasu's shoulder at Mavrin, behind them in the speaking room. "Is he the mastermind of this nonsense, or the other way around?"

Eyasu turned to see Mavrin staring back, mouth open slightly.

"Well?" Jareden demanded, even louder. "Maybe you designed the 'ward' for your friend, eh? Speak up!"

"No," Mavrin managed. "I'm just a . . . I'm as caught up in this as you. I can't offer you anything more than what Eyasu said."

"Then why *are* you here, exactly?"

It took every ounce of willpower for Eyasu not to openly plead for Mavrin to describe what he saw. What he now knew to be true.

But all Mavrin said was, "I can't explain anything here. My involvement is . . . simply a case of unfortunate circumstance."

A familiar, cold feeling settled over Eyasu. *And you refuse to stand with me again.*

Jareden straightened, eyes alight. "So. We've got a sick young woman and a wild story from a heretic. One who openly admits that he channels." She took a step closer. "Tell me. Did you steal your Castoff, or kill someone for it?"

It isn't theft if the item rightly belongs to you. Eyasu had repeated that over and over before recovering his Castoff, but it took a long time after to fully believe it.

"It's mine, as judged by the Aspects Themselves." Despite his hammering heart, he kept his voice steady. "Would they grant my Requests otherwise?"

Jareden grunted again. "You're lucky I'm as good a judge of character as They are. We'll see what I decide about everything else. Move."

Eyasu stepped back further as Jareden stomped past, crossing the speaking room to the house's tiny entrance chamber.

Eyasu whirled toward Mavrin. "We could've convinced her."

"I wouldn't have helped." Mavrin laid his head against the wall with a soft thump.

"Because you still don't believe." Eyasu meant it as a question, but the doubt churning in his gut told him he knew the answer.

Except to his surprise, Mavrin said, "Believing doesn't mean understanding." His brow furrowed. "Why would you tell her everything? About your Castoff?"

"Sometimes the truth matters." Eyasu glanced at Aulina, shifting fitfully as she slept. "I finally have enough evidence to prove we were right."

"Lovely. You can deal with the panic on your own, then."

As he turned away, that churning doubt deadened into a familiar cold acceptance, and Eyasu murmured, "You haven't changed."

If Mavrin heard him, he didn't stop to comment.

Chapter Seven

MAVRIN JUMPS AT THE SLAMMING SOUND OF EYASU'S *palms against the table. Until he saw his friend swing a sword at a young woman's back, he never would've thought Eyasu capable of violence.*

Eyasu's features shift: first wrinkles around the eyes and that three-pronged scar, then the tired but healthy face of a younger man. A large plank table in a Voice's kitchen becomes polished stone carved to resemble five curling appendages, most of the tables empty in a tavern whose name no one could pronounce.

Sun shines through the carefully placed skylights, in the early morning when they only have Calira for company. Except she doesn't weave between the tables today, and later Mavrin wonders if the Presence as Passage conveniently walked her somewhere else.

"I don't understand." Eyasu's voice shakes. "After the work we've done . . . you were the one to discover the first references, Mavrin. What they say . . ."

"None of what's written there could've happened."

"That's not what you said yesterday."

Unlike his friend, Mavrin's voice is hard. "Well, I was wrong yesterday."

The silence seems longer this time. Every second that passes, Mavrin tries to imagine somewhere else to be. It isn't worth using one of those seconds to say something else or go back to the Highest Voices' chambers and refuse to accept their orders. Even a Requester can't change history.

"Have you spoken to Deyeri?"

"Yes," Mavrin says.

"And?"

Eyasu is bringing her up in the hopes she'd change his mind, but he doesn't know she already failed. Or did Mavrin fail her? "That's between us."

"Please, tell me what's going on. I need to understand so I can help you."

Mavrin wishes he could take back what he said next. But it already happened, so there's no way to stop it.

"I don't want your help. And you aren't getting mine anymore."

It took a few gasps for Mavrin to recognize the cramped sitting room he woke up in. He had collapsed onto one of the weathered sofas after Jareden left, and now he regretted spreading his violet cloak over his body, instead of bunching it up to use as a pillow.

". . . and she taught you about the Catalyst?"

Eyasu crouched on one knee in front of the other sofa, clad in travel-worn gray linen. Ohanna sat swaddled in the blankets Mavrin found for her earlier, her hands enveloped in Eyasu's.

"It's the essence of all things."

Eyasu nodded. "That's what it represents, yes. What is the Catalyst's role in the Protector variation?"

"Shields us from harm," Ohanna recited.

"Catalyst as Lifegiver?"

A moment passed. "The ability to heal?"

"For Requesters, yes. And Deathgiver?"

Ohanna pursed her lips tightly, but ultimately shook her head.

"That one is somewhat esoteric, don't worry." Eyasu chuckled, as though the girl was likely to know what 'esoteric' meant. "Would you like to know what the Catalyst as Core represents?"

When Ohanna nodded eagerly, Eyasu said, "It doesn't only allow us to channel. It connects us all, and channeling thrives because of it. Like magic. When we're gone, a part of us continues as part of it."

"My parents are magic now?"

Eyasu smiled. "Yes. The best kind, perhaps."

Ohanna looked over Eyasu's shoulder and her features brightened. Mavrin offered her a tired wave, which he dropped the moment Eyasu glanced at him.

"So that's what you believe in now?" Mavrin asked, his voice croaky and dry. He usually left a glass of water at his bedside when he slept.

Eyasu got to his feet and passed through the interior door, stopping where he'd left his sword and armor. Mavrin offered Ohanna a smile and followed him out, only to find him waiting in the center of the speaking room, expression cold. "Don't pretend like you actually care."

"How could I not?" Mavrin hissed. "It's heresy, Eyasu. When the Highest Voices find out . . ." Something in how Eyasu's eyes flicked away made him pause. "By the Four. They already know, don't they?"

"I refuse to hide my beliefs."

"Isn't that obvious." Mavrin prodded Eyasu's wooden chest plate with his toe, hard enough to make Eyasu flinch. "This doesn't make any sense. Did you steal your Castoff back? How are you not scoured under the Quartered Citadel?"

"I suspect the Highest Voices gave up on hunting me."

"Well, I'm sure they won't hear about this," Mavrin muttered. He looked around. "Where's Jareden?"

"She returned from the orchard while you slept. Now she's speaking with the lawkeepers."

"She's *what*?"

The hint of a smile returned to Eyasu's face; he almost looked smug. "Jareden is appealing on our behalf."

"She's accepted this madness now?" When all that earned was a sour look, Mavrin sighed. "Great, both of you can get banished to the Edgeplains. Don't think I haven't noticed you not answering my questions, either."

"If you're so worried about my past now," Eyasu said, dispassionate again, "feel free to insist the lawkeepers detain me when they arrive."

A few responses occurred to Mavrin, but they tangled in his mind, caught up in the lingering memory of his dream. He settled on snorting and walking to the other side of the room, only to wish that he had more than a few steps to separate them while he stared at the wall. A depiction of Aelda hung at eye level, their broken planet rendered in oil on canvas next to woodboards of the Aspects. No one knew exactly what was left of Aelda beyond the Edgeplains, but most artists depicted it as this one had—like a berrenfruit eaten almost to the core, except with the bottom ending in a jagged, narrow point. The Lifesphere surrounded it in typical violets and blues, encircled by the orbiting forms of the three surviving Aspects, Their scaled bodies and waving appendages rendered in exacting detail. In this case, the Catalyst was at primary, bulkier torso and extra appendages floating directly above Aelda's northern pole.

Mavrin wondered if Eyasu considered how the Catalyst might feel about a Castoff being used by a heretic. He implied They approved, but it didn't feel wise to make assumptions about the beings responsible for humanity's breathable air, workable soil and water drawn from the Winds. Disinterested as he was in Them as a whole, even Mavrin could admit that humanity had a vested interest in appeasing Them, and that appeasement was what Eyasu risked by continuing to channel.

Being right about the Raw didn't mean he was right about everything.

"Mister Leed?"

Mavrin shuffled sideways to peer into Jareden's bedroom, cautiously meeting Aulina's eyes. The faint gold in her veins had mostly faded, and her eyes were clear of everything except fatigue and worry.

"Did . . ." She swallowed. He noticed a glass of water untouched on the floor beside her but when he moved to offer it to her, she shook her head. "Did you know?"

"Know what?"

Her trembling hand touched her shoulder.

Of course not. This sort of thing isn't supposed to exist, Mavrin wanted to say. Except that would have been a lie. He'd dismissed the Raw's existence, but that didn't make them any less dangerous.

Eyasu passed him on his way to the kitchen, armor under one arm, as if to underscore that point.

Mavrin sunk to the ground inside the doorframe, resting his back against it with Aulina to his left. "I'm sorry for what happened. My . . . Eyasu will figure out how to help you," he said, hoping it didn't sound like a lie.

To his surprise, Aulina's lips crinkled with amusement. "I could hear him talking with Ohanna. Do you know what he said to her?" Mavrin hesitated long enough that she added, "His tone sounded like our father. Comforting."

She took a couple heavy breaths. "I don't understand what's happening. He said to fight. But there's nothing I can see to fight."

"Often those are the hardest ones. At least you're not alone." After he spoke, the words felt heavy in the air around him. Especially when he heard the rustle of padding from the next room, as Eyasu put his armor back on.

The words must not have meant much to Aulina, since the next thing she said was: "We used to have the tallest trees. Straight-backed toward the sky."

"I wondered about that," Mavrin said, not minding a change in topic. "Your parents did some sort of cross-grafting?"

Aulina looked puzzled. "Their trunks are strong. Even in winter, before the pears blossom."

Mavrin stared sidelong at her when she mentioned winter. He never heard the middlemonths referred to that way, since there wasn't exactly winter weather like in the Time Before Unity. "You grow pears? I only saw berrenfruit."

She didn't respond right away, expression growing cloudier. When she focused on him again, she said, "Mister Leed . . . make sure Ohanna is safe. Please? Until I can look after her again?"

The sudden shift caught him off guard, but he could imagine how tired Aulina had to be still. It took effort not to glance at her veins. "You have my word," he said, and smirked. "Magician's code of honor."

Aulina's lips crinkled again as her eyes closed. "She really loved your show . . ."

Her breathing became so shallow that Mavrin held his hand in front of her face to make sure it hadn't stopped. He sat near her for a while longer, unsure what to do, until he closed the door halfway and left her to rest.

Heavy footsteps from the front stairs announced Jareden before she thumped inside, looking even grumpier than before. Eyasu reappeared from the kitchen, fully armored.

"Gonna need you two," Jareden said. "Lawkeeper didn't feel like waiting."

She thumped back upstairs without waiting for a response.

Keeping his voice low, Mavrin asked Eyasu, "Why did you agree to notify the lawkeeper?"

"To avoid local trouble, until I can determine how to deal with the Raw." Eyasu didn't bother whispering. When they stepped outside and saw the mob, he added, "Perhaps that hope was misplaced."

Mavrin swallowed and smoothed out his waistcoat, thankful that he left his cloak inside, as the Winds had picked up again. About a dozen people stood in front of Jareden's home. Most wore heavy coats and leather windmasks lowered to droop against their chests. Heavy clouds were approaching to the east, meaning a Longwind on the way, a result of the Catalyst passing by yesterday. Josef stood near the back with Mavrin's trunk and garnills. When he saw all six of their smooth faces staring, he cursed himself for forgetting about them; they would have been expecting to roam his room at the Waystop, and now they were overdue for their protein pellets. Beside Josef, the curly-haired gate guard from that morning held their longstaff across their chest, one foot on Eyasu's rucksack.

Jareden crossed her arms. "One calling at a time's my usual method. Might need you to take numbers."

A gangly, middle-aged man with sepia-colored skin and narrow spectacles stepped forward. "No offense meant, Voice Arric. Just a precaution while we sort out what happened last night."

Jareden grunted. "Lots of people for an investigation, Barris."

"Maybe we need this many." This came from a broad-shouldered woman about Barris's age, with long auburn hair tied back against the Winds and a heavy metal chain around her neck. Her gaze flicked to Mavrin and Eyasu. "My name is Gevian, magistrate of Tanardell. Jareden attempted to explain what happened to Aulina, but I felt our lawkeeper and surgeon should examine her, before we decide what actions to take. I'm sure that makes sense to you both?"

She said it with the sort of diplomatic smile that made it clear they weren't really being asked. Mavrin's stomach flip-flopped a couple times. He glanced at Eyasu, but though his former friend's shoulders were tight, he didn't look concerned.

When no one objected, Barris gestured for two people to follow him into Jareden's home: one of his armed deputies, and a plain-faced, weather vane thin man carrying a weighted leather satchel. Mavrin stepped aside to let them pass, but the lawkeeper paused beside him anyway.

"Stay right there, magician," he said, leaning in close.

Oh, lovely, Mavrin thought, as Barris stepped inside. He caught sight of the cabler strapped to the lawkeeper's belt, ready to catch anyone who tried to run, and decided to do as he was told.

Chapter Eight

AS SOON AS BARRIS STEPPED INSIDE, MAVRIN HISSED in Eyasu's ear: "Maybe we should coordinate more after all."

Jareden faced them with her back to the mob and lowered her voice. "Enough evidence in Aulina's orchard to know you weren't totally lying. Tilting vision, odd noises—but not like when they converted this place." She gestured at her home. "Different flavor, somehow. Doesn't fully explain what happened, though."

"So you're turning us over to the lawkeeper."

"Should be a Requester figuring this out," Jareden grumbled. "Barris wants to look good to Renhollow, and I'm not keen on making enemies of my neighbors."

"Maybe they'll listen to reason," Eyasu murmured, though he didn't sound optimistic. He hadn't stopped watching the mob.

Mavrin kept his mouth shut. Turning them over to Renhollow's Requesters would be worse than dealing with local lawkeepers. Being accused of poisoning or alchemically corrupting Aulina was bad enough, but Eyasu's unsanctioned channeling could see him shackled and transported back to the Citadel, likely for a trial. Wondering if that might be the best thing for everyone made Mavrin feel suddenly ill.

Barris appeared in the doorway, cabler in both hands now. It was old and dented, but the metal dart in the launcher looked freshly sharpened. He fiddled with the wire spooled at the back. "What did you do to that young woman?"

"Us? We went to save her—"

"Your assessment, Lawkeeper?" Gevian called. She and the others hadn't stepped any closer to the porch.

"Surgeon says her blood's contaminated," Barris said. "Doesn't look like a plague but we can't know without a proper assessment."

"The result of channeling?"

"Wouldn't surprise me."

Mavrin wondered if they knew how rare an accidental channeling was, let alone a Request phrased so badly the Aspects provided sickness as their Response. It would require a seriously unfocused or unpracticed mind wielding a Castoff. He had only heard of such occurrences in books, mostly discussing the first decades post-Salvation, when more people could channel but the nuances of Requesting were still unclear.

Gevian sighed. "Bring her to the clinic. We'll transport her from there."

As Barris went back inside, followed by two others carrying a folding cot, Eyasu straightened. "You're sending her away?"

"We don't have a choice," Gevian said indignantly. "Whatever's afflicting her is beyond our means. Either the Bastion or the Requesters in Renhollow will have a better chance."

Jareden muttered something that sounded unsurprised. Mavrin had only heard of the Bastion—Renhollow's science guild was responsible for a lot of the region's innovation, from windtowers to salt batteries, but he had a feeling the Requesters would get their hands on Aulina first. Something about the fear in these people and how they kept glancing at the sky. He wondered what that would mean for Ohanna, and whether Jareden could keep her from being sent off to the Bastion, too.

Eyasu's shoulders drooped. "Magistrate, I don't know a delicate way to explain this to you. Aulina has been taken—"

"By an affliction, yes. I understand."

Her clipped tone told Mavrin what happened. Whatever Jareden explained to Gevian or the lawkeeper, whether that explanation included the word "Raw" or not, they refused to acknowledge the pieces they didn't want to believe. Worse, he recognized the fear in her eyes, because he'd felt the same thing since the orchard.

An image of Eyasu on trial flickered in his mind again. *You're no better than these people.*

Barris and the others emerged from the house, carrying Aulina on the folding cot, thin sheets raised on either side to shield her. Her eyes didn't open as they maneuvered her off the porch.

"Will they help her?"

Mavrin spun around and saw Ohanna standing in the doorway, clutching a blanket. He made it a half-step before Gevian snapped, "Keep back from her, Mister Leed."

Mavrin tried to keep the way his hackles rose from showing on his face. To Ohanna, he said, "Everything is fine, my dear. Go back inside."

She squinted past him at the mob but nodded and shut the door despite what she saw. Barris and the others were already halfway down the road, taking Aulina from sight.

"Magistrate, that young woman is not ill—"

"With all due respect," Gevian said, cutting Eyasu off, "anything more from you should be saved for proper Requesters. We will pray to the Aspects that Aulina's condition improves, but if it doesn't, that will be one more piece of evidence against you and Mister Leed."

"Me?" Mavrin exclaimed.

The gate guard stepped forward. "You strolled into town around the same time as this heretic," they said, pointing at Eyasu. "Aulina was at your show. For all we know, the two of you selected her there as your victim."

"Why would we bring her here and ask for help? Would heretics turn themselves over like that?"

"If they're twisted enough to spit in the face of the Aspects."

"As if They care!" Mavrin shouted and stepped off the porch.

The rest of his tirade died on his lips as he counted six longstaffs raised in his direction. Anyone not armed backed away except for Gevian, whose cheeks flushed bright red.

Except they weren't focused on him. Eyasu stood at his shoulder, with one hand clenched at his side. Mavrin could see glimmering light in the cracks between his fingers.

"Ignorance." The word came out as little more than a breath. His steely gaze swept the mob. "You're frightened. Understandable. But instead of using that fear, you turn it against your fellows, and ignore the real threat."

Gevian swallowed before she responded. "We have proof that—"

"*Proof?*" Eyasu thundered. He shoved Mavrin aside, and the mob scattered backward. "Is the destruction by this Raw not enough? The signs on Aulina's body, marking the creature's presence?"

He surveyed the crowd. "There has been *proof* since Time Before Unity, and it has been willfully forgotten. Would you like more *proof*?"

Mavrin stared open-mouthed as Eyasu loomed over Gevian, ignoring the lawkeepers flanking her, longstaffs trembling in their hands. The Aspects wouldn't help him harm these people, but he could cause other damage if he phrased his Request correctly.

"Wait!" Mavrin stepped between them. He raised a hand toward the crowd and faced Eyasu. "What are you doing?"

"Their ignorance will destroy us." Eyasu's voice was thick with venom. "Always the same. Can't open their eyes. Can't make them *see*."

"No, that's the difficult part, isn't it? People don't like what scares them." His neck tingled, knowing how close he was to being stabbed. "But that's not why we act, is it?" Mavrin wracked his brain for the exact passage from the Words of Aspect. "'They weave the world for us with each of their visages, but only some of us can see the reason for that weaving. We can only encourage, not force, others to understand. The Aspects create a different path for us all.'"

He saw Jareden creeping closer over Eyasu's shoulder but couldn't risk telling the Voice to stay back. Behind him, he could feel the mob's apprehension, the longstaffs still held at the ready. The edges of Eyasu's eyes were wet, the whites noticeably bloodshot. His friend took a deep, heaving breath.

"If we could control everything, we wouldn't need Them, would we?" Mavrin asked him. "Didn't you tell me that once?"

"I paraphrased the Words," Eyasu said quietly. "You misquoted them just now."

Mavrin coughed a nervous laugh. "You were always the better scholar." He fidgeted, and lowered his voice to add, "And you've been right about more than I care to admit. Always have been."

Eyasu's lip twitched. Mavrin stepped forward as he sagged in place and gently put his hand around Eyasu's fist. His friend's thick fingers pulled away slowly and Mavrin scooped the Castoff out. He'd only handled one a couple of times; for a scale fragment from an Aspect, they were always surprisingly cold to the touch. He dropped it into a cloak pocket, and Jareden helped guide Eyasu to sit on the porch, whispering calming words in his ear.

"Maybe we can handle this more calmly, Gevian?" she said without looking at the mob.

"Do you think that little outburst helped?" The magistrate closed some of the distance, either deliberately ignoring Jareden or to make a show of authority. Cheeks flushed, she barked, "You heard what he said? They need to be contained."

"We'll leave in peace," Mavrin said, trying not to sound as desperate as he felt. "Let me collect the rest of our things, and then we'll go. Fine? Send Requesters after us, if you like."

Gevian examined Eyasu before giving him a reluctant nod.

Mavrin cast a stern look at the other townspeople for good measure. Eyasu stared at the ground, his expression blank.

Trusting Jareden to keep an eye on him, Mavrin hurried inside and shut the door. He pressed his hands against the wall, willing some of the shake out of them, before heading to the sitting room.

Ohanna perked up when she saw him and almost smiled when he sat beside her on the sofa, spindly legs splayed in front of him like a doll. She couldn't have seen what happened through the narrow windows and the sound likely didn't carry through the stone.

"Are you leaving?"

Mavrin cleared his throat. "Yes. But you'll be all right."

"Voice Arric said I can stay with her while Aulina gets better. She's sweet. I always like visiting her." Ohanna fiddled with her unruly hair. "I've never had a grandma."

A lovely grandmother who begins the day with whiskey, he thought in his fatigue. And then felt guilty immediately, knowing he could trust Jareden with Ohanna, and his promise to Aulina.

Ohanna scooted closer and wrapped her tiny arms around his midsection. The tender squeeze shocked Mavrin so much that he forgot to hug her back.

"What did I do to deserve that?"

"Aulina says most people deserve one hug a day," Ohanna said softly.

Mavrin stared down at her. His arms remembered to embrace Ohanna of their own accord, since his mind was too wrapped up in fear, guilt, exhaustion, and the sound of a ticking timepiece.

He extracted himself from the hug and crouched in front of her. "I can't promise that I'll visit, but I'll do my best. In the meantime, can you do something for me?"

Ohanna's eyes widened as he produced a large, blue-and-green feather from his cloak and held it out to her. She almost reached out for it but caught herself, and Mavrin couldn't decide if he should be proud or grief-stricken.

"This magic is perfectly fine. See?"

He tapped a switch on the tip of the feather. Ohanna's face lit up as she saw the feather collapse into the simple shape of a bird, wings extended from its narrow frame. Mavrin turned the contraption so she could see, tapped the bird's tail, and suddenly it was a feather again.

"Does it fly?" she asked. "I've seen flying birds in books."

"It does! Though I'd be careful letting it loose outside." He pressed it into her hands. "Keep this safe, as a reminder."

"Of what?"

"That magic is supposed to be good."

The front door opened with a loud bang. He half-expected one of the townspeople, but instead Eyasu walked past, rucksack slung over one shoulder and longsword banging against his hip.

Jareden lumbered behind him. "I told you," she hissed, "I don't have a damn backdoor."

Mavrin caught up to them in the kitchen, where Eyasu rapidly sorted through the items in his rucksack. Without looking up, he said, "I'm going after her."

"It's done." Mavrin tried to keep his voice level, watching for a reaction like what happened outside. "I thought you decided not to fight."

Eyasu grunted. "I'll rescue her peacefully. On the road, perhaps, between here and Renhollow." Satisfied, he closed his rucksack. "The Raw cannot remain inside her."

"She seemed to be fighting it—"

"I'll need my Castoff."

Mavrin regretted his hesitation immediately, only because of the hurt on Eyasu's face. He tried to look apologetic as he handed the Castoff over.

Through the open front door, he heard the distant sound of a scream.

Mavrin was halfway down the road with Eyasu before it occurred to him that he had no business dealing with whatever they were about to find. One encounter with a Raw hardly made him an expert, though he supposed that was more training than Jareden had, and the Voice showed no interest in staying behind, either. After what happened with the mob, neither of them was ready to leave Eyasu alone.

Not that he was anywhere near alone, really. Despite Eyasu warning everyone else to stay behind, most of the crowd followed them toward Tanardell's main avenue. When they turned the corner, Mavrin's next step struck the ground earlier than he expected. Jareden caught his elbow as he stumbled, and through the stars bursting across his vision he could see the Voice's pallor turn gray.

Some of the townspeople murmured and fell back. Eyasu was the only one who continued forward, shrugging off the channeling's aftereffects, toward the wreckage. The three shellwagons they spotted when they entered Tanardell had been tossed across the street, their contents spilled in a dozen directions. One of them sat upside down against a windtower, akrren shell broken into a half-dozen shards; the windtower had been smashed, too, spreading wires across the nearby buildings. Thankfully the cistern attached to the tower's condensers hadn't split open. A crate wedged into the general store's front wall seemed to shift in place every time Mavrin blinked, without any cracks in the stone around it.

The air felt thick as he and Jareden followed Eyasu. The temperature shifted by degrees every step, and Mavrin covered his nose against the reek of burning linen, even though he didn't see anything aflame. A few steps later he spotted a black scorch mark on the road, roughly the length of an adult lying down.

A familiar dented cabler lay beside it, smoke curling from the blackened grip.

Memories of the orchard made Marvin freeze in his tracks, until Eyasu continued forward.

The closer they got to the wagons, the less Mavrin's stomach clenched and the less pressure he felt in the air. Eyasu crouched next to one of them; Aulina's cot lay partially crushed beneath its ceramic shell. Next to it, the plain-faced doctor lay staring at the sky, one hand moving rapidly across his chest in a sign to the Catalyst as Protector.

His other arm was submerged into the road up to his bicep, held in place by hard-packed ground. The lower half of his body disappeared every time Mavrin blinked, so he focused on the man's face.

"Barris, don't let her touch me! No, no, no, he's gone. Where did he go? Please don't see me. She can see me! Barris don't let her touch me! No, no, no . . ."

"I can't counter this," Eyasu said. "A Request might only make things worse."

Mavrin spotted a couple other people staggering away from the wagons, but no one from the lawkeeper's group. These were bystanders caught in Aulina's channeling, and no one would know how many until the aftereffects faded and they figured out who was missing.

Jareden stepped forward and grabbed the doctor's hand. "Great Aspects, who would not wish any harm to this man, or any innocent life that walks the world under your charge, take notice. Let one of your eyes fall upon this man. Hear him, and do not let him be alone."

The doctor's hand trembled like he wanted to wrench it away and keep to his own prayers, until Jareden finished. It stilled as he closed his eyes and his breath steadied.

If the Aspects focused Their attention on the moment he passed, Mavrin didn't feel the difference.

"I thought that holding charm was supposed to keep her under control," he said to Eyasu.

"The Raw is stronger than I expected. And likely reacting to being threatened."

"We'll gather the militia." Gevian had managed to join them, though her face was tight and her breathing slow and labored.

"More threats won't lead to less reaction," Eyasu said with a withering look. "I'll find her. It's too dangerous for anyone else."

He walked away before she could protest, so she turned her attention to Mavrin. "I will not allow heresy in Tanardell. You risk the Aspects' wrath."

"Look around. I'd be more concerned with Aulina's wrath than Theirs." He caught Jareden's eye. "Let's deal with her before we worry about turning ourselves over to the Requesters."

Eyasu called out to witnesses who had been out of the channeling's range. Mavrin marched back to where the original mob fell back from the distortions, specifically Josef, who'd towed his trunk and garnills from Jareden's home. Josef tried to stammer something as Mavrin collected his things, but he didn't stop to listen. Murmuring apologies to his garnills, he opened a compartment under their cage and grabbed their tin of protein pellets. It didn't feel any lighter, so he shook it in Josef's face before holding a pellet out to each garnill, weathering several hard thumps from their snouts in exchange. By the time they'd all swallowed the pellets down their long necks, Eyasu looked to be finished asking questions.

"Things might be uncomfortable a while longer," he warned the garnills. As he carried them away, though, their indignant hoots were directed exclusively at Josef.

Eyasu looked relieved as he approached, but his face quickly hardened. "Mavrin, this situation has gone beyond what I meant to drag you into. You can stay here."

"That's still my coin inside her. Lead the way before I change my mind."

He couldn't be sure, but he thought he saw a glimmer of a smile on Eyasu's face.

Chapter Nine

BY THE TIME THEY REACHED THE NORTHWEST corner of town, tiny pebbles and dirt pecked at the exposed patches of Mavrin's forehead. He clenched his eyes tighter behind his goggles, instinctively trying to protect them further from the Longwind. As it yanked at the edges of his clothes, the extra cord binding his cloak started wriggling loose, forcing him to press his elbow against it with the arm carrying his garnills. Even with the protective flaps dropped over their cage, their hooting made it clear they didn't like being outside any more than he did.

He hadn't stepped outside during a Longwind in years. The last time had been to chase a thief who snatched his patterned bag and the chits inside after a show, and the only reason he caught the urchin was because they both had to hunker down in the same shelter, during which they both decided nothing was worth going outside in that kind of weather. So far, this Longwind seemed less severe, but the speed gauges chimed louder nearly with each step.

Tanardell's mortuary was one of the most obviously ornate buildings in town, partly because it was two stories tall. The people here clearly favored the Hidden as Fatedraw as their variation concerning death: that second story was mostly an open platform, where followers would cry out their entire life history or that of a loved one. The mortuary itself was constructed from polished stone, lacquered to keep from weathering under the Winds, and etched with prayers in alternating squares around the entrance. In addition to the deliberately indistinct characters tied to the

Hidden as Fatedraw, Mavrin saw the reluctant form of Catalyst as Deathgiver and the Presence as Passage in flight with Their appendages outstretched—acknowledging the Aspects' role in the end of life and the soul's journey beyond the material world.

Bystanders said Aulina had disappeared inside. More strangely, no one else had been harmed as she made her way through Tanardell.

"Wait here. If you would." Eyasu stepped from the street and through the front door, one hand on the hilt of his longsword. Figuring the Longwind was safer than bumping into the Raw inside, Mavrin waited as told.

Eyasu reappeared a few minutes later from around the back, gesturing for Mavrin to join him.

The mortuary interior didn't appear damaged. Eyasu led him through the nearly-empty receiving room, past the narrow staircase that led up to the second story, to the stone door at the rear. A patch of white fabric fluttered on the doorframe, and a shallow footprint was visible in the soil outside. A second led between the thick, disordered trees that formed a path into Tanardell's cemetery.

"The last time you faced a Raw, was it this difficult to kill?"

Eyasu hesitated. "In the spirit of honesty . . . I'm not sure I faced one before."

"*What?*"

"I never said I have." Eyasu held up a finger. "You said it would be reasonable for me to have fought the Raw. I agreed." While Mavrin sputtered to find words, Eyasu added, "My research suggests I might have found one—"

"Not a Raw. Lovely. Meaning we're entirely dependent on the Aspects' will to keep us safe." Mavrin didn't mention how he felt about their chances now that he knew the truth about Eyasu's channeling.

At the entrance to the cemetery, the path broke into four separate directions, each of them bordered by dense trees and hedges.

About three meters high, they blocked some of the Longwind's force, but dust and debris still danced across the path and caught in Mavrin's hair. Averblossom hung from some of the branches, mistaking the Longwind for true evening and shedding the sunlight their petals collected that day.

Mavrin didn't see any sign of which way Aulina might have gone. Part of him wondered if, like someone visiting the dead, the Hidden as Fatedraw would bring them exactly where they needed to be.

He pointed down the second branch in the path. Eyasu shrugged and headed that way. Entering the cemetery in the afternoon didn't make the interior any less oppressive, even though the trees were trimmed to allow some light.

"Why do you think it would come here?"

"I'm not sure. Do you remember what we read about the Raw?" Eyasu had to repeat the question once Mavrin stepped closer, to be heard over the Winds.

"Barely," Mavrin said, which wasn't a complete lie—he knew the significant bits but was starting to remember details he thought he'd locked away for good.

"I found more since leaving Veristenok. Evidence that Raw were not only real, but a significant presence in pre-Fracture society. Hints at a society that lived alongside ours."

He tried to imagine people co-existing with the Raw and the scene quickly devolved into screaming and buildings turned to ash. "Where did you find this evidence?"

"From a copy of Uekel's *Accounts*."

That left Mavrin speechless, but the wonder in Eyasu's voice left no doubt whether he believed his own words. Mavrin never thought a copy of that book could exist, even before the Highest Voices convinced him to abandon their research. All they had found were passing references and scraps of information, several of which mentioned a scientist and scholar named Uekel, who lived through the Fracture and recorded his thoughts about the Raw—or "the truth about them," as some later writers claimed.

Mavrin hated feeling in the wrong again. Worse was wanting to know if Eyasu had this copy on him, right now.

His friend seemed to read his mind. "We can examine it once our work is done. I've wanted to share it with you." He hunched his shoulders, as though he regretted sharing that, and Mavrin felt it best not to comment.

Eyasu stopped them at another crossing, breaking in four new directions. One sloped upward to a stone platform for calling out to the Hidden. It would provide the best vantage, but the Longwind was too fierce to risk climbing, so they took the next, another choice either random or left to the Hidden as Fatedraw. Mavrin started to worry that Aulina might exit and leave them wandering the cemetery, and kept an ear open for his garnills, not that he'd likely hear them over the Winds. If the lazy creatures would bother to react.

"It took me a long time to accept why you abandoned our research and left Veristenok. But eventually I understood why."

Despite his decision to follow Eyasu here, Mavrin couldn't think of anything he wanted to discuss less. But this was better than imagining what Aulina might do when they found her. "Go on, then."

"What we considered was incredible. The idea that what we've been taught about our world before the Fracture, possibly the Fracture itself could be fundamentally flawed. I was so focused on truth that I hadn't considered how terrifying this knowledge might be. And I know why it terrified you." Eyasu took his eyes off the path for a moment. "You're a kind man, Mavrin. You recognized the damage our discovery would've caused."

"Of course I did." But it wasn't kindness. Their entire society, even people like him who didn't take much time for prayer and devotion, was based on the idea that the Aspects saved humanity from the worst calamity in its history. Not to save them from themselves, however humanity might have caused the Fracture, or at the expense of *another* species like the Raw. "Why didn't it terrify you?"

"I never said it didn't," Eyasu said, soft enough that Mavrin almost didn't catch it. "If the *Accounts* are true, I believe we're meant to know that truth in full. The Highest Voices tried to prevent that." He held up a hand as he spoke, an affectation Mavrin remembered from their old scholarly debates. "The Aspects are balance incarnate. Testing humanity is part of that balance, through the Hidden."

"While the Catalyst protects us," Mavrin intoned reluctantly.

Eyasu tapped his wooden chest plate. "That balance is where I find my faith. The Aspects ensure the safety of those who believe."

"Even a sanctioned Requester doesn't always get a Response," Mavrin reminded him.

"Would that make for much of a test, if success was guaranteed?"

"I forgot how frustrating you are." Except this time, he didn't mean it with malice. He hoped Eyasu understood that.

They reached another stone platform and this time Eyasu risked a look. Mavrin waited on the path, holding his cloak tight, looking for footprints and wondering if they should have asked Gevian to loan them a proper tracker. Even with the averblossom waking up, spotting signs of Aulina's trail wouldn't be easy.

When he looked up, a figure stood down the path.

Mavrin froze as Aulina shambled toward them. A gasp accompanied every spasmodic step, like keeping balance caused her pain. She lost the struggle after a few meters and fell to her knees with a soft cry, Winds blowing her hair in a snarl.

The wooden box appeared from his left, startling him until he recognized the gauntleted hand holding it. Mavrin pocketed the box and reluctantly followed Eyasu forward.

Aulina didn't look up. Eyasu gestured for Mavrin to stay back and approached at an angle, longsword hanging at his side. Its edges glinted with dariss, just like his knife.

"Time . . . all we need is time."

When she lifted her head, Mavrin grimaced at the golden blotches across her skin and the sunken, weathered texture around her eyes. They burned with the same orange light as before.

"I am resisting," she said to him, almost proudly.

"Against what?" Mavrin asked.

Aulina offered him the same malicious smile from the orchard. She turned her head as Eyasu stepped closer, longsword leveled toward her throat. No other reaction as he touched the dariss-tipped point to her shoulder and pushed her gown aside enough to reveal the ward. Mavrin thought it looked like some of the ink had flaked off.

"Weakening . . ."

The rasp left her voice. Aulina blinked, the orange leaving her eyes, and her face contorted in pain.

"I can feel it," she gasped. "This is the fight."

Mavrin looked at Eyasu. "Can she resist it?"

"I don't know."

Aulina's neck and chest jerked violently. Eyasu stepped back and raised his sword, but she didn't move from where she knelt.

"Foolish . . ." The guttural voice returned, along with the uneven twist to her lips. She gestured at the ward. "This is . . . proof enough. They are . . . helping me."

"Who is helping you?" Eyasu asked sharply.

When her smile deepened, he pressed the longsword against her throat again.

"They will free me." Aulina's eyes closed, and her expression became tranquil. "I can see the clearing . . . the clearing in the cold . . . waters dividing the betrayers' homes." She heaved a deeper breath. "I can reach them."

Holding his sword steady in one hand, Eyasu pulled out his

Castoff and started murmuring a Request. Mavrin stepped further back, rubbing his temple to ward off a sudden pressure. Aulina jerked as the Winds picked up around them and Eyasu raised his voice to a shout.

At the end of his Request, nothing happened.

Aulina lifted her head with an audible click of bone and fixed her orange gaze on him. She flicked her right hand so quickly Mavrin heard the tendons snap and the ground flashed at Eyasu's feet. He leapt aside as dirt exploded into the air, carried away by the Winds. Mavrin stumbled away as a charred branch struck the ground beside him. He raised an arm in front of his face, waiting for another strike.

Nothing came. When he lowered his arm, Eyasu stood between him and Aulina. He held his longsword horizontally in front of him, crystalline edge catching the tendrils of energy from Aulina's fingertips. His friend's shoulders trembled as he held back her channeling.

One of the tendrils broke away, striking the trees to his left with a bright flash. As the smoke cleared, Mavrin wondered why he hadn't thought to duck down the path there earlier.

Because it wasn't there a moment ago.

Another burst of channeling made him scramble backward. He felt slope beneath his boots; when he turned, the path they took earlier was gone, replaced by a raised platform of stone. A statue stood at its peak, even though it was said the Hidden disliked that sort of representation—a statue made of fibrous, intertwining forms, like air frozen into a solid.

Mavrin couldn't move. He stood in the eye of a storm as Eyasu and Aulina created it, watching the world unravel between them. All because he gave Ohanna that coin. He'd only gotten in the way in the orchard. He wasn't a warrior—just a magician.

An idea struck him, and before he could change his mind Mavrin threw himself at Eyasu. He snatched the longknife from his belt and fell back, using Eyasu as cover as he yanked off its sheath and readied himself to throw.

He stepped out again on Eyasu's other side and threw at Aulina's shoulder. Like he expected, the Raw shifted its attention enough to protect the coin, batting aside the sheath with one hand.

By the time it realized its mistake, Mavrin was already driving the knife through the marked flesh.

The Raw shrieked as its channeling winked from existence. Through the pounding in his head, Mavrin felt his body hit the ground—with Aulina on top of him, hands closed over his throat. He released his pressure with the knife.

"No." Aulina looked down at him, eyes wide. Her voice, not the Raw's. "Do it. Now!"

Mavrin twisted the knife. Bright light erupted from where the coin was buried and he stumbled back, watching shadows whirl from Aulina's body as she reeled to her feet and screamed. Mavrin lay there, not sure what to do next.

Eyasu yanked the knife free. He pressed a hand to Aulina's shoulder, silencing her scream with a new chant. Mavrin saw stars from being that close to his friend's channeling. When Eyasu pulled his hand away, Aulina slumped to the ground beside him in silence.

Mavrin looked at the wound he'd made. Through the jagged gash and the blood, the dark circle beneath Aulina's skin was gone.

A moment later, he heard the soft clink of a coin settling into the box in his pocket, and barely remembered to click it shut again.

Chapter Ten

THE LONGWIND'S INTENSITY INCREASED WHILE they tended to Aulina's wounds, choking the cemetery air with dirt, shredded leaves and other detritus. Mavrin and Eyasu carried her into the mortuary, trusting that none of the gravediggers or deadspeakers would show up until the Winds steadied. Color returned to Aulina's face while Eyasu examined her, though she didn't wake up for longer than a few minutes and didn't speak or seem aware of her surroundings.

He cleaned her shoulder with salve and applied a fungal wrap, then built a splint using metal rods and rope from the mortuary's supplies. Her wrist looked to be sprained, not broken, but he tied a splint stick around it with what cloth remained and secured that tight against her chest. Besides some smaller cuts and bruises, Eyasu emphasized her nerves would be frayed for a while. Care would be needed in her presence.

"My Requests for healing haven't gotten any better over the years," Eyasu admitted. "But I'll try when my strength returns."

Admittedly, Mavrin hadn't noticed the dark circles under Eyasu's eyes or the deeper flush to his skin; channeling too much weathered a person's body as well as their mind.

He wrapped Aulina in the spare cloaks and blankets from his trunk and settled down across from Eyasu. Unnerved by the darkness, he rose again to fetch an averblossom lantern from outside. The shadows it cast on Eyasu's face reminded Mavrin of that first glimpse outside his room at the Waystop. The box of coins sat on the floor nearby; neither of them wanted it out of their sight.

"'They are helping me,' it said . . ." Eyasu mused after a while.

Mavrin tried to ignore this as he dug through his possessions. Two days of horror separated by a fitful sleep on a couch were catching up with him, including the return of the crick in his neck. He imagined they should keep a watch between them, in case Gevian or the lawkeepers came looking. They would likely want to send Aulina away still, though weakened and in need of care. He imagined the look on Ohanna's face, the pleading questions as her sister was taken again, and not knowing how to answer them.

Naturally, his garnills started hooting as soon as he sat down. The mortuary was shuttered tight against the Longwind, but Mavrin closed the doors leading out of the receiving room anyway before opening the cage. All six scattered immediately, splitting up to poke their blunt snouts at everything they could. One of the hens hesitantly approached Aulina, only rubbing against her dark hair after the first two nuzzles didn't seem to disturb her.

Eyasu extracted a large sheet of yellow paper from his rucksack, which he rolled out on the floor between them, gently scooting a garnill aside. It was a wrinkled map of Aelda, showing everything from Coaststar to the east, Yarder's Outlook to the south, and the heavy mass of the Grayest Mountains stretching across the north. Around everything, jagged lines marked the dried-out Edgeplains, a pointed way of saying that traveling so close to Aelda's exposed core was not a wise idea. Not that that stopped some people from living out there.

"The Raw said it was going somewhere."

"Eyasu, we should rest." Mavrin's voice felt shaky.

"Think, my friend. The creature said someone 'will free me again . . . I can make it there.' What if it wasn't fleeing when it regained control of Aulina's body? What if it was heading somewhere specific?"

Mavrin shrugged and closed his eyes.

"I thought this Raw was isolated. Everything I read about dariss suggested this. But perhaps it's not alone . . ."

That caught his attention. "Is there more than one of those things in there?"

". . . I don't believe so."

"By the Four!" Mavrin shifted further from the box, barely keeping from kicking it across the room. He heard Aulina stir and held back a string of curses.

Eyasu studied the map, similarly unbothered by Mavrin's reaction—a sign that he was very focused. "Wood functions as a natural ground for a Raw's energy. Between that and the dariss, it should be contained."

"Did you learn that from the *Accounts*?" Mavrin asked. He hoped the question sounded more like talking to fill the silence, and not because part of him genuinely wanted to know.

Eyasu set the map aside and dug into his rucksack again. Near the bottom, Mavrin heard an inner compartment snap open.

Despite himself, Mavrin held his breath as Eyasu withdrew a square bundle wrapped in protective sheeting. He could remember the passing references they found, the ones insisting not only that Uekel was a real person, but that copies of his *Accounts* existed across Aelda, reproduced in different formats. He doubted Eyasu would believe him, but he never stopped assuming they existed—he simply decided they'd been lost over time or destroyed by the Citadel.

Lifting the sheeting away revealed a weathered, leather cover bearing a symbol he recognized: five gears forming an irregular row, struck through with random lines. It had been identified in two different scraps as something like Uekel's family crest.

"The emblem of his guild," Eyasu said. "Uekel belonged to something called the Fifth Progress."

Mavrin used a wand to flip open the cover. The first page was scrawled with faded, tight printing on crinkled pages, identifying the book not with a title, but with an explanation: *Let these words serve as a proper record, and the truest account, of what transpired during our world's greatest devastation.* The subsequent page didn't have a chapter or heading; Uekel simply started writing, with the first paragraph continuing onto the next page.

"An archaic form," Eyasu admitted. "He preferred to complete an idea fully before moving on."

"I assume you tested the age of this?" There was no need to ask; even without proper equipment, Mavrin could tell the pages were unlike the rough, heavily-recycled paper Aelda relied on these days. They crinkled like pure tree fiber, which he had only ever handled in the Citadel.

"It might be Uekel's own hand, though that's only a guess."

Mavrin had the sudden urge to scoop up the book, hide in a corner and pore through its pages from beginning to end. As he turned a few more, though, he didn't register any of Uekel's words. All he could think about was the desperation when he and Eyasu realized they had exhausted the Citadel's libraries, suspecting the Highest Voices likely had more information secreted elsewhere.

"How much does this book confirm, exactly?"

"There are pages missing," Eyasu said. "Others damaged from time. Uekel lived through the Fracture and asserts the existence of the Raw. There was some manner of relationship with humanity. A partnership, perhaps. But fraught. Uekel makes it clear he didn't completely trust them."

"How much did he see of the Fracture?" With how little survived, no one had a clear description of what happened in that span between the Fracture, which ended the Time Before Unity, and the Salvation, when the Aspects arrived to generate the Lifesphere.

"He claims an experiment went awry." Eyasu frowned. "He writes to someone who would understand his references without detailed explanation, so the experiment itself isn't clear. But it utilized dariss, and the Raw were involved. Whatever went wrong caused the Fracture and seemingly wiped out the Raw in the process. Though Uekel asserts some survived."

"Because of the dariss?"

"Yes!" Despite his fatigue, Eyasu's face beamed as he thrust out a hand. "The Raw are beings of energy. Their ability to follow natural conduits was crucial to this experiment, and Uekel suggests they survived by hiding *inside* the dariss. Unfortunately, he mentions no proof."

"Lucky us," Mavrin muttered, glancing at the box again.

Eyasu slowly withdrew his hand. "The dariss is also their bane," he continued more calmly. "Nonconductive materials like wood are useful, but dariss can be used as a shield or deflector, as well as a conduit. Part of my hope has been to prove that it could contain Raw."

Mavrin smirked. "Yes, it seems perfectly natural for you to go looking for monsters." He heard how that sounded too late, and quickly added, "I just mean . . ."

"Neither of us is what the other expected?" Eyasu said mildly.

He stared at the floor almost bashfully, and questions that Mavrin hadn't bothered to ask earlier returned to him now: how Eyasu acquired his armor, where he received that scar on his scalp, even what he faced that *probably wasn't* a Raw. Whether he deserved those stories, though, was the real question.

"They aren't monsters, though. Another species." Eyasu frowned in thought again. "Clearly dangerous, and no friend to us."

Mavrin carefully shut the *Accounts*, the moment to ask his questions carried away like garnill feathers. "No wonder the Highest Voices tried to hide this."

"Underscoring the importance of the search. The existence of Raw, what happened during the Fracture . . . it's a crucial piece of our history, tied to the Aspects' arrival."

"I suspect They know far more about this than we do." He returned to his place against the wall, stifling a yawn. That burst of adrenaline from seeing the *Accounts* was already fading, especially as he tried to process everything Eyasu told him with the whirling emotions it conjured.

Except something bothered him. "You think our Raw was reaching out to others?"

"Uekel suggests the Raw had a collective bond. Look here." Eyasu pointed at the map. "The creature didn't head east, toward Renhollow or Coaststar. Walking through the cemetery means heading directly north."

"Practically a straight line. There's a road nearby it could've taken instead." Mavrin could picture the map in his mind, after two decades of planning performance tours and trying to cut travel time around the Windroutes. The Unity's city-states and the towns dotting their territories were practically old friends.

He followed a direct line in his mind, how a windship might travel if they left the nearby Jesper Windroute—dangerous as that would be. As he focused his mind on benign things like basic geography, he could feel facts settling into place, almost like they had back in his scholarly days.

"What did she say she could see? Something about a clearing?" he asked.

"The clearing in the cold."

"And a division of water?" Aelda didn't have any divisions of water these days; they evaporated away before the Lifesphere appeared, or were siphoned afterward, prompting the invention of condensers that collected water from the Winds.

Mavrin gestured for Eyasu to bring the map closer. He pointed at the top of the Bemner Windroute, used by windships to travel north and south after transferring from the Jesper. Before the Fracture, he knew what would have been there. "A cold clearing set around a body of water."

Eyasu looked up. "Farglade. Almost directly along the creature's path." He tapped his lip. "Dariss is more common there, which makes it a likely destination."

"Or it spoke nonsense."

Eyasu sat back, considering. "Taunting me, perhaps. It may not have realized everything it said. Or if it genuinely believed it has allies, it would have no reason to lie. Possibly even encourage us to take it where it wants to go, by being obtuse."

"I hope you realize nothing you said was comforting or straightforward."

"Something more is going on here," Eyasu said. "I cannot ignore it."

Mavrin let out a heavy sigh and shifted against the wall, leaning an arm on the garnills' cage. Two of them had hopped back inside, long red necks wrapped around each other as their excitement waned like his. They had something he envied: simplicity. His garnills didn't worry about a trick going sideways, or becoming less relevant with age, unable to compete with younger performers. Bonded to him as they were, they trusted him to keep them fed and comfortable, and luckily for them fulfilling that pact was easier to commit to than others.

"It was all a fable," he said softly. "I could decide that Raw weren't real. That the references were wrong, or Uekel was spinning metaphors to explain Aelda's destruction. Maybe the Aspects created the Lifesphere knowing every mess we made, because the Highest Voices are right, and the Aspects love us completely." Not that that meant anyone should give up praying or paying proper respect. "I've always preferred to not think about it."

"Not always," Eyasu said, without any obvious judgment. Simply stating a fact.

One of the garnills poked a rounded snout against Mavrin's finger, soft lips sucking the salt and dirt from his skin. Another adjusted her sleek, flightless wings, waiting her turn.

"Perhaps there's more to Their plan for you, after all."

Mavrin snorted. "Oh, of course. The Aspects want me to go to Farglade so I can correct all my past mistakes."

Eyasu wore that careful expression again, when he was worried about the reaction to what he was about to say. "Promise that you'll come with me."

Mavrin narrowed his eyes. "Why?"

"Because I know you'll let me hold you to your word."

Mavrin pretended to focus on switching fingers with the garnills. Following Eyasu to the mortuary hadn't felt like a decision past today, but he supposed he'd made one without thinking about it. The intelligent move would still be to wish his friend well, satisfied with whatever reconciliation existed between them, and continue to his next performance. Collect as many chits as possible through the middlemonths, then find a town willing to add him to their allotment system and stop touring. But that wouldn't erase the book resting between them, or the memory of him standing outside Jareden's home.

He imagined the compartments and racks inside his trunk. The closest thing he had to weapons were throwing knives, none sharpened to a deadly point. Flash and smoke pellets, wands that sprayed sparks. Other trinkets like the feather he gave Ohanna, or turnspheres that produced weak light. Nothing intended for combat or survival. Eyasu might be better off without him tagging along.

"What about Aulina? Do you think she'll want to return home?"

Eyasu's shoulders sagged. "Even if Jareden could help her recover from this," he said, leaning heavily on the word *if*, "I worry about the Raw's influence. She might not be safe yet." He started carefully repacking the *Accounts*. "Voice Revect in Farglade has helped me in the past. She might be able to help us now, and Aulina, as well. We can ask her when she awakens."

Mavrin blew out a breath. "Fine. Then I suppose you're stuck with me, too."

He expected Eyasu to beam, but his friend looked concerned. "Also promise not to hit me."

"Why in the Aspects' mismatched souls would I want to hit you this time?"

"Because I have two allies in Farglade. The Voice, and . . . a mutual friend."

When Eyasu said who, Mavrin almost hit him.

Chapter Eleven

EVEN FROM THE GROUND FLOOR, THE SOUNDS OF crashing metal flatware and high-pitched cursing from the basement made Deyeri wince. She knew better than to call down to Yeldin or even step away from his shop's front window, though. He asked her to watch the street, not make him feel old, and she'd received too many earfuls from him already.

Through the dust-marred window, Deyeri could see the narrow avenue outside all the way to the nearest intersection. The Watch had appeared from that direction and split up to start knocking on doors. If they followed proper protocol, it would only take a few more minutes for them to reach the T-junction and the repurposed house where she lurked.

Her nose wrinkled when she recognized the lieutenant in charge and some of the Watch with him. When she was Watch Commander, she would have handled each home visit personally, instructions from the Standing Keep and regulations be damned. Or insisted that the Civil Liaisons carry out the edict, instead of Farglade's military branch, but the former's tiny role in city affairs was one of several reasons why Deyeri was guarding an old man's wares and not Commander anymore. At least the Watch weren't armed.

Between sounds of more deliberate, frustrated crashing, Yeldin called up, "How far away are they?"

"Across the street," she called back.

She couldn't be sure Yeldin heard her; the old merchant still made a habit of shouting from one end of his home-turned-antiques-shop to the other even as he gradually lost his hearing. No response either meant he hadn't heard and didn't care or had heard but didn't have any objections.

Some of the Watch admired the commemorative sculpture in the center of the T-junction, an inverted triangle whose corners reflected each of the Catalyst's outstretched appendages. One soldier moved her hand over the names carved into the triangle, from the top left corner to the center, then up to the right, back to the center before pulling her hand toward the sky, each gesture saying farewell to the souls of the departed. Deyeri made a note to tell her craftspeople their work was being appreciated.

Yeldin stomped up into the front room, hefting another crate. The space had been a parlor at one point, until he cleared out any comfortable furniture to make room for display cabinets and a makeshift sales counter, now covered in clay knickknacks and art pieces, old machinery too damaged to be repurposed, and even a small row of books printed on thin composite. He added the crate to a precarious stack of three next to the room's heatwell and dusted off his hands.

"If we're going to fight them on this, why are you still bringing stuff up?"

"Hidden knows they'll probably haul everything away even with you here," Yeldin grunted as he cracked his spine. "Don't let them track dirt on my carpets!"

He disappeared downstairs again, while Deyeri tried to find a spot on the carpets not already thick with dirt.

Outside, two Watch approached Yeldin's shop.

When Deyeri opened the front door, they blinked at her, Lieutenant Havven's mouth hanging open slightly. He finally sported some premature gray, while his hairline continued to slowly recede above his left temple. The woman with him, stocky with wide eyes and large cheeks that made her look young, must have been hired after Deyeri's tenure.

Havven cleared his throat, prominent Adam's apple bobbing. "Commander. I didn't know you'd be here."

"That's sort of the idea, Hav." Deyeri crossed her arms and leaned against the doorframe, making no effort to hide the fact that she was barring the way. "You two having an easy day so far?"

Havven and the other Watch exchanged a glance.

"Glad to hear it. Now you're going to run an errand for me."

"Ma'am?" Cheeks said.

Deyeri cocked an eyebrow at her, and Havven colored a little. "What errand did you have in mind, Commander?"

"I need to speak to Garris."

"*Commander Termot* is busy . . ."

Havven dropped a hand on his partner's shoulder. "Can I ask why?"

"I'm not letting you inside without her."

Cheeks cut in again. "We have direct orders—"

Deyeri didn't look at her. "How many times did you and I ignore orders, Hav?"

The other soldier started to sputter, until Havven waved her away. She spared Deyeri one more glower as she trudged off into the Winds, hiking her shoulders outside the protective cover of Yeldin's threshold.

"Sorry. Caspen is a little . . . headstrong." Havven's smile was fleeting. "People are going to start calling you a nuisance, Dey."

Deyeri shrugged. "You're confiscating people's possessions. Seems worthy of a nuisance." Before Havven could respond, she added, "Don't pretend this sits well with you. Or Termot. Get her down here or we'll have more than a nuisance."

Then, despite their friendship, she shut the door in his face.

Farglade's current Watch Commander appeared at the end of the street about twenty minutes later, stepping carefully around piles of sediment from yesterday's Longwind; the sweepers typically started on the side of the Towers closest to the Windroute and worked their way toward the hills, meaning they wouldn't reach Yeldin's neighborhood until evening. Someone knocked politely at the door, and Deyeri offered Havven and Caspen a beaming smile as they led Garris Termot inside.

"Wipe your boots, please."

Caspen hesitated—the kind of behavior she would have called someone on early in their career—but followed Termot's lead and kicked her boots on the stoop. They gathered in the front room, each person offering a nod to Yeldin, scowling with one arm wrapped protectively over his stack of crates.

In her early forties, Garris Termot was almost a decade younger than Deyeri, but carried extra years in the droop of her shoulders and the crinkles around her eyes. She placed her hands casually on her hips and offered a thin half-smile without ever quite looking her way. "Funny hill to die on, Dey."

Deyeri leaned against a display case of brass wind chimes and crossed her arms, freezing in place when the chimes rattled. Ignoring how Havven hid a smirk, she said, "I had Niena Melur crying on my doorstep two days ago after she handed over the only pitchers she can use for her experiments. Adrike Dren says you took every decoration from his dining hall. And no one from the Keep seems to respond to a message anymore, so here we are."

Hands still on her hips, Termot wandered to the window, so that all Deyeri could see was her pale gold hair, hanging in shoulder-length tresses pinned to her shoulders.

She sighed. "Breck can't honestly expect everyone to give up their possessions—"

"Not just possessions! My wares!" Yeldin kicked the crates beside him, almost sending both him and the stack toppling.

Havven leapt forward to steady the crates. "How am I supposed to operate a business?"

Havven caught Deyeri's eye. They both knew Yeldin's story: that getting his antiquities shop approved came after his husband went looking for a "better life" and he needed a distraction. That his grumbling, ever-flustered attitude was as deliberate as the ways Deyeri projected confidence when she confronted someone in a doorway.

He also knew not to bring that up to Yeldin, so instead, Havven said, "The Lord-Magistrate is appointed on the understanding that we trust their judgment."

"Well, I'm questioning it," Deyeri snapped. That made Termot's head turn ever so slightly, and she realized too late how that must have sounded: was she truly upset for the people, or angry about being shut out of Breck's confidence?

"It would be one thing if the Council changed the allotment on us," she said more calmly. "But confiscating people's things? Unless I missed something, they shouldn't be touching your possessions except in an emergency. Did we find an emergency that needs pitchers and wall plaques?"

She knew they hadn't, even though some of the Councillors she remembered might describe higher trade demands as an emergency. The price of Farglade's independence from the rest of Aelda meant negotiating for things they couldn't easily produce instead of being granted them fairly. It would have been one thing if the Unity demanded more meat or salt; she had no idea why they wanted precious gems and crystal. Farglade couldn't mine enough to meet the new demands, which led to Edict Nine: a new levy on the people, asking for personal possessions made from things like silver, dariss, quartz, or agate, so they could fulfill the Unity's demands. People were promised increased allotments in future months, including luxury chits, but that didn't make up for having to turn over important possessions now.

Havven glanced at Termot, who didn't seem interested in stepping in. With another apologetic look he added, "We're still rebuilding, aren't we? If they want more from us in trade—"

"After they left us to fight the Incursions alone," Deyeri grumbled.

"I'd rather they ask for pretty crystals than our crops. Or my allotment."

Deyeri focused on Termot again. "You're okay with this?"

"Not always ours to wonder why," she murmured lightly, in that way that sounded like she was almost cracking a joke.

"Great. I always worried retiring would mean the Council losing its only person with a backbone." She regretted it even before seeing Havven's sour frown. Worse was when Termot made a light tsking sound under her breath.

In the tense silence that followed, Yeldin of all people spoke up. "Fine. You want to take my *carefully collected* items, be my guest. At least give me time to go through them. There are items in here that have sentimental value, if that means anything to you people."

When Termot didn't answer right away, Deyeri asked her, "If someone tried to carry off your mementos of Cereil, you'd just let them?"

Termot's shoulders sagged a little further. A different person might have lashed out at someone bringing up their dead daughter like that, and Deyeri knew she was taking advantage of knowing Termot wouldn't. But they both knew that sometimes, your last-ditch idea didn't make you feel like a hero.

When Termot turned away from the window fully, she wore a smile like an opponent commending someone on a good move. "Deal."

Yeldin grunted something that might have been thanks.

Termot offered Havven a slight tilt of her head and started for the door. Deyeri opened her mouth to say something, maybe apologize, but she didn't look back as she stepped out into the chilly morning air. Havven, at least, gave her a casual two-finger salute before steering Caspen outside.

Yeldin kicked the stack of crates again, but thankfully they only wobbled a bit. "They could've hauled this away!"

Deyeri cocked an eyebrow. "I thought you didn't want to go through it."

"Didn't think I'd have a choice. And this one's new. From a salvager working the West Chain. Haven't had enough time to grow attached." He sniffed at the top box on the stack. "Help me with it?"

"Much as I'd love that," she said, only half-sarcastic, "I need to go alienate another old friend."

The Standing Keep sat on a large promontory off the Towers, Farglade's eastern district, looking out on the Bemner Windroute and the city's massive airdock. The original settlement established routeside had been replaced over time by four large buildings made of dense, polished dolomite, with deliberate jutting corners and sloping roofs to deflect the greater pressure from the Windroute on the cliffs below. The buildings, a wide stone pavilion and distinct walking paths sat inside a high wall topped with decorative, wrought-iron bars and periodic gaps so the public could meander through at will. Three two-story, rectangular outbuildings sat within the walls as though set by a jeweler, highlighting the delicate beauty of the Gannerthen Building, the large, circular main hall that sat closest to the cliff's edge.

Deyeri didn't bother heading toward the main hall. She knew Breck's schedule by rote; with the morning slipping away, he wouldn't be inside.

Two of the Lord-Magistrate's personal guard stood near

Gannerthen's northwest corner; they wore similar uniforms to the Watch but in gray and black, and were the only armed unit in the city, except for people stationed at the Zerrilen Craggs. Either because of recognition or the determined look on her face, they nodded and let her pass.

Breck stood in a circle of stone benches shielded by a transparent crystal enclosure, close enough to the promontory's edge that someday erosion would toss it into the Windroute. The original had been destroyed during the Incursions, but Breck's predecessor, Pericar, bribed Requesters to recreate a perfect replica when they channeled better defenses to protect the Keep.

Stay calm this time, she told herself again. Except that wasn't always easy with Woldren Breck.

"You know," Deyeri said as she paused on the enclosure's threshold, "too much routine makes you seem older."

Without missing a beat, Breck pointed at his shaggy, white hair. "Figure sheer stubbornness will keep me in shape. Like you."

He took a long sip from a tumbler of water, facing the cracked hills south of the city. Deyeri let out an exasperated breath and leaned against the wall beside him. "People are upset, Woldren."

"That happens."

"Especially when the magistrate doesn't explain things."

"Is that what I'm supposed to do?" Breck grimaced, pulling at the scars on the left side of his face—relics of a time when he wasn't yet Crossed General Woldren Breck, hero of the Incursions from Afar, let alone the city's magistrate. "Explain every decision so the people feel good?"

That dismissiveness shouldn't have surprised her. Or hurt. Except that they hadn't spoken in months, and she could still remember when he would always take her seriously. "You're taking things that matter to people. They deserve more than that."

"Please. People get too attached—"

"They don't deserve to get attached?" Deyeri demanded, feeling her temper rise. Crossing her arms and digging her nails into her bicep helped a touch. "After how many times people almost lost everything during the Incursions?"

She came prepared to rattle off names like she had with Termot, but Breck cut her off: "Would you rather we tear down columns or start stripping roofs?" He gestured vaguely at the Keep, and the ceramic roof tiles bordered in dariss. "I could always take the monuments. No one likes those, right?"

Every other trick she used to stay calm around Breck fled at that point. He was really saying: *Maybe if you didn't leave to go play decorator, we wouldn't be in this position.*

So she responded, "I think the Watch you gave up on feel differently."

Half a snarl escaped Breck's throat before he hid it behind his tumbler. "Says the person who wanted to dismantle the Watch."

"To avoid a military state. People deserve—"

"There's that word again. Deserve, deserve. What does *Farglade* deserve, Deyeri?"

"How about an honest magistrate—"

"They have one!"

"Do they?" Deyeri snapped back.

"When have I ever done anything that wasn't in this city's best interest?" He set the tumbler down hard enough to slosh water onto the bench. "No one complained when I changed Pericar's paranoid curfew laws. Or when I told Coaststar to hop a chasm on that mutual research agreement. Thought people gave me this job because they trust my judgment."

He ambled to the other side of the enclosure, with the gait of someone used to takka riding or marching across the Edgeplains. Even after four years as Lord-Magistrate, he still looked uncomfortable wearing a formal jacket and pants instead of a uniform. And stiff as he walked, which only reminded her how many times they had fought like this.

"Trust doesn't last forever, Woldren."

What she was really saying: *What happened to us should've taught you something.*

"Maybe it didn't for Pericar," Breck said, turning toward her again. "I'm not him."

"You're not," she admitted, making Breck's scowl soften. But even though she knew that—had lived and served under his predecessor's overly hesitant, smile-and-nod bureaucracy, and his sickening deference to the Quartered Citadel seemingly at the expense of any love for the Aspects—she made a point of adding, "Give it time."

Breck's eyes widened like she'd slapped him. The scowl returned twice as deep, pulling those old scars even further. "You have no idea what you're talking about anymore." He held a finger into her face before she could speak. "And don't say it's because I cut you out. You chose to leave the Watch and you know it."

Eyes narrowing, not caring as her temper flared past the ache forming in her biceps, Deyeri snapped, "You cut me out long before that."

"Yeah, well, the Lifesphere might shield us, but we need to shield the truth."

He stared right at her as he said it. Those same words he said during the last Incursion, when he was still the Crossed General and she wasn't even Watch Commander yet. Just someone serving under his command, dried blood flaking to the ground in his command pit as she demanded why Breck had left her people to die, after he promised reinforcements.

Sometimes we need to shield the truth, he'd said, only low enough for her to hear. *If you knew you were alone, you wouldn't have fought so hard.*

Blood pounding in her ears, red seeming to color her vision, she barely noticed Breck tilt his head up to the enclosure's roof and mutter a curse under his breath. Seeing the realization on his features didn't stop her from turning to leave. If he wasn't going to listen, she would go find something else to—

"I'm buying time, okay?" He stomped around the enclosure to block her path, jaw tight like being honest meant forcing the words out. "Until maybe we don't have to keep the Citadel happy."

That made both of Deyeri's eyebrows rise and kept her from shouldering through him to get out.

Except he didn't say anything else, because she was outside his confidence now. The regret in his eyes didn't matter. She remembered the Lifesphere dimming without any sign of reinforcements, and the look on Havven's face when he realized the Crossed General wasn't coming to save them.

"This is the Incursions all over again."

"Dey—"

"Save it. Sorry to take your time, Lord-Magistrate."

He was still quick enough to dodge aside before she could shoulder-check him, unfortunately. Far from the first time between them, she didn't look back.

"The Highest Voices are looking for something."

Deyeri tried not to feel good about the conflicted look on Breck's face. She stayed outside the enclosure, letting the Winds carry away some of the heat in her cheeks and forehead.

Breck rubbed the edge of his scars. "Trade demand is a cover. They're after some artifact from before the Fracture."

"What artifact?"

"Plaque. Memory charm. Old sword. Who knows." He held up his palms. "Look, if I thought people were in danger, I'd lock down the city. All I have are scraps and rumors. Whatever they're looking for, they're afraid of someone finding it first."

She braced herself as the Winds picked up, eyeing him carefully. Anything that worried the Highest Voices likely meant heresy, even if Breck refused to say the word. Growing up in Veristenok, she knew the list of things they considered dangerous was long but specific. Wanting to find it first was the sort of strategic thinking that made Breck effective—and dangerous to anyone who threatened Farglade. "You want to find this thing and leverage it."

"I want the Unity's pressure off our backs."

"Risky."

"That mean you don't want to help?"

Deyeri glowered at his teasing smile until he dropped it.

"Since you're already talking to people, let them know I'm not just bowing to the Unity," Breck said, managing to throw her words back at her even while giving ground. The rest came out in a rush. "Find out if anyone's holding onto things from the Time Before. No one in the Watch knows about this artifact, but I can direct them a bit to speed things up."

That sounded like the sort of work she would give to the newest recruits in the Watch. However, she understood exactly what Breck was offering: the opportunity to be involved in his scheme, even a little. Whether he realized it or not, it was also an opportunity for her to find out everything he wasn't telling her, before something he refused to say caught her by surprise.

"Fine," she said. "Tell me more about this artifact."

She didn't expect that to be a difficult question, but Breck let out a long breath and sat down on the enclosure steps. "You ever hear of the Raw?"

Breck watched as Deyeri disappeared around the side of the Gannerthen Building, knowing she would spend the rest of the day on the streets. That used to be a strength he relied on from her. Now he wondered whether he should have her tracked.

He waved idly at his guards and hoped they didn't notice how much he sagged against the side of the enclosure. The tingling feeling in his jaw wouldn't disappear as he rotated it; admitting even part of the truth to Deyeri took a toll. He glared at the stone beneath his feet, imagining the sanctum below and the creatures inside. They knew he wouldn't have told Deyeri everything—she wouldn't understand, yet—but more information could have helped her find what he needed.

Instead, she would keep believing the Raw were a myth.

Maybe they'll let me show you soon, Dey, he thought, as the tingling in his jaw slowly faded.

Chapter Twelve

BEFORE AULINA WOKE UP, MAVRIN AGREED THAT Eyasu should take the lead on finding out how much she remembered and explaining their concerns and thoughts about Farglade—after he promised not to scare her. That mostly worked, though he emphasized the strength and danger of a Raw more than Mavrin would have liked.

Once her initial daze passed, Aulina didn't seem to remember much that happened when she was under the Raw's control or decided to bury it somewhere deep and not discuss it. Eyasu didn't press her too much, showing more delicacy than Mavrin would have expected, faced with a possible new source of firsthand experience with the Raw. He didn't think she would agree anyway, mostly because of Ohanna, yet Aulina listened intently.

In the end, she said, "I don't want to hurt anyone else. Can you make sure I won't?"

Eyasu didn't exactly lie. "The only way to be sure is through more research."

"Ohanna will want to know when I'm coming back." Aulina glanced at the closed front door. "Except we don't know, do we?"

Mavrin wanted to tell her Ohanna would be fine, but that felt like a half-lie, too.

In the end, she said she trusted Jareden to tell her sister what she needed to know and care for her temporarily. Mavrin figured she knew that returning now was riskier than staying away.

~

As they passed through Vertsa's main gate almost two days later, each avoiding the subject in their own ways, Mavrin finally said, "I've decided something about your channeling."

Eyasu coughed, but otherwise his attention stayed on the thick, metal arch around the sloping tunnel that led into the city. It was stunning, almost enough that Mavrin could believe Eyasu really hadn't heard. Vertsa was the largest town in Renhollow's territory and the oldest post-Fracture community in existence. Most of it lay completely underground, tunneled through the Moderates' stable bedrock, but unlike most other subterraneans, its citizens maintained an extreme illusion of the outdoors. Bioluminescent lichen and fungus grew in cultivated swirls along the tunnel walls, abstractly echoing Aelda's vibrant, pre-Fracture ecosystems. Uneven holes in the ceiling offered actual sunlight, sometimes passing through colored glass depicting scraps of pre-Fracture history. Grinning figures in hoods leading shaggy herd animals shared space with beaded dancers mid-whirl on an island coast, reflecting both the varied peoples who founded Vertsa together and the descendants who now called it home.

They turned a corner down a narrower, winding tunnel into one of Vertsa's many bazaars. Unlike smaller towns like Tanardell, Vertsa adopted electric power almost immediately after Renhollow started trading the technology. Rows of windtowers on the surface powered bulbs in an array of colors, concocted using metals and minerals that weren't needed as much for more practical purposes, or cleverly weaving oil from bioluminescent plants and fungus through the glass. Even the cables snaking throughout the city were splashed with vibrant designs, to highlight the ingenuity of the engineers responsible.

Mavrin and Eyasu's remaining provisions had barely lasted the two days to Vertsa. The first stall they passed, Mavrin handed in three Renhollow chits for the same number of water packs, thanking the vendor profusely as a visitor should. The next stall offered them stone-baked nutroot in wheat wraps, which Mavrin supplemented with a bag of dried berrenfruit using one of his precious luxury chits.

Aulina narrowed her eyes at the berrenfruit and didn't comment as she chewed, studying a wall further down the bazaar. Dozens of mismatched stones painted green, yellow or brown formed a graphic of a tree, standing on a circular patch of uniform blades of grass. Two lamps rotating nearby made the trunk and leaves brighten at regular intervals; when the trunk dimmed, a winding path through mist was faintly visible in wavy lines against the rock, the common image tied to the Presence as Passage.

"Every so often, a Vertsan merchant will pass through Tanardell," Aulina said, brushing her finger over the stones. "People would set aside luxury chits for his trinkets, but I just liked to look."

"What about Ohanna?"

That loving smile Mavrin spotted at his show returned. "She said we didn't need them, when we had the orchard to look at. Your magic, on the other hand . . ." She passed a stall displaying recycled windscarves sewn from patches and one offering sautéed koo beetles, which almost every culture thriving in Vertsa claimed to have originated. "I think I'll bring Ohanna here someday. She deserves to see this." Aulina sighed, a comfortingly human sound after her blank stares and troubled sleep during the journey from Tanardell.

They couldn't pause at any stall for long, as Eyasu cut a path through the bazaar. Having his hood thrown up made him stand out even more than his height and breadth, but he ignored the smiling, energetic people he passed. Their plan wasn't to stay in Vertsa more than a night, which meant securing passage on a windship for the morning, before the hour grew too late.

Mavrin matched his friend's pace. "Aren't you going to ask what I decided?"

Eyasu's placid, mildly curious expression never changed. "You'll tell me regardless."

A gaggle of children pointed at Mavrin's garnills, laughing as they jumped in their cage. They paid him no mind as they scurried away, except for one girl who lingered behind, clutching a bright scarf almost as red as the garnills' matted feathers. Aulina waved with her uninjured hand, but her expression fell as the girl hurried to catch up to her friends.

Mavrin said to Eyasu, "I don't think your channeling is safe."

They turned onto another street, entering a quarter filled with artisanal shops in squat, brick-and-mortar buildings, pressed against the rock walls on either side. A cool breeze ruffled Mavrin's hair from one of the ceiling vents, carrying the scent of takka cooked with merrimor and thyme from somewhere nearby. One of the perks of being nomadic was picking favorite foods in each town and city he visited.

Eyasu said flatly, "That sounds less like a decision and more like maintaining a belief."

"Don't mince my words," Mavrin snapped. "Your channeling shouldn't work, Eyasu. And to be fair, it hasn't worked consistently."

"No Requester receives a Response every time."

"I know that, but what happens if the Aspects decide your . . ." He stopped himself from using the word *heresy* and glanced around the crowded tunnel. "The only reason we didn't die fighting that *being* is because you could match its channeling. What if you can't next time?"

"Then I'll turn to my other tools," Eyasu said, idly tapping the hilt of his longsword. His expression turned solemn. "I hope the Catalyst will save me from relying on them too often."

The sight of that sword, and his armor, and everything else different about him still made Mavrin feel like he'd stepped into an illusion. But this Catalyst as Core bothered him far more. "I don't understand how you believe so strongly in Them while praying to an Aspect-variation that doesn't exist."

"Might not exist," Aulina said. Mavrin had been so caught up in making his point that he didn't realize she was back in earshot. "Isn't the point of variation that they can be unlimited? I wondered that once, but Voice Arric warned me not to follow the idea too far."

"It was debated more before the Fracture," Eyasu said. "The Aspect-variations we know came from the original interpretation of the Words. Many sects died out during the Fracture, and others faded when they weren't promoted by the Highest Voices. The beginning of our communal respect to the Aspects," he added, and Mavrin heard his bitterness in the clipped way he said each word.

If Aulina noticed, she didn't comment. "So that the Saviors know our love," she murmured, eyes flicking to the ceiling.

Much as he didn't want to support Eyasu's point, Mavrin added, "Also to cement power." He shrugged in response to Aulina's surprised look. "Studying at the Citadel lets you see the Highest Voices from every angle."

"You attended the Quartered Citadel?"

The way she leaned on the word *you* didn't escape his attention. Aulina wasn't in awe of discovering that *both* of her new companions studied in Veristenok. She didn't understand how the spindly man in a violet cloak stuffed with what amounted to elaborate toys could have been there, let alone one of the Citadel's prized researchers. He hadn't told anyone about that life in so long that he felt a sudden urge to convince her he wasn't lying, and as a result had no idea where to start.

"Mavrin sought to become either a Servant or an Interpreter," he heard Eyasu answer.

Aulina seemed more confused by that than by the existence of

Raw. She opened her mouth to speak, closed it, and simply gestured at his violet cloak and trunk. Eyasu covered a chuckle.

Mavrin rubbed one of his eyes, wanting to unpack this only slightly more than letting Eyasu do it for him. "Scholars at the Citadel are encouraged to pursue a creative hobby. My father and I enjoyed when the illusionists passed through Hallen's Arch, and it would've made my mother balk. I was passably good back then, but now, witness the master." He flared his cloak, almost tangling someone passing behind him.

"Why did you leave?" She must have noticed Mavrin's expression tighten. "Never mind. What matters is being together now."

"Because I so missed arguing," Mavrin grumbled as they kept walking.

"If the Catalyst doesn't approve of my choices," Eyasu said sharply, "I would have been told by now. If They choose not to Respond to me every time, I'll respect that."

Mavrin wasn't sure he trusted the cold certainty in Eyasu's voice, but he decided to let it go. "Let's hope they don't ignore you again when we're moments away from death." He sighed, finally realizing how he sounded, and turned to Aulina. "I'm sorry. This is likely the last thing we should be discussing around you."

"I don't know that I'd want it discussed away from me, either," Aulina said, studying her feet. Mavrin had loaned her a cloak and spare set of boots, since they had similar frames, but they would need to get her better traveling clothes before they left Vertsa. "Leaving it unsaid doesn't change what happened."

"He doesn't mean to be rude," Eyasu said. "Mavrin is upset."

By the Four. "Why do you think I'm upset?"

"Because I stayed in touch with Deyeri and you haven't. Since you don't want to discuss it, you're lashing out through another subject."

"Why did I ever enjoy arguing with you?"

"I tried to explain," Eyasu insisted. "It was occasional messages and the rare visit when I happened to be in Farglade. Especially after the Incursions . . ."

"No need to explain. You're friends, and friends keep in contact. I understand."

"Mavrin . . ."

"I said I understand."

They walked in silence for a while after that. Since leaving Tanardell, Mavrin kept telling himself not to be angry. Expecting Eyasu and Deyeri not to speak or see each other because he left felt arrogant. But if they made the effort to stay friends, a small part of him wondered why they hadn't tracked him down, too. His name had been written on slate noticeboards across half of Aelda, at one time or another.

He couldn't decide which bothered him more: that Eyasu never tried, or that Deyeri hadn't.

This is what happens when you break someone's heart.

"Am I the only one hearing music?" Aulina asked.

She glanced around furtively, but Mavrin heard it, too. A low, sonorous sound mixed with the tingling of bells. He glanced around, realizing they'd turned onto a street he recognized.

"Mavrin Leed!" A familiar face pushed casually through the evening crowd. His wavy hair and the thin stubble across his jaw looked grayer than Mavrin recalled, but he recognized the beaming grin that practically split the man's round face. He turned quickly to Aulina, hoping the look conveyed the man was as real as the bells.

"You monster!" the man bellowed. "Were you going to pass without saying hello? How dare you!" Cler Landrik grabbed Mavrin by one hand and pulled him into a tight embrace. "When did you arrive back in our dear Vertsa?"

"I, well, a little while ago, actually." Mavrin glanced over Cler's head and saw the bright blue sign of the Lost Myths Respite hanging above his massive, multi-level establishment. The place would have been elegant and picturesque if it didn't tower over every other building in sight, reaching into the ceiling itself. "Did you change your sign?"

Cler spun on his heel, giving Mavrin precious seconds to get himself mentally back in order, showman smile fixed in place the moment Cler turned back.

"Not since you were here last. Though Relliera tells me to clean it more . . . regularly, so perhaps its shine distracted you," Cler said, stuttering partway without losing stride. "Since when are you traveling in the company of others?"

Mavrin quickly introduced the others before a thought struck him. "I was telling them that if we're spending the night in Vertsa, we have no choice but to stay at the Respite. Assuming you have rooms available?"

If Cler noticed Mavrin tap Eyasu's arm to keep him from speaking, he didn't say anything. "For you, my dear Mavrin? I'd kick the . . . dregs out onto the street to make space." He looked at Eyasu. "Your friend here has done me a great service on more than one occasion. My common room is never as full of energy as when the great Mavrin Leed performs."

"Ours is a mutually beneficial relationship," Mavrin said, even as the friendly grip on his arm melted away some of his foul mood.

Behind him, the Respite released a louder series of tones, as the Winds above briefly picked up speed. The tubes pointing out of the building looked motley and random, but they were deliberately placed and sculpted to channel currents through the ground, producing the musical notes that echoed down the street.

Feeling some of his own energy return, Mavrin offered Cler a twirling bow. "My dear Master Landrik, please show us to our rooms."

As Cler pushed his way back down the street, Eyasu leaned in to say to Mavrin, "I'll see about the windship."

Mavrin spotted one of Vertsa's large clocks across the street. "The dockmaster will have closed."

"I prefer to arrange passage personally." Eyasu winked as he handed Mavrin his rucksack. "I thought a well-renowned traveler like you would expect that."

"I don't often travel the Windroutes," Mavrin mumbled. As Eyasu started walking, he called, "Do you want me to find you some ress root? The Respite is usually well-stocked."

Eyasu frowned. "Ress root?"

"Didn't the Citadel quartermaster make you work for how much you snacked on?"

To his surprise, Eyasu cocked his head in thought. "I guess my tastes have changed over the years."

Then he walked away, leaving Mavrin to put down his self-doubt by force, as he and Aulina followed Cler.

Chapter Thirteen

"... COULDN'T BELIEVE HE SAID THAT! AND IN front of the entire group!" Relliera Landrik smacked her husband lightly on the arm.

Cler shrugged and sipped his brandy. "I wasn't going to let that pompous fool carry on. Talking about Ereste's *Greg . . . Gregariousness* like it's political propaganda . . ."

Mavrin nodded absently; he often lost track of which member of the Vertsa community Cler and Relliera were talking about, none of whom he'd ever met. His third glass of expensive brandy—berrenfruit mixed with silverash—didn't help, either. But since his cheeks were sore from laughing, he could live with a reprieve from bawdy jokes and reminiscing on old times.

"I should probably check on Spen and Rikken," Relliera finally said, referring to the two poets under their patronage. She pecked Mavrin on the cheek as she passed, disappearing up the stairs in a flutter of braided necklaces and flowy, multi-colored clothing.

Even in a vibrant town like Vertsa, the Lost Myths Respite stood out. It had started out as one of the town's countless metal-works, until one generation of the family who owned it decided to pursue a different career; Mavrin vaguely remembered a nutcheese shop the first time he passed through town. Cler and Relliera arrived from Coaststar, bought the building, and converted the intricate, almost maze-like interior into a combination inn, artisan commune, and crafting shop.

Since Tanardell had nothing like it, Mavrin explained to

Aulina, "The Landriks offer patronage and lodging to traveling artists, by sharing their weekly allotment."

"Doesn't the local magistrate offer allotments to artists?" She politely shook her head when Cler offered to refill her teacup.

"Of course, but the Landriks believe people should have the freedom to work on whatever they want anytime, instead of being tasked with specific commissions." That was part of why he hadn't stayed with any performing companies after Brennig's Bedazzling Spectacle Troupe. "I've learned that while our system works to keep everyone fed and comfortable, for some even the mildest control from the Unity can feel stifling."

Mavrin met the Landriks because of their crafting, when someone recommended Cler as a designer of "unique mechanisms." He and Relliera earned their allotment on design work for Vertsa and used their spare time to tinker on "special projects" to see if they could be completed. Mavrin had several tools for his show from Cler's workshop, including some of his more eclectic designs that couldn't find a home elsewhere. The workshop took up most of the basement and had changed about as much as Cler: still immaculately organized but dense with workbenches, slates with half-finished notes or sketches in chalk, bins of materials, and a polished wet bar in one corner.

Mavrin picked up a clockwork figure of a sparrow, which looked like a more complicated design of the feather he'd left with Ohanna. "This brass has a different hue than what you built me."

"More . . . refined material," Cler bragged as he poured another glass of brandy from the bar. He gestured at the nearest bins of supplies. "We have a veritable glut, courtesy of the Unity. New trade relations with the south have been good, mostly . . ."

"Anything an old magician could use?" Mavrin asked, before Cler could jump onto another political rant.

The other man snorted. "If you're old, I'm damned ancient."

Glass in one hand, he wandered the room, waving his free fingers in the air as he surveyed his shelves.

Aulina passed one of the workbenches, slowly examining each piece one-by-one. Mavrin wondered if her parents used to tinker like this.

"There!"

An object came flying across the room. Mavrin narrowly caught it before it struck the wall behind him. The ceramic, brown cube weighed more than he would have expected, considering the hollow center; he could see a metal contraption inside, but no obvious indication of what it was supposed to do. Other than a stylized sun stenciled on one face, the cube was unremarkable.

"How does—"

Cler pointed to a switch near Mavrin's thumb. When he pressed it, a tiny flame appeared inside. He brought it up to his face, trying to find the wick or the fluid, and Cler gently pushed his hands back down.

A few heartbeats later, the cube let out a sharp pop, and four bursts of brightly colored smoke popped from each corner on the sun face, one after the other in quick succession. Mavrin almost dropped the cube, but Cler clamped his fingers in place, as a small burst of pink flame erupted from the sun. The entire time, the ceramic cube remained cool to the touch.

"Fanciful, no?" Cler beamed as he ran his finger along one of the edges. "The fuel is hidden within the frame. Tried it with burstpowder, but that was too explosive. Heat triggers the smoke through simple convection. I'm hoping to design a variable timer."

Normally, Mavrin's brain would have been running through scenarios, trying to imagine how he might incorporate the cube into his show. Instead, he saw a figure with golden veins and blazing orange eyes, setting a tree aflame. He deliberately didn't glance at Aulina, in case any fear showed on his face.

"Not sure if I can use this, I'm afraid," he said carefully. "Do you have anything that can be hidden on my person? Preferably along the same lines as that bindcord you made."

Cler squinted at him. "Nothing particularly new. What's the trick this time?"

"I'm not sure," Mavrin said. He couldn't exactly explain his concern about fighting a Raw again. He tossed the cube lightly to Cler, and by the time the tinkerer looked up, he had his showman smile back in place. "Let's brainstorm and see what we come up with."

A while later, Mavrin climbed the stairs to the room he shared with Eyasu, carrying a near-empty bottle of liqueur and that ceramic cube, which Cler refused to take back. Aulina had retired much earlier, on the excuse that she was still recovering, leaving Mavrin and Cler to reminisce about past visits. Between that and the drink, he found himself whistling as he set the bottle on the nightstand and prepared for bed, relying on the colored light cascading through the window and the averblossom lantern in the corner. The Respite's highest floor extended partially aboveground, each room featuring colored glass windows that filtered sunlight or the Lifesphere's glow. He shut his eyes for a long moment, enjoying the unique space, and the occasional notes from the stone pipes running above, to which his garnills hooted in response even though they were fast asleep.

Mavrin carefully folded his cloak and traveling clothes on a table outside; Relliera had offered to have it all cleaned in the morning. Innkeepers and other colleagues in his business were friendly and appreciative, but that sort of kindness was rare. If he went to the Halpeck Opera or attended an annual performers' guild meeting, he knew he wouldn't fit in with the professionals and patrons whose names were legends across Aelda. But in his circuit of performing spaces, he had friends.

They are friends, aren't they?

Usually when he stayed at the Respite, he was so exhausted from a show or the aftermath with Cler and Relliera that he fell asleep almost immediately. Tonight, he stood at the window, gazing at Vertsa's windtowers. The last time he performed here, he incorporated more fables into his act, like claiming one of his wands was passed down from the great Requester Rydlec Oren, to cater to Cler's whimsical sensibilities. Mum told him stories like that as a child, always making sure to remind him that ogrekin and tentacled demons were ridiculous, so they didn't cause nightmares. The same kind of creatures he mentioned with exaggerated gravitas in his show, leaning over the children seated in front and waggling his brows so they knew he was only teasing.

He didn't think he would use those stories again, when he went back to performing.

If he went back to performing.

"Stop dwelling, old man," he said to himself.

Behind him, the lantern light flickered violently.

Mavrin spun around, staring at the empty room. Nothing moved between the two narrow beds, the nightstand between them, or the garnills' cage. He waited for a count of five before he released his breath and ran a hand over his face, blaming drink and fatigue.

As he dropped his hand, something in a corner of the ceiling caught his eye.

Careful not to make any sudden movements, Mavrin tilted his gaze upward. Tinted shadows danced across the wooden boards, conjured by the Lifesphere's glow reflecting off the windtowers outside. Never taking his eyes from the ceiling, he turned the dial below the multicolored window, dropping the cloth curtain so that the only light came from the lantern. The remaining shadows didn't shift as he took a cautious step forward, and another, into the center of the room.

Something creaked behind him.

He whirled too quickly on his wrong foot and slipped to the floor. Waving his hands in front of him, Mavrin kicked backward until he hit the nearest wall. Every corner of the room became a potential hiding place for something horrific, either under a bed or behind the curtains or beneath his trunk.

The lantern went out.

Mavrin stayed perfectly still, heart pounding in his chest. The quiet seemed to press in around him as he waited for his eyes to adjust. It took him a moment to realize why. His garnills were silent. He glanced at the outline of the cage and saw their tiny shapes inside, painted in a faint, blue glow.

A whisper of cold air brushed his cheek, gone as soon as he felt it, the touch familiar and alien at the same time. It felt enough like the gentlest brush of fingertips that he closed his eyes, waiting for something more, like a hand around his throat.

Something heavy creaked, and Mavrin let out a cry, raising his hands in front of his face.

"What are you doing?"

Eyasu stood in the doorway.

"I . . ." Mavrin looked around the room. Nothing unexpected caught his eye, and he became very aware of the almost-finished bottle on the nightstand. "I fell over?"

Eyasu stepped inside and shut the door, one hand lingering near his longsword. He noticed the bottle, too, and shook his head as he jostled the averblossom lantern, prompting the plant inside to resume glowing. Mavrin tried to remember the last time he saw averblossom randomly fall dormant like that.

"I booked passage on a windship," Eyasu said as he started removing his armor. "We'll have time for breakfast before it departs."

"Ah. Good." Mavrin realized he was still on the floor and climbed to his feet, dusting off his pants.

In bed, he tucked the blankets tightly around himself, like he used to when Mum accidentally frightened him with a bedtime fable. He tensed as Eyasu covered the lantern.

When the garnills finally started hooting again, he could consider falling asleep.

Chapter Fourteen

THE NEXT MORNING, MAVRIN WOKE UP IN A DARK room and counted his blessings that Eyasu was already gone. It meant no one heard his yelp, before he realized the curtains were still down and the averblossom had used up its glow.

His cleaned clothes waited on the table outside; he'd showered the road dust away before drinking last night and didn't want to take advantage of the Landriks' hospitality, since they wouldn't accept a chit from him. Before throwing on his cloak, he rolled up his sleeves and strapped the bindcord Cler designed onto his left forearm. On the other, he attached his faded leather drop sheath with a blunted dagger. The latter didn't fit as well as he remembered, but the spring snapped the dagger into his palm with a light flick of his wrist. He finished by adding smoke pellets, trick wands, and more into the pockets of his cloak, carrying out the entire ritual in complete silence.

No unwelcome creaks or whispers reached his ears.

Mavrin wanted to sneak out, rude as that might be, but Relliera waited in the front hall. She wore simpler clothing this morning: one gown instead of several, cinched at the waist, and her customary necklaces, each of which paid homage to the Vital as Sensation and could be unclasped as easily as the wearer liked.

"Cler was up half the night because of you," she said, eyes twinkling, and held out a note between two of her fingers. "He scribbled this."

In her husband's tidy printing, unmarred by drink and fatigue, the note read: *About a half-dozen ideas for you, all of which will need work. On your way back through, drop in to pick them up. And stay for longer! I demand a performance!*

The designs were half brilliant, half unrealistic for his show, but Mavrin's smile felt forced. "Thank you. Tell him I'll visit again as soon as I can."

Relliera squinted at him. "And when will that be?"

"You know the life of a magician." He hoped his shrug seemed nonchalant and jokingly cavalier. "Could be ages. Could be next week."

Could be never.

Relliera pulled him into her usual tight embrace, necklaces jangling, but it didn't make him feel as warm as he remembered. Still wondering why, he stepped outside into the relative quiet of morning in Vertsa. Eyasu and Aulina stood on the street out front, watching the lamps change color to mark the morning cycle. Eyasu's runed armor peeked from a handsomely attached cloak, and Aulina wore new traveling clothes: a dark red shirt under a wool vest, with dark pants and soft shoes. Her splinted wrist was no longer secured to her side, and a leather bag set with sparkly rocks hung over her other shoulder, which he suspected held more offerings from Relliera, and made Mavrin feel guiltier about wanting to sneak out unseen.

Before either of them could say anything, Mavrin pointed at Eyasu's armor. "How early did you have to rise to put all of that on? I'm guessing an hour before me." While Eyasu patted his chest plate, Mavrin started walking. "Never mind, I'm glad I slept through it. There's a little teahouse near the docks that's usually open with the sun . . ."

~

On their way to Vertsa's airdock, Eyasu kept a close eye on Mavrin, even though his friend seemed like his usual self again. Or at least, the usual self Eyasu had adjusted to over the last few days, cursing quietly as his trunk caught on cobblestones and babbling to avoid discussing anything important.

". . . of course, the guilds in each city-state have their own registration requirements, which you have to adhere to if you want to perform in certain establishments . . ."

"Is that why you never made it further north?" Aulina asked.

"Exactly." Mavrin shrugged. "And the Winds are colder there."

Aulina seemed genuinely interested in learning more about things outside Tanardell, letting Mavrin ramble incessantly. Discussing the mundane might have been a useful distraction for them both.

Since that wasn't a distraction they could maintain forever, Eyasu left them to it.

A long, polished corridor marked by small, red lanterns led to Vertsa's airdock. The vendors here offered goods specifically to sailors and travelers, waving and smiling from stone stalls set into the corridor walls. Each alcove between them was decorated with an elaborate artwork in stone or metal, most dedicated to the Presence as Passage, asking for protection for the vessels traversing the Windroutes. A few depicted long-extinct animals or plants or were more abstract; Eyasu had spent some time the night before studying a chair-like construction made from heated brass, stretched and molded into interconnected strips, until he gave up trying to decide why it made him uncomfortable.

The tunnel opened onto a wide platform carved into the side of the Jesper Windroute, which ran along Vertsa's northern edge. Mavrin and Aulina flinched as they stepped back into the Winds; high barriers deflected some of their force, but they were still stronger here than at ground level. For Eyasu, used to months trekking overland on his journeys, the morning Winds barely disturbed his pace. Windships clung to the berths spread out across the platform, carefully tethered and braced; one coming loose could decimate half the airdock before being swept away.

Foot traffic filled the platform; Vertsa was a major hub along the Jesper, which connected the two larger Windroutes running north and south across Aelda. Eyasu scanned faces and clothing as he walked, noting a small detachment of officers in the burnished armor of Yarder's Outlook, likely heading south. No one problematic caught his eye until they were halfway down the platform.

Three figures stood against the metal railing along the platform's edge. Each wore a long, off-white robe with golden gilding on the sleeves and around the hood—not ostentatious like Vertsa's residents, but a subtle accent meant to catch the Lifesphere's muted radiance. Instead of weights on their robes, a heavy chain wrapping across their chest and down their side kept their clothing in place. It also secured them against the Winds by affixing to the ground—and to the bearer's flesh.

Anyone passing close enough offered a nod to the figures or briefly matched their outstretched hands, palms up toward the sky. Paying respect to a Servant of the Hidden—or any Aspect—meant paying that same respect to the Saviors themselves, and by extension the Highest Voices and the Unity that served the people. The three individuals didn't respond, but they weren't expected to; behind the copper masks shielding their faces, their attention was focused inward and above.

Except the one watching Eyasu.

The shieldmask didn't leave an obvious gap for the eyes, but the Servant on the left tilted their head ever so slightly, tracking Eyasu's steps. Most people didn't realize the shieldmask only functioned one way, and that the wearer could see through it perfectly. Several of Eyasu's friends at the Citadel became Servants before his expulsion, though, and he still remembered being challenged to guess who was behind each mask and robe. He'd always guessed correctly, but nothing in this Servant's posture or general body shape reminded him of anyone.

"Do we need to check in or something?" Mavrin pointed at the dockmaster's cabin, nestled into the other end of the platform.

"We may want to avoid them." Eyasu pulled his gaze from the Servant. "Our transport was arranged discreetly."

As they continued walking, the Servant shifted their attention away. Eyasu put them from his mind; he had carefully cinched his robe to cover his armor and sword, and only lowered his hood inside the Respite. Like he told Mavrin before, he doubted anyone hunted for him these days.

Their windship clung to one of the last berths along the platform, expertly secured so that it barely rattled under the Winds. Eyasu had traveled on various mid-sized freighters like it, though he thought this one had a narrower bow than average. The hull's forward shell had been folded open completely, providing the windriders with open air and sunlight as they bustled across the deck. The dorsal and ventral rigging stood fully extended, though the sails wouldn't be unfurled until the windship was ready to depart.

Eyasu stopped at the gangplank and extended a hand to Aulina. She gave him a courteous smile and brushed past.

"This isn't much different than repairing the growing dome," she said, earning a grin from the crewman waiting at the top.

Mavrin stopped two meters away, eyeing the gangplank. "That's awfully narrow for my trunk."

Eyasu frowned. "It looks wide enough to me."

Mavrin still didn't move. "I might have to make more than one trip. Yes, because of them." He gently patted the top of the garnill cage, though if anything the little birds looked excited, poking their stubby faces past each other to get a better look at the ship.

"Does he need help?" A young woman looked up—or down, since she hung from her knees on the dorsal rigging with a tool in each hand. "I can be over there in a minute. I just need a minute!" She pointed at the crewman near the gangplank. "Stay put, Vek!"

Vek snorted and shook his head, making the weighted beads on his shock-white ponytail jangle. Ignoring the dangling windrider's protests, he crossed the gangplank in three confident strides and snatched Mavrin's things, before spinning in a circle and returning to the ship without a single wobble. Vek waved back and wandered away, laughing at the look of horror on her face as she started working the rigging even faster.

"My friend, I believe you can board now."

Eyasu waited, arms crossed, as Mavrin stretched his legs and shook out his hands. He was about to say something again when Mavrin burst forward, quickstepping along the gangplank like he expected it to collapse. He stopped in the center of the foredeck, where he started shaking his hands out again.

"This may have been a question for earlier," Eyasu said, joining him with calm strides across the steady plank, "but do you have a problem with windships?"

"Of course not," Mavrin said quickly. "Just *those*." He pointed at the gangplank. "They're never wide enough."

"Some sort of rope or cage on either side might help," Aulina offered.

Mavrin looked around at the crew. "Will the captain be showing us to our cabin?"

"Be with you in a minute!" the young woman from before called. She dropped from the rigging to help another windrider haul some barrels toward a hatch leading belowdecks, almost losing the first in her eagerness to help.

Mavrin frowned. "That's not the captain."

"She is."

"Eyasu, she's a little—"

"Accomplished, to have a ship of her own at our age?" Aulina looked sidelong at Mavrin with one eyebrow raised.

While his friend sputtered out what sounded like an apology, Eyasu noticed movement on the dock. He left the others without a word and crossed the gangplank back to the platform.

Six strides brought him to the lone Servant, bare hands clasped over their stomach.

Closer, nothing in the set of their shoulders, the way they clasped their left wrist with their right hand, or the cable-straight set to their feet revealed the identity behind the shieldmask. The upper rim of the mask came to Eyasu's lower lip, but he was taller than most. Unsure how to proceed, he defaulted to inclining his head and saying, "May each of Their facets watch over us."

The Servant didn't respond. Their chain was no longer attached to the ground, instead wound onto a hook near the bottom of their robes. The higher end couldn't be removed as easily; beneath the robes, the four hooks would be buried into the flesh around their clavicle, looped around the bone beneath. He could also see the T'var etchings in the shieldmask now, strategically placed so they wouldn't block the wearer's eyes.

"May the scales be ever-balanced," he added, echoing the phrases to the Hidden as Order crisscrossing the mask. He smiled, trying to seem disarming. "Please correct me if I misspoke the blessing."

"The mistaken offer no true blessings." The Servant's voice was soft and of higher pitch, but he didn't recognize it. "Heresy is a worse crime than error."

Eyasu glanced sharply over their head, his disappointment at the strange voice forgotten, but found the other two Servants still in their original place. The one facing him kept their hands clasped over their stomach, either as a sign they weren't armed or a ruse. Unlike many disciples of the Catalyst, especially as Protector, most followers of the Hidden as Order rarely traveled with weapons.

"Heresy is a matter of opinion," he said, eyes flicking around the airdock. He didn't see anyone closing in.

"The interpretations of the Words of Aspect are clear, as are the edicts of the Highest Voices. Anyone advocating an unsanctioned Aspect-variation disrespects Them and threatens us all, Eyasu Temergon."

One hand left the Servant's sternum and reached into their robes, returning with a rolled-up piece of paper. Clearly recycled but being on paper at all signaled the document's importance.

Two hands clasped within the Lifesphere, the stylized official seal of the Highest Voices, caught his eye first. Below that he spotted his name, a physical description, and a warning that labeled him, unsurprisingly, as a dangerous heretic. The note about him being armed was new, however.

"Why are you showing me this?" A former friend might have, but a stranger was less likely.

One hand briefly touched their robes, over where the chain attached to their clavicle. "It is the job of every Servant to convince those who stray to turn themselves over. I am doing *my* duty."

"My duty is to the people of Aelda, the same as yours. Anyone who wishes to debate this with me will be welcomed with open arms," Eyasu said, trying to keep the edge from his voice.

"And duty comes with failure." He thought he heard a sigh behind the Servant's mask. "I will pray that someone else convinces you where I have failed." They started to turn and paused, tilting their masked face back toward him. "Before the Aspects abandon you to your fate."

"Consider in your long hours, Servant, that the real heresy is thinking they would."

The Servant remained stock-still other than the flutter of their robes, as though actually considering his words. Then they turned and walked away.

Eyasu waited until they rejoined the other Servants before stuffing the notice into a belt pouch. He glanced over his shoulder several times on his way back to the ship, but no one else caught his eye.

If that was his last warning, he would be ready the next time someone came for him.

Mavrin and Aulina stood with the captain and Vek. Like when Eyasu met her before, Captain Atera Lavar wore a cotton tunic with a loose, unbuttoned shirt over it, rolled up at the sleeves, and a half-dozen pendants on patterned cords around her neck. Eyasu had asked her politely about them earlier, which was generally welcomed in the old Citen tradition. One pendant signified her calling as a windrider, while another expressed her pronouns and preferences; the others honored specific Aspect-variations, and when they overlapped it was possible to see the interconnected loops of the Aspects Joined.

"—aboard the *Joyous Soul*!" she said with a grin, shaking Mavrin's hand.

"Charmed," Mavrin said carefully. "Forgive me for asking, but—"

"Eyasu! Hi!" Atera bounded forward and wrapped him in a hug that barely made it around his midriff. He chuckled as she coughed and pulled away, brushing straight, fiery hair away from her hawkish face. She adopted a more professional air as she turned back to Mavrin. "Sorry. You were saying, Mister Leed?"

"Yes, I . . ." He ignored a glare from Aulina. "Well, you seem a little . . ."

"Young? Trust me, I inherited good looks from my dad." Atera frowned. "Although, maybe from my mom, too. Neither of them was a redhead, so really, it's hard to tell? Maybe I'm descended from a mephikor." Her snort devolved into a long string of giggles, stopping abruptly when no one else joined in. "Wrinkles don't set in early in my family, is my point."

When no one responded, she spun away, spreading her arms out to encompass the ship.

"Like I was telling Eyasu yesterday, the *Soul*'s been in my family for three generations. She's survived all manner of Longwinds, running aground on cliffs, a couple pirate attacks, and at least one Edge monster." When she saw Aulina's bemused smile, she glanced at the deck and brushed her long hair away from her face again. "Okay, the monster is an exaggeration. But she's survived a lot in her time. And she treats anyone who sails on her with respect. Uh, like a lady should."

Mavrin's mouth started to hang open. He turned to Eyasu with a finger raised.

"Gratitude and pride go well, hand-in-hand." With what he hoped was a subtle look at the captain, Eyasu added, "My friend here learned that over a long and illustrious career."

Atera stared at him blankly at first, until her eyes widened. "That's right!" She grabbed Mavrin's outstretched hand with both of hers, pinning his pointing finger in place. "Eyasu tells me you're *the* Mavrin Leed. The one who's performed in Renhollow and Abergarden?" She shook his hand again, beaming the entire time. "It's—it's an honor! Would you perform for the crew? Eyasu said you would if I asked."

"Well, I—" Mavrin found his stage smile and patted Atera's hands. "I'm surprised you've heard of me."

Atera snorted and waved a hand. "Please, how could I not? You're Mavrin Leed!" She seemed to catch the warning on Eyasu's face. "Right, so . . . after our midday meal, then?"

Mavrin looked ready to refuse, until Atera opened her mouth to say please again. "Yes, fine. I'd be delighted," he said. "In the meantime, can I stow my things in our cabin?"

The captain's smile wavered. "Oh. He didn't tell you?"

Eyasu placed a gentle hand on Mavrin's shoulder. "The *Joyous Soul* is a shipping vessel, but it's the only one heading to Farglade. We've been assured hammocks below with the crew."

"But no hot bunking," Atera added quickly.

To Eyasu's surprise, Mavrin simply shrugged. "Luxury compared to some accommodations."

Vek led Mavrin toward the hatch, but Aulina stood in place, blinking at the captain. When Atera noticed and smiled, Aulina blushed and hurried after the others without a backward glance.

Atera leaned in to Eyasu. "I didn't seem insincere?"

"You did fine."

She blew out a breath. "I'm not a great actor. But I'm excited—I've never seen a magic show. I hope he's good. Is he good?"

A heavy thump and loud cursing echoed from the hatch.

"He's like no one else."

One of the crew called out, "Hatch closing!" and Atera bounded away again. Loud clangs erupted around the deck, followed by a high-pitched grinding as the forward shell closed around them. The *Soul* showed its age with a few clanks as the two halves of the shell met directly overhead, locking into place. Last night, the windship reminded Eyasu of a stretched-out egg with a mottled shell, broken only by the covered forecastle and the twin masts sticking from the top and bottom.

He'd wanted to see the forecastle ever since, and climbed inside after a wave from the helmsperson. The wide window in front of the helm let him see the closed forward shell and Vertsa's airdock around them. A second window above showed the top mast extended behind, secured into place by alloy cables and reinforced braces. The sails ratcheted up its length, in tandem with the ventral sails, and locked into position while Vek and the rest of the crew finished final preparations below.

He had traveled on windships with automatic releases for the sails, but either because of age or habit, someone had to clamber outside and open the *Soul*'s sails by hand. Unsurprisingly, that turned out to be Atera. She'd thrown on a protective jacket, shin guards and what looked like weighted boots, as well as wide, green-tinted goggles and a cap to tuck her braid into. With the nimbleness of someone raised on ships, she climbed the mast almost to the top, using handholds to reach the release lever.

Windships in general fascinated Eyasu. Even after centuries, their entire operation could be dangerous, and detaching from an airdock, especially on one of the major Windroutes, needed to be particularly precise. Simply unfurling the sails while berthed had seemed the logical thing to him, until an engineer explained how doing that would pull on various couplings and attachments and had torn early windships right off their berths. Crews learned to carefully time detaching from the berth and unfurling the sail, which still proved effective for smaller vessels. For even a mid-sized freighter like the *Soul*—and one of the only reasons a windship that size could exist—they needed a boost.

Eyasu tried to feel when the salt-battery engine started thrumming belowdecks, but he couldn't make out its precise sensation over the general tremble of the Winds. One of the crew warned, "Drop in five seconds!" and he braced himself against the forecastle railing.

He *did* feel the lurch in his stomach as the *Soul* fell from the airdock.

The deck kicked under his boots as the engine activated and the turbine beneath them pushed the ship away. Gravity yanked on his wrists and knees as the *Soul* surged forward. From his vantage point, the sides of the Jesper Windroute became a blur of rocky cliffs, the airdock already a memory. Eyasu felt the windship pitching forward, the meager pull of Aelda's surviving core pulling them down. He looked up at the mast in time to watch Atera yank the release lever. The massive, fibrous sails caught the Winds immediately, billowing out to their impressive width with the glory of one of the Aspects soaring above the Lifesphere. Atera slid beneath them, gloved hands held tight to a safety cable until she passed through an open hatch into the forecastle. It snapped shut as she thumped onto the deck, tearing off her goggles with a wide grin as the *Joyous Soul* leveled out beneath them.

Eyasu heard soft groans and clanks around him—the creaks of

age on a much-loved ship. He ran his bare hand over the railing and smiled. A marvel like this windship was only necessary because of a terrible calamity, but it was a marvel, nonetheless.

Chapter Fifteen

ONE DOWNSIDE OF TRAVELING BY WINDROUTE WAS that staring at the passing cliffs could only hold Eyasu's attention so long. He imagined they looked much different in the immediate aftermath of the Fracture, before the plant and animal life of the old rivers vanished. The crisscrossing veins of minerals and karst, or the pockmarked holes and cave entrances being slowly softened by the Winds, were beautiful in their way, but he had seen them enough times before.

More vessels came into view as they approached Iler's Link, the dried-out lakebed that served as a junction between the Jesper, Bemner and Xyger Windroutes. The *Soul* slowed only to carefully navigate the busier windspace in the Link, passing docks and covered enclosures built directly into the walls of karst ringing the lakebed. Eyasu mostly spotted passenger vessels or other freighters clinging to the docks, the latter often licensed by an official guild instead of operating on contract; he had used them for passage in the past and discovered they stuck to a more ponderous schedule. As the *Soul* coasted onto the Bemner Windroute heading north, he caught sight of a trio of Nesevar hideblimps, relying on the Presence's will to guide them along, and even a sleek, pointed vessel from Renhollow that surged past faster than anything else on the Windroute, likely using salt batteries for an extra boost.

The crew bustled around him until evening, eager to finish necessary checks and chores and be able to watch Mavrin's performance. He would use the foredeck as his stage, since that was the largest space available.

Eyasu waited near the forecastle while the crew gathered. One offered to store his rucksack, unaware that five people had already asked. He didn't intend to watch the show but imagined the person he needed would arrive before long.

When she did, Aulina stopped beside him, leaning on one of the metal railings staggered across the deck. They were meant as emergency handholds, but she held on tight with her uninjured hand, and her tawny complexion looked a little sallow.

"I don't think I like windships." She swallowed. "Or maybe they don't like me."

"You can return below where it's more stable. Mavrin won't be offended."

Aulina managed a small smile. "I wanted to try and watch . . . but I don't think I'm comfortable with magic anymore." She shook herself. "Were you going to stay?"

"I was looking forward to the quiet below."

He told himself it wasn't a lie. It simply omitted that he'd been waiting for an opportunity to test something, and Aulina joining him below would provide perfect timing.

The *Soul* dipped to the left, sails catching a rogue current. Aulina swallowed again and gestured with her free hand, now wrapped in tight bandage instead of a full splint.

On their way belowdecks, Eyasu spotted one of the crew emerging from the engine room at the rear, where the salt batteries hummed as they charged. He had a basic understanding of how the small turbines on the *Soul*'s hull generated power, using a fraction of that kinetic energy to power the ventral turbine that helped keep the windship aloft. Yet how the grayish-orange block of salt compound stored that energy for later use went beyond him, along with why it only lasted a certain length of time before the charge dissipated. He remembered thinking as a child the design must have been channeled into existence, only to discover it was one of the Bastion's many inventions.

As they entered the crew's sleeping area, he heard the cheer that signaled Mavrin stepping out for his performance. Empty hammocks swayed on either side as he walked toward the row of footlockers bolted at the rear. The lack of portholes made the space dim, but he had collected an averblossom lamp on the way down, which came to life inside the shadowy interior.

Aulina sat with her back and shoulders pressed against a nearby support post. Eyasu placed his longsword against another.

"Why are you always carrying your rucksack?"

"Some of my possessions are precious to me," he admitted.

"You don't trust the crew?"

Eyasu instinctively wanted to shake his head—no one on the *Soul* had given him a reason not to trust them yet—but he realized that would have been a lie. "I've learned to be careful."

He set the rucksack down beside the footlockers and opened the top flap. "I can work elsewhere, if you'd prefer to be alone."

"I'm fine." She glanced at the wall. "Even if I did, I feel safer in company. For now."

Eyasu nodded. Had she wanted solitude, he would have left, and looked for another time for this test. Her caution pricked at his nerves, but if he thought any of them were in danger right now, he would be handling things differently.

With slow delicacy, he emptied the rucksack's contents, placing them one-by-one on the footlockers. Most of his equipment was benign: extra knives that weren't inscribed or coated in dariss, dry rations, generic herbs and healing rubs, and essentials like a waterskin and tinderbox. His pouch of chits was light; since he didn't claim citizenship anywhere specific, he gained his allotment through labor in the communities he passed through, usually offering to help with particularly difficult or tedious work. He supposed it wasn't that different from how Mavrin lived.

Below that were the less mundane possessions. Pouches of rarer herbs and reagents, like the blend he used to cloud the Raw inside Aulina. He hadn't been entirely sure that would work, which made him feel more confident about the others. Then, carefully wrapped relics—the closest thing he had to mementos or heirlooms. A narrow, marble bracelet inscribed with a prayer to a defunct Aspect-variation, the Hidden as Test. A chunk of bone supposedly from a rukharek, believed to have died out before the Salvation. Other small artifacts from the Time Before Unity—pieces of history the Highest Voices might someday pretend never existed, if they didn't already.

When he reached the wooden box containing Mavrin's coins, he closed his eyes and felt for the lingering effect of his channeling. It came as wafts of churned soil and crushed serrn needles, thrown over graves to help decomposition. The box went to the left of everything else. Out of the corner of his eye, he noticed Aulina watching.

The rucksack's lowest compartment was designed to be waterproof. Eyasu ran his fingers along the spines of the books inside, thinking back to the circumstances that led him to each one. Only scraps of how much knowledge had been lost in the three centuries since the Fracture; in some cases, like Uekel's *Accounts*, possibly the last copies in existence. He thought about the prayers on his chest plate as he tapped the edge of *Protections and Wards, on My Deathbed*. Or the ward he envisioned to contain the Raw, based on the fragmented excerpts from Damisar's treatise on channeling and the Aspects. Scholars rejected by their peers; histories considered unofficial or suspect. People like him, which meant he could trust them.

Anyone advocating an unsanctioned Aspect-variation disrespects Them and threatens us all, the Servant of the Hidden said. Eyasu couldn't believe the Aspects wanted humanity ignorant or complacent. During the Salvation, They reshaped Aelda to be survivable, but only if humanity investigated the transformed plant and animal life they offered or how to pull water from the air. Curiosity and challenging norms created windships, salt batteries, and more; innovative thought conjured the system of allotments that provided everyone with the means to live, instead of forcing them to scrape for subsistence. The Catalyst as Core was how he showed his devotion to the Aspects, not his disrespect. Along with wanting people to know the truth about their world.

"Aulina," he said. "I'd like to examine the coins. I can do so elsewhere, though."

This was the second part of the test.

She shifted against the post. "Isn't that dangerous?"

"Possibly." Eyasu refused to lie to her—only the necessary omissions. Keeping his movements deliberate, he opened the pouch containing his Castoff. "I'll be careful."

She rubbed the bandage over her injured wrist, eyes never leaving the box. "I feel like I'm afraid of everything now," she said. "Seeing them again might help. To think of them as just coins."

"They aren't simply coins," he reminded her gently. "You must never forget the danger they pose."

That warning wasn't part of the test. Her grimace was another good sign, though, as she nodded for him to continue.

Eyasu closed the sealed compartment over his books, returned most of his possessions and set the rucksack aside. He made sure his longsword was within reach if needed. The box went directly in front of him while he knelt, since sitting cross-legged wasn't possible in his armor. He took a moment to put his gauntlets back on—the only piece of armor he'd removed since boarding the *Soul*—and held one hand closer to his Castoff.

His hesitation at this part of the test surprised him. He needed to know how the coins might react if released. Having Aulina nearby would dismiss any lingering doubts about her freedom from the Raw's control. Eyasu couldn't think of a more logical way to approach this, but that didn't keep his pulse from speeding up.

May the Catalyst as Core stand over my shoulder and guide my hands. Your strength to my tendons, to my bones, to the heart that beats in my chest. Feed my body and my mind as I face that which would seek to harm the world you so carefully protect for us all.

He removed the lid from the box.

Even in the dim hold, the coins sparkled as though bathed in sunlight. Eyasu leaned over them, hands on his thighguards. He still didn't know the significance of the interconnected lines scratched into their surface; they might have been a dialect of T'var he didn't know. Most Requesters stuck to familiar, memorized phrases for channeling, but Eyasu followed the teachings of the more masterful Requesters, spending years memorizing syntax and other subtleties, so that he could improvise when needed. The Quartered Citadel didn't teach prayers directly relevant to fighting Raw, after all. But his studies didn't help with these scratches.

"What are you doing?" Aulina asked softly.

"Examining. Testing," Eyasu said simply, hoping she didn't realize he'd been waiting for her to speak.

"They wouldn't like that."

She pulled the collar of her shirt tighter against her throat, staring at the box. Eyasu didn't straighten, or move his hands away from the box, not wanting to give away how much those four words concerned him.

"What do you mean?" he asked mildly.

Aulina blinked at him. "About what?"

Before he could respond, the averblossom blinked out.

When Eyasu reached for his longsword, he found open air and the solid support post. Instead of waiting for his eyes to adjust, he snatched an alchemical flare from his belt and scratched it against his armor.

In the sparking, orange light, Aulina stood only centimeters away. Her mouth twitched, trying to form words. Every breath came in short bursts, chest pumping like they'd stepped into thinner air.

"We're alone," she managed to say. "They've abandoned us."

Her eyes moved away. Eyasu risked a quick glance, but only saw hammocks and bulkheads. The coins sat unmoving in the box.

"It's your fault." Aulina's eyes locked on him again. "That's why I'm alone."

"Aulina. I promise you're not alone."

It didn't feel like a lie; he hoped it didn't sound like one.

"No one is safe, Requester."

Aulina formed the words, but that rasp wasn't her speaking.

Eyasu reached for his Castoff. Her fingers clamped onto his wrist like a vise.

"I didn't wish this." She took a shuddering breath, staring through him. The rasp suddenly returned: "No one wishes to be alone." Only her face moved, expressions shifting faster than Eyasu could track. "Your kind are traitors and destroyers. You severed our connection to the whole."

"Who am I speaking to?" He knew what, but if the creature wanted to speak, he could listen.

Except Aulina's natural voice returned. "It's too much. It isn't meant for me. Make it stop." Her entire body shuddered, loosening the grip on Eyasu's wrist, but he didn't move yet. He waited for her to freeze again, the Raw's voice returning: "I understand why the cleansing is necessary. Why the retribution is necessary." Her eyes widened. "You are fools."

And then she screamed, "No!" as the *Soul*'s deck suddenly lurched to port.

Either Aulina or the Raw released him and Eyasu went tumbling past, left shoulder striking a support post. He looped his arm around it while the other drew his Castoff. Through the pounding in his skull, he watched hammocks and storage bins phase in and out of sight. For one terrifying moment he hung in the open air, looking down at the dark bottom of the Windroute, but he fixed the image of the *Soul* in his mind, clinging to where he was supposed to be in more ways than one.

Words flowed from his lips. T'var felt more natural than the Collected Tongues sometimes, with its repetition of roots: *Protector's protected protection, bless with blessing, shield against the threatened and threaten via the shield.* He focused his Request on the windship, trying to counter the Raw. Warm energy radiated from his Castoff, joining what came from the core of his body, and then vibrating from his knuckles into the space around him. No matter how much it seemed to be, that space wasn't empty. Nothing under the view of the Aspects could be.

And he wasn't alone. In that purest moment of channeling, between making his Request and the Aspects' Response, he felt Their attention on him—or part of that vast intelligence, at least. He knew their precise locations, through sense instead of sight. The Presence, coasting high above the eastern Moderates. The Hidden, far to the south within eyesight of Yarder's Outlook. The distant, muted form of the Vital, body encased below the Quartered Citadel. And the Catalyst, beyond the northern True Edge on the other side of the Lifesphere, far from his mortal location but not from his channeling.

They knew him. They knew his Request. They would know Their decision, before he finished asking for Their help.

He felt the deck leveling beneath him, but not pulled by the Aspects; the crew had the helm under control. Eyasu felt the Aspects' attention shifting, centering on Aulina, standing rigid next to footlockers with her eyes and fists clenched. Their focus on her felt strange—like They stood at a remove, analyzing her from all angles, creating a distance between her and Them that should not have been there. No one and nothing should have been that alone.

Eyasu started another Request—if the Raw wouldn't speak to him, he needed it contained again—but before he could manage more than half a phrase, the Aspects pulled on the world around him. Aulina gasped and started to fall. Eyasu abandoned his channeling and leapt to her side, catching her before she struck the deck. There was a flash of light beside them, and when it cleared, the box's lid was back in place.

There were tears at the corners of Aulina's eyes as blue averblossom light filled the cabin again. "I don't know if they heard me," she said.

Eyasu glanced at the box, realizing she meant *they* in the singular. "What did you say?"

"That we didn't mean them any harm." She was pale and trembling, like that night in the mortuary but not as severe. "I could *feel* them. This flood of emotions . . . pain and rage and . . . loneliness. It seemed like the kind thing to say."

After making sure she could stand on her own, Eyasu collected his longsword, which had rolled to one side of the cabin with his rucksack. The box didn't seem to have moved, but the wood was no longer plain. A symbol was carefully etched onto the lid, reminding him of the root for *shield* in T'var. He wondered what it was meant to stand against.

"There's a connection still, that I can't see." For clarity, he said, "Between you and the Raw. I needed to see if we severed this in Tanardell. I'm sorry."

If the admission bothered her, Aulina hid it behind a steely gaze. "But you can remove it."

Eyasu frowned. "I don't know."

Aulina's face fell.

"There shouldn't be a connection here," Eyasu told her. "Not with the coin removed and my previous Request. But according to most sources, there shouldn't be Raw at all."

"I thought I came with you," Aulina said, voice shaking, "to make sure I was safe."

"You are safe. And not a threat to anyone, as far as I can tell."

That didn't calm her like he hoped. "As far as you can tell?" She crossed her arms and took a step away from him. "You led me down here to get a reaction from me—or from the Raw—didn't you? Except you had no idea what was going to happen."

Unsure what to say that wouldn't make things worse, Eyasu simply shook his head.

"You could have asked," she said quietly, reminding him of Ohanna in the orchard, wondering why her sister was angry. "I had to decide to trust you, you know."

"You can," Eyasu said, though it felt more like a lie than he liked.

"Then never do that again. Or you're no better than *them*," Aulina said, flicking her chin at the coins. "No matter what their reasons are."

"I give you my word." He tried to catch her in the eye, but she ignored it. "I prefer to be honest, when I can."

"Then tell me when I can go home."

She had asked for the entire truth. "I don't know if you'll be able to."

Aulina held a hand to her mouth, shoulders shaking. "But Ohanna can't . . ."

Her sister was with Jareden, who understood exactly why she and Aulina couldn't be reunited yet. Jareden's home was a safer place than most. Eyasu knew that, like he knew to trust in the Aspects, but he realized that wasn't something Aulina needed to hear.

"I'm sorry," he repeated.

She shook her head, and he couldn't tell whether she rejected the apology, or his presence, or having decided to leave Tanardell at all. He wanted to ask, but she marched away before he could form the question.

The door to the crew quarters slammed open and Atera hurried in, Mavrin trailing in the doorway behind her. "Are you two all right? We're not sure what—"

"Fine," he heard Aulina say, as she pushed past the captain.

Atera turned a curious look on Eyasu. When he didn't offer a response, she quickly examined the room from the door, noting everything that had been tossed about, and disappeared back into the corridor.

Mavrin didn't step any further inside. He took in the mess, too, and when his gaze reached the box, he let out a knowing sigh.

"Whatever you were doing down here ruined my show. Can you save any further chaos for when we're on the ground?"

Eyasu sighed and sat down on the footlockers. "I'll do my best."

Mavrin huffed and walked out, leaving Eyasu feeling as close to alone as he had in days.

Chapter Sixteen

THE WINDS HAD PICKED UP THROUGH FARGLADE again, making the speed gauges whistle at Brace, two levels below Shelter. Deyeri left home wearing her heavier, plainer coat, which hid her salt lamp without the activator bulging out too far. She wanted to be unassuming and casual for today's trip, and the weather made it convenient to cinch a wool cap under her chin and duck her head low as she approached the Keep.

Heavy tarps suspended on metal racks created a path from the street to the Gannerthen Building. Civil Liaisons, bureaucrats, and everyday citizens coming to petition the Council still needed to access the Keep, regardless of wind levels. Today, there weren't as many people navigating the tarpway as Deyeri would have hoped. She hung close to a knot of chattering students from the Technical Academy, sporting heavy scarves bound at the throat with the intertwined stylus, torch, and gear of the Vital as Talent. Together they approached the main entrance, consistently flanked by two Watch since the last Incursion. Deyeri kept her head down, trying to seem like she was engaged with the students' discussion of adapting new turbines to the large geothermals on the Towers outskirts. The huddled students were too engrossed to notice her as they passed through the wide double doors, nodding at the Watch as they hurried inside. Deyeri stared straight ahead, trusting the Watch wouldn't take a second look.

Inside, bureaucrats and petitioners lined the long entrance hall, their voices and footfalls echoing off the twelve-foot dolomite ceiling. As the students turned toward the learning commons in the southeast wing, Deyeri casually peeled away, looping around the wide, circular monument engraved with the names of Farglade's previous Lord-Magistrates. She learned during her tenure as Commander that the design was based on a "fountain," some sort of feature that used to pour water from its curving arms—simply as decoration. Absurd as that sounded, the monument's weathered stone arms helped heat the interior now, connected to the Keep's geothermals through pipes and tubes running from the basement.

Deyeri strode with fake purpose toward the Office of Legal Grievances, with its too-narrow doorway and perpetually ignited gas lanterns. Someone shouting inside about arson caught her attention for a moment before she sidestepped through a narrow doorway halfway down the corridor.

She waited at the bottom of the stairs beyond for the sound of footsteps behind her, wrinkling her nose at the dry, musty air. Deyeri didn't know the extent of her permissions as a former commander, but no one told her she *couldn't* wander the basement without an escort. Most of the storerooms were wasted on old files, anyway, as opposed to emergency supplies like she'd suggested years earlier.

Except that according to an old contact working for Trade Commissioner Jenneri, this was where everything confiscated under Edict Nine was being stored. And that so far, almost nothing had been shipped to the Unity. Another point of confusion, but at least an opportunity to figure out what Breck still wasn't telling her. Meeting with a few people around the city had helped ease tensions, but that would change as the Watch kept collecting. And she couldn't shake the feeling he'd sent her to market without any chits, whatever he thought of her ability to help.

Unlike upstairs, the basement corridors couldn't accommodate more than two people standing side by side. Deyeri had to hunch to keep her head from scraping the ceiling and watch for uneven patches in the floor. The occasional hanging lantern kept the place from becoming pitch black; Farglade had power to spare courtesy of the massive windtowers along the Bemner, letting technicians loop lazily hanging cables along the ceiling here. Once or twice, hairline veins of dariss glistened along the unfinished walls, reminding Deyeri of how much unmined crystal still existed under the city. If collapsing a street weren't a legitimate concern, they might have found enough to stave off the Unity entirely.

Shaking that thought, Deyeri checked each storeroom, passing one unremarkable metal door after another, noting the stenciled numbers above them as she peered inside. The tiny, ovoid windows didn't give her much of a view, even when she took out her salt lamp and wedged it against the bars. Several rooms housed shelves and boxes of parchment, whatever reports had been considered important enough to record permanently. Another held containers that glinted under the lamp's light, but quickly turned out to be pieces of outdated observation equipment from the Keep's sentry towers. She couldn't always make out all the objects, especially in the corners, but she didn't want to crack open every locked door and keep breathing the stench of musty uniforms or tattered parchment rolls.

Somewhere near the basement's southern edge, Deyeri caught a glint of an object shining differently than copper or lead. Storeroom Twenty-One, she noted. After pausing to listen for footsteps or voices in the distance, she pulled out her old lockpicking set—one of many skills that came in handy in the Watch, not that she ever publicized it. She blamed how long it took on the age of the lock and the bits of rust along its edge.

Unlidded crates filled the room beyond. The salt lamp crackled as she held its glass globe above her head, reminding her that the battery inside didn't hold a charge as well as it used to. She looked through the nearest crates and found a wide assortment of objects: ceramic plates, silver candlesticks, a couple quartz statuettes, even weapons with silver or bronze filigree. Plenty of dariss, as well; in fact, the longer she looked the more dariss she saw. The crates further back looked dustier, and a black streak marked each one except a few closest to the door.

This weird hoard made less sense than when she'd imagined it. Her feelings about the Unity aside, Farglade wasn't completely self-sufficient; they needed to maintain some sort of trade relationship with other city-states. She tapped her finger against a dariss chalice inscribed with some family's crest and tagged with the name and address of its owner. She wondered if Breck was holding out for a better trade deal, trying to get something extra beyond the artifact the Unity really wanted. Or maybe he hoped to get away without handing anything over at all and return these possessions to their owners. If that were the case, Deyeri owed him an apology. Except for not telling her.

She kept puzzling as she opened the door to leave.

Havven stood outside, arms crossed over civilian clothes.

Deyeri forced her muscles to relax. "Please don't tell me I'm losing my touch."

"Oh, I would never suggest that." He glanced down at her free hand, still on the doorknob. It took a moment for Deyeri to smile and pull out her picks again.

"There are five rooms so far," Havven said once she relocked the door. "I suspect they'll open a sixth soon, since our orders are to keep collecting."

Deyeri let out a low whistle.

He took a turn peering through the tiny window, and she gave him time with his thoughts. It reminded her of those rare calm stretches during the Incursions, when they sat studying something innocuous, like a single undamaged street or a pockmarked wall that survived the Fracture. Havven had been the first one to hear her suggest adding more monuments to the city, back before she ever considered leaving the Watch.

"How'd you know I'd come here?" she asked.

"This would be the first place you'd tell me to look." He frowned. "You weren't wrong at Yeldin's. About the edict."

Deyeri hesitated from revealing what Breck told her. After their conversation at the enclosure, she'd spent the evening wracking her brain for everything she remembered about the Raw. The only person she heard mention them since Veristenok was Eyasu, and she regretted ignoring most of what he said; his wild ideas might have helped her find this artifact now. Still, Breck had a point about spreading his secret too far. Even mentioning the Raw skirted heresy, and she didn't know enough to put Havven at risk.

"I'm sorry that I can't . . ."

Deyeri shook her head to stop him. "I also told you to pick your battles. Leave the nuisance-making to me."

"Termot and I are asking questions," Havven said. "Those black marks on the crates aren't being left by the Watch."

That meant Breck wasn't working alone. He would never handle something that tedious personally. Realizing there was someone else in his confidence shouldn't have bothered her as much as it did.

"Did you notice how much dariss is in there?" When she shook her head, Havven added, "More than anything else. Why would the Unity want so much?"

Dariss is a natural conduit, Eyasu told her once.

"Maybe someone believes the wilder stories about the Time Before."

Havven's wry smile confirmed what would happen if she started talking about the Raw. Until he said, "How much do you think Breck is keeping from us?"

In official meetings or within earshot of the public, Havven would never refer to him as anything other than "Lord-Magistrate." Within closed quarters, they both had a different attitude toward Woldren Breck; he had left them out there on the Edgeplains, after all. Even so, she needed to be cautious—for Havven's sake.

"Same as always," she said, hating the omission as much as a lie. "Which is always too much with him."

Struck by the calm in her own words, she realized she was behaving exactly like Breck: holding information back out of presumed necessity. You couldn't tell your people everything, but as Watch Commander, Deyeri always told them as much as she could and whatever they needed to be safe. She hated the fact that, either by accident or on purpose, Breck was making her behave more like him.

Deyeri knew she'd stayed down here too long already and gestured for him to follow her out. He didn't budge, hooking a thumb behind him.

"Best if we're not seen together," he said, which made her proud and a little sad simultaneously. "I'll keep asking questions where I can. Termot, too. I imagine there's no point in asking you to be careful?"

She shook her head, keeping to herself that there was no point in asking the same of him and Termot. "Just make sure to save my ass if I slip in the dust somewhere."

He tried to hide a grin before heading further down the corridor. Deyeri held down everything she hadn't told him, wondering if she deserved the loyalty of the people who trusted her.

~

She spent the rest of the day connecting with more of her contacts around the city. As she called in favors past sunset, she told herself that despite everything, Breck always had Farglade's best interests at heart. They survived the Incursions because of him, after all. The problem was, this was still *her* city. And she had learned to trust her instincts.

A delivery crate waited at home, secured in the metal delivery cage beside her front door. Deyeri glanced up and down the street, but this late at night the other townhomes were quiet, especially with the heavier Winds that day. She relaxed when she saw how old and ramshackle the container looked, and the random swirls of green lichen paint along the side: Yeldin's personal signature.

Being gone all day, she had left the heatwell in her sitting room unlit. She turned the dial on that first; its blue light was enough for her to see by as she dragged the room's only chair over to the box and cracked it open.

Yeldin left a note on top: *Some of that new stuff you didn't take with you. You're welcome.* Deyeri snorted at his version of a thank you and placed it aside.

She noticed a dagger first, longer than average and with a narrower tip than she was used to. The metal glinted strangely when she rotated it, specifically the dark blue material forged along the edge of the blade. Dariss.

"Great. Now they can confiscate it from me."

She found dariss twice more. Either Yeldin hoped she'd start another fight with the Watch, or he saw some sort of value in these things and didn't want them taken. One was a small figurine of a juvenile akrren, which Deyeri thought showed solid craftsmanship, though she wasn't much for knickknacks. The other was a long wooden box with a glass top and soft wool lining. Three dariss coins rested inside, each imprinted with a bunch of interconnected lines forming a symbol she didn't recognize.

Deyeri plucked one of the coins from the wool lining and twirled it in her finger. If the imprint had significance, it meant nothing to her. For a moment she thought she could feel extra warmth coming from the coin, tickling her fingertips while she stared. The dariss seemed to glitter more than the dagger or the figurine, making the sitting room dimmer by comparison.

Maybe you're what the Unity is after?

Working that thought in her mind, she leaned back in her chair and kept staring.

Chapter Seventeen

TRAVELING THE WINDROUTES CUT A WEEKS-LONG journey overland to under two days, and Mavrin couldn't decide whether to be happy about that. After performing for the crew, he slept through as much of the journey as possible or simply hid belowdecks, refusing to admit that anything besides the gangplank made him nervous. When Atera proudly announced they were nearing their destination, Mavrin's stomach flip-flopped like it had at the Wayward Waystop.

He found Eyasu at the stern, watching the chasm walls slide past through the rear portal. Mavrin placed both hands on the back of the bench, tapping his fingers while he decided how to ask.

"What would you like to know about her?" Eyasu gave him a knowing smile.

"Who says that's what I want to talk about?"

"You could drum your fingers more until you think of something better."

Mavrin rolled his eyes. "You would've told me if she wasn't well?"

"You wish to know if Deyeri is well?" Eyasu barked a laugh as Mavrin threw up his hands. "It was several years ago, but yes, she was well the last time I saw her. She had decided to retire, in fact."

"Retire from what?"

"Serving with the Watch."

Mavrin frowned, trying to imagine Deyeri wielding a weapon and marching in formation. He remembered a free spirit, quick to speak up or defend someone in need, but he didn't think he'd ever seen her hold something as simple as a longstaff. Then again, he would never have expected Eyasu to walk around in wooden armor.

"I suppose she retired to spend more time with family, or some such." He tried to sound casual.

"It wouldn't be my place to say."

"No, of course not," Mavrin said softly. He tried extremely hard not to imagine Deyeri surrounded by small children or sharing evening tea with some faceless individual in a pressed shirt and shiny boots. "As long as she's happy, I suppose."

"You'll be able to ask her soon."

"I will, won't I?" Mavrin murmured. "Won't that be lovely."

He spent the rest of the afternoon in the crew cabin, idly sorting and re-sorting objects in his trunk. He figured Fargladeans enjoyed entertainment like anyone else; being the only city independent from the Unity, he didn't expect to encounter as much of the close-minded nonsense they faced in Tanardell.

As he rolled the device Cler gave him in his hands—he'd named it a firecube—someone knocked on the support beam behind him. Atera leaned around it, wearing a hesitant smile. "Are you preparing for a show?"

"I wish." He caught himself and cleared his throat. "Sorry, I mean this is a different kind of trip. But I like to be prepared."

"Right. I shouldn't have assumed. Wait, you're probably down here because you want to be alone." Atera ran a hand through her fiery hair. "Eyasu said where you were, and I thought that meant I could come find you, and . . . did you want to be alone?"

Mavrin gestured at the hanging cots, one-third full of sleeping windrunners, and the two middle-aged women playing dice in a far corner. “Did you need something, Captain?”

“Oh, nothing, really. We’re close, that’s all, and sometimes travelers like to watch from the deck.” She backpedaled twice while she spoke, then nodded to herself and leaned forward more confidently. “You said you’ve never been to Farglade before.”

Mavrin looked down at his trunk, which could probably be reordered a fourth time if he tried hard enough. His garnills studied him with barely disguised disdain, probably because they’d been cooped up for too long again.

“I suppose fresh air is good for the old lungs.” He feigned leaving for three steps, earning indignant hoots from the garnills before he scooped up their cage.

It took a while to climb to the foredeck, since Atera kept stopping to speak to a crewperson or help with some mundane task most captains wouldn’t worry about. She didn’t seem to deliberately make a point or lead by example, but simply liked keeping busy. And the crew clearly enjoyed it as well, joking and laughing like they did with anyone else.

“. . . and we only get here a couple times a year, but honestly, it’s my favorite dock to visit,” Atera said as they reached the foredeck. “Except for Coaststar. And maybe the Point of Careful Attention. Actually, I think there’s something I like about each of them.”

“How long have you been windriding?” Mavrin asked, shifting the garnill cage in his arms again.

“Three years as captain since my dad passed, but he pretty much raised me on this deck, so . . . forever?” Atera straightened her shoulders and grinned.

“Visiting the same places hasn’t gotten boring?”

“Of course not. I’m sure you’re not tired of magic.”

Oh, I don’t know about that.

The forward shell unfolded as they stepped on deck, whipping a light breeze that ruffled the edges of Mavrin’s cloak and the garnills' feathers. North of the Moderates, the air was noticeably colder; as Mavrin understood it, the Winds gradually lost both moisture and heat as they traveled north. Through the gap, he saw the final curve of the Bemner Windroute disappear behind them, as the crew deployed the *Soul*'s brakes for their final approach to Farglade. The shell stopped opening halfway, and Mavrin suspected Atera ordered it open to offer her passengers a better view.

Or perhaps for Aulina specifically, who stood at the furthest railing, staring down the Windroute. Atera tapped the iron bar next to her white-knuckled grip, with a playful smirk that brightened the other woman's expression. Mavrin had noticed the two of them talking after Eyasu's experiment with the coins, and again this morning. He had no idea how much Aulina might have said; Eyasu hadn't sworn them to secrecy, and it was Aulina's story to tell whoever she liked. If she had, it didn't seem to have scared the captain away.

After what Eyasu told him happened belowdecks, his rational brain howled to keep his distance from Aulina. Whether it was because of Ohanna or because he was a fool, he didn't see much point in that, so he stood on her other side at the railing, hoping she couldn't sense his unease.

The *Soul* coasted along the highest level of the Windroute possible, giving them an early glimpse of Farglade as they approached. The city's two major districts had possibly the most literal names Mavrin ever heard. To their left on the Windroute's western side, the Tiers climbed the side of one of the Grayest Mountains, streets layered one above the other like shelves. Except for a single wind barrier at the end of each street, the Tiers looked largely open to the elements. To the east, the Towers looked even stranger: three- or even four-story buildings that often didn't extend underground, according to Eyasu. Mavrin couldn't imagine standing inside one, let alone living there, with only his faith in their builders to convince him the Winds wouldn't knock everything over. But one thing commonly said in the Moderates was that while Renhollow pushed the boundaries of science, Farglade pushed the boundaries of sensible living in a post-Fracture world.

Most impressive, though, was the massive bridge spanning the end of the Windroute to connect the Tiers and Towers. Windships of all sizes meandered between the stone support pillars, following colored flags hung under the bridge to denote entrance and exit.

Mavrin pointed at the support pillars extending to the Windroute's floor. "Those must be, what, forty meters thick?" he asked Atera.

"Something like that. Are you a mathematician *and* a magician?"

"Gauging distance is important for some of my tricks." Mavrin guessed the Windroute at about a half-kilometer across where the bridge sat. "I've heard stories about this bridge. What's it called again?"

"The Unyielding Walkway," Eyasu boomed as he stepped up beside Mavrin, leaving their things on the deck nearby. "One of the Aspects' more spectacular Responses."

Mavrin rolled his eyes. "Lucky happenstance that anyone ever needed it, if you read your histories."

Early in his time at the Citadel, Mavrin became fascinated with Aelda's architectural wonders, specifically the ones channeled into existence. Creating something of that scale required a combination of clarity and ingenuity that even the Highest Voices admitted only the most talented Requesters could properly articulate to the Aspects. Mavrin remembered reading that the settlers who discovered Farglade's ruins partially intact after the Fracture also found the Walkway waiting for them. An inscription nearby identified the person responsible as Gannerthen—one of the first Requesters, possibly the very first, who used the Castoff he found without understanding the limitations the Highest Voices would learn later. The exertion required to create the Walkway left Gannerthen with barely enough strength to leave the inscription, which bequeathed the Walkway to whoever repopulated the area in the future.

Atera's hand brushed the pendants around her neck, lingering on the four loops of the Aspects Joined. "You don't think the Aspects knew Farglade would be rebuilt?"

While he puzzled over how to answer without sounding like an ass, Eyasu said, "My friend believes Their influence is more indirect."

Mavrin went back to studying Farglade, letting Eyasu play diplomat. Every city-state had a distinct atmosphere and character, partly from centuries of cultural intermingling and paying homage to different "official" Aspect-variations—partly at Veristenok's encouragement, so Aelda collectively showed respect to Them all. Coaststar splashed the entire peninsula in deep blue symbology tied to pre-Fracture sealife, as a gesture to the Hidden as Substance. Renhollow's scientific achievements and determination to encourage "progress" were as much a point of pride as a way to show respect to the Vital as Growth.

Farglade didn't pay homage to a specific variation as far as he knew, like Atera wearing multiple pendants. That didn't mean the city didn't stand out. The crystalline cannons glistening below a promontory to their right were obviously channeled into existence, likely via the Catalyst as Protector. The massive keep above them caught his eye not because of its size, but because of glistening blue crystal lining the roof. Mavrin pushed his goggles back and peered to either side of the Windroute, catching a blue glint every few seconds, from columns, statues, windows or simply embedded in the walls. Veins of blue even stood out on the sides of the Windroute.

Eyasu had underexaggerated how common dariss was here.

Beyond the Unyielding Walkway, the Windroute widened into a massive, circular chasm that had once been Bemner Bay.

Farglade's engineers repurposed it for their airdock, which offered at least twice as many berths as Vertsa. The *Soul* didn't slow nearly as much as Mavrin expected at first; he realized why as the windship pitched to the right, circling the bay.

"They direct the Winds using those!" Atera pointed at massive, alloy panels attached to the cliffs, angled like sails. "Isn't that amazing?"

Mavrin nodded weakly.

Aulina's bandaged hand brushed his knuckles. "Just think of clouds," she said. "Clouds are calming."

He hadn't seen a cloud except in drawings as a child, but he tried anyway.

The deck vibrated less and less as the windship slowed, airbrakes squealing as Vek steered them toward an open berth. Mavrin stifled a cry as several cables fired from the docks, the large claspers on their end thudding against the *Soul* with enough force to rattle the deck. With a tug, the cables wrenched the windship to a stop and yanked it against the berth, as Atera called an order and the sails collapsed against their masts.

While the crew leapt onto the dock to help tie the *Soul* down, Atera asked, "How did you enjoy the voyage, Mister Leed?" She frowned. "It wasn't too bumpy, was it? I know we take the turns hard—"

His stomach needed solid ground to finish settling. "Pleasant the entire time, Captain." Though he'd never admit it to Eyasu, the young woman's excited energy shook off some of his unease. "I'm surprised you're not tying down the ship, like you do everything else."

"Oh, I learned how to do that a long time ago," Atera said with a wave of her hand. "Besides, the captain is supposed to see her passengers off. That's what Dad always said."

Eyasu inclined his head. "May the Aspects' guidance follow you and your crew, wherever you travel next."

Atera blushed and tried her best to completely encircle him in a hug. Next, she threw her tiny frame so hard against Mavrin that he almost fell to the deck. With Aulina she was gentler—mostly because they both hesitated, making jerky half-movements until they settled on a handshake, once they noticed Mavrin and Eyasu pointedly staring.

It took one swallow and swing of his arms before Mavrin sprinted down the gangplank to the dock. Vek materialized on his heels, putting down Mavrin's trunk and garnills with another wink. Nearby, the dockworkers and crew finished securing the *Soul*; the cables that struck the windship weren't simply claspers, but had large, square magnets on their ends, attached to plates on the hull he hadn't noticed before.

After thanking Vek, he took in the sight of the bustling airdock. It consisted of two levels, with the berths spaced out so no windship hung directly above or below another. They stood on the higher level, which let him see the motley collection of freighters and passenger vessels scattered around the bay. The barriers here were lower than at Vertsa, forcing Mavrin to tie his cloak right away to avoid being yanked off into the open air. He clung to every handhold or railing he could until they reached a tunnel into the cliffside, busy with windrunners, merchants, and all sorts of travelers. A container sled pulled by an adolescent akrren momentarily separated Mavrin from Eyasu, and as he waited, he noticed Aulina even further back, studying the sky.

"See something interesting?"

"No clouds." Aulina frowned. "I've only been imagining them."

"There wouldn't be, even here." Clouds sounded like a lovely phenomenon, but he wasn't sure he'd want to lose his view of the Lifesphere. "The Winds don't change that dramatically this far north, besides their temperature. Surely they teach that back home."

He meant it as a jest, but Aulina's brow furrowed. "No, you're right." She shook her head. "Of course, there wouldn't be any. I don't think I've ever seen a cloud."

Eyasu emerged from the tunnel. "Is something wrong?"

"Nothing," Aulina said sharply, almost snapping at him. She glanced back at the *Joyous Soul*. "I don't think I should be walking around. Especially so close to . . . them." She gestured at Eyasu's rucksack.

"I believe what happened the other day was incidental," Eyasu said. He tried to sound reassuring but ruined it when he added: "To be fair, I can't know for sure without more research."

Aulina sighed in annoyance. "Maybe I should wait for that."

"Voice Revect will want to speak with you."

"That can happen later, can't it?" Mavrin said, stepping between them. "Aulina might have a point."

"I could stay on the *Soul* while you research." It sounded more like a decision than a suggestion. "We can discuss what you find after."

Eyasu pursed his lips. "You'll remain on the ship?"

"She isn't a child," Mavrin muttered. Her sister was the child, abandoned back home. Not that Ohanna would be returning home, unless Jareden brought her to collect her things. He hadn't even considered what would happen to the orchard with Aulina gone; a growing dome couldn't be left untended forever, and Magistrate Gevian didn't seem like the patient type.

Eyasu dipped his head. "I apologize. You may do as you wish. I mean no judgment."

"Thank you." It sounded half-hearted, and Aulina still seemed troubled as she walked away.

"She doesn't trust me," Eyasu said glumly.

"She has reasons not to trust," Mavrin said. He rapped his friend's shoulder. "Don't take it personally."

At the other end of the tunnel, there was a brief conversation with the dockmaster about their business in Farglade, which Eyasu described as "scholarly pilgrimage" and Mavrin claimed was "a mission to encourage drunken revelry and the worship of evil." The dockmaster's eyes widened and they looked like they were about to summon assistance, until Mavrin laughed and presented his guild token, marking him as an independent performer.

The neighborhood he and Eyasu entered looked like it serviced the ships and crews passing through Farglade; besides the storage houses lining the cliffside, there were stalls offering local food samples to incoming windriders or visitors, specifically not requiring a chit in exchange. Mavin spotted one cookhouse offering takka flank scorched over an open heatwell with steam-boiled hessa grubs, which would have smelled incredible if his stomach had recovered from the *Soul*'s docking.

They stopped in an isolated alley between two small warehouses, where he and Eyasu could pause without being in anyone's way. Even sheltered there, the Winds felt more intense and colder than he was used to, especially after spending time inside the *Soul*.

"I will visit Voice Revect. You will find Deyeri." Before Mavrin could protest, Eyasu placed a firm hand on his shoulder. "The longer you delay, the more agony you'll experience."

"How will you abandoning me prevent agony?"

He scanned their immediate vicinity and lowered his voice. "Of all Aelda, the Raw wanted to come here, and *we* are the two individuals who discovered their course. The Aspects' grip is in this, as with everything."

"More like an overactive imagination," Mavrin muttered. He glanced at his garnills and brightened. "What about my things?"

"I'm more than capable of taking them." Eyasu knelt beside the cage and whistled three quick notes. To Mavrin's amazement, the nearest garnills straightened, fixing their attention on him. "You see? We're developing a rapport."

"Traitors." When they ignored him, he started pacing in front of the alley. "I'm assuming you know her address, having stayed in touch?"

Without looking away from the cage, Eyasu produced a tiny slip of paper and held it out.

"You're a pain." He made it two steps away before another thought occurred to him. "Wait, how will I find you after?"

"You don't think Deyeri will be able to direct you?"

"I . . . well, depending on whether she . . ." Mavrin didn't look up, worried that Eyasu would see the many terrible outcomes flashing through his mind. "Just in case, I mean."

Eyasu gestured for Mavrin to join him at the mouth of the alley. He pointed across the Windroute at the Tiers, specifically at a stone tower taller than any structure had a right to be. Mavrin counted four stories, which baffled him even with the four iron loops of the Aspects Joined displayed from its domed roof.

"I'll wait for you there." Eyasu started collecting their things. "Good luck."

Mavrin clutched the slip of paper tighter and watched him go. "Yes. Because I have plenty of that these days."

Chapter Eighteen

EYASU'S DIRECTIONS DIDN'T INCLUDE ANY STREET names besides Deyeri's. Below that, he'd scribbled a series of instructions that began at the airdock, but only said things like "walk two blocks, turn left" and "past the yellow nutcheese vendor." As much as Mavrin wanted to waste time wandering, he knew that if he did, he would never find his way back to where the directions started. Which was likely why Eyasu wrote them that way.

As he made his way through the Towers, though, he paused to examine one of the unnerving, multistory buildings that gave the district its name. The smooth bricks along the base caught his eye immediately; that was pre-Fracture design. He crossed to another building and found the same bricks forming the entire three stories, topped by a ceramic roof lined with glittering dariss. Mavrin knew that post-Salvation Fargladeans tried to preserve as much of the original city as they could, but he hadn't realized the extent of their efforts. The bizarre design of their city wasn't new construction emulating the past; it was almost entirely made from the past, with the additions of speed gauges, condensers, and wind barriers carefully added to not damage Farglade's heritage. Unnerving as it was, Mavrin could appreciate that.

He barely looked at the Unyielding Walkway as he crossed, holding his cloak tight against his body while walking as straight as he could along its center median. The granite walls on either side were barely waist high but the locals walked without concern. He didn't encounter a lot of Fargladeans on his travels, so he forgot how their clothing didn't sport obvious weights like the ones dangling from his cloak; instead, they sewed panels of stone or metal directly into the seams, making them almost impossible to see. To Mavrin, they looked like people asking to be swept away during a Longwind.

Heavy patches made from composite and fungal glue covered several areas of the Walkway, since the curling, turquoise stone Gannerthen channeled wasn't immune to erosion. Steering away from one patch, Mavrin almost walked into a statue being built partway along the Walkway, the completed torso tied down with ropes and a larger tarp that fluttered in the Winds. After that, he picked up his pace even more to the other side.

Finally reaching the Tiers, two switchbacks brought him to the level he needed. He had to walk against the Winds to reach Deyeri's neighborhood, but surprisingly didn't need his goggles; the metal barriers at the street's southern end deflected the Winds better than he expected. Deyeri's street turned out to be a row of elegant townhomes with ceramic roofs and post-Salvation mottled brick, set almost flat against the curving face of the mountain. Tall iron gaslamps every few houses flicked on as evening approached, adding a shine to the glass renga loops secured to the eaves of almost every house. The homage to those long-extinct vines was popular in Hallen's Arch, too; one of many cultural scraps passed down from forebears to descendants after the Fracture.

He had to count houses, since Eyasu wrote *the thirteenth house on the block* instead of the actual addresses chiseled above each stone doorway. Halfway down, he spotted a small group of uniformed figures in slate and blue talking in a tight circle at the other end of the street. Mavrin spent a minute watching passersby give them nervous glances and wondered what they were investigating, mainly because he had reached Deyeri's front steps. A small, inverted triangle of quartz above the doorway served as the only unique touch, but what it signified was lost on him.

First, he shook his hands out and took deep, measured breaths.

Second, he checked his pockets to account for every item on his person, smoothing out his tunic and cloak when he finished. He cleared his throat a few times, swept his cloak back and forth, to loosen it for potential flourishes. The entire suite of pre-performance routines, which he hadn't combined in years, didn't help him feel any better.

By the grace of disappearing rings and illusory flame, walk up those damn steps and get this done.

Mavrin squared his shoulders, smoothed out his tunic one last time, relaxed his shoulders, and *then* climbed the steps to Deyeri's residence.

Oh dammit, what if she isn't home?

That thought entered his mind after he knocked on her door, and with a giddy rush of nerves he figured she probably wouldn't be home. It was late enough in the evening that she was likely out somewhere, or maybe she went to bed early. He could wait a ten count and collect himself some more before—

The door swung open.

It went wide, as though the person on the other side didn't worry about being bothered by strangers. But of course, the woman standing there wouldn't. She stood slightly taller than him, which meant Mavrin's line of sight went directly to her mouth. He moved his eyes away instinctively and found the soft lines that had formed along her cheekbones, and the streaks of distinguished white cutting through her auburn hair. It hung shorter than he remembered, a little above her shoulders, which seemed rounder than he remembered, unless that was an effect of her woolen shirt, which was considerably fuzzier than anything he remembered seeing her wear.

When he found the courage to look her in the eye, he saw a mixture of astonishment, doubt, hostility, and other emotions he wasn't confident finding a name for. He told her once that those eyes carried "a depth unlike anything I've ever seen, beyond my mere human comprehension." Not because he used to think poetry was an effective way to court, but because sometimes, he genuinely hadn't a damned clue what Deyeri Renn was thinking.

"I . . ." He cleared his throat. "That is to say . . ."

Deyeri's lips formed a hard line as one of her hands tapped the doorknob. Mavrin felt his chest constrict and imagined dropping dead of a heart attack in the middle of the street, like his father had.

"Take your time," she said, leaving the door open while she disappeared inside.

Mavrin blinked furiously and waited for his heart to stop. Faint clattering inside shook him from his daze, and when his first step didn't kill him, he kept walking until he entered a combination atrium and sitting room. A single stuffed chair sat in the corner between the window and a boxy stone and metal device he figured was a heatwell, part of the geothermal system that kept Farglade's buildings warm. Everything looked comfortable but carefully organized, even the crate placed beside the heatwell. A doorway left of the heatwell opened onto a staircase that thankfully led down, meaning Farglade's architects at least had some sense.

A narrow plaster wall with open doorways on either side separated the sitting room and kitchen. Sheets of composite covered most of its surface around eye level, with scribbled writing or what looked like architectural diagrams. He hadn't seen that much brainstorming on paper in a long time. Deyeri must have negotiated recycled sheets into her allotment, somehow.

She stood over a woodstove in the kitchen with her back to him. The vague smell of cloves came from the pot, which she used to fill a ceramic cup.

"You came in here to make tea?"

"Can't let it oversteep."

"Of course." Mavrin noted the narrow shelves mounted on the

wall, a cabinet with cooking supplies and a small table with two chairs. No sign that anyone but Deyeri lived here.

She leaned against the counter, completely nonchalant, and pointed at him with her cup. "Looks like you're doing well."

For the first time, his waistcoat and cloak felt like a disguise. "I'm considering retirement, actually." He offered a nervous smirk that felt about as far from his showman smile as possible. "I've managed to avoid dying in a ditch somewhere, at least."

She nodded and shrugged. Mavrin fiddled with his cuffs.

"Am I really supposed to take the lead here?" she asked, heat creeping into her voice.

"What? No, not at all . . . give me a moment . . ."

Deyeri shook her head. "You show up after who knows how many years—"

"Sixteen," Mavrin muttered.

"—and you didn't even prepare some badly written speech out of a street play? What the fuck are you *doing* here, Mavrin?"

The sudden, vicious anger in her voice made him tense.

"I'm worried you might be in danger?" Before she could respond, he took a step forward, hand outstretched. "Well, not just you. The city. We're worried the city might be in danger, and we're here to make sure it isn't."

"We?"

"Eyasu. He brought me here. Told me where to find you." Mavrin winced. "Try not to be angry with him. Even though this was his idea."

Deyeri fixed him with a dubious look. "You're saying you're here out of the sky because you and Eyasu aren't only speaking again, but you're on one of his damned quests? Did you take up hard liquor as a hobby somewhere down the line?"

"The thought crossed my mind recently. But I'm serious, love. We—"

"Don't," she said sharply, "*ever* call me that again."

She slammed her cup down and marched back into the sitting room.

Damn it. Mavrin stood in the kitchen running his hands through his hair, cursing Eyasu and the Aspects and the performer who gave him those coins and the Highest Voices and a bunch of other random people who had nothing to do with anything. The person he needed to curse the most was himself. But that could wait.

Deyeri leaned one elbow against the mantle above the heatwell, idly tapping her boot against the crate. She had turned on the room's two gaslamps, with the Lifesphere dimming to its darkest shade outside. When she didn't look at him, he stepped hesitantly to the crate's other side. It looked like a random collection of trinkets, mostly crystal that caught the heatwell's light.

"Are you just going to stand there?" she asked.

"Eyasu should have come with me," he said half-heartedly.

"Should've done all your talking for you back then, too?"

Mavrin let out a long breath. "Possibly."

The crate's contents rattled from her boot. A silver goblet rolled aside, revealing a long wooden case, about wide enough to hold one of his wands. Beneath it, he spotted an unsheathed dagger, its blade glinting blue like Eyasu's sword. More dariss.

"Eyasu thinks there might be Raw here. Or something equally dangerous." Realizing what he just blurted, he tried to slap his performer's face on.

He dropped it as Deyeri's gaze snapped toward him. "Raw aren't supposed to be real."

"They're real."

Something in the way he spoke must have broken through her anger, because she held back whatever she wanted to say next. Her intense stare made him more uncomfortable.

"What happened to you?" she asked, matter-of-fact. Not like she spoke from actual concern.

Before he could figure out how to answer, someone knocked at the front door. Deyeri grumbled something incoherent and kicked the crate harder. She waved for him to wait, but Mavrin barely noticed. That long wooden case had tipped over, revealing the edge of a glass top.

Inside, he heard a familiar clink.

Very carefully, he crouched and picked up the box. Three coins rested inside, sealed behind the glass top. Each of them made from dariss and imprinted with the same symbol as the ones he carried.

Mavrin shot to his feet as Deyeri swung her front door open. He heard her say, "This really isn't a good time, folks. Try again in the morning."

Three Watch stood on her stoop. The young, stocky woman in the center sneered. "Sorry, Ms. Renn. We're on direct orders."

Then they stepped inside.

Chapter Nineteen

"I'M SURE HE'LL BE FINE," EYASU SAID AS HE WAITED for the row of shellwagons blocking his path. "Did he ever tell you about Deyeri? They had something special in Veristenok."

The garnills paying attention blinked at him, which he decided meant "no." The others stared at the trio of painted, steel-reinforced shellwagons—about half-again as large as the ones he saw in Tanardell—making a slow turn across one of the Tiers' narrow streets on their way to the airdock. One of the wide-bodied takka snorted mist from all four nostrils as it snuffled at the ground, following the wagon ahead of it by scent and vibration. Something crystalline rattled under the wagon's dome, and Eyasu wondered what Farglade was shipping away for trade.

Once the last carriage passed and the foot traffic resumed, Eyasu said to the garnills, "Whatever was said between them, Mavrin was a different man. I meant it that I don't blame some of his choices. I'm certain Deyeri felt the same. Their reunion will work out for the best."

The garnills ruffled their sleek feathers, probably because they had doubts.

"Did he let you stretch your necks in Vertsa, little ones?" That seemed to get a more positive reaction, as the others swiveled toward him. "We'll see what we can do about that."

It didn't take long to get to the Outreach once those carriages passed. Navigating Farglade's twisting streets was simple enough if you knew where you were going, especially on the Tiers. Eyasu had been able to maneuver from memory, describing Farglade's design features to the garnills along the way. The Technical Academy had added more speed gauges to the taller buildings in the Towers district, he thought, sticking to the design made from four separate rings spinning on independent axes. He counted gauges on every fifth or sixth building, usually one or two buildings away from one of Farglade's condensers, collecting moisture from the Winds and funneling into cisterns at ground level.

"They use their geothermals to capture additional moisture," he told the garnills. "And not only because of the drier Winds here. Less reliance on the Unity has been their goal for some time."

The Outreach stood on the Tiers' lowest level, at the end of a narrow pavilion sheltered from the Winds by dense hedges. Between those and the burnished wind barriers around each neighborhood, the Winds were nothing more than a tickle. He'd pointed out similar barriers to the garnills in the Towers, bent into curving shapes to deflect the Winds away from ground level, like around the airdock.

As he walked the pavilion's cobblestone path, Eyasu noted several new machines dotting the smoothed ground on either side, each at least a foot taller than him. He stopped to study one in the shape of a figure holding a torch, its extended arm lifting and lowering with deliberate motion. At first, he thought it was being moved by the Winds, until he heard hissing and spotted the cables attached to the machine's legs. It was using heat from Farglade's geothermals to move the figure's limbs, letting the warm air pass against a motor inside the skeletal frame. Voice Revect had found a new project since he last visited, possibly taking the Catalyst as Core to heart.

The Outreach loomed over the residences around it, and Eyasu suspected some channeling had been responsible for stabilizing it against Longwinds. The brick walls were smooth and solid, carved with symbols to every Aspect-variation approved by the Highest Voices. Nearby, a pair of children pointed excitedly at the roof, where the four loops of the Aspects Joined rotated in place, catching the Winds with nearly invisible netting inside their design.

"The efforts we take to prove our devotion," Eyasu murmured to the garnills.

Climbing the front steps and passing through the Outreach's tall double doors brought him into a sweeping antechamber covering the ground floor. He remembered a mostly empty interior, but now benches and oval tables dotted the space, inside the ring of aged stone pillars. One of Voice Revect's earliest creations still covered the walls and ceiling: an intricate latticework of glass tubes, melted and curved to recreate the Aspects' path around Aelda. Sand mixed with ground-down bits of colored minerals flowed through the smooth tubes, moving on tiny currents brought in through valves on the Outreach's exterior.

Eyasu watched a flurry of brown and rusty orange sand pass directly overhead, along the route the Catalyst would take during Their final pass of the month, somewhere above the northern True Edge.

"You here for words, pie, or both?"

The acolyte at his left seemed to tower over him, either because of the broad shoulders beneath plain, dark green robes or the severe facial features, topped by a curly mop of hair. Other figures in green navigated the room; unlike smaller communities like Tanardell, Farglade's Voice shared their duties with several acolytes.

He frowned. "Did you say pie?"

The acolyte pointed to a long counter across the room, where several pies had been laid out. A young couple cut into one while they listened to an acolyte wearing a woven vest similar in nature to Jareden's sash, though depicting a different journey. Nearby, another visitor poured what looked like berrenfruit juice from a heavy cask.

"People get comfortable with food and drink." The towering

acolyte shrugged. "You'd think speaking to the Aspects instead of your neighbor would be enough, but what do I know?"

Eyasu tried to adopt a polite smile. "Voice Revect has always liked to be different."

"Different *was* one way to put it."

Eyasu's heart dropped. "She's accepted the touch of the Aspects."

"Second Summer, two years ago." She fluttered her fingers toward the sky at chest level, reflecting the Hidden as Deathgiver, followed by expressing her pronouns and title. "Voice Kedar Kalle. Afternoon."

Eyasu tried to decide what disappointed him more: losing someone he considered a friend, having one less person in the world who believed in and supported him, or that his chances of learning more about the Raw and helping Aulina might have drastically diminished. That last point bothered him the most, he realized, remembering the look on her face when he warned about going home.

Kedar furrowed her thick brows, and he realized he hadn't introduced himself.

"My greetings, honored Voice. I'm . . . Mavrin Leed, scholar from the Avergarden chapter." Unable to walk back that sudden choice, he added, "My apologies. I haven't seen Voice Revect in some time. Her passing is a shock."

"For me, too. Thought that old bird would outlive the Unity." Kedar leaned back slightly as she considered him. "Scholar? You here to research something specific?"

"I . . . yes. Voice Revect used to help me." Having already spun half-truths, others came more easily. "The research is sensitive and discreet. I can explain in private, perhaps?"

"So no pie, then?"

When his confused expression earned a deep-throated laugh, Eyasu wondered if maybe he should have brought Mavrin with him after all.

"Y'know, if you told me more about your research, I'd be able to help you better."

The Outreach's second floor looked more familiar than downstairs. The expansive room was filled with two rings of tall, stone bookshelves encircling more ovoid tables for reading. The shelves practically burst with tomes and rolled documents, mostly printed after the Salvation. Older texts used paper and parchment, but anything since would be on composite. Eyasu wondered if this new Voice was any better organized than her predecessor. The cataloguing system he learned in the Quartered Citadel wasn't universal.

"I prefer to keep my theories close, until I've verified my evidence," Eyasu said. That had been typical of some of the established researchers in Veristenok, sometimes even encouraged by the Highest Voices, so he doubted Kedar would question it.

To his surprise, she said, "Of course, can't possibly talk openly with a Voice, of all people. It's not like we both studied in the same place or anything." She let out a long, low whistle and added, "Citadel on high, and never mind the rest of us."

Eyasu paused between two sections of the inner ring of shelves. Voice Revect used to say something similar, about how sharing information used to be a guiding principle at the Citadel.

"You can understand my hesitation," he said carefully. "Disproving heresy is delicate work."

"Don't worry, I'm more offended you didn't want any pie," Kedar said mildly. She led him across the center of the room, veering left past the reading tables. "You knew Revect pretty well?"

"I visited twice during her tenure. For help with previous research," Eyasu said. It had been seven times, but Voice Revect didn't record the visits, as far as he knew. "She passed peacefully?"

"In her sleep."

Kedar brought him to a set of shelves on the far side of the room. The books he needed had moved since his last visit, and the thick wooden panel covering their new home surprised him. Kedar unlocked it and swung the panel up. "Every heretical text currently in the Outreach. Admittedly, not much."

Eyasu's heart sank. There were about half as many books as he remembered, not even filling an entire shelf. Worse, each book bore a red ceramic strip across the top of the spine: officially marked as *dangerous heresy* by Citadel guidelines, like his copy of *Protections and Wards.* "Have items been lost over the years?"

Kedar shrugged. "Had a couple disappear. A few others fell apart, and I never replaced them. Not much point, right?"

"No, I suppose not," Eyasu muttered. Choosing his words carefully, he asked, "Voice Revect maintained a more private collection. Does it still exist?"

"Thought you weren't interested in open talk."

Her menacing tone didn't register quickly enough. As Eyasu turned, Kedar already had one hand on his shoulder. He managed to wriggle away, but not before she deftly yanked enough cloak away to reveal a wooden pauldron. Eyasu bumped against the shelf and recoiled.

Kedar didn't follow, eyeing his armor without a hint of surprise. "Revect wasn't much for openness, either. At least, not at first." Then she crossed her arms over her robes and added, "Let's try this again, Eyasu."

Chapter Twenty

AS THE THREE WATCH PRACTICALLY PUSHED PAST her, old instincts screamed at Deyeri to go for the sword she kept leaning by the doorframe, or the one tucked discreetly behind the heatwell's mantle. Or grab the Watch with the noticeable cheeks—Caspen, the young woman she met with Havven—by the wrist, spin her around and march her outside. Mavrin's arrival had her mind whirling.

Since these were still her people, and this wasn't the Incursions, she settled for calmly shutting the door behind them.

Caspen and the other two Watch, one man and one woman, formed an organized line in the middle of her sitting room, with Caspen in the center. She looked Mavrin up and down and discounted him. Deyeri noticed he had picked up something from Yeldin's crate.

"Sorry for barging in, Ms. Renn. This is official business related to Edict Nine."

Deyeri tried to ignore the way Caspen addressed her. She had accepted that someday she would be nothing more than a nameplate in the barracks. Being retired, even with her record, meant you started to fade. But they still heard enough stories to treat her with some deference—often more than she thought she deserved—except this Caspen. And she must have been acting on her own; secrecy aside, there was no way Breck or Termot would specifically send the Watch to her house.

"Want to take bets on how quickly she gets promoted?" Deyeri asked the other two. The man, whose untrained stance would allow

Deyeri to knock him on his ass before he could blink, looked at the floor; the woman, not much better but at least with her blade at ready, tried to stifle a smirk. "With that attitude, I predict lieutenant within a year. Any takers?"

Caspen sneered at her. "Now that promotion comes from actual merit, I'll be fine."

"Okay, three years."

Mavrin let out a choking sound, but she ignored him. Caspen turned purple and clenched her fists.

Ah. That sparked Deyeri's memory. The Watch went through rigorous evaluations after the Incursions, as they transitioned back to a guard and protection force as opposed to a military one—or as much as they could, without knowing if the most recent Incursion was really the last. The person you wanted fending off a scuttleboat wasn't the person you wanted making safety calls during a Longwind. Deyeri had tried to keep as many of the former out when she was in, and the idea that soldiers like Caspen simply waited for her to retire only made the ill feeling of Mavrin showing up worse.

"Careful, Caspen," she said evenly, deliberately not using her rank. "Hope you learned to control your temper."

Caspen tried to cover her surprise with a fresh glower and squared her shoulders. "We're here on direct orders from Watch Commander Termot, on behalf of Lord-Magistrate Breck, to fulfill your contribution to Edict Nine."

Her tone confirmed that everything except the last was a lie. Deyeri put a hand to her mouth. "Really? I couldn't have guessed."

While Stance openly gaped, that got a snort from Smirk. Caspen glared at her. "Search the premises."

Smirk shrugged in the universal gesture of someone following orders without context. "Sorry, Commander."

"*Commander?*" Mavrin repeated.

"A lot can happen when you leave," Deyeri told him. She pointed at the crate. "Don't bother. It's all in there."

Mavrin fidgeted harder, mouth opening and closing.

Caspen motioned for Smirk to collect the crate. "How do we know that's everything?"

It didn't include any of her personal possessions, but she hoped it was enough to get rid of her visitors. "Trying to make things easy for whoever came by. Now get out of my house."

As Smirk bent to pick up the crate, she noticed the box in Mavrin's hands. "Sir, does that belong in here?"

"No," Mavrin said, at the exact moment Deyeri said, "Yes."

Mavrin shot her a look that he had no right to cast her way.

Caspen looked between them with a glimmer of amusement before focusing on Mavrin. "Sir, are you a citizen of Farglade?" When he shook his head, Caspen continued, "Then the edict doesn't apply to you. Anything belonging to a citizen is subject, however."

"I see. Unfortunately, this does actually belong to me, so—"

Seeing Deyeri's confusion, Caspen made a *tsk* sound and crossed the room. She snatched the box and examined its contents, making the coins inside clink.

"Deyeri . . ." Mavrin said quietly. "We should really get Eyasu."

Whatever about the coins bothered him so much didn't matter; they would end up thrown into Gannerthen's storage rooms with everything else. She needed to find out what he knew about the Raw, but the only way to do that was to get Caspen and these shit-trained Watch out of her house.

"Are these some collector's item?" Caspen looked for how to open the box. "I can see why you'd want to hide them."

Three things seemed to happen at once:

Caspen found the latch and pushed it with her thumb.

Mavrin shouted, "Wait!" and flicked his wrist, shooting a

multicolored rope from his left sleeve. It snaked around Caspen's forearm, wrenching it sideways.

The front door flew open as Havven strode inside, practically bellowing, "By the Four, I told you to wait—"

Everyone froze. Caspen recovered first, crying out as she tried to jerk her arm free. The box slipped from her hand and struck the floor with a crack, the unlatched lid popping open and releasing the coins. Caspen ignored it, going for her sword.

"Hold!"

Deyeri had been halfway to snatching Caspen's sword arm, but she stopped along with everyone else. She couldn't remember hearing Havven sound that commanding before, and the shocked silence left her room to feel impressed. A vein pulsed under his receding hairline as he looked from the Watch, to her, to Mavrin and the rope, one end still hidden beneath his sleeve. Mavrin blinked at his outstretched hand as though surprised at what he'd done.

Havven cleared his throat. "Would someone care to explain?"

"He assaulted a member of the Watch!" Caspen screeched. She snatched for her sword again, using the opposite hand. Mavrin tugged on the rope and it went slack, which only caused Caspen to scramble more furiously.

Havven stepped forward. "I said *hold*, Corporal." When Caspen stilled, he added, like he was speaking to a child: "I'm sure this is a misunderstanding."

Deyeri tried not to roll her eyes. She turned to Mavrin, wanting to tear into him, but the words died in her throat. He looked terrified.

Havven raised an eyebrow her way. As she tried to figure out how to explain, Caspen scooped up the coins in her black uniform glove. Mavrin let out a sharp breath and stepped away, even though the corporal didn't seem interested in drawing a weapon anymore.

"The old man was fighting over these, Lieutenant." Caspen

picked one up between her thumb and forefinger. "Maybe they're more valuable than they look."

And she tossed Havven one of the coins.

Chapter Twenty-One

THE WATCH GRABBED MAVRIN'S CLOAK AS HE TRIED to rush forward, jerking him back.

Caspen stepped between him and the lieutenant. "Assaulting a member of the Watch, *again*?"

"You need to take that coin back." Mavrin tried to wrench free. "Take it from him now!"

He glanced desperately at Deyeri, but despite the alertness on her face, she didn't move.

Havven studied the coin in his palm. "They don't look like much," he said softly. A slight shudder rippled up his arms, as though he was shaking off the last chill from the evening Winds.

Something in the way he spoke caught Deyeri's attention. "You all right, Hav?"

Clear, brown eyes blinked back. Nothing changed on his face except an understanding smile. "Caspen, give me the other two coins. We'll sort this out."

She slapped the other two coins into Havven's outstretched palm, beaming like a puppy. Havven nodded his thanks absently, rolling the coins in his palm with a sort of bemused look on his face. "This is good work, Caspen. You always do good work."

"Thank you, Lieutenant." She shot a smug look at Deyeri.

The skin around Havven's eyes crinkled, like he was pleased at something.

"Deyeri!" Mavrin choked out, and the Watch yanked him closer.

"You were always good. Even when your mothers didn't ask."

Caspen frowned. "Sir?"

"The seedbarn." Havven brought his other hand up to his temple and winced. "Yes, the barn. And the cats. You kept the seedbarn free of cats, didn't you?"

Caspen's face paled.

"I'm sure you remember. Entire families of the things, hiding from every Longwind. Nowhere else to go after . . . yes, after Ryten Forest died." That made Havven's smile widen. "Mother asked you to chase them out, but they came back. Then one of them scratched you. They shouldn't have done that." Havven cocked his head. "Definitely not."

Finally, Deyeri turned her wide eyes to Mavrin, but it was too late without Eyasu here. Not because of what Havven said, but because of how the tenor of his voice changed, from the clipped tone when he entered to something velvety and smooth.

"Did you apologize?" Havven closed his eyes, concentrating. "Yes, of course you did. You were sorry for brutalizing those poor creatures, but your mothers wouldn't hear it. Oh, and things were never, ever the same."

Mavrin tried to speak, but the words caught in his throat.

Havven's eyes snapped open, boring into Caspen. "Would you like to ask forgiveness again?"

Caspen's eyes widened. She almost tripped over the crate as she pressed her back to the heatwell's mantle. Havven followed her, a knowing smile on his lips.

"Ask your mothers' forgiveness, Caspen. Everything will be fine."

The air around them charged. Mavrin finally found a breath, but forced, like pushing against a Longwind. Nothing slanted around him, nothing pounded at his head, but the jittery feeling against his skin was unmistakable: Havven was channeling.

Or rather, the being inside him was.

"I . . ." Tears ran down Caspen's cheeks. "Please. Forgive me."

Mavrin could have sworn he saw the whisper itself float between the two, like a translucent piece of sickly orange cloud. It faded against Havven's cheek while he closed his eyes as though in rapture. His free hand touched Caspen's shoulder.

"Your forgiveness is granted."

Caspen let out a long, despairing cry and dropped to her knees, shattering the coin case's lid. She shook so violently that Mavrin was amazed she stayed upright, rooted in place as though her knees were glued to the floorboards. One last rattling breath issued from her lips as she raised her hands, either to cover her gasping mouth or claw at her hair or beseech the Aspects for assistance. Mavrin never found out, since her hands abruptly dropped to the side and she slumped in place, the horror replaced by a vacant stare.

The charge left the air. No one else moved.

"That was almost worth waiting for." Havven rolled his shoulders. "I wonder how original those life choices are."

"By the Saviors . . ." Deyeri breathed.

Mavrin tensed as Havven's gaze fell on her. New veins appeared from under his light brown hair—not gold like Aulina, but a darker color, like old iron. They spread down his face, twisting around his sly smile and down his throat, appearing on the tips of his fingers. In the span of an eyeblink, Havven's eyes filled with a deep, purple glare struck through with flecks of dark amber.

"What's happening to him?" the Watch holding Mavrin managed to whisper.

"A Raw." It was Deyeri who said it aloud, before Mavrin could.

"There's no such thing," the other Watch spat from across the room, raising his sword while Deyeri waved frantically for him to stay still.

When Havven rolled his head that way, Deyeri called, "Can you hear me, Hav?" Her fingers twitched where a sword might hang from her belt.

"Oh, your friend is preoccupied." The Raw closed Havven's

eyes again. "So many thoughts in this one's mind. More than I would expect for someone of his station. A quieter mind would have been easier." He chuckled. "Do you want to know what he really thinks of you? You might be surprised."

"Let him go," Deyeri growled.

"Where are you? Ah, there . . . Watch Commander Deyeri Renn. Hero of the Incursions from Afar. Do you wonder what people under your command think of you?" The Raw gestured at the side of Havven's head. "Or did you wonder, I suppose. I'm catching up." He kicked one of Caspen's knees, not getting a reaction. "There are layers to Havven's respect for you, Commander. He might not remember the nightmares he's had."

Mavrin cycled through everything in his pockets, not sure what he could use that wouldn't get them killed. He didn't have anything like Eyasu carried. No reagents, no dariss—

Except in that crate. He measured the steps to it.

"I wonder if anyone else shares dear Havven's thoughts?" the Raw mused. "Shall we find out?"

Havven's hand flicked out and the woman holding Mavrin stiffened, releasing him. One step to the crate and the room tilted. For an instant, Mavrin stood in the Citadel's courtyards, surrounded by scholars debating the finer points of Unity politics. Then he was in a performing pit in Yarder's Outlook, buffeted by harsh jeers and the Winds driven across the different stages.

Deyeri's sitting room returned, with the Raw standing centimeters from the Watch as she opened her mouth to say something. Havven's head shook back and forth ever so slightly, looking genuinely apologetic.

The Watch screamed so loudly that Mavrin flinched away. It cut out as she dropped to her knees, wearing the same, blank stare as Caspen.

"Well, she didn't share them," the Raw said, almost absently. "What about the next one?"

His gaze settled on Mavrin.

He wasn't sure what he expected. Maybe the cold hand of death. Instead, the air seemed to grow warmer, like sitting in front of a roaring fire on a dark winter's night. Havven's head cocked slightly, and for a second Mavrin thought he saw the face of his mother, blue eyes sad but accepting that she might never see her son again. The image flickered, becoming Deyeri, younger, features contorted with anger and betrayal. That didn't last, either. When Havven's face returned, the purple-filled eyes narrowed.

"Very curious. You've been touched by someone else. Recently, I think?"

Mavrin couldn't even shake his head.

"You remind me of a human from long ago. He didn't mind my kind's touch. Called me by name, even." Havven's hand flicked in the sign of he pronouns, almost absently. "Has the ability to hide from us been lost?"

When Mavrin still didn't respond, Havven's smile twisted maliciously. "I sense my sibling's touch on you, and you will tell me where—"

He staggered as Deyeri struck his right hand, the one holding the coins. When his fingers flew open empty, she blinked in surprise. Havven flashed her an indulgent smile and smacked her with enough force that she flew backward into the wall between the sitting room and the kitchen. Papers fell to the ground around her as she coughed, spitting up blood.

Ignoring every instinct to run to her side, Mavrin sprang toward the crate. He scooped up the dagger he spotted before and flicked it at the Raw.

The blade sunk into Havven's shoulder halfway to the hilt. Unlike with Aulina in the mortuary, this Raw simply frowned at the smoke hissing from the wound.

"Not wanting to ruin your mind doesn't mean your body is safe, magician."

He raised his hand and Mavrin felt his body move without permission. His head struck the doorframe leading into the kitchen and he landed hard on the floor, halfway between both rooms, cloak tangled around his limbs.

When he regained his senses, Havven faced the last Watch, clutching the other man's neck as they stared into each other's eyes. Neither of them said anything; the Watch simply let out a quiet yelp and crumpled to the ground like the others.

Mavrin looked for Deyeri and saw her crouched at the kitchen's other doorway, eyes darting around the room.

Havven turned in a circle, staring at nothing, muttering under his breath. "Searching for minerals . . . rich resources to keep them safe . . . sneaking your liquor allotment in the middle of a patrol, naughty girl . . . too fast, you always ate too quickly at dinner . . ." He grunted and rubbed his forehead. "Settle yourselves, please . . ."

Caspen started to stir. Her cheeks were deathly pale, brows knit in confusion.

Mavrin tore through his pockets, until his fingers brushed the firecube. In a flash of what he hoped was inspiration, he locked eyes with Caspen and pointed. "Incursion assassin! Protect the city!"

An expression of clarity crossed Caspen's features. She surged to her feet, drew her sword in a smooth motion and threw herself forward. The Raw snarled and backed away, seeming to direct Caspen's first strike askew without needing to touch her. The other two Watch stirred, going for their weapons like automatons.

As they converged on the Raw, Mavrin ducked through the kitchen and grabbed Deyeri by the arm, tugging her out of the sitting room. "Do you have a back door?"

She pulled away. "We can't leave them."

Someone screamed in the sitting room, short but bloodcurdling, followed by a heavy thump as the dividing wall took another blow.

"Those soldiers are already dead, and we need to get out of here. *Now where is the damn back door*?"

Deyeri gritted her teeth. "Downstairs."

She led him back to the doorway closest to the stairs. When she looked around the doorframe, she closed her eyes and cursed, then bolted. Before he followed her downstairs, Mavrin glanced back and saw the Raw standing with hands raised above the three Watch. His eyes were closed in an expression disturbingly close to bliss as they spasmed on the ground, blood pooling around them.

Havven's stolen eyes peeked open, fixing directly on Mavrin.

Mavrin pulled Cler's firecube from his pocket. He pressed the switch on the object's frame and threw it—not at the Raw, but into Deyeri's heatwell.

Mavrin slammed the door shut behind him and practically leapt to the bottom of the steps. A few seconds later, the device triggered and the fuel inside ignited, creating a heavy boom upstairs that rattled the door.

Deyeri grabbed him. "Did you blow up my sitting room?"

"Later?"

She cursed again and crossed a narrow hallway that spanned the floor, passing a bedroom and storage room to the right. The "back door" was a window slit at the end of the hallway, leading to whatever open space lay between Deyeri's home and the mountain. She grabbed a sword from beside her bed and some sort of wrist-guard from a stone dresser, shattered the window with the latter, and hoisted herself up. Mavrin's first attempt to follow didn't work, heels scrabbling against the stone wall.

Something almost like laughter floated down the stairs, as Deyeri caught Mavrin's wrist and dragged him out into the night.

Chapter Twenty-Two

IGNORING MAVRIN'S PROTESTS, DEYERI CIRCLED around the row of townhomes and crept back down her street. Her shoulder blades and lower back screamed where they'd struck the sitting room wall, and she felt blood sticking to the sweat on her brow. But a familiar energy coursed through her, too; as much as she wanted to close her body off from it, she knew she needed it now.

"We need to find Eyasu—"

"Quiet," she snapped. She took a moment to test the balance of her sword, one of several she kept around her home but hardly practiced with anymore. The wristguard she grabbed from the mantle wasn't her favorite either, but the padded inside fit snugly around her sweater's sleeve, and the pounded iron exterior would catch most weapons. "Stay here."

Sticking close to the windwalls and covered gardens nestled between each home, Deyeri hurried back down the street. She'd seen two other Watch outside when she opened the door for Caspen; if she could draw Havven away, they could rescue the people in her home. The ones mauled by a creature that was far from a myth, regardless of what lies Breck told. She'd deal with that later.

One of her neighbors stood outside his front door, rengan memory charms half-unspooled as he stared down the street, likely having heard Mavrin's explosion. She waved frantically at him to go back inside. Rounding the bend to her home, she saw the two Watch hustling up her front steps, a moment before her front door swung open to reveal a uniformed figure. *Havven. Shit.*

Before Deyeri could call out a warning, two hands closed on her shoulders. She tried to shake them off, not caring what Mavrin hissed at her.

Someone screamed, and one of the Watch fell onto the street, armor clattering against the stone. The other went for their weapon, but Havven was faster. Within moments, a new scream echoed down the street. The air around her house wavered, several glass vines cracking suddenly from the pressure, but luckily Deyeri wasn't close enough to be affected by the channeling. The channeling that shouldn't have been possible.

Through the wavering air, Havven stared down the street at her.

"Hidden's breath, do you have a death wish?" Mavrin said.

As she glanced at the two soldiers lying in the street, and imagined the three in her home, Deyeri thought she might. Except that despite keeping things from her, Breck taught her some useful lessons during the Incursions. Like the fact that you couldn't avenge anyone if you passed beyond.

She let Mavrin pull her away.

Violet cloak billowing behind him, he sprinted ahead, glancing back every few steps as though he expected her to break off again. At the end of the street, he veered toward the nearest ramp, leading to the Tier below them, but Deyeri steered him the opposite way.

"Eyasu is at the Outreach," he protested.

"Just shut up and move, Mavrin."

She led him behind the next row of townhomes, leaping over fat geothermal pipes that burrowed into the mountain. At the end of the row, she ducked under the wide beams supporting a condenser and threw her throbbing shoulder against the door of the next building, a standalone brick structure dominated by wide, crystal windows. The single room inside looked exactly like she remembered: nutroot plants tied together in dense pods, sheltered from the Winds while getting sunlight through the crystal and water from narrow tubes connected to the condenser outside. Besides a rack of gardening equipment against one wall, the interior looked empty.

"What are we doing here?" Mavrin asked.

"Isn't everything multipurpose where you settled down?" She realized she didn't have a clue, but the host of thoughts behind that needed to wait until she got them out.

Deyeri brushed carefully past the nutroots' tall stalks, making sure not to step on any of the tubers poking up from the soil on her way to the center of the room. What looked like a strategic or even artful planting arrangement disguised a hatch set into the floor. She threw it open and gestured for Mavrin to follow, shutting it above them with as light of a clang as possible.

"Found these after they resettled the city," she said before Mavrin could ask. Phosphorescent lichen lined the uneven rock walls, averblossom's cousins providing barely enough light to see the tunnel sloping sharply downward toward the Grayest Mountains. Snatching a salt lamp instead of her wristguard might have been more useful. "The tunnels date to the Time Before Unity. More of them survived the Fracture intact than people expected."

The tunnel curled away from the mountain after about a hundred paces, traveling under the next lowest Tier. Mavrin lagged shortly after the turn; she thought he was being cautious on the sloping ground, but he'd stopped to study the carvings set into the walls. He brushed a hand over a vaguely humanoid figure with a shield covering their lower body: the Catalyst as Protector, back when the Highest Voices allowed the Aspects to be anthropomorphized. Deyeri tugged him away; Havven knew about these tunnels, having used them for shelter or quick travel during the Incursions, so she had to assume the Raw knew about them now, too.

The tunnel curled twice more before leveling out at a dead-end of collapsed rock. Deyeri snatched a handle riven into the ceiling and used her weight to unlock the hatch. The Lifesphere's glow illuminated a short metal ladder, which she sent Mavrin up first. They emerged in an alley on the lowest Tiers; the tall barrier shielding it from the Windroute loomed ahead.

Foot traffic thinned with the sun going down, but the gaslamps lining the street still highlighted every potential casualty if the Raw caught up to them. Airdock workers in heavy coveralls. A merchant offering leftover biscuits to passersby, trailed by three children who looked like siblings, their hair braided up using small shells and wax. An adept from the Technical Academy holding a hydrometer into the Winds.

That adrenaline from fleeing her home and pushing through the tunnel twisted into a familiar terror she hated. They needed to get off this street.

Deyeri steered Mavrin toward the barrier wall, hoping no one noticed them as she searched its surface. She spotted it a hundred paces to their right: the outline of a door, barely visible against the barrier unless you knew to look for it. Mavrin huffed at her side as she raced down the slope toward it, bracing himself against the wall when they stopped.

"What's . . . on the other . . . side of this?"

A heavy metal bolt secured the door, and only the Watch had the keys. The nearest civilians were far enough away that she gripped her forearm with her other hand and slammed her wristguard against the lock, wincing as the impact rattled her wrist bones. On the fourth strike, the lock snapped free.

The Winds buffeted her as soon as she opened the door, and she grabbed the length of rope she knew was there before they sucked her off the platform. Mavrin cursed, bracing himself with both hands against the doorframe and staring at the Windroute below.

"Where in the abyss are you taking us?" he screeched.

"Grab on!" she ordered, pointing at the harness hanging from the heavy bronze pole in front of them. When he didn't move, she gestured at the sailboard attached to the bottom of the pole, currently tied to the platform using cords and magnet clamps. The top of the pole ended in a loop with an alloy cable strung through, stretching both ways along the barrier, as far as one could see if they dared to look for long enough.

Mavrin shook his head violently.

Catalyst, give me strength. She couldn't hold onto the rope and move her arms enough to illustrate what they needed to do. Instead, she stepped onto the sailboard, looped her arms through the harness, and stuck one foot through a strap that slipped over her boot.

"Get on or stay here!"

Pulling a release on the pole snapped out its miniature sails, which immediately billowed out. Deyeri felt the board being pulled and yanked Mavrin forward by the elbow. He grabbed onto her instead of the harness as she used her free foot to kick the magnet clamp, releasing them from the platform. Mavrin's howl echoed in her ear, but Deyeri knew the board could hold; she'd used this in an emergency with two other Watch before, everyone wearing armor. The barrier wall surged past to their left, the distant lights of the Towers to their right as the board carried them along the cable.

She risked a glance back. Without goggles she could barely see, but she thought a figure stood on the platform, straight-backed against the Winds and watching them escape.

By the time they reached the streets nearest the Outreach, Mavrin had shaken the headache from the Raw's channeling, but not the images of the Watch writhing on the ground, or the tremors in his limbs from sailing along the Windroute with Deyeri. Glancing down every alley they passed, watching for shadows or flickers of movement in the gaslamps' glow, didn't help. Every few glances he spotted something made of dariss and edged away from it.

Needing a distraction, he asked, "You were really a commander?"

Deyeri didn't respond.

"Those soldiers called you 'Commander.' What sort of commander? Not Commander of the entire Watch, certainly."

Her eyes narrowed. "What do you mean, 'certainly?'"

For a moment Mavrin couldn't decide what terrified him more: facing down a Raw, crossing the Windroute on a flimsy sheet of metal, or Deyeri's glare. "That would be a political position, wouldn't it? You hate politics."

Deyeri shook her head and kept moving.

"I suppose I should apologize about your house . . ."

"I don't remember you babbling this much."

"Eyasu hasn't said anything about that."

Deyeri's hand closed on the front of his cloak. Not gruffly or violently, but enough to stop him in his tracks.

"Always having a quick response, I *do* remember," she said evenly. "Not with me. Not with at least five of my people dead, and maybe a sixth who happens to be a friend. Not until I find out everything you and Eyasu know about the Raw, and maybe not even after that."

She let him go and picked up her pace.

"Understood," Mavrin whispered, even though she hadn't asked.

When they finally approached the Outreach, he thought there were people milling on the front pavilion, but the dark shapes turned out to be skeletal machines made from twisted metal. What seemed like an effect of the Lifesphere's glow turned out to be actual movement, like the rearing takka turning its four-horned head back and forth on some convection-powered piston.

Deyeri didn't spare them a glance, marching up the front steps to the Outreach's double doors. As she pounded on them, she said, "Kedar's acolytes don't live here, but her residence is upstairs."

"Let's not wake her up."

Mavrin wanted nothing more than to pretend he hadn't heard the smooth voice behind them. When he turned, the Raw stood halfway across the pavilion, next to the takka construct. A line of blood coated the front of Havven's uniform, but the dagger wound had closed. There were no obvious burn marks from the firecube exploding.

Mavrin started banging underhand against the door.

The Raw spread his hands. "This is embarrassing. To run all this way and get stopped by a door?"

"Do you have any weapons on you besides rope?" Deyeri whispered.

"Eyasu is the warrior. I'm the magician."

"What do you mean you're the *magician*?"

A sharp laugh cut across the pavilion. "Interesting as your squabble might be, I'd like to know where I can find my sibling. Please."

It took Mavrin a moment to figure out what was happening.

"You don't know where they are," he said. "You can't sense . . . your sibling at all, can you?"

The crooked smile on Havven's face didn't change. This Raw seemed to have better control over human features than the one inside Aulina had, which made Mavrin worry about the rest of his capabilities. What he demonstrated already was terrifying enough.

Eyasu had to be inside. He needed to stall, like in the orchard.

He stepped forward, pulling his cloak around him. "I'm right, aren't I? The big, powerful, dangerous Raw can kill people with a thought, but he can't find the one thing he's actually after?"

"Perhaps. But I still have my *tricks*."

The Raw raised a hand toward Deyeri. Without thinking, Mavrin stepped between them.

He heard Deyeri gasp, and her sword clatter to the ground.

As Mavrin tried to move toward her, the world around him seemed to slow. On either side of the cobblestone path, the skeletal constructs stood straighter, and then taller. A humanoid figure holding a torch stretched in place as though its metal frame was turning to gelatin, while the rearing takka's limbs arced further into the air, becoming more like an akrren's long, barbed foreclaws. The Raw stood in the center, eyeing the constructs warily with one hand twitching at his side.

The faint sound of hissing gas became a whine so high-pitched that he tried to clamp his hands over his ears, except his limbs still wouldn't move faster than a crawl. The Raw seemed unaffected, back-pedaling away from the Outreach and the moving constructs, waving his hands to channel again. Before he finished, a sudden pop replaced the whine as gouts of fire shot out of every construct, forming a maelstrom around the Raw.

As heat washed over his skin, Mavrin's limbs returned to motion. He spun to Deyeri as she gasped, face pulsing red, and he realized that for those brief seconds she'd stopped breathing.

A firm hand pushed him toward the doors. Eyasu tugged one open and shoved him inside, where he tumbled in next to Deyeri. The door slammed behind them, Eyasu's tall figure flickering in the antechamber's blue light.

"The doors were open the whole time?" Mavrin managed to gasp.

"Of course not." Eyasu turned a lever to relock them. The atrium beyond was lit by tiny blue gaslamps that illuminated tables, some sort of bar set-up at the back, and an elaborate network of glass tubes filled with sand along the walls and ceiling. "The short version of your latest adventure, please."

When Deyeri didn't offer an explanation, Mavrin rambled out,

"She had another set of coins. The Raw inside escaped. Followed us here, since he knows we have another one. His sibling maybe?"

Deyeri coughed. "Whatever that thing is, he can attack your mind."

Something that sounded heavier than a human hand or foot slammed against the doors.

"I hoped we could start by talking this time," Eyasu murmured. He pointed toward the bar. "Get my rucksack. Hide the box."

"What about you?"

Eyasu threw off his cloak and drew his Castoff as he faced the double doors. When Deyeri stepped beside him, Eyasu gestured at the longknife on his belt. The dariss glinted on its edge as she held it aloft in the hand with her wristguard, holding her short sword in the other. Seeing them stand together only surprised Mavrin because of how natural Deyeri looked, readying herself for a fight. Even in a torn woolen sweater.

He scurried around the bar as instructed, finding Eyasu's rucksack. New books filled the top, with a round stone marker bearing the joined hands of the Voice. Mavrin tossed those aside as he dug for the box, frantically wishing his friend organized his things in a way that made sense.

Heavy wood boomed and cracked, crashing into the room. Mavrin peeked around the bar and saw one door lying on several crushed tables, while the other hung from half its hinges. Colored sand trickled from several cracked glass tubes on the wall behind it.

The moment the Raw stepped into the atrium, Eyasu started chanting in T'var. Mavrin caught phrases related to banishment; Eyasu was trying to drive the Raw back outside, since extracting him from Havven's body would likely be impossible, at least at first.

As Eyasu finished his Request, the glass tubes along the walls rattled.

Nothing else happened. No tilting or slowing of the world, no pounding headache behind Mavrin's skull. Eyasu stared in shock as the glow faded from his Castoff, and the Request went unanswered.

When the Raw's eyes flashed, Eyasu gasped and fell backward with a heavy thud. His longsword clattered beside him as he clawed at his chest armor. Mavrin waited for the channeling to wash away like it had in Tanardell, but Eyasu kept writhing—his wooden armor wasn't protecting him. Deyeri rushed forward with the longknife and the Raw raised his hand again, forcing her sideways into a stone pillar, where she slumped unmoving to the ground.

Sheer will kept Mavrin from calling to her. He dumped the rucksack over, spotted the box and scooped it up, tucking it into his cloak.

"You're more focused than most. But your doubt must come from somewhere . . ." The Raw stood over Eyasu's feet and closed his eyes.

He couldn't run for the front door and hiding upstairs seemed like a terrible idea. Figuring Eyasu used another entrance to circle around outside, Mavrin spotted a narrow, wooden door at the back, with a circular, barred window.

"Ah, there we are," the Raw cooed. "Has life always been that unkind, false Requester?"

As Eyasu gasped in pain, Mavrin froze beside the bar. A flick of his wrist dropped a blunted dagger into his palm—but then his eyes locked with Eyasu's, long enough to see the fractional shake of his friend's head. Telling him to leave. Deyeri stirred nearby, starting to rise.

Who knows this fight better? Cursing, Mavrin broke into a sprint toward the door.

Except when have you listened to him before?

As he pushed the door open, Mavrin whirled, blunted dagger ready to hurl at the Raw's head before he fled.

Tingling erupted across his flesh and one ankle caught the other, turning his spin into a fall through the doorway, yelping onto the cold dirt outside. The feeling came back to his legs immediately and he scrambled out into the Winds, reaching the swaying frame of the Voice's speaking tower. It was as tall as Jareden's in Tanardell, held by support beams riven into the ground and the low stone wall between the enclosure's edge and the Windroute.

A hand grabbed Mavrin by the cloak and whipped him around, slamming him against the stairs. The Raw loomed over him. "I'd like my family, please."

"Family?" Mavrin felt the box poking him in the hip. "I didn't think monsters had families."

"Such hubris. If only you knew." The Raw cocked his head. "We will pass our test and be given what we deserve."

"*Your* test?" He glanced at the open doorway. *Keep talking.* "Please, I want to listen. What test?"

"Let me show you."

The Raw showed no sign of channeling, but Mavrin felt the world swirl. This was different than when they faced the Raw inhabiting Aulina; it wasn't reality shifting around him, but a flood of images blanketing his vision, tangibly from somewhere else. People in light clothing, with no weights to counter the Winds, surrounded by machinery he didn't recognize: quartz screens, metal cranks and levers, cables snaking across the floor and burying into a wall of dariss. Someone with thin hair past their neck, braided in an unfamiliar style, looking him directly in the eye and speaking; he knew the person lied and meant him harm, despite not hearing the words. A familiar symbol on his coat: five gears with lines cutting through them. Sensations mingled with images so alien he couldn't fathom them: a zigzagging tunnel of light he could feel with his fingernails, then a static charge directing through his limbs, from a source he didn't recognize. It was the sky, but not the sky; he could see the stars clearly, without the Lifesphere's comforting haze, and that static came from above somehow. And then pain, more pain than his body could possibly hold, frozen in place like the throbbing of a fresh bruise but continuous on every inch of his body.

When the images receded, Mavrin knelt on the cold dirt, holding the box out toward the Raw. Flat on both palms like an offering, since a being so powerful and so *wronged* required that gesture—no, *deserved* it—

Something blurred behind the Raw and he whirled, catching the dariss-coated longsword one-handed, so that the blade buried into Havven's palm. Deyeri stumbled as the Raw used that hand to wrench Eyasu's sword from her grip. It clanged against the speaking tower's handholds and landed in front of Mavrin.

Blinking confusion from his mind, he scooped up the longsword and stabbed without aiming, sinking the point into Havven's back. The Raw inside howled as Mavrin yanked the sword out, stumbling with its weight. Deyeri slammed into the Raw with her shoulder, driving him past the speaking platform. Whether it was surprise or stumbling over Mavrin, the creature couldn't manage a counterattack before he pitched over the stone wall.

His howl faded into the Winds, leaving them alone on the platform.

Chapter Twenty-Three

EVERYTHING ABOUT BEING LORD-MAGISTRATE involved meetings, and Woldren Breck hated it.

Committee meetings with specific Councillors. Inspections of new geothermal vents or repairs to the Unyielding Walkway. Petitioners who wanted his ear—which he used to not mind, since the people were why he accepted the appointment, until they started needing to screen anyone taking issue with Edict Nine. During the Incursions, his special position as Lord-General meant he could run things as he wanted, putting lieutenants in charge who he knew didn't need supervision, while he focused on overall strategy. Now, even the people he trusted most expected regular meetings, simply because. Like the Legislative Council, seated around the table with him right now, determined to remain until they finished every item on Councillor Oreel's checklist.

It was late, and he wanted to be in bed.

The oozing green pustules on the ceiling didn't help, either.

They varied in size, from smaller than a luxury chit to the width of a dinner plate. Sickly green droplets fell from the ceiling every few seconds, burning holes into the council room's table or the floor. When Watch Commander Termot reached for her tumbler, one sliced cleanly between her thumb and wrist. She didn't react to the burning hole it left, which disappeared the next time Breck blinked.

You're not the only one who's bored, he thought, unsure if the Raw under the Keep could hear him at this distance.

". . . and the airdockers want a twenty-two-meter gap beneath each berth in the new expansion, instead of the usual twenty." Oreel never looked up from his ledger while he spoke, as sizzling droplets he couldn't hear, feel or see plopped onto the back of his neck.

Trade Commissioner Jenneri leaned forward to argue with him, as usual, clacking her rings together on the table in frustration. Breck only paid partial attention to what she said, carefully waiting for when he could step in and settle the debate. He compared it to preparing a surprise attack: too early and someone would pipe in with a new argument, sometimes useful but sometimes not; too late and some of the Councillors would have already dug in their heels on some asinine point.

". . . let us receive shipments more rapidly from the Unity, you must see there are concerns with . . ."

As Oreel stood from his seat in that pretend-polite way when he argued, the pustules disappeared and his throat opened, gushing thick blood across his tunic. His wizened russet flesh grayed as the blood left his body, showing an attention to detail the Raw hadn't managed with their illusions yet.

". . . and if we take those provisions, the time and materials should not be prohibitive to complete the project . . ."

"Let's do that," Breck said. Jenneri tried to interject, almost like clockwork, but he continued over her. "Our usual captains will want to compete for the new berths. Organize a lottery or something so it's fair, and if anyone doesn't like it, tough. Safer and larger docks are good for everyone, right? Our engineers know the safety protocols."

It had taken years of practice to moderate the way he used to snap at soldiers to something more measured. More importantly, the Council understood his ways, too. Everyone around the table nodded and started folding up ledgers and slates.

Except Oreel. The old man placed his hands on the table, one over the other, fixing a placid expression on Breck. The other

Councillors gradually noticed and either stopped moving or sat back down.

"Before we depart, Lord-Magistrate, has there been any further communication from the Unity?"

Breck had been waiting for this. He shook his head. "Nothing beyond the usual."

The usual being the Unity's ambassador giving him the same prepared lines from their superiors, about how Farglade's existing trade deals treated the Unity unfairly and needed to be changed. He knew Jenneri didn't like trade discussions coming directly to him, but Breck took advantage of the ambassador's preference for going above the Council. That gave him something truthful to say when the Raw wouldn't let him say more.

"While we respect your strategy toward the Unity," Oreel said, his wheezing voice careful and meticulous, bothering Breck a little more every day, "we are concerned about antagonizing them too much."

"Shipping some of the items today was a good step," Jenneri added. "The ambassador will expect more, and soon, based on the new allotments they're demanding."

"And there is increasing public frustration with Edict Nine."

Breck prided himself on being difficult to surprise on a battlefield, but the slate Termot pushed across the table caught him off guard. The polished stone was scrawled with statistics on Watch reports, written in Termot's blocky handwriting.

"More people speaking out," Breck muttered as he read. He didn't expect Deyeri to have much effect with the Watch continuing to collect possessions, but he had hoped. "Any arrests?"

Termot shook her head, but her lips were pressed tight.

"Expecting some?"

"People will only hand over so much before they expect something in return," Oreel said. "A relatively simple equation. If we could perhaps pause our collection—"

Breck held up a hand without looking in Oreel's direction.

Termot shrugged. "Too early to tell."

Great, Breck thought. If more people spoke out, Oreel would push to temporarily withdraw Edict Nine, before he found the artifact he needed. He didn't want to ship anything else away, either; despite what the people might be thinking, he'd rather return every collected item with an apology. But anything he did now would lead to more questions he couldn't answer.

Among the Council, he counted Termot as one of his closest allies, but a united front between the Commander and Oreel told him he'd borrowed too much on their service together. He scanned the table; when Jenneri and Yveln, the Technical Academy's chief administrator, didn't meet his gaze he knew who else to worry about.

More than anything, he wished he could simply tell the Council what was under the Standing Keep and how he planned to use it. Except as soon as he considered that, that staticky tingling crept into him again. Worse, he saw the illusion of crackling electricity, like the broken end of a windtower cable, behind each councillor's head. The Raw weren't exactly subtle.

"Let me know if it gets worse," he said, sliding the reports back to Termot with more force than necessary. "Go easy on people, but make sure they follow the edict."

"Lord-Magistrate, if we could discuss this matter further . . ."

"Not much more to discuss, is there?" Breck asked Oreel. To the entire Council, he said, "Look, I understand your concerns. The Unity wants more from us than we can give. More than we *should*. I don't know why they're increasing their ask, but I'm hoping I can find out before we hand over everything. If we're lucky, we can return some of what we've taken from our people."

Technically nothing he said was a lie. That was another key to leading, both in the council chamber and on the battlefield. Give people the truth while letting them believe they had the entire thing. Like he had with Deyeri.

"We support your direction," Oreel said, and though the others nodded in agreement, Breck heard the unspoken addition: *For now.*

The thumping of slates resumed as everyone filed out. A couple Councillors made a point of thanking him for some decision or confirmed they could meet with him later about something. Breck nodded and smiled and gritted his teeth until everyone left, paying close attention as Oreel pulled a couple Councillors aside to whisper on their way out. Termot didn't join that gathering, and Breck couldn't decide what to make of that.

When the room emptied, he sagged against his chair, finished his water, and decided to leave before Idriks came with something else needing his attention.

His assistant appeared even before the chamber doors finished closing, and Breck held back a curse. Idriks carried several slates in his arms, along with sheets of paper that held more important, permanent records.

"I need a stretch before I do anything else. What time is it?"

"Apologies, Lord-Magistrate. Voice Kalle is here to see you. She says it's urgent."

She shouldn't be saying anything is urgent, Breck grumbled. *That's how people get suspicious.*

Kedar entered in an obvious rush, the top of her hair rattling the alert bell next to the door. She almost reached Breck by the time Idriks shut the door behind him.

"What's the problem?" Breck checked his tumbler, found it empty, and leaned over Termot's to see if she left any water behind.

"Revect's old friend is in my library."

That made him look up sharply.

"Tried to bluff me." Kedar huffed, massive shoulders heaving, like she sprinted from the Outreach. "Didn't realize Revect told me about him before she passed. He says he's researching the Raw."

"Tell me you didn't show him anything."

"Only what's left there." When Breck opened his mouth, she added, "He knows I have other books. Don't worry, I didn't tell him you're involved. Though if he stays in town more than a day, he'll figure it out."

Breck's mouth stayed open, entranced by the blackened skeleton Kedar became while she spoke. The illusion wore her green robes and the four loops cinching them at her waist. The bones even looked as thick as he imagined her skeleton to be, under her muscled frame.

"You want to, I don't know, do something about this?" The skeleton's jaw managed a frown somehow.

Breck turned in his chair, hoping the Raw kept the stone walls bare while he thought. They didn't know much about Eyasu Temergon other than a name in Revect's journals, and the fact that he openly practiced heresy. That made him unpredictable.

He had thought Deyeri was going to be his greatest challenge.

"We need to move faster," he decided. "You haven't found anything else to narrow the search?"

Kedar had been the first person he went to when he learned about the Raw, before they inserted themselves further into his mind. The only thing he didn't tell her was the extent of the illusions. No one could know that.

"Not sure there's anything to search for," she said, folding her arm bones. "If Uekel had a way to make dariss react when there's a Raw inside, he might never have written it down. We were lucky enough finding a way to bind the things."

"You said you weren't sure you could bind them."

"Well, I'm not. We'll need some luck there, too."

Breck grimaced, remembering too many moments in the

Incursions that came down to a gamble. "I hate needing to be lucky."

The alert bell by the door started clanging. Breck leapt from his chair, barely noticing that Kedar's flesh had returned. That alert system, with bells strung throughout the Keep, hadn't been used since the last Incursion.

Idriks came back in before he made it two steps. The young man looked pale, but his attention focused on Kedar, not Breck. "Honored Voice, we have reports of a fire at the Outreach."

Chapter Twenty-Four

"WE MUST RETURN TO AULINA." MAVRIN HEARD Eyasu say.

"The Tiers' brigade will be here soon," Deyeri repeated. "That'll give us a chance to—"

"Draw more innocents into danger."

"Wait, you're saying that fall didn't kill him?"

Mavrin turned away from Eyasu and Deyeri, realizing he hadn't grabbed his garnills. Instead of the Outreach, he saw a narrow alley between two of Farglade's unnerving, three-story buildings. When had they left the Outreach?

Something dragged him off-balance: the garnill cage was in his hands.

"I can't speak to your friend's life. But the Raw will keep his body alive . . . with enough intact."

"One more reason to go to the Keep."

"The Raw will expect that."

Through the alley, a street of comfortably shorter buildings stretched into the distance, with a plume of smoke rising behind them. They left something burning at the Outreach, but Mavrin couldn't remember what. A garnill hooted at him, squeezing her nose through the cage's top to brush his fingers. *Those constructs in the courtyard. Yes, thank you.*

"Aulina is still connected to the Raw in these coins." Eyasu tapped his rucksack's strap. "If this new Raw can sense that, Aulina's in danger."

"Can we come up with specific names for these things?" Deyeri asked.

Their names are important to them, Mavrin thought. The man in his vision, with the thin hair in a braid, used a name and pronouns to address the Raw. He couldn't remember either, though.

"We get Aulina first, then head for the Keep," she continued. "It's secure, closer than the Watch barracks and . . . there are people there who can help, I think." Her next step made her wince. "Hopefully the healer's still awake."

Something clattered against a storage barrel nearby and Mavrin jumped. The garnills leapt inside their cage, startling him a second time. "The Keep is a bad idea."

"Excuse me?"

He hadn't meant to speak. A gaslamp directly overhead hissed like one of those machines in what he thought was a laboratory, though not like any laboratory he'd ever seen before. The thin-haired man's coat might have been like the gowns they wore in the Bastion. Mavrin had never been in the Bastion, but he met some of their researchers when he performed in Renhollow—

"I believe Mavrin means," Eyasu said, with a quick glance his way, "that because this Raw is controlling your friend, he knows Farglade's strategic places."

"Figured that already, thanks. The Watch still needs to know what's going on," Deyeri said. "If they don't already."

"What would they know?" Eyasu asked, frowning.

Deyeri sighed. "You're not the only one in Farglade looking into the Raw."

She started to explain as they kept moving, but Mavrin only caught half the words. He didn't like the idea of going anywhere the Raw might follow. Certainly not without his trunk, which he must have left behind in the Outreach. He opened and closed his free hand to make sure it wasn't there.

"Mavrin." Eyasu placed a hand gently on his shoulder. "Let's go."

His friend looked worried, but that was good. Mavrin was worried, too.

The pain in Eyasu's ribs was oddly comforting as he walked. It gave him something to focus on, puzzling over how they felt like they developed a will of their own, turning inward to crush his organs when the Raw channeled. Or how his armor didn't protect him the way it had against Aulina's channeling. Or why Mavrin had been left in such a daze that he needed to be guided around gaslamp posts and benches.

He kept his attention on Mavrin, trusting Deyeri to follow the quickest path to the Unyielding Walkway. She led them mostly in a straight line, switching between the three parallel streets making up the lowest Tier. After a few switches, Mavrin stopped muttering and started watching his surroundings more closely, though Eyasu couldn't tell how astutely. He wished he had the time to interrogate Mavrin about what he experienced. Clearly the Raw showed him something, which could be useful when they faced the creature again.

More than anything, they needed information. Every scholar knew the search for it never ended; the closest you came was *enough for now*, and Eyasu realized he had been wrong to believe he reached that stage before Tanardell. It was possible this Lord-Magistrate Breck knew something to help contain the new Raw—which might help assuage the heavy feeling in his gut, from the Catalyst not Responding to him tonight.

They barely saw another living soul as they approached the Walkway; Eyasu suspected Deyeri knew how to avoid anyone braving the post-sunset hours. Eventually they turned a corner onto a wide, cobblestone street that merged with the Unyielding Walkway ahead. Two spiraling glass columns flanked where the channeled stone began; Eyasu recalled that the flames inside were lit each day and fed by tiny openings in the bottom, using the Winds without letting them snuff the light. Their orange glow illuminated two Watch standing sentry.

"Shit," Deyeri muttered, but didn't break stride as she led them forward.

The Watch on the left raised a friendly hand as they entered the columns' light. "Bit late for a stroll, Commander?"

"Life lesson, Preare—sometimes second careers keep weird hours."

Deyeri's laugh sounded forced to Eyasu, but Preare smiled along with her; the other Watch joined in, clearly not wanting to be left out. As they reached the edge of the Walkway, though, he glanced at Eyasu's armor and Mavrin's ragged appearance.

"History people," Deyeri said to him, leaning in and lowering her voice. "They're a little weird, too."

More curling columns lit the Walkway, driving the smoke from their flames high above the thoroughfare. Deyeri steered them to the right side of the waist-high, stone median dividing the center of the bridge, past a small construction site made of wooden beams, ropes and pulleys, with a half-finished statue partially concealed under a weighted tarp.

Mavrin paused in front of the statue. "This bridge is something of a mess."

"My team doesn't always understand deadlines," Deyeri grumbled.

"Your team?" Mavrin snapped his fingers, eyes lighting up as he shook off the last of his fugue. "Those sketches. Are you some sort of architect?"

"Overseer. Other people design and build. Trying to preserve and honor our history." Deyeri shook her head. "Not that this is the time to discuss it."

"I thought you were retired."

"Not the time, Mavrin."

He fell back beside Eyasu, letting her lead by a few paces.

"I have a feeling," Eyasu said, lowering his voice, "that your reunion didn't go smoothly. Before the Raw, I mean."

Mavrin snorted but didn't respond.

"'When time is needed, time will be offered.'"

Quoting the Words of Aspect didn't feel as natural as usual. He touched his Castoff's pouch, resisting the urge to remove it and confirm its latent glow. Though he didn't want to ask, the first step to gathering information was posing questions.

"Why do you think I didn't receive a Response earlier?"

They reached the middle of the Walkway before Mavrin answered. "I can think of several, but there's only one that matters. Maybe the Aspects have finally had enough of you."

Eyasu stopped. In the light of the nearest column, he tried to find anger or judgment in Mavrin's eyes. If anything, his friend looked solemn. Possibly even sad.

"Which part of this 'reunion' do you want to know about? The old magician showing up with empty, shaking hands, or when I couldn't stop a murderous Raw from crushing her against her blood-soaked house." Mavrin stared after Deyeri as she marched, clearly expecting them to keep up. "But surely you're right, and the Aspects want me here. Just like they want you worshipping an Aspect-variation you *invented.* The fact that you've managed to Request at all is, well, miraculous."

All the support I've given, and you still haven't learned to trust me. "The Catalyst has supported my entire journey." Saying it didn't feel like a lie, yet. Even through the pouch, Eyasu could feel the Castoff's familiar grooves. "Even before my exile, I knew I prayed to a different variation."

"And you still don't realize how dangerous that is? You almost died back there, Eyasu."

He wanted to say the Aspects wouldn't have let him. Every Requester knew they might not receive a Response; the Interpreters in Veristenok spent their lives wondering why. Maybe the person you wanted to heal had reached the end of their life. The structure you wanted to create came from pride or ambition, instead of the common good. A mistake or a lapse in judgment needed a subsequent opportunity to learn. That was written in the Words of Aspect, as well.

What mistake have I made, then? Eyasu wondered.

Anyone advocating an unsanctioned Aspect-variation disrespects Them and threatens us all.

He set his jaw against the masked Servant's words. "I don't believe They would abandon me."

"Then you're a fool." Mavrin set down the garnill cage so he could sweep his arms out. "Everything here belongs to Them. They give us the air. The water. The soil. Keep us from freezing or roasting or whatever would happen without the Lifesphere. I might not agree with the Highest Voices on most things, but wanting to keep the Aspects happy? Feeling respected? That's not the mad idea here."

Deyeri waited a few meters ahead. "We don't have time for this, either."

"This is an old discussion," Eyasu said, barely keeping his voice level. "He pokes me at every turn with his . . . dagger of madness."

"It's my fault?" Mavrin's voice rose. His hands shook at his sides. "I understand you, Eyasu. Always trying to do good. And I'll admit, your channeling has been useful. But it's an unknown factor and relying on it is dangerous." His shoulders slumped. "You need to know what you can rely on."

"Calm down," Deyeri said sharply. "I realize I'm still catching up, but if anyone has a chance against that thing, it's Eyasu. You degrading him doesn't help. Nor is it *nice.*"

"And here we are all over again," Mavrin nearly sneered. He turned away, hugging his cloak tighter against his body. A disbelieving cackle escaped his lips, and he gestured at the horizon. "Showing up to prove my point."

Eyasu followed his gesture across the Windroute and the empty plains to the southeast, recognizing the distant, glowing mass of one of the Aspects. He hadn't been tracking the days as closely as he should have, he realized. They were almost a week from when the Catalyst passed over Tanardell; moving north placed them more in line with the Hidden's path over the edge of the Moderates, only visible until morning and far enough away not to rouse people from their homes for a glimpse.

"Much as I hate it," Mavrin said, directly into the Winds as they tossed his hair askew, "Theirs is the only power that matters. Everyone on this husk of a planet knows it."

Footsteps behind them made Eyasu turn, spotting a tight knot of figures marching down the Walkway from the Tiers. Their slate and blue uniforms caught his eye immediately.

"Authorities to the rescue," Mavrin murmured.

Before Eyasu could stop him, he started walking. Deyeri offered a sympathetic look and followed in Mavrin's wake, shaking her head.

Five Watch made up the approaching group. Eyasu saw they had weapons drawn—three bearing swords and two holding metal tubes about the length of a dagger, with grips like a cabler. Not unexpected, if they came from the fire at the Outreach. He was surprised they caught up so quickly without stopping to investigate, unless they decided to look for the people responsible and got lucky, helped along by the sentries Deyeri bluffed past.

Mavrin spread his hands out toward the Watch. "I suppose I should apologize, but I have to report—"

The lead soldier, a woman with dark, curly hair, said something Eyasu didn't catch. Mavrin cocked his head, confused.

Then she grabbed him by the throat, as the other Watch rushed forward.

Chapter Twenty-Five

"I SUPPOSE I SHOULD APOLOGIZE, BUT I HAVE TO report—"

"Enemy of the Lord-Magistrate."

Mavrin barely registered the Watch's flat tone before she grabbed him by the throat and lifted him into the air one-handed. Her arm trembled under his weight, but she didn't show any sign of discomfort.

"Get the item."

The other four Watch moved past her, weapons raised and faces blank. Mavrin noticed a dark bruise on the woman's temple and a line of blood running from her hairline to her neck, still dripping from the edge of her collar.

Weapons crashed behind him, but he couldn't turn to see how Eyasu and Deyeri were faring. The Watch rifled through his pockets while he pried uselessly at the hand squeezing his windpipe. Kicking at her armor barely made her stumble as she pulled out his tools one by one and dropped them. Desperate, Mavrin growled and scratched at her face, but she simply tightened her grip on his throat. He scrambled at his pockets, choosing a pouch at random and slamming it against her cheek.

The burst of glittering dust made her cough and let him go. Mavrin gasped as he hit the ground, knocking his scattered equipment aside. He kicked out when the Watch reached for him, batting her hand aside and then striking her knee. Whatever kept her from feeling pain didn't hinder how her body functioned; she stumbled forward, and before she could bring her sword to bear,

Mavrin swept her other leg out from under her and backpedaled away, knocking his discarded equipment aside in the process.

Nearby, the other Watch had split into pairs to face his friends. Eyasu batted aside their attacks with his longsword, seeming hesitant to deliver a return blow as they pushed him toward the Walkway's edge. Deyeri stood next to the tarp-covered statue, trying to reason with the two Watch approaching her. It seemed to be working, until one of them raised his tube-like weapon. A crack filled the air and Deyeri stumbled backward, clutching her sword arm. Gritting her teeth against the pain, she tossed the sword to her other hand and cracked the hilt against the Watch's face.

Mavrin made it two steps toward her before something overhead caught his eye. His mouth dropped open as the curly-haired Watch landed in front of him, two folds of taut fabric unfolded beneath her arms. The makeshift wings snapped back into her armor as she advanced. Her first strike sliced cleanly through his waistcoat. Mavrin jumped back to avoid the second and rolled beneath the third, feeling like he was back in Brennig's Bedazzling Spectacle Troupe. His next leap took him over the stone median. Before the Watch could clamber after him, he flicked his wrist, launching his bindcord like he had at Corporal Caspen. He wanted to catch her arm, but the Winds blew the cord askew, letting her vault the median unimpeded.

Deyeri's voice rang out: "Mavrin—down!"

He dropped to his knees, just before a crack sounded behind him. The Watch staggered away, touching a dart-like object embedded in her throat. The wound only confused her for a moment before she came at Mavrin again. Like in the Troupe, he grabbed her wrist and flipped her over him. Deyeri rushed past, and by the time he scrambled to his feet she had pushed the Watch into one of the gaps between the Walkway's wind barriers, tossing her out into the Windroute.

A war cry tore through the night from the other side of the Walkway. Eyasu's opponents had him pressed against the barrier, and to Mavrin's amazement, his friend was tiring. He still hadn't drawn his Castoff.

Mavrin scooped up the Watch's fallen sword and ran toward the statue's tarp. He hacked at one of the ropes, trying to hold the tarp in place with his other hand. Deyeri joined him, catching on to his idea. As soon as the last rope snapped, the tarp practically dragged them into the air as it caught the Winds, but they held it in place long enough to aim it.

Deyeri's voice thundered over him. "Eyasu—down!"

Neither Watch made a sound as the tarp wrapped around them and dragged them to the ground. Eyasu rose to step calmly over their writhing forms and swept his longsword overtop. Two strikes each and they stopped moving.

Deyeri sagged against the stone median, wincing as she pressed a hand to her arm. The wound wasn't bleeding much, but Mavrin suspected she would need a bandage. He scooped up the tube that wounded her; it was about half again longer than his hand, with a now-empty cartridge and some sort of pneumatic mechanism along its length.

"Bladetubes. Supposed to be locked in a weapons cache," Deyeri said through gritted teeth. "Only for emergencies." She stared at the gap she'd pushed the Watch through. "What did she say to you?"

"There was something wrong with them," Mavrin said. He noticed blood under his fingernails and hastily wiped them with a handkerchief from his cloak. It became a gift to the Winds but couldn't carry away the feeling of clawing into flesh. "No reaction to pain." He shuddered.

"Her name was Fraller. She made corporal after the last Incursion." A haunted look crossed Deyeri's features as she studied the other fallen Watch. "I know them all."

"The Raw must have crossed their path," Eyasu said as he joined them, one hand clutching his side. "Possibly at the Tower."

Mavrin started forward but didn't see any blood under Eyasu's gauntlet. He backed away, heat rising in his cheeks, remembering some of what he said minutes earlier.

Eyasu dismissed it with a shake of his head and focused on Deyeri. "This Raw's specialty is our mind's conduits. Those people were being controlled. Their deaths are not your fault."

Deyeri shook herself. "We need to get out of here. That thing will be—"

Voices shouted in the distance. Eyasu and Deyeri raised their weapons, turning toward the Towers' side of the Walkway. More uniformed figures jogged toward them, enough to fill one side of the bridge.

Mavrin realized right away that these Watch looked wary, not expressionless. Deyeri raised a hand as someone ordered them to drop their weapons and stay where they were. Mavrin realized he still had the bladetube and tossed it away.

"Hold!" someone bellowed.

The Watch parted, admitting a man wearing a formal jacket and pants instead of street armor. He looked a little older than Mavrin, with shaggy white hair and old scars crisscrossing his rugged features. He surveyed the scene and cocked a disbelieving eyebrow at Deyeri.

"Woldren," she said, offering him a wry smile. "Nice timing."

The shaggy-haired man grimaced as he studied Mavrin and Eyasu. "Looks like you've had quite the night. What do you say we go chat about it?"

Chapter Twenty-Six

MERCIFULLY, THE RAW UNDER THE KEEP WERE either dormant or not paying attention while Breck sat in his office. The bronze timepiece clicking on his desk reminded him he should have been asleep, too; trying to cover his reactions to their illusions would have been difficult fully rested, with Deyeri facing him.

She stood at attention while she told him what happened. The cuts and bruises didn't seem to bother her, but he'd seen her bear worse without a grimace. He leaned against the wall and tapped his boot against the wide, stone desk—the Lord-Magistrate's office was annoyingly small—figuring she would misunderstand his impatience and frustration. Nothing she told him bothered him as much as knowing this new Raw was loose in the city, instead of under his control. Years of preparation and searching scoured like dust out a window.

When she reached the end, he said, "And you made for the airdock."

"Seemed like the best plan."

"Whose plan?"

"Does it matter?"

Breck shifted in place, feeling too familiar and off-balance at the same time. "You're not Watch anymore, Dey."

"You've been lying to me like I am."

As clear as one of the Raw's many illusions, he felt another layer added to the barrier between them. Worse, he understood why because he had watched Deyeri forge it, sheet by sheet, ever since the Incursions. She had never accepted that he needed to cut people out of his trust back then, keeping any guilt and repercussions squarely on him. When the Windroute was overrun, someone needed to decide where to send their reinforcements, and a battalion halfway across the Edgeplains fell from the list of priorities. Trying to explain that later hadn't helped, even when he couched it by adding that he trusted her and Havven to hold on longer than anyone else, especially if he let them think help was coming. People fought harder when they had hope.

Impossible situations and hard choices, they always said. That mattered now more than ever, but Deyeri wouldn't be able to see it.

"Don't worry about adding anything now," she said. "Knowing there's a dangerous creature somewhere in the city, I'd keep it to myself, too."

She didn't bother hiding the sarcasm. Breck heard the question under that comment, too, and decided that he needed to tell her *something*. Maybe by being careful, he could.

"Only Kedar knows. Everyone else thought Edict Nine was about trade."

"You approached her?"

"Had to." That was true, too. "I barely believe what's happening."

In hindsight, the weary sigh and faint smirk weren't likely to make her relax. Deyeri's eyes grew harder while she tapped a finger against one bicep and waited him out. She wanted to see how much he would say, now that she'd discovered most of the truth on her own and almost died because of it. Which felt too like the Incursions for his liking.

Remembering that made the decision for him. Alone in his office, telling her everything would be simple, if the Raw really weren't paying attention. Besides, he would have to tell her and her new friends more soon.

As easy as thinking it, he started speaking. No eruption of tingling stopped him from telling Deyeri everything he knew about the Raw, and the danger they posed to Farglade. About the sanctum he found beneath the Keep. What he and Kedar discovered about dariss and the power it possessed, beyond simply trapping the Raw. About how Pericar knew them first, and learning more from Kedar, and spending every sleepless night since worrying about things spiraling out of his control. Which they had, maybe because Deyeri hadn't been the first person he confided in.

Telling her felt even better than he expected.

When he finished, she reached across the desk and stabbed him in the throat.

Breck collapsed against his chair, slipped from the seat, and landed on the floor behind his desk. He'd seen people die from neck wounds during the Incursions; his body writhed and jolted more than he expected. Deyeri circled around while he lay there twitching and gurgling and looked down at him with more anger than he'd ever seen on her face.

"Nothing to say for yourself, then?"

He blinked and braced himself against his chair, the illusion gone as quickly as it arrived, replaced by Deyeri still standing across from him. Her frown slipped as more seconds passed, while he tried to ignore the feeling of static electricity at the back of his skull.

Luckily, she helped him by shaking her head and saying: "Saviors' breath, Woldren. You must have had a backup plan if the Raw got loose before you found him."

"Right. Backup plan." He had one, or rather Kedar did, even though things were never supposed to reach this point. Instead of explaining to Deyeri for real, he said, "Maybe we should trade slates. You're the one with a Requester on your side."

"Don't stall."

"Who says I am?" Picking something to grumble about helped him stabilize. He tried to decide what message the Raw were sending. Did they want him to say nothing, or just be careful with what he said? He decided on little pieces of careful truth. "Any of my plans don't mean much now that one of these Raw is loose."

Deyeri snorted. "You always were a sharer only when you had no choice."

He could still feel the Raw, studying him from their sanctum. "Fine. I didn't want to tell you about the Raw because I didn't know how you'd handle it. Happy?" That earned a wry smirk and shake of her head, which raised his hackles up for some reason he couldn't place. "The part about beating the Unity to finding it was true."

"To use it?"

"So the Unity can't."

"Typical." Deyeri shook her head. "This isn't some new blend of salt battery you can hoard, and we're not fighting the Incursions anymore. You haven't seen what this Raw can do."

Breck almost told her she was wrong and that he had, but that vision from before held his tongue. He wondered if that was the Raw's point, so instead he told her, "We have research. Details your Requester friend might not. Like where the Raw came from."

When all Deyeri did was cock an eyebrow, and his body didn't explode with shocks, he almost let out a sigh of relief.

"I'll tell you and your friends everything downstairs." Using the word *everything* was obviously a lie, but the next thing he said was genuine. "I shouldn't have kept as much from you as I did."

"Teach you to neglect your best asset, right?" Deyeri didn't say it with malice, and Breck wished he could trust the hint of a smile on her face as something real.

He closed his eyes as soon as she left. The tingling passed down the back of his neck and faded, as the Raw reminded him of their attention one more time.

"... we ended up here," Mavrin said as he settled back on the bench. "And I came to see you." His eyes flitted to the side.

Deyeri tried not to pace while he described his last few days with Eyasu and Aulina. While she "explained things" to Breck, he and Eyasu had been treated for their wounds and offered food and water, then were told to wait in a quiet corner of the southeast wing, near the Lesser Historium. Eyasu apparently left immediately for the airdock with a Watch escort, leaving his rucksack in Mavrin's care.

He pulled out a metal sphere made of interlocking pieces and started fiddling. "It's been a strange few days."

"Seems simple enough." The words came out as a grumble, especially after talking with Breck. His caginess always bothered her, but especially now. "Raw are real. All those rumors you chased from before the Fracture might not be takka shit, and now one of them is running around my city controlling one of my friends. Did I miss anything?"

Mavrin's fingers paused. "I don't think so."

Without the distraction of people barging into her house or Raw trying to kill her, Deyeri could finally get a good look at the man she hadn't seen in almost two decades. It *was* Mavrin, but with worn, creased skin that didn't quite hide the uneven crinkle of one eye or the turn of his lip. The sunken cheeks and heaviness under his eyes spoke to fatigue, but the lines on his sharp, pointed features and the stiffness when he walked were more telling. Mavrin Leed hadn't defended a city against relentless, unexplained Incursions, but he'd been marked by a life on the road. As a magician, of all things; even seeing the garnills sleeping behind him, she couldn't think of him as anything other than a scholar.

He had been quick-witted and charming, back then, commanding a room with rhetoric. Annoyingly chivalrous but accepting zero nonsense from people who thought they were his betters. Deyeri supposed some of that could have translated into a career as a performer.

The tumble of conflicting emotions across his face now made her want to run, cry, knock him on his ass, and protect him from the gray that surrounded him. All at once, without reason, and it made her want to scream.

"You didn't do half-badly out there," she found herself saying.

Mavrin seemed to brighten for a moment. "Thank you. You're quite the warrior yourself."

"I might've had some practice," she chided. He didn't laugh.

The Watch down the hall straightened to attention, pulling her focus, but it was only Eyasu and his escort. They were joined by a young woman who must have been Aulina. She wore a cotton shirt and pants under a threaded vest that, strangely, reminded her of Mavrin's waistcoats, if only with a lot more color.

Aulina nodded politely during introductions. Eyasu excused himself and continued down the corridor to the Lesser Historium, taking his rucksack with him. Mavrin offered to pull some blankets from his trunk while they waited, even though Deyeri kept telling him it wouldn't be long, now that Eyasu was back.

"Eyasu tells me you fought another Raw?"

The faint tremble in Aulina's voice told Deyeri all she needed to know. She hadn't shaken the feeling of her lungs suddenly closing outside the Outreach; every few breaths, she took one in a little deeper. It would have been perfectly natural for Aulina to run screaming from the city, but here she was.

"Honestly, the Keep is probably the safest place in Farglade," she said, putting on a comforting, if not reassuring, smile.

"I'll get us some more water," Mavrin said, straightening the extra blankets for Aulina. "Sorry to take you away from Captain Lavar."

She blushed a little, which released some tension from her features.

"Eyasu didn't find anything at the Outreach," Aulina guessed, her smile dropping as Mavrin wandered away.

"I guess not." Deyeri shrugged. "Voice Kalle will be at this meeting. I get the feeling she hid some things from Eyasu earlier."

"That sounds like a Voice," Aulina said, managing a smirk. "My parents like Voice Enar, but they always say he isn't very forthcoming."

Deyeri frowned. She could have sworn Mavrin mentioned Tanardell's Voice by a different name. And she was certain he said Aulina's parents were dead.

She checked her timepiece again, hoping Breck would summon them as soon as the Watch reported Eyasu's return. Leaving Mavrin to fuss over Aulina, Deyeri went after him.

The Lesser Historium was another section of the Keep designated mostly for the public, containing display pieces from before and after the Fracture to entertain people while they waited for appointments. Anything truly valuable or precious was kept in the Greater Historium across the Towers, but there were significant items here, like fragments of an ancient Teehar orrery and a claw from the last mephikor to emerge from the Edgeplains. Seeing some of the newer displays installed after the last Incursion was part of what inspired Deyeri to start her work with the monuments.

Eyasu stood at a long, stone table in the center of the room, seeming to ignore everything around him. She would have expected the scorched and dented remains of the scuttleboat across the room to capture his attention. Installing that had been Breck's idea, to remind people of how they climbed cliffsides during the Incursions. A complete scuttleboat would never have fit, but the few meters of wreckage displayed the segmented legs on either side and the gearbox in front that made the vehicle function. Deyeri would have kicked it if not for the metal barrier designed to keep visitors from doing exactly that.

Eyasu didn't look up from cinching one of his wooden bracers. The motions were methodical and almost unconscious, except she could see the ties slipping from his fingers because of how much they trembled.

After the third try, Eyasu let out a heavy breath.

"Would it hurt your pride if I offered a hand?"

"If you think it would, it's been too long." He held out his arm.

Deyeri planted one hip on the table while she fastened the bracer. The motions came back easily enough. When she finished, she snapped her fingers for his left. "That was a hot breeze on the Walkway. Before we were attacked, I mean."

Eyasu shrugged his other shoulder. "Mavrin has his beliefs, and I have mine. We need more time." He glanced at her. "Hopefully the two of you will have that, too."

She held back a smile. Eyasu was still Eyasu. "Don't try to insinuate things. You're not good at it."

"He was more concerned about seeing you than anything else we have faced."

"Oh yeah?" Deyeri cinched the last tie tight enough to make Eyasu wince. "Sorry. More time might not help anything."

He started removing items from his rucksack, resorting them along the table's length. "Don't be too certain." He sighed and murmured, "We cannot be certain about anything."

She was tired enough that it took effort not to say, "Okay, out with it" or something along those lines. "You okay?"

He turned one of his books over, studying the red wax strip on the spine. "Have you ever questioned the one thing you believed above all others?"

Every day. "Sometimes."

She noticed the book wavering in Eyasu's grip as he set it down. "I have spent most of my life researching the Fracture. Grappling with ideas no one else believes in. Gathering knowledge that should have prepared me for what we're facing."

"Except tonight, that knowledge didn't help you."

"Not simply tonight."

Eyasu delicately removed his Castoff and placed it on the table. Deyeri had only seen one or two up close; the last had been with the Requesters who helped repair the damage from the Incursions, and they hadn't exactly passed them around. She always wondered why a scale from one of the Aspects would be small enough to fit in someone's palm.

"My first Request to contain the Raw didn't work." He left his Castoff and picked up a book, dropping it back into the rucksack. "People were killed. Not because of their ignorance, but because my Request was flawed." He added more books, each with a heavier thump. "Aulina's connection should have been severed, but clearly it remains. And then tonight, my Request was ignored outright."

More of his gear went on top, almost slamming into place. When Eyasu looked up at her, he looked stricken. "Why would the Catalyst not aid us?"

Deyeri had no idea what to say. She trusted the Aspects, but she had never been much for prayers or devotions. People moved to Veristenok to serve or study at the Quartered Citadel; people born there, like her, weren't always the most actively religious. Her more recent issues with the Requesters didn't help, either.

"You're the one who keeps saying the Aspects have a plan." She shrugged. "Maybe you don't understand it yet."

Eyasu didn't seem to really be seeing her, so she stepped forward and grabbed one of his hands. "Hey. Whatever's going on, you're not doing this alone. All right?"

His gaze shifted over her shoulder. The stricken look on his face faded. "I know."

Mavrin stood in the doorway. He straightened his cloak. "Your magistrate is ready."

"Give me a moment to finish," Eyasu said, patting his rucksack, "and I will meet you there."

Deyeri caught up to Mavrin halfway down the corridor. Without looking, he said, "He never fought a Raw before Tanardell."

"You saying he doesn't know what he's doing?"

"None of us do. Even with everything we've learned, we can't understand the Aspects. Or how They view our actions." He shook his head. "I sound like a damned philosopher."

"Or a scholar, maybe?"

That didn't get a smile from him, either. Mavrin sighed as they reached the fountain monument. "I'm worried about him."

For some reason, that made Deyeri's hackles rise. "Seems he's been doing all right without you."

"I'm not so sure," Mavrin said quietly, and continued down the main hall.

Chapter Twenty-Seven

TWO OF BRECK'S PERSONAL GUARDS, IN HEAVIER armor colored blue and black, escorted the group through the atrium into what turned out to be a modest learning commons. Mavrin felt like he had truly stepped back into his scholarly days. Instead of the audience facing a lectern, the bench seats and tables sat in three concentric rings; whoever sat in the innermost ring would be involved in discussions with the instructor, and everyone on the outside watched and listened. In Veristenok, the people sitting in the center would cycle between lessons, enforcing the free and supportive exchange of ideas that helped humanity thrive after the Fracture.

Humanity only, Mavrin thought. *At the expense of the Raw. Or to protect against them?*

A massive sculpture overlaying the torch, stylus and gear of the Vital as Talent's academies hung overhead, directly beneath a skylight inscribed with prayers in T'var. Mavrin thought he saw phrases for stability and an educated future. Beyond, he could barely make out the Lifesphere's midnight hues through the glare of the room's gaslamps.

Three people sat together around that inner ring. Breck rubbed his chin as he listened to who Mavrin assumed was Commander Termot. Pale gold hair hung past her shoulders, free of the shoulder clips even Fargladeans knew to wear outside, and her slate and blue Watch uniform bore extra brass bars on the shoulders and wrists. A tall, muscular woman in green robes sat at a separate table to Breck's right; that would be Kedar Kalle. As Mavrin,

Eyasu, Deyeri and Aulina descended the steps cutting through the commons, the guards filed out quickly and quietly, shutting the door behind them.

Following Deyeri's lead, Mavrin and the others stood facing Farglade's three officials, and they quickly went through introductions.

"That your assistant?" Breck looked at Eyasu but pointed at Mavrin.

Before he could get indignant, Eyasu stepped in, "Mavrin was a colleague of mine at the Quartered Citadel, during our scholarly days."

"Never saw a scholar with that much flair." Kedar gestured vaguely at his cloak and fresh waistcoat.

Mavrin smiled and reached behind Deyeri's ear, producing a Renhollow chit and disappearing it back into his sleeve, as he waved his fingers. Termot smiled; Breck and Kedar glanced at each other uncertainly before their attention shifted to Eyasu and Deyeri as they sat down. Trying not to appear sullen, Mavrin put an empty table between him and his friends. Eyasu shot him a narrow-eyed look that he steadfastly ignored.

Aulina took the other seat at Mavrin's table, either as support or because she didn't want to be near Eyasu, either.

"Before we waste any air," Breck said, "let's make it clear that me and Kedar know the basics about the Raw. What they are and were, and some of what the Highest Voices denied happened before Unity. Now Garris knows." He offered the Watch Commander an apologetic smirk.

"You promised to show me Voice Revect's missing research," Eyasu said carefully. "What you removed from the Outreach."

It didn't escape Mavrin's notice that this might have been the first time he sat down with a higher authority who shared his understanding of the world.

Kedar reached beside her and produced a book, tossing it across the gap between their tables. Eyasu caught it and froze, as though he'd been given a lit firecube. He turned the cover so Mavrin could see.

"By the Four. You have a copy of Uekel's *Accounts*."

This one looked less beaten than Eyasu's, likely in part because it didn't live in a rucksack. The five gears of the Fifth Progress stood out in dark embossing, though most of the random lines cutting through them had worn away with time. When Eyasu flipped the cover open, the crinkled, yellow pages looked remarkably intact. Mavrin craned his neck to see if the style of Uekel's writing matched.

"Don't trust him."

Mavrin turned to Aulina. No one else seemed to have heard her whisper, so he pitched his voice low. "Which one? The magistrate?"

Aulina blinked at him. "What if the magistrate isn't in charge?"

". . . Revect's collection away from prying eyes." Kedar's proud voice caught his attention as she spoke to Eyasu. "You wouldn't have been the first koo beetle from Veristenok poking around."

"Was it something in this research that led to you looking for dariss?" Deyeri asked them.

"The books came later," Breck said. He paused, gaze slipping into the middle distance for a moment. "Revect wasn't the only one interested in heresy. Pericar was, too."

"Pericar knew about this?" Deyeri asked. Once she noticed Mavrin's confused look, she quickly explained that he was their Lord-Magistrate before Breck.

"Remember how erratic he seemed near the end? I started searching and found out he'd learned things about dariss. Didn't realize until I asked her that Kedar inherited a bunch of knowledge from Revect." Breck gestured at the Voice as he spoke. "When the Unity were explicit about dariss in their trade demands, I had a feeling it might be connected. Turns out I was right."

Mavrin thought that sounded a little self-important but kept silent. Deyeri didn't seem put off by Breck's attitude as she asked Eyasu, "Could the Highest Voices be hunting for the Raw?"

"I believe they've always known the truth," Eyasu said. "Or some of them, at least. I don't know why they'd be actively searching now."

"Maybe a bunch of Requesters will come help us fight this thing." Deyeri's tone made it clear how she felt about that.

Termot's soft voice cut across the room. "Describe it."

No one had to ask what she meant.

"Not to be melodramatic, but more terrifying than anything from the Incursions." Deyeri told them how the Raw manipulated the Watch in her home and on the Unyielding Walkway. The only moment her voice cracked was when she mentioned Havven. Mavrin fought down the urge to change seats to be closer to her. *Sixteen years*, he reminded himself.

"Can't believe these Raw can channel," Kedar mused. "Especially without a Castoff."

"The Raw were locked away before the Salvation, and before we received the first Castoffs," Eyasu said. "The abilities we've seen carry similar side effects to our channeling. It might simply be that Uekel and others couldn't make the same comparisons we can."

"Channeling without needing to Request." Breck blew out a breath. "What was it like?"

Mavrin wasn't sure who he was asking, until he followed Breck's gaze to Aulina. She straightened when she noticed his attention.

"They changed the trees," Aulina said softly. She lifted one hand in front of her, pressing her fingers together and apart. "Tiny motes inside us both. They combined the motes to burn the trees."

When no one responded, Aulina shrank back into her chair again. She looked smaller than Mavrin had seen her yet. He leaned toward her again, trusting the others to continue without him; they hadn't needed his input yet, after all.

"Did you want some more water? We could leave them to this if you—"

Her chair suddenly scraped against the marble floor, until the legs thudded against the raised ring behind them. Mavrin followed her wide-eyed gaze to Eyasu and Deyeri's table. He had taken out the wooden box for Kedar to see.

"Containment," Aulina breathed out. "Control."

Mavrin waved at the others that everything was fine. Only Termot kept staring at Aulina. Not with the wariness he expected, given that everyone present had been told what happened to her, but with an almost protective level of concern.

Kedar traced a thick finger along the symbol on the lid. "Looks like a prayer of warding."

"It was provided by the Aspects," Eyasu said, "when they answered my Request to seal the box."

Breck leaned on one elbow with his chin in his palm, eyes fixed on the box. "The other Raw knows you have this."

"That's part of why we should decide our next action quickly," Eyasu said. "The Raw was weakened at the Outreach. That won't last."

Breck rubbed at his lower lip. "Can't think of a better place to stash it than here. We'll keep it safe."

Deyeri and Termot protesting at the same time—one much louder than the other—knocked Breck out of his reverie. He rubbed at the left side of his face, near the scars Mavrin noticed earlier. Something in Breck's distraction stood out to him, but he couldn't focus on it and Aulina at the same time.

"We don't know how much time we have," Eyasu cut in. "Unless one of us has some secret weapon, we need more information. Yes?" He focused on Breck. "You said Lord-Magistrate Pericar became interested in these subjects during the Incursions. Why?"

"Edgeplainers didn't attack us for everyday resources," Breck said, almost automatically. He blinked, as though surprised he had spoken. "Pericar thought they wanted dariss."

"They can't recover properly," Aulina murmured. When Mavrin asked what she meant, she didn't respond.

Deyeri pointed at Breck. "You figured this out and didn't say anything?"

"We drove them off, so it wasn't worth bringing up."

Eyasu broke in again: "You never determined who the attackers were?"

Deyeri shook her head. "They never identified themselves. The ones we captured never said a word. Not even when they started to wither away . . ."

"People tied to our world, like we were." Aulina drew Mavrin's attention, shaking her head. "*They* were. I'm we, they're *they*."

They have names and pronouns, Mavrin remembered from his vision.

Aulina grabbed his hand, pinning it to the side of her chair. "The conduits."

"What conduits?"

"Power. That's all anyone wants." Her gaze flicked over his shoulder at the box.

". . . had mining equipment during those first two Incursions, remember?" Breck looked at Deyeri and Termot. "Pericar noticed those attacks were near some of our old dariss veins."

"Dariss is a natural conduit," Eyasu murmured.

"More than that."

It took Mavrin a moment to realize he had spoken. Aulina locked eyes with him and nodded, urging him on.

To his surprise, Breck asked sharply, "How do you know that?"

One of the visions from the Outreach came back to him: the laboratory, with the strange machinery he couldn't understand. The details remained clear in his mind, far more than many of his own memories, and he realized what he'd missed before. That machinery seemed so strange because it wasn't all metal. Crystals sprouted from panels and switches or glowed on the walls above the machines. Blue-black crystals, specifically.

Someone else must have asked a question, since Kedar was saying, ". . . notes we found that dariss is some sort of huge energy source. Not sure how, but before the Fracture people knew how to feed electricity or heat into dariss to harness its potential. Sort of like what we figured out with salt batteries."

Eyasu opened his mouth to ask something, but she cut him off. "Engineering was my hobby at the Citadel. I'm a little rusty, but Uekel's notes describe dariss being used a bunch of different ways." She snorted. "Too bad the Highest Voices would call it all heresy."

"Aulina," Mavrin said quietly, "I'll need to relearn my tricks without fingers."

She didn't release the pressure on his hand.

"That may explain part of your attackers' interest," Eyasu said, eyeing the box, "and possibly the Raw's, as well. Before we left Tanardell, they made it clear they wanted to come here. I thought it was because they sensed more of their kind."

"They want reunion." Aulina finally let Mavrin go. She circled around to Eyasu and Deyeri's table and placed her fingertips against its surface. Her nails made a scraping sound as they inched toward the box. "Trapped for so long. Betrayed and alone. I can't imagine . . . being away from someone you love for that long."

She started suddenly, eyes wide, like someone who had fallen asleep and briefly forgotten where. "Mister Leed, I don't think I should be here."

The others watched her with varying expressions of alarm. Mavrin shot to his feet before anyone with a weapon—which he realized was almost everyone—did something rash.

Aulina yanked herself away from the table, almost knocking

him aside as she backpedaled. "I should be gone somewhere . . . somewhere else, I should be home . . ."

Her heel caught the commons' steps. As she fell back, her palms flew out in front of her. "Not my words! Not my thoughts . . . I need to see her face again, please, let me see her . . ."

"Saviors help us," Kedar breathed. "She can still feel it."

Aulina clenched her eyes tight. "They never left. Who am I trying to see?"

Mavrin lowered to a crouch, keeping a few meters between them. Breck stepped up on his right, hands in his pockets feigning nonchalance, but Mavrin saw his jaw working, pulling at those scars on his face. He finally asked, "Who's they, exactly?"

"The Raw isn't a monster. They're a person. Not like humans. One Raw alone isn't supposed to happen." She wrapped her arms around herself. "My mother's good with puzzles, I should be speaking to her."

Eyasu approached from Mavrin's left. "Aulina, where is Ohanna right now?"

"Ohanna?" Her brow furrowed. "My sister. She's at home."

"With whom?"

"My parents." Aulina shook her head again. "No. They're gone. She's . . . Ohanna, I mean. She's with the Voice."

"Who's the Voice in Tanardell?" Deyeri asked suddenly.

Aulina opened her mouth, closed it again. Seeming embarrassed, she shook her head helplessly.

"Thought you said their connection was blocked." Breck looked sidelong at Eyasu. "So much for containing it."

"The Raw is poisoning her memories," Eyasu agreed grimly. "They haven't released her."

"I keep thinking of them," Aulina said. "They keep thinking of me, too. *I don't want to feel them in my mind.*"

She launched herself at Mavrin, falling to her knees as her hands tightened on his wrists. Breck didn't so much as budge as

Mavrin tried to pull away, expecting golden light to crisscross her veins again.

Instead, her very-human eyes turned to Eyasu. "I want this *fixed* so I can go *home*."

"I tried to sever the connection. I don't know if a more complicated Request would be successful." He studied the markings on his gauntlets. "But I will try."

Breck stirred, catching Eyasu's eye and nodding in approval. Eyasu considered before adding, "Aulina, while I do this, I'd like to glean what information I can from the Raw. We won't allow them to harm you. Would you be willing to help me, before we sever the connection?"

Aulina took a breath and nodded. "But then I want to be free."

Unsure whether it was only in his mind, Mavrin could have sworn he heard her voice drop several octaves when she spoke.

Chapter Twenty-Eight

THEY PUSHED MOST OF THE FURNITURE ASIDE, leaving two chairs and a small table in the center of the commons, directly beneath the Vital as Talent sculpture. If the tables weren't stone, Mavrin would have suggested carrying them out of the commons entirely, to remove potential weapons if the Raw re-emerged. Breck must have been thinking similarly; he whispered a question to Termot about the sword strapped to her hip, but she politely shook her head and kept it sheathed.

Eyasu took a few minutes alone with his Castoff, pacing a corner of the room with it clasped behind his back. He seemed thoughtful instead of nervous, but Mavrin knew he was practiced at keeping things beneath the surface. After the bad luck with his recent Requests, trying to speak to the Raw was an incredible risk, let alone trying to sever their remaining connection to Aulina.

Mavrin sat down opposite her while they waited. "I know Eyasu said he wasn't sure about you returning home. I'll try my damnedest to see that happen."

"Home would be nice." Aulina sounded tired. "Maybe we can pick up something from Vertsa on the way. For . . . Ohanna."

He tried to pretend her hesitation came from nerves. "I'm sure she'd like that."

As Eyasu approached, Mavrin scooted out of the chair and went to stand with Deyeri. Kedar sat a few tables away, with a composite notebook and pencil open in her lap.

Eyasu placed the box on the table between him and Aulina,

watching her reactions carefully. At her nod, he lifted his Castoff between them, cradling it in both hands.

Mavrin closed his eyes as Eyasu murmured in T'var. The phrases mostly focused on protection and guidance, to keep him and Aulina safe and steer them toward the information they needed. Surprisingly, he didn't feel the room tilt or sway. He realized Eyasu wasn't trying to channel any protections; he was simply praying.

As he finished, Eyasu lifted the lid from the box and set it aside.

Aulina didn't react at first. When her hand reached toward the coins, Mavrin held his breath. She stopped at the edge of the box, fingertips pressing against the wood where the lid would rest.

The light from the gaslamps flickered. Mavrin realized the blue flames weren't changing; it was the shadows around them writhing back and forth, not quite matching their source. Like the Winds if they were visible to the naked eye.

Or like waves. He couldn't be sure, but he thought that's what ocean waves were supposed to look like.

"Painful," Aulina said softly.

"What's painful?" Eyasu asked.

"Separation." Tears trickled down her face, but she didn't so much as blink. "I don't understand why I feel so lonely."

"Who is suffering this?" Eyasu asked.

"We share it." Aulina clenched her eyes shut. When she spoke next, her voice was halfway to that low croak Mavrin remembered from Tanardell. "It was quiet for so long. Nothing but darkness." Her regular voice returned. "When they woke up, they felt connected. That connection's gone, and they remember loneliness."

In a whisper, she added, "It's okay. I'm lonely, too."

At least for now, Aulina didn't show any physical changes. No gold flooding her veins, and only white in her eyes. The only evidence of the Raw was in her speech. It dawned on Mavrin that she was functioning almost like a Voice in reverse, with Eyasu in the role of the Aspects.

"Do you have a name?"

The smile was crooked. "You're so concerned with identifications." Her voice shifted back. "They didn't have names at first. Not like we'd understand." Aulina looked surprised for a second. "Other than the name we gave them."

Eyasu frowned. "The Raw?"

"That was one. That came later." Aulina looked him in the eye. "First it was the Purity. Before the world fell."

"And which do you prefer?"

"They say they are Raw now."

"You keep saying 'they.' Do you mean this Raw," Eyasu indicated the box with his chin, "or their kind in general?"

"I don't understand." It didn't sound like Aulina was responding to him. Eyasu waited for her to speak again. "They adopted them. Names, I mean. They . . . came up with a system? To make it easier on us. Names and pronouns." A smile teased at her lips. "Violet-Twenty-Four-Ten. That's the name this Raw chose."

Mavrin glanced at the others, but no one seemed to understand the significance. Until Kedar looked up from her notebook and exclaimed, "Wavelengths. Like how the Bastion describes electrical current from a windtower."

When no one seemed to follow, she added impatiently, "The Raw are beings of energy? Must have come up with names using some system from the Time Before Unity. Maybe to do with dariss. Or something." Facing blank stares around the room, she grumbled, "Not important, I guess."

"Not so different from us," Deyeri muttered.

Mavrin nodded. They had effectively gone through the same process anyone on Aelda did, confirming or clarifying their name and pronouns when it felt right.

Aulina's fingers twitched against the box. "Violet-Twenty wants to speak directly. To you. I shouldn't do that. Should I?"

"That wouldn't be a good idea," Eyasu said cautiously. "We don't want a confrontation. Perhaps there is another—"

"Liars." Aulina practically spat the word out. She reeled back as far as she could without losing contact with the box. "*Confrontation* is all you know."

Her voice dropped octaves again. Eyasu managed not to visibly react, which was more than Mavrin could say about himself, as his knees trembled under his cloak.

"I had little choice before," Eyasu said. "You were hurting my friend. People died in Tanardell."

"Nothing compared to how many died before. You broke the world. Lied to us, used us, destroyed us." Aulina took a deep breath, but Mavrin didn't think she was the one feeling it. "We endured. They are out there, and they have survived."

"You mean the other Raw. Your kind. They're trapped in dariss, yes? Like you?"

"Yes." Aulina's entire body trembled and she gritted her teeth. "Betrayed."

"Wait," Breck said, half-rising out of his seat. "How much more of this are you going to make her endure?"

Aulina's head snapped toward him. In her voice, she said, "You don't know how much worse holding this in would be."

Breck opened his mouth to say something more, but Termot stepped into his line of sight. He sank back into his seat.

"How did this happen?" Eyasu asked, drawing Aulina's focus back. "How were you trapped?"

It was the Raw that answered. "You wanted power. The dariss was not enough. We agreed to connect with something deeper. We were supposed to share it. This core."

Deyeri started. "Do they mean *Aelda's* core?"

"We know," Eyasu said to Violet-Twenty, "that an accident

damaged our planet. We call this the Fracture. Is that what you're describing?"

"No accident." Aulina's head jerked back and forth. Her arm shuddered as she pressed harder against the box. Her own voice returned in a gasp. "They're so angry. I've never imagined so much . . . it's anger and not at the same time."

"Aulina. If you wish to stop, we'll stop."

Breck nodded his agreement, but Kedar looked up sharply from her journal. "We don't have enough."

"Let them finish." Aulina took a deep breath. "I feel something like . . . movement. Passing through something harder than air. Harder than water."

"Like a tunnel of light," Mavrin said without meaning to. Deyeri gave him a look, but he ignored her, because Aulina was suddenly looking at him, too.

Her eyes were the same ones he'd seen in his performing space, and when they spoke briefly in Jareden's home. But he was sure there was something else there, too. Possibly Aulina letting the Raw see a little of what she could, to satisfy them enough that they didn't take her over completely. How she could manage that much control, he had no idea.

"You've seen him," Aulina said. "The man they're telling me about. The one they trusted, but who never trusted them. The betrayer."

Thin hair, in a braided style Mavrin hadn't recognized. A coat marked with five gears. The symbol of the Fifth Progress.

"Uekel?"

Her lips twisted, close to how they had when the Raw possessed her fully. "They pushed too far. He insisted. Broke our planet."

Eyasu caught Mavrin's eye, and his stony expression spoke volumes. Their research suggested both humanity and the Raw were involved in the Fracture. Uekel insisted he couldn't trust the Raw. They had been so amazed at what they read, so excited to confirm that Uekel existed, that they didn't stop to consider that what he said about his "monsters" might have been a lie.

"We wouldn't intentionally destroy our world," Eyasu said cautiously.

"You would intentionally destroy us." Aulina's voice curled into a snarl, and she shuddered. "He warned us not to trust you, in the end. We didn't listen."

"Who warned you?"

"He took the identity Azure-Seven-Seven. Out of respect and adoration for the betrayer. Then his faith broke with everything else."

That must have been the other Raw, the one inhabiting Havven. Knowing his name, even knowing more of what happened didn't make Mavrin fear him any less. If anything, understanding that anger made him fear more.

When Aulina spoke again, her voice lost its lower pitch but picked up in pace. "I can feel . . . they're showing me the pain. Being trapped. They felt it happen. I don't understand . . ."

"You're still with us." Eyasu's Castoff started to glow brighter as he closed his hands.

"Wait." Aulina straightened, staring over his head. "They were trapped. Held in the dariss they used for the experiment. They should've been able to leave, but . . . the betrayer forced them to stay."

"Someone held them in the dariss?"

Aulina looked down at the coins. "You were angry. Betrayed. You wanted answers, but you never got them. And then you were separated."

"By the Four," Deyeri murmured. "Am I hearing this?"

Mavrin couldn't respond. When the Highest Voices summoned him to their chambers, they made it clear that any assertion about the Raw, any heretical views on the Fracture or the Time Before Unity, risked the safety of everyone on Aelda. He thought they meant the need for collective worship, that even they didn't believe the Raw ever existed. But they must have known at least part of the truth. Not only who really caused the Fracture, but why the Raw suffered afterward. They were right to fear that knowledge.

The Aspects couldn't possibly know. Why would they create the Lifesphere if they knew what we did?

He couldn't imagine how people would react to the truth. His mother lived her entire life thanking the Catalyst as Lifegiver for her only child, the Presence as Passage for their health and happiness, even to the Hidden as Fatedraw for his father's death being quick and painless. She had *known* the Aspects loved and protected her. If They were to turn on her . . . he supposed it wouldn't matter for long, and glanced up at the skylight, and the Lifesphere's faint shimmer beyond.

"Why did you want to come here?" Eyasu asked. "To find Azure-Seven-Seven?"

When he asked again, Aulina gasped, "They don't want to tell me."

Eyasu moved to respond.

"I won't force them," Aulina snapped. She gasped, wavering in place. Eyasu rose halfway from his chair as she steadied herself. "There's more. Something else they want . . . something else they can feel . . ."

"Requester," Breck said from the stairs. "If she loses control . . ."

Aulina reached forward for the coins, but Eyasu was faster. He tugged the box away, slamming the lid back into place while his other fist held the Castoff out, a Request already spilling from his lips. Bright, yellow light filled the commons, so sudden and violent that Mavrin had to shield his eyes.

When he lowered his arm, Aulina was encased in light. She looked as shocked as Mavrin felt, as the entire commons wobbled around them. The misshapen shadows curled against the walls, seeming to collapse on themselves, and for a moment he thought he saw a thousand eyes staring at him from within their darkness. They winked from existence along with everything else in the room: the furniture, the steps, the skylight, even Eyasu and the others. Everything except Aulina.

As the glow faded, he saw a second source of light: a thin, winding tendril of energy like the one passing from Caspen to Havven when he snared the corporal's memories. The tendril jerked forward like an adder but couldn't pass through the glow encasing Aulina. It withdrew, sinking toward the wooden box and into the coins. As the last bit of that tendril sank away, the rest of the commons returned.

Aulina sat back in the stone chair, arms at her sides as her lungs heaved, staring at the closed box.

Eyasu gently put down his Castoff and collapsed into the other.

Breck spoke first. He had slumped down onto the second tier around the commons. "Did you kill them?"

"No." Eyasu said that like it should be obvious. "I invoked nothing about the Raw. I asked for Aulina to be protected from that which would harm her. And the Catalyst Responded."

"Meaning they're trapped," Deyeri said. "Again."

"For now," Mavrin replied, and didn't stop watching the shadows.

No one said much after that. Termot left immediately, and Mavrin briefly wondered if she was summoning Watch despite Eyasu's assurances that they were safe. Instead, she returned with a cup of tea that smelled like nutroot and something sharp Mavrin couldn't place, and a heavy takka fur blanket. She offered both to Aulina, which was when Mavrin realized she'd been sitting at that table shivering since Eyasu walked away.

"Good for fevers, too," Termot said to Mavrin, indicating the tea with her chin.

Mavrin couldn't think of anything smart to say to that. He asked Aulina, "How do you feel?"

She gingerly sipped the tea. "I don't know." Her voice sounded hoarse, but from overuse as opposed to being contorted against her will.

Not wanting to pressure her, he wandered away, unable to stop repeating what the Raw had said over and over. It seemed like Kedar was in a similar state; she'd retreated to one of the tables they pushed aside, poring over her notebook and adding to whatever shorthand she used. Breck and Deyeri picked a different corner to talk, and Mavrin didn't even have the energy to wonder about that, or why he wasn't figuring out something to say to Deyeri instead.

He finally joined Eyasu in front of the exit, sinking onto the top step. Eyasu stared at the ceiling, but not out the skylight or even at the Vital as Talent's sculpture. His eyes seemed to focus on a corner of the room's high walls, facing roughly south—approximately in the direction the Hidden would be as it disappeared from Farglade's view.

"I can't decide whether I'm surprised, horrified or simply tired. Likely all three."

"We should go to where these coins were found," Eyasu replied.

"Yes, this is sort of—wait, what?"

The smile Eyasu cast down reminded Mavrin of when he stepped out of his room at the Waystop, to find his friend waiting beyond the door. "You were right on the Walkway. We can't rely on tools we don't know will help us."

"Your channeling seemed fine just now," Mavrin admitted.

"I meant my armor."

"Of course you did," Mavrin grumbled. "Maybe we can find someone reckless enough to encase your head in wood."

He didn't mean it as a joke, but Eyasu chuckled as he gestured for Deyeri to join them. Breck followed.

"Deyeri, how did the coins end up in your possession?"

"Yeldin. He's a merchant in town—"

"Hoarder," Breck muttered without looking.

Deyeri shot him a look. "Gets a lot of random trinkets from salvagers. He's also sanctioned to evaluate finds from the Edgeplains. The coins were in his last shipment."

Mavrin had heard of that sort of operation. Most buildings, technology, and artifacts from the Time Before Unity hadn't survived the last three centuries, often needing to be reused or repurposed afterward. The exceptions were significant cultural or historical artifacts, either preserved by their surviving people or, if they had been wiped out by the Fracture, saved in museums. The only place where things hadn't been completely recovered was nearest the True Edge, and independent windship crews still risked skirting it, hoping to find intact artifacts.

"Given what we know," Eyasu said, "it seems likely whoever possessed these coins originally knew what they contained. Would you agree, Mavrin?"

"Quite the coincidence, otherwise, carrying around a Raw."

He realized what he'd said and glowered.

"You're thinking if our mystery attackers knew more about the Raw than we do," Breck said, "there might be more information out on that wreck?" He smirked. "Innovative thinking."

"It's possible." Eyasu raised a hand, summoning his internal academic again. "We could hunt down Azure-Seven-Seven and rely on what weapons we have. Except I doubt we'd succeed. Information has been my ally, and I suspect more is needed here."

"Eyasu," Deyeri said carefully, "there's wishful thinking, and then—"

"The information must exist somewhere."

"There's a way to bind them," Breck said. Kedar perked up

across the room, eyes wide, but he waved a calming hand. "We don't know much. One of those fragments from Uekel's book says he knew how to use dariss against the Raw, for more than containing them."

"Not something you want us to know?" Deyeri asked Kedar.

"Only because we don't totally understand it yet," Kedar insisted as she joined their group. "I could barely grasp the waves and currents Uekel described in his notes. Lots of missing pieces. But it sounds like dariss could be used for all sorts of things, if you ran a current through it properly. Like binding."

"Binding how?" Eyasu asked, but Kedar simply shrugged.

"What are you suggesting?" Mavrin asked, recognizing the look in Eyasu's eyes. "We explore this old wreck and look for something else as unlikely as those coins, while the Raw roams the city?"

"We know what he wants," Breck said, half to himself.

Deyeri caught on first. "If we bring the box with us, Azure-Seven-Seven will come after it. Even if we don't find anything, I feel a lot better about fighting him away from the city than here." She looked across the room at Termot. "We can't bring too many Watch in case the Raw visits here first. One squad, maybe?"

Termot smiled at her.

"Oh, shut up. I'll get the location from Yeldin while you organize everything else."

As she headed for the door, Breck said, "Didn't realize we were sending *ex*-Watch on this little adventure."

Deyeri swung around, her eyes hard. "How has cutting me out worked for you so far?"

Mavrin felt the sudden urge to scoot from the path of that glare, but Breck simply acknowledged the point with a reluctant nod. "Fine. Under my authority as Lord-Magistrate, blah-blah, you're reappointed to the field rank of Lower Commander. Second-in-command answering to Garris and me. Congratulations."

"Great," Deyeri said, without much enthusiasm.

Breck looked at Termot. "Put together a squad and a ship. I'll take care of everything here."

"You don't want to come along for the ride?" Deyeri asked.

"Believe me, I'd rather," Breck said sourly. "But you're right, someone needs to keep an eye on the city. Update the Council. Besides . . ."

Mavrin followed his glance toward Aulina, still sitting with her hands clasped around her tea. She didn't seem to be listening.

With roles settled, Deyeri left first. Kedar followed shortly after, saying she would gather some things from the Outreach now that the fires were under control. Breck and Termot discussed the minutiae of dispatching the Watch.

"I should rest, for a change," Eyasu said. That latest Request had left darker circles under his eyes and even hollowed his cheeks.

Mavrin touched his arm. "I'm not going to get sentimental or anything, but I went too far on the Walkway."

Eyasu shook his head. "Not the first time we disagreed. Nor the last."

As he left, Mavrin realized he was the only one without some sort of task to prepare.

Aulina glanced up when he sat across from her. Tea finished, she looked halfway to falling asleep. He couldn't blame her; it had taken effort to get up from those steps, and he had only watched things happen. Staying up through the night was becoming a dangerous pattern.

"That was courageous, letting Violet-Twenty speak through you."

"They needed a voice." Aulina shrugged. "We all do, sometimes."

"Ohanna will be very proud of you."

Her confusion could have been fatigue. Until she said, "I hope so," and Mavrin wasn't sure Aulina knew who they were talking about.

Breck made it halfway across the main hall, heading for the stairs to his office, before Kedar approached from the corridor leading to the Office of Legal Grievances. He glanced around but only saw the distant Watch guarding the main entrance. They wouldn't think to question the Lord-Magistrate and Voice having a private conversation, any more than they might question this entire midnight meeting and the strangers wandering around the Keep. Even so, Breck beckoned Kedar away, toward the entrance to the Lesser Historium.

Kedar leaned against a plinth bearing a cracked Watch helmet from the Incursions, covering the name of the person it belonged to. Breck tried not to bristle as she casually brushed her hand across the windguard at the front.

"You bothering me for something important?"

Kedar rarely glared at him, but he earned one now. It always reminded him that she stood almost a head taller than he did and bore a lot more muscle.

"Why'd you tell them about the binding?"

Breck sighed. "The minute they look through our copy of the *Accounts*, they'll figure it out."

That had been his plan for the entire meeting, besides letting Kedar handle most of the talking. He'd felt the Raw beneath the Keep the whole time, tugging at the base of his spine when he tried to mention their existence and pushing him to intervene before Aulina could reveal it.

"Besides, it helped convince them that leaving the city makes sense."

"Convenient to get them out of the city," Kedar said, tapping her foot idly against the plinth. "Made it seem like their idea, too."

"You're going with them."

She stopped tapping. "You know," she said, shaking her head ruefully, "every time we talk, you make it clearer why we won the Incursions."

Breck's hands tightened in his pockets enough to crack his knuckles. Planning to leave Deyeri out on the Edgeplains with Eyasu and the magician, even temporarily—worse, letting her go out there thinking she had his support—felt too much like the past. Except he couldn't see another way to re-establish control of this situation, and Farglade's interests came first.

"I don't want them hurt," Breck said through clenched teeth. "Figure out a way to leave them behind and we'll get them once this is done."

"And if Deyeri's right and Azure-Seven-Seven follows us?"

"Might be worth practicing that binding, wouldn't it?"

He knew he shouldn't be short with her, but lack of sleep combined with the Raw's pressure was making him irritable again. All he wanted was a nice glass of reserve brandy and the warmth of his bed. "As soon as we have those coins, we bring the other Raw into the sanctum and finish this. Your equipment down there is ready?"

"Don't touch anything and we'll be fine." As she pushed away from the plinth, she added, "What Violet-Twenty-Four-Ten said back there. About how the Fracture really happened."

"Doesn't change anything." He imagined he could smell the tang of iron from the helmet between them. "Bigger concerns right now than what happened before."

He couldn't tell how much of the bothered look on her face came from hearing the truth from the Raw, or how they planned to trap the Raw exactly like Uekel did. Either way, she left without another word.

As he straightened the helmet on its stand and moved his hands in the sign to the Catalyst, he briefly saw dark coins outlined against the back of his hand. The Raw in the sanctum knew he was close to fulfilling their agreement. Meaning he couldn't afford any more delays.

And that meant using Deyeri all over again.

Chapter Twenty-Nine

THOUGH THE WATCH KEPT ITS MAIN HEADQUAR-ters and barracks near Farglade's outskirts, the senior staff worked out of the Lyarnen Building, one of the smaller rectangular structures on the Keep's grounds. The white walls and lack of ornament hadn't changed since Deyeri retired, but the level of activity inside reminded her of the Incursions, with officers hurrying from one room to the next to organize Breck's search of the city. The main barracks would be twice as busy, as Lower Commanders received orders and dispatched squads to search for the Raw.

She had managed a couple hours of restless sleep after waking up Yeldin and getting the information she needed, while dodging his questions about why it mattered. No sign of the Raw made her hope Eyasu was right, and Azure-Seven-Seven needed to regain his strength. That made her imagine Havven's broken body lodged somewhere along the Windroute, which wasn't much better than listening for screams from somewhere inside the Keep or a distant explosion from the airdock. She might as well have been sitting on the Zerrilen Craggs, watching for scuttleboats.

As she descended to the mortuary—one of only a couple underground rooms in the Lyarnen Building—the stuffy interior smothered what little energy she'd recovered. Like the weapons caches across Farglade, they had dug several rooms like this during the Incursions, as somewhere to temporarily stack bodies until the deadspeakers made time for them. This was the fullest any of them had been in years. Dark green fungus wraps already covered the bodies of the Watch who died at her home, but the slate beside each one carried their names: Cerril, Jayen, Pren, and Wilaw. Fraller and the other Watch who died on the Unyielding Walkway lay next to them, bodies cleaned but not yet wrapped.

Before she left, Deyeri stood over each soldier and moved her hands in the sign of the Catalyst as Protector.

She had hoped to never make that sign over someone again.

Back upstairs, she hesitated at the doorway opposite the mortuary, ultimately forcing herself to enter the recovery room. Simple beds lined the walls, separated by oval side tables bearing hooded averblossom lanterns; their natural light provided a more soothing atmosphere than electric lamps. A single heatwell occupied the center of the room, kept low under a cylindrical shield. Painted versions of the Catalyst as Lifegiver hung between the beds, with the signature healing flames around Their appendages and tail. Each was strategically placed so that as the sun moved past the windows, it would always catch at least one.

Corporal Caspen lay on her side, heavy breaths showing she wasn't asleep. As Deyeri pulled over a stool, her eyes opened halfway, tugging on the stitches down both sides of her face.

A flicker of recognition faded into a frown of confusion. "Did I fall asleep?"

Deyeri had spoken with enough soldiers suffering head wounds. "No, I don't think so."

Her upper lip twitched. "I thought I was dreaming. That's a shame."

"How are you feeling?"

"Sore. Like recovering from a fever." She spoke very matter-of-factly. Without the bluster from before, her voice sounded almost child-like. "Am I a soldier?"

That question caught Deyeri for a second. "Yes. You're a member of the Watch."

"I always wanted to be a soldier." Caspen's frown returned. "I don't remember why."

Deyeri could still hear Havven talking in her living room, in those first moments when his voice shifted into the velvety tone of Azure-Seven-Seven. "Maybe to make someone proud?" When Caspen's confusion deepened, Deyeri added, "You, uh, told me once about your mothers. If you don't remember, that's okay."

Caspen rubbed her forehead, letting Deyeri see the thick bandages covering her fingers. She reached out and placed a hand on Caspen's shoulder. "I'm sorry this happened to you."

"Thank you. I guess," Caspen said, without any malice or sarcasm. "You healers are really apologetic."

Deyeri left as quickly as she could after that, not making eye contact with anyone she passed. In the sea of people scurrying between rooms, she was just one more person in uniform. Except wearing the Watch colors didn't comfort her like it used to.

Ending this nightmare would.

~

"Why in the Four are we using *this* ship?"

Mavrin gestured at the bow of the *Joyous Soul*, as the crew finished preparations to get underway. Eyasu was somewhere onboard talking to Atera, Deyeri nowhere to be found yet, which left Commander Termot to voice his concerns to. And *someone* needed to listen.

"You must have realized this is a civilian vessel." Mavrin spread his arms out to encompass the entire airdock. "Didn't Farglade repel an entire armada of those scuttleboat things? Why aren't we taking a caravel or a dreadnought or something?"

Termot offered a slight shrug. "No dreadnoughts."

"You don't have dreadnoughts? Yarder's Outlook has dreadnoughts." When Termot didn't respond, Mavrin sighed. "Are you really telling me there isn't a single military vessel available for us?"

Termot pointed at the assortment of nearby vessels wobbling in their berths. The only ones bearing the Watch's slate and blue were small scoutsleds that could barely hold six people and, according to Deyeri, were mostly used to patrol the Craggs. Among the other windships, Mavrin counted several passenger ships and a sleeker narrowcraft designed by the Bastion.

"Yes, I can see there are none docked at the moment, but surely . . ."

"We need something fast," Termot said, and somehow her forced whisper made Mavrin clamp his lips shut. "We need something now. And Captain Lavar could've said no."

Deyeri's voice came to him from the nearby tunnel. "Winds be damned, now he's interested in strategy."

That wasn't his point at all, but the flip-flopping that had worsened all morning stalled when he saw Deyeri. She had changed into a set of Watch armor, but not quite the same style as Termot or the others. Smaller overlapping plates covered her arms from pauldrons to bracers; the latter sported larger hooks that he suspected could catch a blade if necessary. The top of her boots narrowed to a point at the knee, giving added protection while seemingly leaving her able to move.

This must have been the armor she wore as Watch Commander, or maybe during the Incursions. Between that, the swords strapped at her sides and her hair braided back, she completed the warrior image he glimpsed last night. The glimmer in her eyes as she noticed his pause was the Deyeri he remembered, though.

Until it suddenly vanished. "Looks like we're the last," she said, matter-of-factly.

This time, Mavrin didn't so much as blink as he climbed the gangplank. He refused to admit that it had anything to do with Deyeri watching him. When he looked back, though, she was leading Termot away from the ship, standing out of the way of the airdockers and windriders meandering along the docks.

"... apologize for bringing up Cereil. That was low."

Termot's whispered response didn't carry over the *Soul*'s railing, but whatever she said made Deyeri smile. Mavrin realized he was eavesdropping and hurried away, only for that nervous flip-flopping to return twice as strong.

Several of the crew waved or smiled at him as he crossed the deck; if his lack of response bothered them, he didn't notice. He tapped one of them on the shoulder and asked about Atera, only to learn she was hanging from the lower hull, reattaching a cable on the bottom mast that came loose during their arrival. Unsure where to vent his nerves next, his marching led him to the rear observation pad. Eyasu sat on the long bench like before, eyes closed. His rucksack propped up his longsword, plus an extra blade about half the length.

"We shouldn't be drawing Atera into this."

Eyasu didn't open his eyes. "She wishes to help."

"Did someone tell her everything?"

"Yes."

"And?"

"She wishes to help."

Mavrin realized his pacing brought him closer to the stern railing and moved back to the bench. "They're just young, Eyasu." He caught himself. "Atera is, I mean. The Edgeplains are dangerous on their own, even without—"

"Would you feel better with a weapon?"

Eyasu grabbed the extra sword and held it out. When he waggled it like showing an iron rod to an akrren, Mavrin reluctantly took it. The sword was lighter than expected, with a comfortable pommel and a curving guard to protect his fingers. He drew it from the leather sheath, revealing an elegant, polished rapier. The way the pointed blade shone, he thought it was from some noble's collection, until he noticed the blue gleam. The rapier was coated in a thin film of dariss.

"Where did you get this?"

"Breck accumulated quite the collection in his search for the Raw." Eyasu hid a mischievous smirk.

He produced a second weapon from his rucksack: a dagger, also coated in dariss, engraved with some family crest sporting a pre-Fracture crustacean. It looked about the right size to fit the drop sheath tucked under Mavrin's sleeve, opposite his bindcord.

Mavrin set both weapons down on the bench. "I have mixed feelings about this, Eyasu." His friend waited patiently for him to continue. "The Raw, the Fracture . . . we had no idea back then, did we?"

Eyasu pursed his lips. He reached into his rucksack again, producing a copy of the *Accounts*—not his, but the one Kedar showed them in the learning commons. "Combined with what Violet-Twenty told us, it's clear now that Uekel was not simply a chronicler. He was involved with trapping the Raw in dariss and learning how to weaken them further. By splitting them in things like your coins."

"Not quite the noble scholar we thought he was." Mavrin tapped the book against the bench. With Eyasu's permission, he tucked it into his cloak so he could read it later.

Eyasu was silent for a moment. "I considered releasing the Raw yesterday."

He should've chastised his friend, but knowing what they did now, Mavrin understood. "You couldn't risk them possessing Aulina again. Or someone else."

"Unless they could hold their form separately. That ability isn't clear from these fragments."

Mavrin sat down on the bench but couldn't quite look out past the *Soul*'s hull. "Centuries trapped in dariss. What if they were aware all that time? The way Violet-Twenty spoke of loneliness . . ."

That led his thoughts in a direction he didn't want to travel.

"We have no control over what happened in the past," Eyasu said.

"No, but we should think carefully about what we do now."

"And how we choose to fight?" Eyasu lifted an eyebrow, deliberately patting the pouch holding his Castoff.

"Oh, yes, because a made-up Aspect-variation is an example of good judgment." Mavrin regretted his words immediately. "By the Four, I didn't mean that . . ."

Studying the deck didn't help reorder his thoughts. Atera and her crew risking themselves wasn't even the main thing affecting his mood. Nor was the lack of sleep. Poking at Eyasu was simply easier than being honest.

"You don't understand why I still believe," Eyasu said finally. "In Tanardell, Violet-Twenty said they were being tested. I've always thought we are, as well. Ever since the Fracture, and possibly before. The Aspects are benevolent and kind, but maybe They expect us to keep earning that benevolence."

"We aren't doing so well at that," Mavrin muttered.

"Are we not? Look at our world. We innovate, in a way that doesn't damage Aelda further." He gestured at the propellers visible at the rear, and the cables that funneled power from them into the salt battery belowdecks. "These inventions are part of a pattern that began with the Salvation."

"That pattern includes more than a little in-fighting." He remembered hearing about the first Incursion, unable to understand why anyone would wage battles like that anymore. Immediately after the Fracture, when resources were scarcer and the Unity only an idea, Aelda saw plenty of fighting. Yarder's Outlook still dealt with raiders from the southern Edgeplains occasionally, but that came from a disagreement as long as Farglade's independence from the Unity. He wondered what the Aspects thought, seeing the pockets where "unity" didn't mean much.

"The Aspects know why we act," Eyasu said, somehow reading his mind again. "Like They know what's in our hearts." Mavrin finally turned to look at him. There was more in Eyasu's expression, but he was too tired to understand.

"Not everyone's heart is that pure," Mavrin said, feebly. He wasn't sure whether he meant the Highest Voices, Uekel, or himself.

Eyasu shrugged. "They give us the chance to prove otherwise."

"By abandoning us?"

He didn't intend the question to sound as harsh as it did. Eyasu's deep intake of breath reminded him of Tanardell, and he immediately started to apologize again. When Eyasu spoke over him, he sounded calm, even though he was avoiding Mavrin's eyes now.

"They answered my Request to protect Aulina. They didn't allow Violet-Twenty to crash this ship. When I truly need Them, the Catalyst as Core stands at my side."

Mavrin shook his head. "I wish I understood your faith."

"I wish," Eyasu said, with heavy gravitas, "that I could make one of your garnills disappear."

He started moving his hands, as though he was manipulating a small animal in one and a cloth in the other. Lips pursed, he made a passable attempt at mimicking the cloth moving over the animal, though his fingers looked more like a four-legged spider than a bird.

"Are you two day-drinking?"

Deyeri stood across the deck, staring at them.

Eyasu froze with his elbows sticking out and the wide-eyed expression of a child caught sneaking cane sweets. Mavrin sputtered, covering a laugh with his hand, which made Eyasu start to chuckle, low in the middle of his barrel chest. Before he knew it, they were both laughing so hard that Mavrin ran out of air and started coughing.

When he looked up, Deyeri was smiling. Not sardonically or

by force, but a natural smile that only slightly pulled at the corners of her lips, like she kept most of her amusement to herself.

How often does she wear that smile? Mavrin wondered. *How often does he laugh that loudly?*

Easily as that, the thing he'd been avoiding wouldn't let him ignore it anymore.

"I'm sorry."

He couldn't even explain what he was sorry about. There was a sudden ache in his diaphragm that wouldn't leave. It had come and gone since they reached the Keep, while he tried to distract himself by ranting and arguing, exactly like Eyasu accused him of in Vertsa.

"Sixteen years, thinking nothing you and I discovered mattered," he said to Eyasu. "How could I have thought anything would happen?" He couldn't stop his voice from shaking. "Except we might have stopped this. You shouldn't have been alone," he said, finally looking at Deyeri. She didn't wear the pain on her face, but he felt it anyway. "And now people are dead. Your people."

Not only dead. And like that, what he'd been avoiding since yesterday came rushing back: his makeshift stage in Tanardell, and the gentle smile on Aulina's face as Ohanna gasped at the sight of floating petals.

"She doesn't remember her sister."

He couldn't shake that look of unknowing on Aulina's face. The scars gouged into Eyasu's scalp and the way his shoulders shook as he faced Tanardell's mob. He heard the hurt in Deyeri's voice as she told him to never call her *love* again, and her gasp of pain outside the Outreach as the Raw closed off her lungs.

"I don't know how to apologize for it all," he said, as that ache in his diaphragm stole the last of his breath. "Eyasu says we can change, but I've only faded."

Deyeri crouched in front of him and took his hand in both of hers. He waited for her to call him a fool, or slap him, or tell him he had no right to try to apologize. He deserved all of that and worse.

"Mavrin."

Her eyes glimmered. Before he could blame himself for that, too, she said, "It's okay."

For an instant, he was back in Veristenok, sitting in her bedroom. Long before he faced the Highest Voices. When he told her he was researching something that scared him, she leaned against him and he knew she understood, because of two simple words.

Only this time, those words made that ache in his diaphragm burn.

Deyeri kept holding his hand. Eyasu gripped his shoulder.

And Mavrin hung his head, as old tears fell at his feet.

Chapter Thirty

AFTER *THE JOYOUS SOUL* CLOSED ITS FORWARD shell and opened its sails to the Winds, Mavrin retreated belowdecks, hoping to spend their journey sleeping even if that meant being awake through the night again. When that only worked for a couple hours, he went back to the foredeck and stood at one of the portholes. The curving glass covered the wall and a section of deck, letting him see the dried-out salt patches and ribbons of old sediment below, carrying ahead into the glowing horizon.

With Yeldin's information, Deyeri and Termot pinpointed an exact location where his salvager found the coins. The salvager claimed he found Fargladean and Edgeplainer machinery less than a day into the West Chain, which meant the coins could only have come from one place: a tall collection of rocks marked on Watch maps as "Location Seven West."

The deck noticeably shuddered under Mavrin's feet as they entered the Edgeplains. The Winds were more unpredictable at higher altitudes, growing worse closer to the True Edge. He remembered a poem written by a follower of the Hidden as Substance, describing the hard rock and massive features here as evidence of the Aspects' anger; if They could generate the Lifesphere and will Aelda's flora and fauna to thrive in this new environment, They could have smoothed the land or cloaked it in mist or something else to save humanity from the sight. Unless the Aspects wanted people to see how close humanity came to destruction.

Mavrin couldn't recall the exact phrasing, but the point felt clearer, now.

"You ever make it out this far?" Deyeri asked, stepping up beside him.

"Not many requests for performers out here." He studied a particularly large fissure through the glass at his feet. "Geographers think this was all ocean, in the Time Before Unity. Very easy to get lost in there, I suspect."

She handed him a metal cup. Mavrin sniffed it, surprised at the sharp tang of whiskey.

"Sorry it's not berrenfruit brandy. That still your drink of choice?"

"Yes, though I don't partake as much these days." Straight whiskey wasn't always to his liking, but the oaky burn of this vintage was smoother than what Jareden had offered. "Are you still an ale person?"

"Even tried making my own once. Didn't take." Her smile turned rueful behind her cup. "Funny how we still remember things like that."

Mavrin had thought of dozens of questions to ask on the way to Farglade, only to add more since he arrived:

Did you ever marry?

I'm guessing the Incursions were difficult?

How did you like being Commander?

How much did Eyasu tell you about why I left?

What's your best friend's name? Everyone has a best friend.

Deyeri asked, "Any family to notify if we all die?"

Mavrin tried to cough out a response, settling for shaking his head. Once the whiskey cleared his lungs, he asked, "And you? I suspect I would've seen a spouse or children by now."

He regretted the question as soon as he asked it.

"Wow, you used to be smoother." She didn't look upset, as Mavrin scrambled. "I was engaged once. Long time ago."

"What happened?" He paused. "I mean, if you want to tell me."

Deyeri cut him a side glance. "Turned out I couldn't trust him the way I thought." She threw back the rest of her whiskey. "After the Incursions, we both had other things to worry about."

Mavrin's next thought simultaneously brought a warm feeling to the back of his neck and a swift garnill flutter in his stomach. With slow deliberateness, he asked, ". . . Breck?"

"Don't ask like we're children."

"Right. Sorry."

"It happened between Incursions," Deyeri explained. "The third and fourth. One of those whirlwind battlefield romances that didn't last."

"And you still served as his Watch Commander?" He knew he was prying, but he couldn't imagine volunteering to spend that much time with an ex-partner. Which had nothing to do with analyzing the two of them right now.

"Served Farglade, not him. Someone needed to." Deyeri shrugged. "Woldren was tolerable, at least for a stretch."

"Was there anyone after?"

"Subtle," she murmured. "But no, Vital as Sensation didn't bless me much."

About a half-dozen sympathetic phrases occurred to Mavrin, but since he didn't know whether he was part of her bad luck, he kept them to himself. "You've been happy here, though?"

"Yeah," Deyeri said, a little wistfully. "I mean, take out the Incursions and it's been good. Farglade is quite the city."

"And the Watch?" he asked, sensing there was something she wasn't saying.

"It gave me direction. The problem was when we didn't need a Watch anymore." Mavrin waited for her to fill the silence. "Woldren insisted we couldn't disband in case of another Incursion. Expanding the Watch was always supposed to be temporary, but he wouldn't listen. That was the last bit of pressure, so I stepped down."

He wasn't foolish enough to equate that to when he left Veristenok—he had fled, as opposed to leaving the role that gave her purpose. "What about your work now?"

"Needed to do something other than sit around collecting my allotment," she said wryly. "But I love it. Every monument or statue we put up feels like . . . protecting memories." She glanced his way. "Not that I know anything about channeling or the Raw, but Aulina might get her memory back. Given time, right?"

"One can hope." The final shot of whiskey burned his throat probably as much as he deserved. "She resisted their control more than she should've been able to."

Deyeri had a thoughtful look on her face. "If their control isn't perfect, that might be worth investigating."

"Presuming we don't all get killed."

Behind them, the Watch started gathering in front of the forecastle with Kedar.

"Let's make sure that doesn't happen."

". . . no interior maps, so we could face any kind of layout. We're looking for anything significant: locked boxes, slates or papers, maybe even cultural artifacts. Use your imagination. Salvagers have been through the site at least once, so we might need to dig a bit."

Deyeri paused as she studied the Watch, but as far as Mavrin could tell, none of them looked perturbed by the briefing so far.

"This is where it gets strange," she continued. "Touch nothing with your skin. Especially dariss. Gloves or gauntlets at all times."

That caused a murmur around the circle.

"As usual, I can't tell you everything." Mavrin wondered if her glance at Kedar was for the Watch's benefit. "You've heard rumors about what happened last night, so you can guess this isn't an average mission."

"Would you've put your knitting away if it was, Commander?" someone asked, prompting another round of chuckles.

Deyeri gave them a sign that definitely wasn't Aspect-approved. She pointed at Eyasu and, to Mavrin's surprise, at him. "They speak with my authority. You see anything unusual, you report to one of us immediately. But I'm the one you answer to for taking unsanctioned risks. Understood?"

There was a chorus of nods and Deyeri dismissed the Watch to load their armor. Feeling his stomach flip-flop, Mavrin touched her shoulder as the Watch dispersed. "I have *your* authority? I'm not even sure I should be here."

"You wanted to be useful. And don't let them hear that."

Mavrin felt his heart start to race. "Yes, but I expected to be carrying boxes or keeping an eye out for call signals."

One of the crew shouted about looking for somewhere to land, and Deyeri gave Mavrin's arm a reassuring squeeze before striding away to help. Mavrin watched her go and murmured, "Maybe I should stay on the ship after all."

"We stay together," Eyasu rumbled. He turned Mavrin away from the activity crisscrossing the deck. "And you have skills to offer."

"Narrowly avoiding death isn't a skill."

"Do you truly believe your life's work is so worthless?" Mavrin thought he meant scholarship, far removed as Mavrin was from that, but Eyasu leaned down to look him directly in the eye. "What are the most important skills for a magician?"

"Misdirection," Mavrin said immediately. "Sleight of hand. Showmanship."

"Skills I don't have, nor does Deyeri, in the same way," Eyasu said. "I could always childsit you, if you're determined to feel useless."

His uselessness was a fact, not a feeling, and Mavrin wasn't the one being a child. Whatever Eyasu thought, he had only survived facing the Raw so far because of sheer luck, stronger friends, and the fact that their powers weren't infinite. Though if they weren't infinite, that was a place to start. His fingers itched, as they always did finding a new magician's puzzle to unravel. Their powers had limitation. Like the fact that wood muddled their perceptions, for example, keeping him from becoming another charred patch in Aulina's orchard.

"Misdirection," Mavrin murmured, turning over that thought. He pointed at Eyasu's rucksack. "I need the box."

Handling it still made his stomach flip-flop, but he put that from his mind and examined the ward provided by the Aspects, simultaneously listing materials in his head. Some he could have pulled from his trunk, back at the Standing Keep, but he was sure he could find something similar on the *Soul.* Before he turned away, he noticed Eyasu's smug smile.

"Oh, go ride a Longwind," he said, and hurried away to see if his idea would even work.

If geographer theories about northern Aelda were correct and this lifeless patch had once been an ocean, Eyasu suspected Location Seven West must have been an island. From a distance, the towering spire of rock looked like it had erupted from the old seafloor, dragging several smaller protrusions with it. As Vek carefully steered the *Soul* around the spire, Eyasu wondered what structures the jagged top might have supported, before centuries of erosion from the Winds.

More contemporary wreckage was visible, too. The first was a large sheet of brassy hull, likely Fargladean, wedged at the base of the spire. Smaller reflective bits caught his eye, as well, too small for him to clearly identify but heavy enough to not have been carried away by the Winds. Eyasu craned his neck looking for pieces of a gearship or scuttleboat, even though Deyeri said they'd be painted black.

The *Soul* finished its first pass of the island and turned slowly to port. Atera had disappeared for the middle of the voyage, explaining when she emerged that she wanted to consult her father's old maps in her cabin. She warned them that finding somewhere to land might take time; neither she nor her father had ever equipped the *Soul* with the sort of docking equipment salvagers used. Behind Eyasu, the base of the topmast clicked as its sails rotated, setting them at an angle to the Winds. Once they locked into place, a noticeable thrum through the deck announced the salt engine activating, feeding power to the ventral turbine to keep them aloft as they circled.

Kedar joined him on the foredeck. "You're lucky Revect told me you could be trusted."

She placed a rolled-up sheet of recycled paper on the railing between them. Eyasu didn't need to open it to know what the notice said, or the four loops it bore along the top.

"Helps that Breck wouldn't want to hand you over to the Citadel," Kedar said.

"Clearly he thinks I'm more useful here," Eyasu said wryly. "And you, honored Voice?"

"You and I wonder the same things, I think." She tapped the inscription on one of his gauntlets. "Why we're taught to be no different than a takka, yoked around by the Citadel while the Aspects do what They want. Or don't do anything, sometimes."

"The Aspects aren't omniscient. They see and Respond," Eyasu said, feeling strange pointing this out to a fellow acolyte.

"So it depends on what we say to Them? How is that right?" She snorted. "Funny how we both speak to the Aspects, but you're the only one who ever gets an answer."

Eyasu could hear Vek and the lookouts arguing through the forecastle's hatch. "The purpose of a Voice is to speak our concerns. An answer is never expected."

Kedar slapped her palm against the railing. "Be nice to get one, though."

They suddenly lurched toward the ground. He thought something had gone wrong, but Vek leveled them out with distance from the bottom. Leaving Kedar and her complaints, Eyasu moved quickly to the side of the ship, peering to see their direction.

Using wind brakes and turning the sails, Vek slowed the *Soul* to a crawl near a collection of tiny plateaus near the central spire. None of them looked wide enough to land on, but Eyasu spotted their destination as they came alongside a narrow shelf jutting from the island, barely long enough for the Soul to anchor to and high enough not to snap the ventral mast against the ground.

He had no idea how Vek could have guided their approach from the forecastle—until Atera came bounding up from the lower decks, still wearing her protective coveralls and carrying a helmet in one hand.

"We're secure!" she called, seemingly to everyone. "Wasn't that exciting? I've never done that before!"

Across the deck, the crew lowered the gangplank to the shelf while the Watch gathered. Mavrin appeared last, cradling something wrapped in what looked like old sailcloth. He winked at Eyasu and pulled him to the side of the gangplank, where he revealed a box that looked remarkably like the one holding Violet-Twenty's coins. Not wood, but the compressed fungal material used by the windriders, which was close to the same color. Mavrin had even carved the Aspects' ward into the top.

"Misdirection?" Eyasu tried not to sound smug.

"Misdirection," Mavrin said, grinning. "Just need to compare."

He laid the real box and the fake one side by side, each with matching scraps of sailcloth. While he finished, the Watch gathered near the gangplank. Deyeri brought them in close to issue some final instruction, and Eyasu caught the words "channeling" and "Raw" right away. Mavrin rapped on his boot to get his attention and handed back the box, now completely shrouded in sailcloth. He rattled the decoy in his hands and Eyasu heard something clatter inside, completing the illusion.

"Might work long enough to catch Azure-Seven-Seven off guard."

When they joined the group, Deyeri was saying, ". . . since we don't know what we might find in there, watch each other's backs." She focused on Kedar. "Any suggestions on where we should start?"

"The big sign that says, 'Magic Weapon,'" the Voice said, totally deadpan. She surveyed the soldiers, looking for a reaction, but didn't earn a smirk. Most of the Watch looked distant or uncertain, some with an expression like they were working out hard mathematics.

"Commander, are we really dealing with storybook stuff here?" one of the Watch asked tentatively.

"Nothing storybook about it," Deyeri said. Her voice took on the gentle assurance of a comrade. "This is real-world danger, people. But we handled the Incursions, and Farglade's survived everything else. We can handle this."

Someone thumped a boot against the deck, and the rest of the Watch followed suit. As they started to disembark, Atera hurried toward Eyasu. She had replaced the coveralls with a worn leather jacket, patched in several places and tattered on the right sleeve.

"Who should I report to?" Atera asked smartly.

Mavrin stepped between them, eyeing the short sword slung across her chest and the leather bracers on her wrists. "Aren't you staying with the ship?"

"An average captain would." Vek appeared behind her. His

ponytail jangled from the back of a stiff bronze skullcap. "You ask for our captain's help, she's damn well gonna help you."

Atera straightened but couldn't quite hide her blush.

"That's a generous offer, Captain," Eyasu said, turning her so she couldn't see Mavrin's panicked expression. "Perhaps you could remain with Mavrin? I'm sure he would appreciate a familiar face."

Atera beamed at Mavrin, who sighed and gestured for her to precede him. As she and Vek clomped down the gangplank, he shot Eyasu a glare. "She should remain here."

"That young woman is older than some of Deyeri's people," Eyasu said. "She isn't Aulina."

Mavrin's glare deepened before he scurried down the gangplank.

"You two really are friends, aren't you?" Kedar said.

Eyasu smiled as he watched Mavrin stumble onto the shelf, notice the sheer drop beside the gangplank and start scrabbling in the opposite direction. "Still, it seems."

"It's important, having someone to rely on."

She walked away before he could ask what she meant.

Chapter Thirty-One

"CLOSE THE KEEP. SEND EVERYONE HOME, EVEN THE Council," Breck ordered. "Have the Watch maintain a perimeter outside the walls. Gather my guard for other orders. If we're in danger of another attack, this is a likely spot, especially after sunset."

He had to give the orders with his eyes closed, hoping everyone thought he was tired. Which he was, after being up most of the night and through the next day. But the purplish thorns and twisting vines sprouting in and out of the council room table were the real obstacle to speaking coherently.

"You wish to send us away, Lord-Magistrate?" came Oreel's wheezy rasp.

Breck realized he mentioned the Council like they weren't sitting in front of him. Forcing his eyes open, he didn't see any vines and hoped the Raw under the Keep would finally leave him alone for a bit. *Let me get this done,* he thought.

He tried to speak calmly. "For your safety. If that's all—"

"We won't be leaving."

Breck straightened. "What?"

Oreel shared a look with Trade Commissioner Jenneri and rose from his seat.

"You've forgotten things, Lord-Magistrate. Or willfully ignored them. For example, that the Legislative Council is meant to be privy to everything you are." Oreel looked around the table, and several other councillors nodded their support, including

Jenneri. "Please provide a *complete* briefing about what happened on the Walkway and at the Outreach last night. Now."

A vine erupted from behind the old councillor's teeth, ducking back into his mouth as he closed it. Another coiled around the base of his throat.

Breck rubbed his hands together, not sure whether the tingling in his extremities was real or imagined. "Until the Watch finishes investigating, I have to—"

"You choose to." Jenneri clasped her hands in front of her, connecting the interlocking rings on her fingers into the curving, ephemeral shape of the Presence as Passage in miniature. "Why you're handling things personally, without the support of your Council, I don't know. But a Lord-Magistrate doesn't simply dictate." Her rings clacked again. "Do they, Woldren?"

A couple councillors shifted uncomfortably in their seats and looked away. The others watched much more carefully, even people Breck considered friendly. He wondered how Termot would have reacted if she wasn't out coordinating the search. Only his assistant, Idriks, looked surprised and insulted, but he stayed silent off to the side.

For a moment, Breck wondered if the Raw had gotten better at creating illusions. As he stared open-mouthed at the Legislative Council and the vines disappeared, he realized this was real. He had used up the last of his goodwill here. Or the Raw had, since if it wasn't for their influence, he would have told the Council more long before now.

Would you have, though? he thought.

He settled into his seat, trying to hide how unbalanced he felt. "Anything else you want to know?"

"Commander Termot reported last night's assailants were killed, and that today's curfew is a precaution while the Watch searches for potential accomplices." Oreel gestured a liver-spotted hand at Termot's empty seat. "Except I have it on good authority that Deyeri Renn has been reinstated to lead a detachment north. Would you care to explain why?"

Roof tiles and mortar clanged against the ceiling with enough force that Breck expected dust to fall from the stones. When no one else in the room reacted, he gritted his teeth. "Their mission is . . . sensitive."

"I thought we established the Council is meant to be privy to things." Oreel glanced around the table, as though making a point to the others. "And the rumors that this detachment included a Requester?"

"Are rumors all you track, Oreel?"

Jenneri's rings clack-clacked a little faster. "We have to, thanks to you."

Breck looked between her and Oreel, who bickered during every other meeting, and wondered how much of that had been an act. Or if distrusting him made them look past their dislike for each other. At least when he sat at a table with his lieutenants, they had better things to worry about than politicking.

"Things have gotten out of hand, and we believe you know that," Oreel wheezed. "We listen to the people, Lord-Magistrate, and they're afraid."

"Afraid of what?" Breck grumbled. He didn't want to deal with these people, not when he couldn't tell them anything. They wouldn't know how to handle the truth even if he did.

"Reports of severe headaches and ghostly sounds around the Outreach. Evidence of channeling, if I'm not mistaken. Strange noises and lights near the airdock early this morning. Some people even claim to have seen a monster."

"Monsters," Breck muttered. He wondered how easy it would be to coax the Council into mentioning the Raw on their own. The less he needed to say, the more he might be able to reveal. It hadn't worked as well with Deyeri as he hoped, but so many people had seen the dead Watch or the destruction at the Outreach already.

"Sometimes the rumors are worse than the real thing," Jenneri said, more imploring than anything Oreel said yet. "What's going on, Woldren?"

I can't tell you. If he did, if the Raw let him, the Council would demand a full explanation. To see the sanctum. Maybe even lock him up and send word to Veristenok, while murmuring that he'd lost his way, like Pericar. He couldn't risk that.

"I understand your concerns, but this is a military operation. There's no point telling you more when there's nothing for you to do."

He said it flatly, like a Crossed-General would.

The table erupted.

"With all due respect, Lord-Magistrate, that simply isn't—"

"Given our precarious position with the Unity—"

"The Watch was never meant to replace our civil workers—"

As the noise washed over him, Breck started counting, waiting to continue his appeal until the Council calmed down.

He stopped as new figures swept into the room. They wore an old military uniform he wouldn't have recognized without noting it in the Lesser Historium earlier. Yet, not quite. The massive, six-pointed windguards over the helmets echoed a time when Fargladeans tried to mimic the Aspects in every design, but the blood-red stain to the armor didn't match the relic downstairs. Or the weighted broadswords they raised one-handed, as each one stood behind a Council member.

With their free hands, they lifted the windguards. Breck saw his face in every helmet, smiling ear to ear.

As one, the broadswords swept through the Council. Oreel fell gasping against his chair, pierced through the chest. Jenneri hit the floor, practically carved in half. Heads rolled across the table and blood splattered the walls and ceiling. The entire Council, dead in seconds.

Idriks landed at Breck's feet, eyes wide.

"Lord-Magistrate!"

One eyeblink and the bloodbath disappeared. Breck saw the eyes of the Legislative Council on him, everyone but Oreel silent and shocked. Probably because Breck wasn't in his chair anymore. He felt the stone wall pressing against his back as sweat ran behind his ears.

No tingling from the Raw this time. They had made their point, again.

This needs to stop.

"You remember the Incursions," he said, surprised that his voice felt hoarse, like he'd been screaming. "Lots of need-to-know matters? Pericar hiding in his chambers, talking to no one except when his appointed Crossed General demanded he open up." He stepped forward and planted fists on the table, trying to let the polished surface ground him. "I'm not Pericar. I got us through the Incursions. I'll get us through everything else. That's why *the people* gave me this chair."

No one spoke. Oreel and Jenneri shared another glance.

"You've got your little areas of responsibility. I've got mine. You want to remove me and handle everything on your own? Say the word. Until then, meeting adjourned."

He expected someone to object as he stalked away from the table, but their whispered voices didn't pick up until he was half-way down the corridor. He ignored them. They couldn't remove him quickly, even if they agreed to. They'd have to bring Termot in from coordinating the search, and she wouldn't listen, anyway. More likely, the Council would debate and argue until long after Kedar came back. Then he could show the fools exactly what he'd accomplished for Farglade, and they'd leave him alone for good. Maybe he'd copy Deyeri and retire, so he could spend his days out on the hills.

To get that far, he needed to focus. To stay in control.

And he knew who could help him.

"Am I not safe here?"

Breck threw a casual smile back at Aulina. "Mavrin said to protect you, didn't he? There's a little corner of the Keep most don't know about. Come on."

The truth was such a delightful tool.

As they crossed the grounds facing the Windroute, Breck grimaced at the voices echoing from the other side of the Keep. He had ordered the Watch to close the grounds to petitioners, but they hadn't started clearing anyone else from the buildings; that would happen shortly, since he doubted the Council would risk people's safety simply because of his behavior upstairs. The only other people in sight were two of his personal guard, told to keep an eye on the Windroute for potential intruders. If they were lucky, the only likely intruder was far from here. Breck had strapped on his sword anyway.

He stepped into the crystal enclosure and pressed the switch inside. Aulina stepped back as a section of stone floor fell away, revealing the staircase beneath.

"Like I said—somewhere not everyone knows." Breck beckoned her to follow but she didn't move.

"I might be afraid of the dark. I don't think I always was, but . . ."

Breck held out his hand. "It isn't dark down there."

She didn't take it but started down the staircase anyway. *Good enough.*

The underground staircase was familiar against his feet, after countless visits to the sanctum. When they reached the bottom and stepped into the passage beyond, Aulina disappointed him by not reacting. He couldn't remember what the series of caverns and tunnels truly looked like anymore; the Raw liked to change what he saw each time he visited. The first time, following Pericar, was the only instance it appeared to him as bare stone. Sometime after that, the floor was covered in jagged crystal that didn't pierce his boots. Weeks later, strange creatures with bulbous eyes, glossy scales like adders and no limbs floated behind translucent walls; a little research told him they had been fish.

This time, the walls looked like polished marble and the air around him had a strange, pink glow. He stayed near the base of the stairs as Aulina stepped forward, brushing the wall with her fingers. There was phosphorescent lichen lining the tunnel, like the others discovered under Farglade over the decades, but Breck wasn't sure if it was pink like what he saw.

"What is this place?"

"The old Lord-Magistrate called it a sanctum."

"A sanctum for what?" Aulina spun toward him, eyes narrowed as though she already had her answer.

Breck didn't offer one of his own. "Do you feel anything?"

"No."

"Oh," he said, and pointed ahead. "Let's keep going."

Aulina didn't move until he did, glancing furtively over her shoulder. She stopped again, eyes drawn to the ceiling. "I recognize these designs. They're from Before."

Breck had forgotten about the carvings that lined the central cavern and couldn't remember what they looked like. He wondered why the Raw weren't playing with Aulina's mind like they did with his. Everyone else who came down here felt something. "Feel anything now?"

"No."

He clenched a fist at his side. "Try, maybe."

"What would I feel, exactly?" she asked, crossing her arms and arching an eyebrow.

"The Raw."

She made a great attempt at trying to hide it, but he noticed

Aulina's attention flick over his shoulder. They had made it far enough that he knew the staircase was out of sight behind them; one more curve would bring them to the end of this cavern, with the sanctum waiting beyond.

"Let me explain," Breck said, holding his hands out toward her. No tingling anywhere along his body yet. "You have a connection to these things, right? I don't. Not in a way that lets me understand them the way I need to."

"Except they're not things," she said, like he should have known that.

Breck blinked. "Right. People. Beings." He caught himself before adding *whatever* to the list. "I think I know what they want, but I need to be sure. You communicated through that one in the coins. I need you to do that here."

"Because there are more Raw down here." Aulina didn't sound surprised. If anything, she sounded disappointed. In him.

Time for a little more truth, then.

Breck pointed around that final bend. "Let me show you."

Aulina shook her head. "I don't want anything to do with this."

"You won't get hurt."

"I've already been hurt," she snapped. "Eyasu promised—"

"That fool?" Breck snorted. "He has no idea. None of them do. But you've felt the Raw's pain, like I have. Seen their thoughts. You can help me negotiate, and I need—"

"Need what?"

The whispered voice came from behind him. Breck pivoted, back against the wall so he could keep Aulina in his peripheral while he focused on Termot, a few meters back down the cavern. Aulina didn't look surprised by her appearance, either. When she glanced over his shoulder, she'd been looking at Termot.

"Shouldn't you be out looking for something?" Breck asked her wryly.

"Did that." Termot shrugged. "Led me here."

It didn't take much to realize what had happened. "Keeping an eye on me for Dey?"

"Still hiding things?"

Breck's response died in his throat as the cavern shifted around him. Glistening gold streaks cut through the white marble, zigzagging like cracks. They yawned open to either side, like the interior was breaking apart.

"I can't tell you everything," he said, forcing the words out as that damned tingling returned. "You have to trust me, Garris."

Except Termot wasn't looking at him. She was studying Aulina, taking in the obvious fear on her face and this strange tunnel around them. Breck knew right away what the Commander was thinking even before she extended a hand.

Aulina darted forward. When Breck tried to grab her arm, his hand slid off like from a pipe slick with condensation. Termot stepped between them, raising her voice for the first time since the last Incursion, telling him to stop.

Her voice cut out with a grunt as Breck slammed her against the wall.

The vibrations stopped but the fissures in the wall remained, shifting slowly to either side of Termot's head.

"Don't tell me you can't see it," Breck hissed. Static coursed through his entire body, so intense he was surprised his hairs weren't standing on end. Except the static was no more real than what happened around channeling. "Look at it! This is what I'm protecting us from."

Termot shook her head, not understanding. She grimaced, teeth wet with blood. Stepping back, Breck's eyes widened at his sword buried into her chest. Straight through the only seam in her chest armor; hitting that point by accident was practically impossible.

"Sorry," Termot gasped, glancing toward Aulina. Then she slumped to the ground.

Breck heard Aulina's footfalls as she ran. He didn't bother following. She couldn't leave; only Breck and Kedar knew how to trigger the door from inside. Even if she figured it out before he caught up, his guards would bring her back. They hadn't only been told to watch for intruders.

There was no escaping, for any of them, so Breck sat down opposite Termot and waited.

Chapter Thirty-Two

BEFORE THEY PARTED WAYS AT THE AIRDOCK, Termot had said to Deyeri, "Don't let our past haunt you out there."

Her friend's words hung in the air as Deyeri faced the narrow tunnel in front of her. Location Seven West was riddled with these passages, either hollowed by the ocean long ago or as the karst left behind was weathered by the Winds. Too many to follow without dividing her people too thin, so she quickly matched teams with herself, Eyasu and Mavrin, guiding hers down the tunnel furthest to the left. The unexpected benefit was that almost no one got to see her pause at every junction, pretending she was assessing the terrain, when really this place reminded her too much of where she and Havven almost died.

The Lifesphere shimmered through fissures above, where parts of the island broke away over time, illuminating a dead-end alcove filled with broken crates and debris. Scavengers must have dragged away most of it, but they left behind bits of fabric and wood they wouldn't eat, and a pair of iron swords with Fargladean pommels. The latter caused a chill that had nothing to do with the Edgeplains' cooler temperatures.

She hadn't known anyone who died at Location Seven West, but that didn't mean they weren't her people.

"Nothing here for us," she said to the Watch behind her, and willed herself to turn around.

Backtracking to another branch revealed a jagged passage where more ceiling had collapsed. Deyeri turned sideways to try to wriggle through, but her armor made it impossible.

"Ryld, hold my pauldrons."

The short-haired corporal didn't hesitate; Deyeri had made far stranger requests when they'd served together. Once the pauldrons were balanced between their left hand and right wrist—Ryld lost the hand during the third Incursion—Deyeri said to the other Watch, "You're giving me a boost, Emar."

Emar was studying the far wall. "Commander, you said to look for dariss, right?"

Deyeri grunted as she tried to wriggle through the opening.

"I haven't seen any." They pointed their salt lamp to illuminate the walls above her. "Not even veins, like we have back home. Weird, right?"

Deyeri filed that away for later as she braced herself against the narrow gap in front of them, sticking one heel back for Emar to grip.

"How are you planning on coming back?" Ryld asked.

"Hoping there's something to climb on the other side. If not," she said, offering them a wink, "you're in charge."

When Emar hoisted her up, Deyeri pressed her palms against either side of the tunnel to catch herself. Thanking whoever designed the Watch's armor for making it light and durable, she kicked her legs and let gravity carry her forward. Her toes touched the collapsed rocks and she pushed off, dropping nimbly to a crouch on the other side with a pointed shard of metal less than a meter from her nose.

She straightened carefully, eyeing the length of scrap. Light from a wide tear in the ceiling revealed the metal frame of a scuttleboat widening away from her. It filled the passage beyond after a few meters, which was the first clue that this wasn't Fargladean; not even a scoutsled could fit in here. Even in the dim light, she recognized the dull, nonreflective hull and the mangled gear assembly at the back, which would have operated the segmented legs on the scuttleboat's sides.

Wondering how it got here, Deyeri lifted herself onto the nose and felt a stronger gust of air against her forehead. She stepped carefully into the main bed, mindful of gouges in its belly or jagged edges where the bench seats were torn apart. By the time she reached the aft, the pressure against her was strong enough that she needed to brace against the cavern walls. The tunnel floor continued a few meters past the wreckage, ending at a T-junction where the floor dropped away some unseen distance. She inched as close to the junction as she dared, tugging on her goggles as she poked her head over the threshold.

By this point the Winds felt almost as powerful as in the Bemner, and she realized she had found a natural Windroute, although on a much smaller scale. The tunnel, only fifteen meters wide but at least three times as tall, must have cut through most of the island, if not the entire thing. That would explain how the scuttleboat found its temporary berth: someone meant to come back for it.

Who that person might have been, no one in Farglade knew. She wasn't even sure she understood the Incursions, anymore. And she had only just made peace with the lives and sense of security lost.

Those thoughts chilled her more than finding those swords, as she made her way back to Ryld and Emar.

~

"That's simply disconcerting."

Atera stepped up beside Mavrin. "Why are there so many faces?"

No matter which angle he chose, he couldn't catch a glimpse of the eyes. Eight brass faces encircled the lip of a large bowl, mounted on a platform that had fallen sideways into a crevasse. He didn't have the courage or lack of self-preservation to climb down and remove one of the old strips of leather covering them.

The parts of Mavrin's brain that first led him to scholarship tickled at the sight of a sculpture unlike anything he'd seen before. The faces might have been humanity, the leather strips reflecting their unwillingness to see something—there were certainly a lot of things humanity didn't understand. But even before the Fracture, most of Aelda's cultures focused their architecture on other beings, including ones consciously discarded after the Aspects arrived.

"Maybe worshipping something other than Them," Mavrin mused.

Atera brushed her fingers against her pendants, lingering on the one representing the Hidden as Order. "Would the Aspects tolerate something like that?"

He thought about his conversation with Eyasu on the way here. Allowing the Incursions made sense but letting an entire culture worship something else surprised him. He wondered if that was because all he had ever known was the Unity's strictness.

"I have no idea what They're willing to accept anymore," he admitted. His old scholarly curiosity faded away. "Maybe we'll get lucky and stumble upon all of our existential answers in this gloomy place . . ."

Atera stared at the glimmers of sunlight through the ceiling. "I think we'll find what we need."

As she led the way down the next tunnel, Vek sidled up to Mavrin. "Learned optimism from her father. Hard bastard, that one, but he always believed. Redrew the Catalyst's lines on the hull every week, like you should, and dropped ointment over the railing for the Presence. All to protect Atera. And she's twice as good a captain."

"How so?" Having seen how she handled the ship, he was curious about Vek's perspective.

"Never gives an order that don't make sense. Listens to us.

Even gives away extra chits." Vek shrugged. "Just wants to be out on the Winds, seeing the world."

The next tunnel opened to the outside, forcing them to hunch against the Winds across a narrow shelf. Mavrin spotted one of those scuttleboats below, which at a distance seemed to be mostly intact but empty of cargo. When he turned to ask Atera's opinion, she'd already reached the shelf's other end and ducked into the next tunnel. Inside, he joined her in a wide, square chamber, half of its roof open to the sky. To their left, another tunnel led deeper into the island. Bits of debris were scattered about the chamber: a rusted shield beside the remains of some barrels, and two more painted pitch black. Mavrin poked at a collapsed pile of metal beams that looked like they had formed a stand or weapon rack.

A crooked fissure cut through the floor near the center of the chamber, dropping into darkness. Mavrin turned his ear to the ground and thought he heard air currents whipping around distant stone.

Shadows flickered in front of his nose. Mavrin whirled, almost falling backward into the fissure—but it was just Atera, her salt lamp's light playing off the rock.

He shook the nerves from his fingers. "I should've stayed back in Farglade. Only an angry Raw to worry about there."

"What do you think about them? The Raw, I mean," Atera said as they crossed the chamber.

Mavrin wasn't sure how to answer. He was about as certain about the Raw as he was about the Aspects. He told Atera as much, adding, "Much as I understand their rage, I can't condone the harm Azure-Seven-Seven—"

"You know his name?" Atera asked, surprised.

"And more than that." Mavrin tried not to dwell on the Raw's voice or the visions he shared at the Outreach. "The lives he's taken don't balance what was done to his people."

"Balance is a matter of perspective," she murmured.

"More wisdom from your father?" he asked, but she didn't answer.

A rough metal sheet, looking like the same material as the scuttleboat's hull, rested against the wall on the opposite side of the room. Someone had affixed a hinge on an iron pole worked into the stone; it reminded Mavrin of his early attempts to make mechanisms for his shows, before he turned to tinkerers like Cler. Except that this door worked, swinging open with a soft grind.

Onto an empty alcove.

As Atera turned away, her lamplight wobbled against the rock. Mavrin asked for the lamp and held it further into the alcove until he found the reason: a sliver of open air around his eye level. Mavrin tracked the sliver up and down the rock wall, thinking about how he would hide something important in this faraway island.

"Captain, did you ever figure out how my disappearing bottle trick works?"

"No." Atera's voice picked up. "Are you going to explain it?"

"The key with simple tricks is you never actually hide anything from the audience. Everything is in plain sight, but how you present it makes the audience *think* they understand what they're seeing . . ."

He handed Atera's lamp back and ran both hands along the wall, ignoring Deyeri's voice in his head telling him not to touch anything. It didn't take long to find what didn't belong: metal latches, like the makeshift hinges but painted to blend into the rock.

". . . when in fact they're being misled," Mavrin said, and pushed against the center of the stone.

It slid a couple inches before his muscles seized and he stepped back, panting.

"Can the magician get an assistant?"

Together, he, Atera and Vek heaved against the rock until they made enough of a gap to pass through. On the other side, they found a small, natural chamber converted into a storage room. A larger blindfolded brass face loomed over a collection of sealed boxes and scroll cases, coated in years worth of dust.

"Perhaps we should all be optimistic," he said to Atera, unable to hide a beaming smile.

Shouting at the top of his lungs eventually brought Eyasu to them, barreling from the other tunnel. He and the two Watch with them had their weapons out, and even Kedar looked ready for a fight. When they saw that Mavrin and Atera weren't in any danger, Eyasu looked like he wanted to scold them.

Until Mavrin explained what they found.

While they waited, he and Atera had poked through some of the containers. Most of the rolled-up parchment was scrawled in a language he didn't recognize, but the format reminded him of manifests or inventories. He found one book with lines upon lines of tighter, detailed printing, and brought it for the others to examine.

"Do you understand any of that?" Mavrin asked Kedar.

"Remember the part where they never spoke to us?" She pointed at the makeshift door. "Maybe let's see what else they left behind?"

As she headed that way, Eyasu lingered with Mavrin, the excitement on his face quickly falling. "There might be nothing useful here."

That had crossed Mavrin's mind while he searched, but he knew this entire mission was a gamble—and that drawing Azure-Seven-Seven away from Farglade was the more likely outcome. "If there isn't, we'll keep looking. Like the old days."

Mavrin hoped the sincerity showed on his face. Not because it wasn't genuine, but because he couldn't shake the feeling that he still needed to make up for that past.

Eyasu clapped him heavily on the shoulder and headed after Kedar. Noting the tight conditions in the storeroom, he ducked out for a moment to place his rucksack beside the door. Mavrin listened in the alcove, to see whether they came to the same conclusions he had: that finding something they could use against the Raw would likely take more time than they had. Eventually he wandered away, examining the pile of metal poles and wondering where the weapons might have gone.

"I thought channeling wasn't supposed to have limits," Atera said nearby.

"Ask Eyasu later. He can provide a long treatise on what we can and can't Request," Mavrin replied. "Requesters aren't all-powerful, after all."

"That is very good to know."

Something in Atera's tone made Mavrin turn.

Only to feel her sword plunge through his side.

Chapter Thirty-Three

MAVRIN FELT THE SWORD SLIDE OUT OF HIS BODY as he fell to his knees.

Atera's smile was cold and gleeful as she yanked the sword back. "Using this felt positively vulgar, but that *was* satisfying."

"Captain?"

Vek stood nearby, eyes wide. That un-Atera smile froze on her face as a wisp of light appeared above Vek's head and passed into his forehead. His face contorted and his limbs curled in against his body before he struck the ground, hard enough to send his skullcap flying. The two Watch whirled, looking for an attacker, before each let out a short, pained scream and tore their helmets away to claw at their faces.

Azure-Seven-Seven appeared from the shadows, stepping over the three dying men like they didn't exist. Despite the fall from the Outreach, Havven's body only sported bruises along his chin and receding hairline, though the Watch armor was noticeably scuffed and stained. Atera didn't budge as he approached, hands hanging limp at her sides and a vacant expression on her face, as Mavrin's blood dripped from her sword.

"Too bad you'll remember all of this," Azure-Seven-Seven cooed at her, and still, she didn't react.

Mavrin couldn't summon strength back into his legs, even if he could tear his hands away from the wet patch of blood at his side. He could only watch as the Raw crossed to Eyasu's rucksack and upended it, catching the wooden box in midair while the other contents scattered across the ground.

Azure-Seven-Seven paused, considering the box and its sail-cloth wrap.

Eyasu burst from the alcove, longknife and Castoff already drawn. Kedar stood behind him, eyes wide. Mavrin couldn't help but be impressed as Eyasu lurched forward, throwing himself at someone he knew he couldn't defeat. Phrases in T'var spilled from his lips faster than Mavrin had ever heard them.

Please. Please, just help him, he called into the ether, not caring who was listening.

The channeling that erupted from Eyasu felt so powerful, he wondered if the Aspects heard. In one eyeblink, Havven's body disappeared, replaced by an indistinct silhouette the same blue shade as the Lifesphere. When Havven's form returned, the stone at his feet glowed red hot, as though Eyasu was trying to recreate the Fracture. The Raw stumbled with a snarl, and a burst of air like a Longwind thundered across the chamber, knocking Mavrin onto his side hard enough to blast stars across his vision. When they faded, he saw Atera staggering but still upright, and a whirl of green robes as Kedar fell backward into the storage room.

Eyasu braced against the onslaught. His longknife fell from his fingers, winking out of existence halfway to the ground, and he clasped both hands around his Castoff, barely forcing another Request through his gritted teeth.

All pressure left the air in an instant. Azure-Seven-Seven stumbled, knocking into the still-catatonic Atera, but otherwise he looked unaffected as the Request passed.

Eyasu wavered in place. When he opened his hands, his expression turned from disbelief to horror. It took Mavrin a moment of bleary study to figure out why.

It wasn't a Castoff in his friend's hands, but two pieces. One shard in each palm, no longer catching the light from anywhere around them.

"Poor, broken thing," Azure-Seven-Seven hissed, stepping forward. "You thought They would save you? Even now, with everything you know?"

Eyasu didn't react as the Raw plucked the shards from his hands. He didn't even look as they were tossed aside, making dull thuds as they struck the floor.

"They have chosen, false Requester."

The Raw's eyes flashed and Eyasu crumpled soundlessly to the ground. He didn't rise as Azure-Seven-Seven marched away, unwrapping the sailcloth from his prize.

Mavrin managed to croak, "Wait! Don't . . . release them . . ."

Disgust spread across the Raw's stolen face as he approached, holding out the box—which he promptly crushed one-handed. The fungus composite Mavrin used for the fake fell away, as three ceramic bolts from the *Soul*'s engine room clattered to the ground. The Raw didn't waste any time yanking Mavrin to his feet and digging the real box from his cloak, still wrapped in sailcloth. He dropped Mavrin back to the ground and snorted.

Azure-Seven-Seven's fingers froze halfway to tearing the sailcloth apart. His brows knit together as a faint glow outlined his body, like what had encased Eyasu in the Outreach. He turned sluggishly and Mavrin saw a shard of dariss floating in the air behind him, crackling with charged energy. Kedar stood behind it, holding a second crackling shard toward the Raw.

"Enough of that."

The loose shard shot through the air. Mavrin thought it tore through Havven's throat at first, but as the Raw whirled he saw the crystal embedded in the side of his host's neck near the jugular. Azure-Seven-Seven flailed at it, carving a thick gash into Havven's flesh, but when he touched the crystal a spark erupted from his fingers and he snatched them back like he'd been burned.

"I thought," the Raw gasped, "this knowledge was lost."

"Not quite." Kedar squeezed her eyes shut and the crystal in her hand crackled, while Azure-Seven-Seven squirmed, hands trembling and fingers flexing at his sides.

Mavrin stared, his hands held feebly against his wound. Kedar was holding the Raw, using the dariss to bind him like Uekel's notes described. Except she and Breck had insisted they didn't understand how that worked yet.

"Pretty simple, once you piece it together," she said, noticing his attention. "Feeding enough power into the dariss activates it. Then all you do is focus . . ." She cocked her head and Azure-Seven-Seven twitched. "Makes them some level of defenseless."

She stepped right up to the Raw and pressed her hand to his throat. His glare contorted into a grimace of pain as smoke rose from both crystals, blackening Havven's flesh in two places.

"Hurting you isn't my plan," Kedar told him. "We can release you, if you cooperate. Along with the rest of the Raw in Farglade."

"Your kind always lies," the Raw spat.

"Not this time."

She stepped away and Azure-Seven-Seven sagged, able to move everything except the hand clutching the box, which stayed rigid at his side. He fixed his glare on Kedar, but nothing else happened. The Raw couldn't channel.

"Wish there was another way, but you won't trust my word. Bring Violet-Twenty-Four-Ten and we'll settle this."

The Raw snarled in place. Rolling her eyes with a lack of fear Mavrin couldn't understand, Kedar concentrated again and forced the Raw's feet to turn toward the tunnel, marching him awkwardly out of the chamber. Atera followed in a daze, still yoked to his control, and thereby Kedar's—who made no move to free her, either.

Kedar glanced at Mavrin. "If it makes you feel better, I'm really on your side."

"Is that so?" he sneered.

"The Aspects should know the truth," Kedar said, as though

that should be obvious. "Then we'll find out what They think of us. Don't worry. I'm sure you'll see Their answer from here."

She struck him across the skull, and everything went black.

Even before the echoing screams faded, Deyeri knew she was too far away. Taking the left branch when she split their group placed her as far away from Mavrin as possible, and she hadn't covered enough distance after she heard him shouting for Eyasu, even once she started running. *Shouldn't have split us up at all.*

Deyeri drew up short, staring down the latest side tunnel they passed. When Ryld asked what was wrong, she held up a hand. After testing the breeze with her cheek, she turned that way, telling them, "Keep down the main passage!"

She wouldn't let Ryld and Emar risk what she was planning. It was the sort of impulse she would have followed during the second Incursion, before Termot convinced her to think before she leapt. There wasn't time to think now. Only leap.

The air pressed harder as she advanced, forcing her to lean forward to keep pace. By the time she reached the end of the passage, the Winds howled in her ears, which was exactly what she wanted. Four steps from the edge, she snapped on her goggles. Two steps away, she slapped the trigger on her chest plate, activating her armor's wings as she cleared the final meters and sprang out into open air.

Her wings finished unfolding and billowed under her triceps, tugging her down the miniature Windroute. Deyeri raised her arms, bending her elbows at ninety degrees like she'd been taught and letting her feet dangle behind her. The salt lamp on her belt didn't offer nearly enough light but luckily the tunnel seemed straight enough that she could keep to its center by feel.

Turning her arms, she managed to angle her path closer to the right, waiting for a gap in the wall. She spotted one a few heartbeats later and snapped her right arm to her side, collapsing the wing to let the Winds push her that way.

Her aim was a little off. The goggles took the impact against the tunnel's ceiling and her legs swung forward, thankfully with enough momentum to clear the Windroute—and land hard on her back. Even losing all the breath in her lungs and some of her dignity, she thanked the Presence as Balance for lending a hand.

Deyeri tore her cracked goggles off and brushed the glass shards away from her eyes. Ignoring the throb in her spine, she climbed to her feet and jogged down the new passage she'd found, hoping it led somewhere close to her friends.

As she rounded a thick stand of stalagmites, Kedar stepped into the tunnel about fifteen meters ahead. She turned when Deyeri called her name. The frown on her face didn't make any more sense than the dariss shard crackling in her hands, as Havven appeared behind her.

Deyeri didn't have time to scream before crushing pain closed around her skull, ten times worse than hitting that ceiling. Agony came in the form of long-forgotten memories: the sharp crack of her right arm breaking when she fell as a child, the dazing blow of a concussion during an attack on the Craggs, stabs and cuts from Edgeplainers and criminals and training accidents, plus other wounds she'd forgotten until now. She felt blood and bile at the back of her throat as the physical pain mingled with the emotional, reliving the cutting misery of Mavrin leaving her, the emptiness when Breck abandoned her in the Edgeplains, and the despair of every death under her command.

When she collapsed to her side, gasping and numb, Kedar and the Raw simply walked away.

Chapter Thirty-Four

DEYERI RECOGNIZED SECONDS TICKING BY.

Garris is going to give you such a look for lying around.

The last time she'd lain like this was in an old takka pen, one of the last in Farglade to be made entirely from wood. Not well maintained, either, leading the plank floor upstairs to collapse beneath her when she ran. Even though she couldn't hear the footsteps over the wind gauges whirling outside, she'd known her quarry was doubling back. She hadn't thought about that in a long time, but the tingling in her shoulders, the throbbing of her sprained ankle and the half-dozen bruises felt fresh now. Along with the dread of knowing the only repeat killer she ever faced in Farglade was coming to finish her.

He would have, too, if she hadn't imagined Breck standing over her. Not even telling her to get up because, as he would put it: "I shouldn't have to. You're Watch, right?"

She could hear him now, but this time it didn't help her move.

Deyeri knew she had to get up, but her body wouldn't let her.

I'm worried you might be in danger.

It took two tries to get one palm flat against the ground and lift her body enough to free her other arm. Her vision swam, so she closed her eyes while she levered herself to kneeling. That took longer than it should have, since she needed to remember that she broke her leg ten years ago, not ten seconds.

Getting to her feet helped shake off the Raw's attack. By the time she made it to where Kedar first appeared, her body stopped wobbling.

When she reached the chamber beyond, she broke into a run.

Pools of blood surrounded the two Watch, their eyes vacant. Vek was the same, except with a wide-eyed, frozen expression on his face. Mavrin lay nearby, wrapped in his ridiculous cloak, with Eyasu at the back of the chamber.

Deyeri rushed to Mavrin first. Blood soaked through one side of his cloak, but not as much as on the others. His eyes were closed, lined face almost as white as his hair.

The moment she touched his shoulder, his eyes snapped open. He gasped and tried to roll away from her, almost falling into the fissure nearby before she tugged him back. "It's me. I'm real," she said, remembering the illusions still fighting her mind.

"Why is getting stabbed this painful?" he hissed between labored breaths. "By the Four, it's like someone's rummaging my insides with a hot poker."

Deyeri eased his cloak aside and gently pulled on the blood-soaked waistcoat and shirt. After she found the wound, she felt his eyes on her, confused, as she searched his pockets. Her fingers closed on something blocky and dense, pulling out Kedar's copy of the *Accounts*, gouged through the middle and soaked in blood.

Mavrin laid his head back. "Of course, the damn thing saved my life."

Deyeri bunched up his cloak against the wound. "Keep holding that." One of the fallen Watch had a field kit slung over one shoulder, but she needed to check Eyasu first.

He didn't stir when she rolled him onto his back. His chest armor made it difficult to see whether he was breathing, but holding her hand over his nose, she felt something faint. When she pulled her hand away, Eyasu's eyes were open.

Deyeri sighed. "What happened?"

He didn't speak. She reached for her sword and his eyes tracked the motion. Not a single emotion played across his face.

"See to Mavrin," he said. "It's over."

He went back to staring at the ceiling.

~

No matter how Mavrin moved, he felt the fungal wraps pulling at his flesh. Or he could imagine the sickening moment of torn flesh and willed his organs to stay where they belonged. At least death might cover the pungent smell of the wraps; with all that innovation Eyasu liked to praise, he didn't understand why they couldn't scent medical equipment. Deyeri worked fervently, slapping his hand away whenever he touched his side, while he quickly recounted what happened before Kedar left with the Raw.

"I'm surprised he didn't kill you," she murmured as she repacked the field kit.

"Kedar stopped him. Not sure why."

Mavrin glanced back into the chamber where they left Eyasu, sitting upright now but refusing to talk or budge. He hadn't responded when Deyeri collected the halves of his Castoff, so she brought them to Mavrin. Neither of them could fathom what to do about that, so both pieces sat in his pocket for now.

He asked Deyeri, "Why would she come here with us, if she could already control the Raw? And why not kill us?"

"Tactically, it makes more sense than I would've given her credit for."

Deyeri snapped the field kit shut and gestured for him to follow. They passed along the exposed shelf where Mavrin spotted the scuttleboat, realizing that he should have noticed something was wrong with Atera when she failed to show interest in it. If he had, he could have tried breaking the Raw's control.

Through the next winding passage, they discovered three more dead Watch. Only the two from Deyeri's team had survived; they reported seeing the *Soul* drift overhead, circling the island before heading south. Mavrin assumed the rest of the Watch got in Kedar's way or had been tricked into boarding the windship.

Deyeri left the bodies where they'd fallen, grimacing as she moved her hands over each in a sign to the Catalyst as Protector.

As she led him forward again, she said, "This was never about research. This was about getting us out of the city, and about securing that other set of coins."

"Trying to lure Azure-Seven-Seven away," Mavrin mused. "To capture him away from an audience."

Deyeri paused at a tunnel he recognized, an almost triangular shape that led back to where the *Soul* had anchored. She chewed her lip. "You're sure Kedar said *our* terms? Not her terms?"

Mavrin wished he could say otherwise. "I know you and Breck—"

"Let's figure out how to get back first," Deyeri said flatly, and Mavrin set that topic aside.

She led him out onto the shelf. All they found at first were gouges in the rock from the *Soul*'s docking clamps and scrapes from the gangplank. Deyeri stood at the edge, barely budging under the Winds, while Mavrin searched the empty space, wishing blankly that something had been left behind.

Surprisingly, something had.

Mavrin slid to a stop at the shelf's far corner. Atera mumbled incoherently as he dropped at her side; her eyelids fluttered, and every few seconds her body jerked.

"Almost like she's dreaming," Deyeri said, joining him. "Captain, can you hear me?"

"Why isn't she dead?" Mavrin asked frantically. "Why leave her here?"

Deyeri thought for a moment. "The Raw doesn't need her now, if he has her crew."

Too bad you'll remember all of this. Mavrin imagined Atera trapped in her own mind, unable to warn anyone about

Azure-Seven-Seven's presence. She'd been the perfect choice: someone they all trusted who hadn't encountered the Raw yet.

Mavrin grabbed Atera's arm and shook her gently. "Time for you to wake up, Captain." She twitched again, but not in response to him. "There's a tear in the mainsail and a Longwind on the horizon!"

Nothing changed. Mavrin started pulling items from his pockets, discarding anything that couldn't help. Which proved to be everything, until his cloak was empty and flapping at his sides. The only things left were his hands, which he pressed into the rock until his knuckles ached.

"Mavrin."

Deyeri pointed at his side. When he saw the soft glow emanating from his pocket, Mavrin scrambled backward, thinking one of his toys had broken and caught fire. Except the only things he hadn't flung to the ground were the halves of Eyasu's Castoff, still tucked into the pocket where he used to place a coin when he performed.

He'd never felt comfortable holding a Castoff. When he tested for a connection to the Aspects, he remembered blanching at the grainy texture, and how the underside felt smoother than glass. The Servant made him hold it longer than seemed necessary, reminding him that the single physical contact everyone had with the Saviors was a blessing. Mavrin the child had been happy the Castoff didn't glow, since that meant he'd likely never handle one again.

Eyasu's Castoff glowed now. Not as bright as when Eyasu wielded it, but more than its natural shine, emanating from both pieces as he held them out.

"I don't understand," he said to Deyeri, and himself, and no one in particular.

The percentage of people on Aelda who could connect directly with the Aspects was incredibly small. Supposedly it had been more common when the first Castoffs fell, though whether the ability became diluted as Aelda's population recovered or because the Aspects didn't want too many Requesters in the world, no one knew. The ability was so rare now that the premature death of any Requester terrified the Highest Voices, and so finite that Requesters received larger allotments and fiercer attention when they were injured, sick or missing. Their channeling was as much a gift as the Lifesphere, treasured for its rarity.

Castoffs did not glow in anyone else's hands.

"There something else you never told me?" Deyeri asked, hushed and half-joking.

Mavrin's gaze turned to the sky. He didn't realize why until a moment later, when he registered a slow, creeping feeling at the base of his skull. It passed across his shoulders and down his arms, terminating at his palms and fingertips where they touched the Castoff. Different from the feel of the Winds, but similar in that he knew something was there even if he couldn't see it.

The sensation lifted as slowly as it arrived. Starting with his neck again, down his body, lingering at his fingertips before it passed completely. With its absence Mavrin felt a surprising longing, like the immediate aftermath of being held by a loved one. The air left his lungs in a brief sigh as he wished for a sign, any sign, that he hadn't imagined that sensation.

It came from Atera, as the frantic movement under her eyelids stilled and her breathing evened out. When her eyes opened, they were bloodshot and confused. "Mister Leed?"

She started to shake, shoulders curling inward. "Oh, what did I do . . . ?"

Then she clung to him, sobbing but somehow alive. Over the top of her fiery hair, he saw the Castoff's glow fading, as the Aspects' attention shifted elsewhere. But for a moment, it had been centered on *him*.

A moment later, he realized why.

As the glow vanished completely, he thought to murmur, "Thank you."

Naturally, no one answered.

Chapter Thirty-Five

"YOU SURE SHE CAN GET THAT THING WORKING?" Deyeri asked as they walked back through the island.

"She's a windrider with a stolen ship. She'll fix it. Quickly, I hope." Mavrin glanced back at the shelf where they left Atera. "She curses much more than I'd expect."

The captain had sat in silence for a while after she calmed. She didn't ask to see Vek. Mavrin and Deyeri gave her space, but before long Atera was on her feet, declaring that she wanted to see the scuttleboat "for real this time." After leaping across its deck and scouring its frame, she declared the hull intact enough to handle a journey, once she repaired the cables that moved the turbines.

"Besides," Mavrin added, "she needs the distraction, and she has your people with her. Let's worry about our other problem."

Eyasu sat cross-legged where they left him, facing the storeroom. Its makeshift door still hung open; Mavrin looked inside to confirm that Kedar had left with a bunch of the texts, the rest incinerated by Azure-Seven-Seven. Eyasu hadn't moved except to take off his armor and toss it haphazardly nearby.

"Better you do this," Deyeri said. "He's your best friend."

"Yes, I suppose so." Mavrin looked at her. "I haven't asked if you're all right."

"No, you haven't." A flicker of a smile crossed her features, disappearing behind the mask she'd been wearing since she bandaged him up. She nudged him forward.

Eyasu didn't look up when Mavrin sat across from him. One

thumb traced tight circles on his other palm, while his shoulders trembled beneath his padded shirt.

"I know what you're going to say. I don't need to hear it."

Mavrin cocked an eyebrow. "Is that so?"

"That there are people in danger. That we need to press on. That there is hope," Eyasu said, his voice flat. "You're wrong."

"Eyasu, we can't—"

"*Did you not see what happened?*"

As his bellow echoed around them, Eyasu's chest heaved.

"They don't care," Eyasu said, his usual octave sounding like a whisper compared to that bellow. "Not anymore." His voice shook as he finished. "I'm the one with hubris. To think the Aspects believe in us without reservation."

Mavrin placed the two halves of his Castoff on the ground between them, next to his discarded chest plate. They lay dormant as Eyasu grimaced.

"Pick it up."

"There's no 'it' any longer."

"They haven't abandoned you."

Eyasu's face scrunched so tightly that it pulled on the scars lining his scalp. "I failed the test," he grated, as his thumb worked against his palm. "The Aspects have chosen the Raw, and I don't blame Them."

"Why not?"

"I tried to destroy Azure-Seven-Seven. I saw what he did to you and the others, what he must have done to Atera, and . . ."

A narrow line of blood wound its way down his palm.

Mavrin reached out, saying, "Hold on, there's still—"

"You think to tell me what's real?" Eyasu shouted, surging to his feet. Mavrin scrambled upright as his friend raised a bloody finger toward him. "You never believed! You turned your back the moment you learned the truth!"

"And haven't you been calling me a fool, all this time?"

"One fool convincing another."

"Now listen—"

"No! Not anymore!"

He swung, and for some reason Mavrin raised his arm to catch the blow. Eyasu's fist struck his open palm and he stumbled backward, feeling something tear under the fungal wraps. A thick backhand struck him across the face, knocking him to the ground.

When the stars cleared, Eyasu stood over him, wide-eyed with horror. He fell to his knees again, staring open-mouthed at his hands.

Mavrin hurried to his side, ignoring the tingling in his jaw as he laid a hand on the back of Eyasu's neck and placed the other on one massive shoulder.

"You're wrong," he said softly. "I'm so sorry, my friend."

"I've been wrong for a long time."

"That's not what I mean, dammit." Mavrin broke away and looked Eyasu in the eye. "You were right about the Aspects. The Catalyst as Core. You were *right* to believe, and I was wrong not to listen. But the Aspects have been listening all along."

He pointed at the two Castoff pieces, kicked aside when he fell. "I felt *Them*. Out in the Winds, They healed Atera."

"She's alive?" Eyasu asked, disbelieving.

Mavrin nodded. "I didn't save her. The Aspects chose to help. Somehow They heard me ask." Eyasu's brow furrowed. "I know how that sounds, but They're *paying attention*, Eyasu. Maybe to everyone, but especially to you, and I think They wanted me to know."

When he shook his head, Mavrin added, "Think about it. In Tanardell, your Request to bind Violet-Twenty succeeded. Why? Because the Aspects didn't understand what you were fighting. They've been watching ever since, picking and choosing the moments when it felt right to help you."

Eyasu was still breathing heavily. "They see our intentions in the instant before we do."

"But They aren't all-knowing." He tapped the side of his head. "Think about every time the Aspects helped you, and every time They haven't. What if there's a pattern, and we simply didn't realize?"

He and Deyeri worked it out while Atera recovered. After the Aspects helped him subdue Violet-Twenty, even if the first attempt didn't quite work, Their attitude toward his Requests changed. They protected the *Joyous Soul* on the Windroute and helped isolate Violet-Twenty further but didn't harm them or cut them off completely. They didn't answer Eyasu's Request in the Outreach, which would have caused Azure-Seven-Seven harm, but helped protect Aulina in the learning commons. Their actions so far weren't random, nor were they meant to judge Eyasu. The Aspects were learning about the Raw and avoiding taking a clear side. At least so far.

Eyasu eyed him. "You don't believe this."

"I do."

"Why?"

"Because now I know. They haven't abandoned us," Mavrin said, grinning. He pointed at the Castoff shards. "I'm betting They'll prove it to you."

The entire time, from measured speech to bellowing, there hadn't been a trace of hope in Eyasu's eyes. Mavrin saw that familiar flicker return now, enough to soften Eyasu's features and finally steady his breathing.

He snatched up both pieces of Castoff a lot quicker than Mavrin expected. Neither of them looked down.

Which meant that Mavrin saw the yellow light reflected on Eyasu's face first, before it illuminated the chamber. For a second, he thought he felt something, too, like he had outside. A passing glance, maybe, like from someone across the room. When the light faded back to its familiar glimmer, Eyasu's eyes were wide, staring down at the single, reforged Castoff in his hands.

Mavrin grunted. "I didn't entirely expect that to work."

"You aren't serious."

"Well, every trick has a margin for error," Mavrin admitted. "This one wouldn't lose me a thumb, so the odds were worth it."

Eyasu shook his head ruefully. "For once, I don't know what They expect me to do."

Now it was Mavrin's turn to give him a look. "The same as always, I imagine."

"Except we have no way of returning to Farglade."

From somewhere outside the chamber, an unmistakable whoop of triumph carried on the Winds. Mavrin grinned.

"Get your armor on. I think we're about ready to leave."

Chapter Thirty-Six

BRECK SAT IN HIS CRYSTAL ENCLOSURE AND thought about Pericar.

The last Lord-Magistrate hadn't been good at keeping the Raw secret. Knowing the truth, even less than what Breck knew now, broke the poor man's hold on reality. People explained away the strange behaviors and odd working hours as the result of four Incursions, until they continued and worsened long after. It was Deyeri wondering aloud about calling a new People's Vote that made Breck pry into Pericar's activities, discovering his notes about the Raw and then following him to the sanctum.

Deyeri had been right, of course. Breck knew as soon as Pericar told him he wanted to turn everything over to Veristenok and let the Requesters prowl the sanctum at will. Pericar insisted he was working in Farglade's best interest. Breck decided he was wrong.

It hadn't been the first time Breck sacrificed someone for his city's future, but the first time he'd used his own hands. Good people were always the ones he sacrificed. Like the ones who died during the Incursions, while he played strategy. And Termot, who had been as loyal to Farglade as anyone Breck knew. Except not loyal enough.

No one would find her body. Breck remembered where a few of the sanctum's side tunnels ended, and which ones plummeted into darkness. The chasm he chose went deep enough he didn't hear the impact.

As the sun set and the Lifesphere shifted to darker blue, messengers from the Lower Commanders came to report on their search for Azure-Seven-Seven. He offered the shortest responses he could, glad that they assumed and didn't ask whether their reports would make it to Termot. No one commented on his mood, but he doubted anyone noticed.

After all, he was Woldren Breck.

Someone new stopped outside the enclosure, and once again it wasn't anyone there to arrest or depose him. They didn't know he'd done anything wrong. As the guard approached, Breck noticed the dirt begin to vibrate, radiating outward from the enclosure. He knew without the guard's lack of reaction that only he was seeing this; the smell of char filling his nostrils gave away the Raw's sudden interest and excitement.

"Lord-Magistrate, the Voice is at the gate. With Lieutenant Havven."

Breck slouched back down when the guard didn't mention anyone else. He gestured half-heartedly, and she hurried away. Kedar and Azure-Seven-Seven appeared through the gloom shortly after, not looking much worse for their time in the Edgeplains. She held a familiar wooden box tucked under one arm. Havven's body looked different, and Breck realized he wasn't used to the lieutenant matching his eye level; the Raw wasn't bent at all under the Winds.

The ones in the sanctum below kept up a steady vibration in his bones, but he ignored them. He waved the guards away and stepped closer to Azure-Seven-Seven. "You know, it's damn eerie staring into a face I recognize, seeing someone else look back."

"I've been wondering something." That velvety tone was even stranger than the smile. "What if someone doesn't want to raise these koo beetles? Your allotment system provides everyone's basic needs, but assumes the able will contribute. What if the beetle keepers' children all want to be artists? Have you considered what would happen?"

Kedar rolled her eyes. "Been doing that since we left the island."

Breck studied the dariss shard pulsing softly at the Raw's neck. "You bound him?"

"Just like we read about. Fed enough energy through the crystals to link them together." Kedar looked a little too smug as she showed him the matching crystal looped around her wrist, but Breck couldn't be bothered to care. "Hasn't completely dulled his senses, but most of his power is limited. Energy suppressing energy, basically."

"Sort of like you're channeling," he mused.

Kedar fidgeted, as though the idea made her uncomfortable. "Not quite."

"Not sure I like the idea of one more Raw in my head."

"Inside anyone's, actually." Azure-Seven-Seven rolled his head languidly toward Kedar, making her flinch, before snapping his attention back to Breck. "You convinced yourself Pericar was a different person by the end, no? Almost a mercy, you called it?"

Breck stepped right into the Raw's face and was disappointed when he didn't react. "Want to show me something? Pretty sure I've seen worse."

Kedar stared at him. "Woldren. That isn't a good idea."

"You seem to think you know what you're doing," he growled, suddenly more tired with the Voice than he realized. "Take a little of that suppression away. I want to see."

He expected her to refuse and hoped that she could see how serious he was—that he would take the crystal from around her wrist if he had to. Whatever Azure-Seven-Seven mustered couldn't be worse than the other Raw. If he proved he could handle this, maybe they would all leave him alone.

Muttering a very un-Voice-like curse, Kedar closed her eyes and concentrated on her connection to the dariss.

When Breck looked away, it wasn't the Raw standing beside her anymore. It was Deyeri, looking exactly like she had during the last Incursion, when she marched into his command pit: younger, harder-edged, and her eyes full of hurt and betrayal. Her appearance shifted, the physical wounds healing while a cotton shirt and pants replaced her armor, and he knew which Deyeri she'd become. The one who realized her mistake trying to be more than comrades, since he didn't think they were ever really friends.

"You betrayed me again. Coward."

Breck growled and leapt forward, drawing his sword. Deyeri disappeared and the empty air around him filled with mangled, bloody figures in ruined Watch armor. Missing limbs, puncture holes peppering their bodies, or electrical burns across their exposed skin. Betrayal and rage contorted each face, and he recognized every single one.

The dead disappeared in a ring of crackling flame. The side of Breck's face started to burn; when he touched his cheek, he felt bubbly wetness instead of old scars and yanked his fingers away. Warmth spread down his body, like it had on the Craggs during the first Incursion, when he was certain the burning Towers would be the last thing he ever saw.

Someone gasped, but it wasn't him. The flames vanished and in the sudden darkness he pawed for his sword, finding it in the dirt a few meters away. As his eyes readjusted to the Lifesphere's midnight glimmer, Breck saw the Raw kneeling a few meters away, clawed hands halfway to the crystal embedded in Havven's neck.

Kedar stood with her crystal outstretched, crackles of blue energy rippling around her wrist. "Satisfied?" she asked Breck.

The guards stood further back. Neither of them looked his way as he struggled to his feet and sheathed his sword. Even trembling, the Raw forced out a malicious grin. Breck ignored it. He was still in control, and that's what counted.

He waved Kedar into the enclosure. "Deyeri?"

"Left her behind like you wanted. Alive."

Part of Breck wished he had told Kedar to bring her back.

He still wanted to explain things to her, if he could. Once they finished, he'd take a windship back to the island personally. By then he might have figured out how to include what happened to Termot when he told Deyeri the whole truth. When he finally helped her see why he made these choices, for Farglade.

Breck could feel the Raw watching as he crouched and pressed the switch hidden in the enclosure floor. Havven's tongue clicked in mock amazement as the hatch slid aside.

The sharp comment that came to mind fell from Breck's lips as twirling, multicolored lines appeared on the enclosure walls. They coalesced into stick drawings that reminded him too much of people being torn apart by wolves. Within seconds the humanoid figures vanished, and the wolves paced across the stone, impatient for another meal. The Raw didn't bother with static this time.

He turned to Kedar. "Keep a tight hold on that box."

"I would be happy to teach you more about our ways, in exchange for releasing Violet-Twenty-Four-Ten to my care," Azure-Seven-Seven said. When Kedar snorted, he added, "There are always deals to be made. You should know."

Kedar glowered and opened her mouth, but Breck snatched the box from her.

"Enough," he snapped. "Just remember who's in charge." He shook the box for emphasis and turned his back to the Raw, heading underground.

This time, the sanctum matched the crystal enclosure outside. Smooth walls and ceiling replaced the rough-hewn stone from before, giving off a soft natural light close to early morning under the Lifesphere. Kedar barely looked around beside him, per usual; the one time he asked, she said she never saw anything but natural stone. They passed the carvings to the Aspects, which he still couldn't see, and turned the corner toward the massive chamber that served as the sanctum's heart.

He heard scratching and noticed Aulina yank her bound hands

away from a tiny stalagmite, at the bottom of the steep, sloping path into the chamber. Breck checked that she was still bound and tugged the rope a little tighter.

She inched away when she saw the box in his hands.

"Don't worry," Breck said, gesturing back at Azure-Seven-Seven. "Found a new negotiator."

Surprisingly, Aulina didn't ask what might happen to her now. "I'm sorry for you. Losing your way like this."

Breck ignored her and led the others inside. When the Raw saw the massive, curved walls and ceiling, dariss shining under the averblossom lamps, he smiled so wide that Breck worried about Havven's jaw. They climbed the path onto the wide dais, where the ground had been smoothed long before Breck discovered it. Three metal tables at the opposite end of the dais supported Kedar's equipment: panels with buttons and switches that resembled the operating stations for Farglade's defense cannons, except with different-sized dariss crystals connected in places. Cables curled over the edge to the sanctum walls. Uekel's notes mentioned crystal screens that could display information, almost like a slate, but Kedar couldn't recreate them based on his passing references. Instead, she would have to play with the controls and monitor changes in the dariss by sight and sound, hopefully with Azure-Seven-Seven's help.

The crystal illusion didn't extend here; Breck always saw the pure dariss deposit that encircled the room. Faint, smoky shapes moved along the surface, darting away whenever he looked directly at them. He had never been able to count them, but knowing what they did now about the Raw, trying didn't seem important.

He held up the box, gestured at Azure-Seven-Seven and called out, "Finally found what you're looking for."

The Raw in the deposit didn't respond, either with visions or pressure on his mind.

"Next step is to release you. But let's discuss some terms first—"

Something heavy and loud boomed against his temples. Breck winced as a dozen images of death and pain flashed through his mind, each one more imaginative than the last.

He waited for it to pass. “Don’t take this the wrong way,” he said, managing a crooked smirk, “but I wouldn’t blame you for incinerating me and Kedar as soon as we start setting you free. We don’t want to harm anyone, but your kind stay bound until I’m sure our arrangement stays amicable. Understood?”

Nothing else buffeted his senses. Along the dariss, the shadowy shapes moved more slowly. They seemed to be waiting, and he took that as a good sign.

“Let’s start, Kedar.”

She didn’t respond.

A powerful hand grabbed Breck’s shoulder and spun him around. Before he could reach for his sword, Azure-Seven-Seven tore the sheath from his belt and flung it away. He grabbed the wooden box next, tossing it to Kedar. Her expression was flat as she caught it one-handed. The dariss crystal crackled on her other wrist.

“Everything we’ve learned, and all you want is power.” Kedar tucked the box back into her robes. “You know you’re pathetic? No different than the people who nearly destroyed Aelda in the first place.”

“What in the abyss are you doing?”

“What I thought you’d do, with all your talk of freedom from the Unity.” She gestured at the dariss around them. “The Raw don’t deserve to be used again, by anyone.”

Breck tried to break from Azure-Seven-Seven’s grip, but it was like a vise. He pointed at the crystal lodged in Havven’s neck and gave Kedar a withering look.

“He needs a demonstration of trust. I can understand that. Showing the Aspects the truth will be enough of one, won’t it, Azure?”

That sent an unexpected spike of panic through Breck. "Thought the idea was They never have to know."

"Your idea, maybe. The sooner They find out everything, the sooner we know our place." She looked at the ceiling, but Breck suspected she was staring further than the dariss. "Can't trust Their love if it's based on bad information."

The details of the sanctum wavered around Breck, obscuring his sight. As Kedar circled the dais, Azure-Seven-Seven turned him in place; it wasn't long before he lost track of where he stood relative to its edges.

"You didn't do too well convincing them, by the way," Kedar said, gesturing at the sanctum walls. "Especially after I took a turn. But I actually listen to people. You just murder them."

"I'm no murderer," Breck said, even as he imagined the weight of Termot's body in his hands, and Pericar's look of shock before the bladetube plunged through his neck.

"Oh, please. People are usually more honest with a Voice." Kedar closed her eyes, hearing something Breck couldn't. "Time to work, Woldren. I won't make you wait around. Toss him outside."

Breck looked around as he stumbled, hoping to get some sense of what was really under his feet. Except everything stayed blurry, right up to the moment Azure-Seven-Seven grabbed him by the throat and lifted him into the air.

Chapter Thirty-Seven

MAVRIN BARELY FELT THE JOLT THIS TIME AS Deyeri steered the scuttleboat around another massive crevasse. One hand pressed tight to his fungal wraps, he felt his skeleton rattling apart from the constant vibrations of the vessel's legs striking the ground, thump-thumping like a giant millipede. He had no idea how anyone could manage an attack after reaching Farglade in one. Even though it moved faster than he would have expected, an hour of this made him wish for a windship.

Not for the first time, Atera half-stood to peer around the cracked glass screen at the fore, her braid whipping behind her as she searched the horizon. "What do you think Kedar wants with the Raw?"

He had to shout over the Winds. "If we're lucky, something that takes a lot of time."

When the *Joyous Soul* still didn't materialize, Atera sat back down. This was the third time she'd checked for her ship, even though she must have known it would've reached Farglade well ahead of them. She noticed his attention and shifted uncomfortably in her seat.

Mavrin patted the scuttleboat's hull. "This old wreck is holding up better than I thought." When Atera didn't brighten as much as he hoped, he added, "A little wear can be a strength sometimes. Isn't that right, Commander?"

Deyeri didn't respond, but she wasn't paying him much attention. She hadn't been any more pleased about leaving her fallen people behind than Atera had about Vek, but even if they had time for the dead, the scuttleboat barely accommodated the six of them.

And then there was Eyasu, sitting silently between Ryld and Emar on the bench closest to the helm. Every now and then, Mavrin noticed his hand on the pouch where he kept his Castoff. The tightness in his face betrayed his whirling thoughts, but not with the same pain as the two outbursts Mavrin had witnessed. His friend was recalibrating, he guessed, and he could only hope Eyasu was ready when they reached their destination.

Atera stood at the bow again, pointing. "How long was I unconscious again?"

In the distance, the horizon glowed. Except morning was still hours away, and the bluish tint looked more like one of Farglade's heatwells than the sun.

Deyeri cursed loud enough to be heard over the Winds, and the scuttleboat's legs hammered harder against the ground.

It was the dariss.

Deyeri could tell even before Farglade's northern buildings sharpened in her vision. Her architects built their first Incursion monument along the Zerrilen Craggs, facing the Edgeplains for any future attackers to see, along with the imposing cannons the Requesters created. Three times the size of the inverted triangle near Yeldin's shop, it glowed bright blue against the Towers, like someone set a gas flame in the center and cranked the valves to full.

Eyasu stood up sharply, rocking the scuttleboat and making Mavrin cry out. "We lost too much time."

Beyond the Craggs, everything melded together into solid blue radiance, impossible to count individual light sources. For all she could tell, every individual pillar, wall, or statue of dariss in the city had started to glow. She leaned harder on the control levers, willing the scuttleboat to pick up more speed, refusing to accept that they were too late. At her nod, Ryld and Emar waved toward the cannons, to catch the attention of the Watch on duty. Even without a flag or markings, the scuttleboat was unmistakable from afar.

None of the cannons so much as budged. As they reached the Craggs, nothing moved on the platforms around them. They passed into the Windroute without being challenged, and as they entered the airdock, Deyeri didn't see any Watch along the walls or the sailboard platforms. In fact, she didn't see anyone. Only the glow of the dariss, while they searched for a cliff to scale.

Woldren, please don't be responsible for this.

"I see the *Soul*!" Atera pointed west, where her windship hung from one of the upper berths. Its forward shell was closed, and the barriers around the berth made it impossible to see if anyone stood around it.

"We need to get to the Keep," Deyeri snapped.

At the captain's hollow-eyed look, a crack broke through the familiar, focused energy that overtook Deyeri since the island. She was thinking tactically, fixated on one goal: getting to Breck. Not the Keep or the Raw, but to him. Despite everything, he still managed to get her thinking like him again.

To the hells with that. Calling out for everyone to hold on, she steered the scuttleboat sharply to the right, directly for the Windroute walls.

Scaling the Windroute wasn't as straightforward as Deyeri hoped, even having seen it done during the Incursions. Mavrin cursed her the entire time they rattled up the cliffs, pausing only to holler in terror when the scuttleboat's starboard legs slipped on the rock halfway up and they almost flipped backward to their deaths. By the time they ground their way onto an empty berth, bending the wind barriers in the process, the gearwork engine spewed steam from places it shouldn't and one of the control levers had snapped off in Deyeri's hands. The scuttleboat settled with a heavy thud, legs refusing to fold together like they should have. Despite its place of origin, Deyeri patted the side of the hull as they disembarked.

Without the clatter of the scuttleboat, Farglade's silence sunk in. No shouts or screams in the distance. No panic. That alone made her tense, along with a totally different unease she couldn't quite identify, separate from being surrounded by glowing dariss.

Eyasu paused nearby, slowly studying the city around them, but before she could ask if he felt the same thing he wandered away, murmuring under his breath.

She noticed too late Atera racing across the dock. The *Soul*'s gangplank sat against the platform, though the access door was shut. Atera burst inside as soon as she unlocked the door, and Deyeri signaled Ryld and Emar to keep watch while she and Mavrin followed.

They found her only a few steps beyond, staring around the *Soul*'s deck. She swayed in place as she took in the half-dozen bodies scattered about, including one leaning limply against the ladder to the forecastle. Mavrin placed a hand on her arm to steady her, while Deyeri crossed to the person at the ladder, someone about Atera's age wearing a miniature spyglass around their neck.

They had a pulse.

"I did fight him." Atera needed to swallow before she could finish. "He was going to hurt them, and . . . I could've stopped this."

Deyeri took in the subtle twitches and rapid eye movements among the crew. "No one could stop this," she said.

Except she didn't mean it. Someone could have stopped this, and that person was standing impotently on an airdock, days after she should've grabbed Breck by the shirt and held him over the Windroute, until he told her what he was hiding.

"Commander!"

Deyeri raced back outside, following Ryld's pointing to the nearest tunnel entrance. The two dariss pillars flanking the entrance had started to glow. Eyasu stood watching them from a few steps away. Joining him, Deyeri saw the stone floor near the pillars ripple like water. As the bizarre effect transferred to the walls on either side, she could have sworn she saw something move along the pillars' surface, like a shadow.

"Please tell me Azure-Seven-Seven isn't this strong."

"No." Eyasu's eyes widened, sounding steadier when he added, "There must be more Raw."

Once he said it, that unclear feeling in her gut crystalized. She'd felt it before, on the Edgeplains with Havven during the Incursions: that certainty that an approaching force was about to engulf your own, and there was nothing you could do. Her sword arm jerked, and she reached to steady it.

"That is what Azure-Seven-Seven and Violet-Twenty wanted," Eyasu continued. "More of their kind. They're being freed."

Huge sounds crashed in the distance, like a building collapsing. As Deyeri searched for the source, she spotted figures emerging from the next tunnel over. She counted a dozen Watch, all of them armed with swords and cablers, led by a corporal she recognized: Klennen, a square-faced man with ochre skin and a nervous twitch. She placed a hand on her sword, remembering the Walkway, until Klennen snapped his hands back and forth in the sign of the Catalyst as Protector—with more vigor than any other Watch she knew, per usual.

"Klennen? What in the hells is going on here?"

"You taught me not to guess without evidence, Commander." Klennen gestured at the pillars. "This has been happening for almost an hour. Lord-Magistrate Breck ordered everyone indoors, but we have no idea—"

"Is Breck still at the Keep?"

"As far as we know. We haven't received orders since."

His clipped tone wavered as he said it, and the same uncertainty marked the faces of the other Watch. Termot should have issued orders in response to this, but she could think of a half-dozen reasons why none had come, liking each one less.

"Four Incursions," she reminded them. "That's how many we beat." Klennen's back straightened, and several others followed suit. "Maintain your patrol. Make sure no one is on the streets." She wished she could assume Breck ordered the lockdown to help search for the Raw, but at this point she wasn't assuming anything. "Incursion protocol stands. Spread the word."

Klennen looked surprised but snapped a salute and led his squad away.

"Incursion protocol?" Mavrin asked, emerging from the *Soul* with Atera.

"Means we lock everything down. No answering individual requests for help." Deyeri tried not to think about someone in their home, watching a Raw materialize from their dariss front door, but anyone trying to help would only put themselves in danger.

"Meanwhile we head for the Keep." It wasn't a question, and the hard edge to Mavrin's voice surprised her until he added, "We left Aulina with Breck."

"We need to go." Atera stayed at the top of the *Soul*'s gangplank, watching her crew, hand visibly trembling against the access door. "Will they . . . ?"

"If we can contain the Raw," Eyasu said, "your crew should be released." His normal baritone returned more each time he spoke, but Deyeri noticed he didn't offer to Request a solution. Either he didn't think it would work, or he didn't think the Aspects would answer. "We won't judge you for remaining here."

Atera touched the quartz disc framed in silver that symbolized the Catalyst among her pendants. She said to Eyasu, "The Catalyst as Core is all about connection, right? That we all have a purpose?"

For the first time Deyeri had seen, Eyasu looked uncomfortable being asked about his Aspect-variation. "Yes."

"Then don't try to talk me out of coming," Atera said, and locked the access behind her.

Not every piece of dariss in Farglade glowed, but more than enough to bathe the entire city in blue. Mavrin watched crystal specks blink along the side of a two-story residence, the height of which no longer made him nervous compared to the dariss fused through its body. In the distance, the buildings along the Tiers looked hazy, like the dusty air that preceded a Longwind. Mavrin wracked his brain for any specific mention of something like this in the *Accounts*, but either he couldn't remember or there wasn't one. Possibly because Uekel deliberately left that out, or Kedar removed those sections from her copy.

He kept expecting to hear screams. The silence surrounding Farglade closed in on him with this terrifying finality, considering the obvious evidence of either the Aspects turning on humanity or something beyond Their power. Somehow, he would have preferred the panic he always envisioned during his research with Eyasu.

A few blocks from the airdock, he discovered the reason. Two men in long, sleeveless coats stood facing one of Deyeri's inverted-triangle monuments. Mavrin noticed the tattoos on their arms and necks immediately—their life stories, inked for the Hidden as Fatedraw—bathed in the harsh blue glow from the monument. Neither of the men reacted when Deyeri called for their attention. Mavrin circled around to look them in the eye, some instinct warning him not to focus on the dariss.

Neither man reacted, mouths hanging open slightly and eyes unblinking.

Ryld started toward them, but Mavrin waved them back. "Too risky. The Raw are taking hold of them."

"Like the coins," Deyeri said. "When I looked at the ones Yeldin gave me, it was like staring into a puzzle. Almost didn't want to look away."

Mavrin's exhaustion, his injuries, and his terror all began to jumble. He couldn't think of a way to help the two Fatedraw followers without getting too close to the dariss; yanking them away with his bindcord might not break the hold on them, and that was his least ludicrous idea.

"We must continue," Eyasu said, soft but determined. "We must be strong."

Blinking back tears, Mavrin nodded and followed him away.

When they reached the Keep, Deyeri waved for them to skirt along the outer wall. Each gate they passed was closed and locked. Mavrin didn't see any guards, but Deyeri told them to hunker beside the gate as she and Ryld climbed over, wiggling between the wrought-iron bars on top. Not that there was much shadow to hide in if someone approached from the street. A few minutes later, a section of wall nearby swung open, revealing a doorway like the one Mavrin and Deyeri used to access the sailboard.

Her expression was carefully neutral. "The grounds are empty except for two guards stationed around back. By that pompous enclosure."

"Deyeri—"

"Stay low and close. Keep your eyes open," she said in a tight voice, and led them through the doorway.

Mavrin matched Eyasu's stooped posture and rapid pace as closely as possible across the grounds. They stuck close to the covered tarps raised around the path to the Gannerthen Building, how they shuddered under the Winds hopefully muffling their footsteps. Mavrin couldn't see a single light in any windows; even the gaslamps around the pavilion were dim. The dariss here didn't glow, either.

Deyeri stopped them at a corner so she could peer around at the entrance. She flashed a command at Emar and Ryld with her trailing hand and gestured for everyone to follow her forward.

The two guards outside the enclosure stiffened, hands lingering near their swords.

"Ma'am, you're not supposed to—"

"Where's Breck?" Deyeri demanded. She stopped outside of their sword reach. "Or Kedar. I'll take either."

The guards exchanged a look, clearly uncertain—and not controlled, thankfully.

"Eyes on me," Deyeri snapped. "What about Lieutenant Havven? Either of you seen him?"

Both guards' eyes went wide.

Deyeri's shoulders drooped. When she spoke again, her voice lost some of its sharpness. "You've seen the dariss out there? I need to speak to the Lord-Magistrate. Please."

One of the guards moved his hand from his sword. "Voice Kalle said she left you behind. Didn't mean for us to hear." It was clear on his face how much he liked that. "They went below. Lord Breck, the Voice, and Lieutenant Havven. A couple hours ago. Then the dariss started glowing."

What about Aulina? Mavrin wondered, but before he could ask, Eyasu stepped forward. "Below where?"

The guard pointed at the center of the enclosure. "There's a hatch hidden there. It closed after they went through. I didn't see how he opened it."

While Eyasu examined the stonework, Deyeri said to the guards, "What about Commander Termot?" The two men shook their heads. "Okay, stay here. If Termot comes back, let her know where we are. If Breck or Kedar come out, detain them. Understood?"

The guards nodded, and Deyeri directed Emar and Ryld to take position with them.

Mavrin heard something grind inside the enclosure. Eyasu stepped back as a wide patch of stone tile slid aside, revealing a staircase descending into the ground.

"Ancient construction," Eyasu noted. "Possibly from the Time Before Unity."

"It seems less likely that Breck is innocent in this," Mavrin said to Deyeri.

She drew her sword. "Let's find out."

As she descended, Mavrin asked Eyasu, "Shouldn't we figure out a plan?"

"Until we see exactly what we're facing, any plan is merely guesswork." A ghost of his old hopefulness crossed Eyasu's face. "For now, simply have faith."

At Mavrin's desperately bemused look, he added, "In the four of us."

Chapter Thirty-Eight

THE STAIRS DESCENDED DEEP ENOUGH AND TURNED in enough places that Mavrin wondered if the cavern at the bottom led beneath the Windroute. He'd read accounts of damp, humid tunnels like this, where early explorers post-Fracture went looking for water deposits after the lakes and rivers dried out. This tunnel was bone dry, however, like the one Deyeri brought him down to escape Azure-Seven-Seven. *And now we're likely marching right to him.*

There was no phosphorescent lichen here to light their way, but the natural minerals shone under Eyasu's alchemical flare and Deyeri's humming salt lamp. No one spoke as they continued, until Mavrin spotted familiar carvings in the rock overhead, spaced at regular intervals. The first was ovoid, about half a meter wide and long enough to span the cavern. In the center, the ancient figure of the Catalyst as Protector held a diamond-shaped shield in both hands, so that its outer side pointed down at the floor.

"Pre-Fracture iconography," he told Atera.

"And the Hidden as Test, here." Eyasu pointed at the ceiling several meters ahead.

Mavrin joined him and saw the familiar Aspect-variation, holding a scale in each hand. "Unusual combination, these two."

"Some cultures argued the Hidden as Test controlled the world's unnatural forces." Eyasu pointed toward the first carving. "And that beseeches protection."

"What do these say?" Atera traced her finger under an inscription carved around the Hidden's hands, written in T'var.

Eyasu said, "Mostly names, I believe, with an epitaph . . . 'those who sealed away our doom.'"

Deyeri had continued even further. "Wasn't this carved on that book of yours?"

Mavrin wriggled past the others to see what she meant. Scratched into the side of the wall, instead of the ceiling, were the unmistakable gears and interconnected lines of the Fifth Progress, Uekel's guild.

"I've never seen this in the other tunnels," Deyeri said.

Whatever Breck kept secret down there, Uekel had hidden first.

Past the carvings, different branches of the cavern twisted further into the bedrock. Mavrin and Atera followed one to a dead end, where the wall was spiderwebbed with lines of dariss, likely snaking toward the surface. When they rejoined Eyasu and Deyeri, they learned that another branch veered sharply to the right before dropping into an open chasm.

From there, the passage continued for another sixty paces or so before sloping upward into a larger space, lit from within by a soft, blue-white glow.

Someone with shaggy white hair lay crumpled near the foot of the slope.

Deyeri beckoned Mavrin to follow her. He held the sheathed rapier with one hand to keep it from bouncing against his leg. Deyeri managed to move without a sound.

Fresh scrapes and bruises crisscrossed Breck's face, and dried blood matted his hair. His eyes snapped open and he started to pull away, until Deyeri grabbed his arm. She tapped her ear and pointed up the sloping path. Mavrin tilted his head to listen, and eventually caught it: the low sound of a voice, somewhere in the chamber beyond.

Together they hoisted Breck to his feet and helped him back around the bend in the tunnel. When they released him, he sagged to the ground and rubbed the side of his head. "Should've known you'd make it back somehow."

Deyeri crouched in front of him. "What are you and Kedar doing?"

Breck started to rise, but Eyasu loomed over him, arms crossed. "We don't have time for this."

"And why's that, Woldren?" Deyeri snapped, her firm affect slipping. "If Kedar is in there with your new friend, why are you out here looking like the bad side of a bar fight? And no more of your *bullshit*."

"We were supposed to contain them together." Breck blinked, as though surprised at what he said.

Mavrin saw Deyeri's stern expression crack, and realized that up until that moment, she hadn't fully believed he was involved. Her voice turned cold. "What have you done?"

"We *don't have time—*"

"Then speak fast."

Breck wiped blood from the corner of his mouth. "Before I do . . . you have to believe I wanted to tell you. They wouldn't let me."

"The Raw," Eyasu said.

He nodded. "Got into my mind. Like they did with Pericar. I tried to tell you in my office, Dey, and they . . ." He looked stricken, no longer the blank-faced leader they met in the Keep.

Mavrin expected sympathy on Deyeri's face, but her expression only hardened. "Tell me."

"Our plan was to contain the Raw. Kedar found more notes from the *Accounts*. Things we didn't share with you, about how Uekel used dariss. Creating energy and trapping the Raw. Without needing to channel."

"How?" Eyasu asked, his posture shifting as he grew more alert.

"Damned if I understand it. Kedar said she could only figure out some. Which might've been a lie." He stared down the tunnel.

"There's a dariss deposit down there *filled* with Raw. Uekel trapped them. They could feel more of their kind nearby, so I thought if I offered to reunite them, they'd let their guard down. Then Kedar could draw them from the dariss."

"You were going to let them go?" Atera asked, eyes wide.

Mavrin snorted. "Of course not. He would've destroyed them."

"For the dariss," Eyasu finished, his hushed voice betraying his horror.

Breck looked imploringly at Deyeri. "Untapped power, Dey. A resource the Unity doesn't have. We'd be free of them completely, with something even the Bastion would be desperate to get their hands on."

Deyeri stared at him the same way she'd looked at Azure-Seven-Seven in her sitting room. Seeing that pain broke Mavrin's heart. His boot twitched as he thought about kicking Breck into an abyss.

"Why did Kedar betray you?" Eyasu asked.

"Said the Raw don't deserve to be betrayed again." Breck wouldn't meet Deyeri's eyes anymore.

"She's releasing them," Mavrin said to the others. "That's what we're seeing in the city. The Raw preparing to break free."

He had no idea what would happen after. If the Raw couldn't survive outside some sort of host, they would take control of an untold number of innocent civilians. If their rage compared at all to Azure-Seven-Seven's, they might simply destroy Farglade and move on. Unless the Aspects passed judgment first.

Or if you decide to step in . . . Mavrin thought into the ether.

Deyeri stepped away from Breck, dropping her grip on his arm like a discarded weight. "Garris and Aulina?"

"They have the girl in there. Garris . . ."

As he trailed off, Deyeri's expression somehow turned even colder. Mavrin's instincts told him to step between her and Breck, but he didn't care to.

"What else could I do, Dey? The Lifesphere shields us, but we have to shield—"

Deyeri grabbed him by the collar, and Mavrin thought she was going to punch him. With a growl, she let him go, shoving him hard against the wall. She veered away from everyone, eyes searching, until she found a random patch of stone to press her forehead into while she let out a long, slow breath. Mavrin let two heartbeats pass, but before he could say anything Deyeri started walking again, and all he and the others could do was follow her around the bend.

They left Breck sitting against the wall.

Mavrin stayed within a couple strides of Deyeri, but his mind whirled with too much—the Raw, Kedar, Aulina somewhere in here, and more. Until he saw Deyeri stumble, ever so slightly, and Atera catch her elbow for a moment, and realized that he couldn't fall to pieces now.

Beside him, Eyasu sorted through equipment from his rucksack and started attaching extra knives and pouches to his belt, though none of the former were as large as his lost longknife. Seeing that methodical process return helped Mavrin shake off a few of his nerves.

"Now you have more knives?"

Eyasu actually smirked as he double-checked his longsword. He handed over several pouches, which Mavrin recognized as packed with the reagents he used in the orchard. "If I should fall, please take my Castoff away from here."

That jarred a sour look from Mavrin. "You should know I'm not running off without you. Not again."

Eyasu's smile wasn't large or filled with mirth, but it was better than nothing.

Deyeri and Atera had stopped ahead, whispering about twenty meters from where they found Breck.

"Atera will keep an eye on him," Deyeri said, pointing back down the tunnel. "I need someone I trust making sure he stays."

Mavrin didn't like the idea of leaving anyone alone at this point, but Atera looked determined. "Whatever needs doing," she said, touching her pendants as she moved back down the corridor.

The sloping path ahead led to a stone dais, naturally created by its uneven edges, hanging over a massive, spherical cavern. Dariss covered the entire ceiling and floor, lit from within by the Raw. Shadowy shapes moved beneath the surface, reminding him of how Violet-Twenty manifested themself in the orchard. Wherever the Raw passed, Mavrin spotted T'var phrases etched into the dariss, either a component of the binding or simply for the comfort of Uekel and his accomplices.

As Deyeri led them up the sloping path, Mavrin drew his rapier as quietly as possible, cursing the soft whoosh of metal on leather.

He spotted Aulina first, seated on the ground to his left. She looked physically unharmed, bound by rope she was trying to break against the rock behind her. To her credit, she didn't make a noise when she saw them, instead tilting her head toward the three tables at the dais's other end. Kedar leaned over these with her back to the entrance, examining an unfamiliar collection of machinery. Mavrin could see nodes made from dariss, between the size of a fist and a takka skull, some of them attached to cables that snaked between the machines and out across the dais. He wasn't sure he could figure out what the equipment did even if he could examine it, but it did remind him of something: the vision he received from Azure-Seven-Seven, of the Fifth Progress researchers.

In a rough, almost disinterested voice, Kedar said, "Too late. It's already started."

"What's started?" Deyeri asked.

"The conversation. The only one that matters."

Mavrin didn't see Azure-Seven-Seven. He stepped to one side and glanced over the dais, tracking cables running down to the stone floor, their ends melted to fuse with the sanctum walls. A stack of books stood to the left of Kedar's tables, supporting a familiar wooden box with three faintly glowing coins inside—Violet-Twenty waiting inside to be freed, along with the other Raw.

"You want to know if we've earned Their love," Eyasu said, stepping closer. He held both palms out, longsword sheathed at his hip. "My fear is similar. Voice or Servant, even we can doubt."

"This isn't about doubt." Over her shoulder, Kedar's face looked red and splotchy. "It's about truth." One of the machines sparked, drawing her attention. While she made an adjustment, her other hand pointed at the dariss surrounding them. "You haven't heard it yet, so you don't understand. But you will."

"We all know what happened," Eyasu said, taking another step. "There are other ways to solve this." He hesitated, attention flicking back to Mavrin before he added, "The Aspects *are* listening, Kedar."

"Not to the right people."

Are you listening now? Mavrin wondered. Were the Aspects paying attention to this moment?

"You're using them, too," Aulina said. Deyeri crouched beside her, working to remove her bonds. "Think about it. Where's the kindness in turning the Raw against the Aspects?"

Kedar whirled, expression hard. "Can't just release them. They wouldn't survive. If I recalibrate this equipment, build on Uekel's instructions, the Raw can speak through the dariss. Like waves without a cable. The Aspects will hear them." Her shoulders sagged. "They'll probably destroy us. But we deserve it."

"We can find another option," Eyasu insisted. "The Aspects are not ignorant."

"No, that would be us." Kedar turned her back again. "Make them go away."

A breeze against his neck was Mavrin's only warning. Turning, all he could see was Azure-Seven-Seven's grin, close enough that he could smell salt and damp rot from Havven's body. He froze as

Eyasu stepped in from the left, only to be shoved backward. Deyeri went sprawling next, leaving Mavrin on his own.

"This would be much easier without limitation," the Raw said languidly, gesturing at the crystal wedged into Havven's neck. Kedar didn't respond, focused on her machinery again. "Alas."

Mavrin didn't know what to do. Or really, he didn't know what *They* wanted him to do. For the first time in sixteen years, he was actively waiting for a sign from the Aspects. He'd asked, but he didn't feel that shiver of attention like before.

"We can help you," he heard himself say to Azure-Seven-Seven.

With a sneer, the Raw lunged forward. Instinct screamed at Mavrin to run. Instead, he flicked his right wrist, loosing the dagger from his drop sheath when it touched his palm. As the Raw caught it without looking, Mavrin threw one of Eyasu's pouches into his face, followed by a pellet at his feet. A thick plume of gray smoke filled the space around Azure-Seven-Seven as he hissed in surprise.

A crack sounded and the Raw staggered, blood bursting from a pebble-sized wound in Havven's cheek. Deyeri dropped the bladetube and drew her cabler, but before she could fire, the Raw raised a hand and she crumpled, clutching her chest. The dagger Mavrin threw hadn't been caught, but its blade sunk into Havven's palm, steam issuing around the wound.

Azure-Seven-Seven narrowly sidestepped a sweeping chop from Eyasu. Mavrin suddenly found himself locked in an elaborate dance: Eyasu twirling his longsword, Mavrin following with basic thrusts, mindful of his wraps, and the Raw twisting left and right to avoid them. Every strike caught air or a piece of Havven's tattered clothing, until Mavrin feinted to one side and cut forward, slicing through the hip almost exactly how the Raw had stabbed him. Azure-Seven-Seven yanked sideways, tearing a chunk of Havven's flesh free as he evaded Eyasu's wide sweep. He grabbed Eyasu by his armor and threw him backward with enough force that he practically bounced off the dais's surface. Eyasu clattered down the sloping path, almost toppling into Deyeri, face tight with pain as she clutched her midsection.

Mavrin snapped back to see the Raw pointing at his skull. He felt warmth climbing the sides of his neck, like he had in Deyeri's living room.

"No need to fear, magician," Azure-Seven-Seven cooed. "You'll feel better once I've taken that maelstrom from you."

Rope snapped, and then Aulina stood between them, and the warmth was gone.

Her shoulders shook under her vest, but her hands were steady as she held her palms toward the Raw, as though she intended to fight barehanded. The Raw's eyes flicked between both palms, brow furrowed. Behind him, Kedar looked up from her work, attention drawn by the momentary quiet.

When Aulina's fingers came level with her shoulders, Mavrin saw it: a glimmer outlining her skin, like someone traced the outside of her body in phosphorescence. Like the light that encased her in the learning commons.

I asked for Aulina to be protected from that which would harm her. And the Catalyst Responded.

Azure-Seven-Seven's confusion flicked away, and he surged forward.

Eyasu roared as he slammed into the Raw from behind. Azure-Seven-Seven tried to turn, but Eyasu kept pushing, using speed and momentum to reach the edge of the dais.

And then followed the Raw over the side, plummeting to the rock below.

Chapter Thirty-Nine

SHOUTING AND THE CLATTER OF WEAPONS ECHOED down the tunnel, drawing Atera's attention. Breck kept his gaze on her.

"Deyeri's wrong. Not smart to hold anyone in reserve."

"My family's in danger because of you," Atera said, her eyes fixed toward the fight. "My home."

He could hear the tremble in her voice.

"You really want to risk losing anyone else?" Breck asked.

Eyasu landed on the Raw, the rattle of the impact almost knocking him senseless. He rolled away, empty hands searching for his longsword. The moment he felt the hilt under his fingers, a fist struck him in the jaw, beating him into the nearest wall.

Havven's shoulder and spine cracked as Azure-Seven-Seven set bones back into place. Only three fingers and part of the palm remained on the hand he rose to brace his neck, the rest torn away with Mavrin's dagger. Steam rose from the gaping wound.

Eyasu held his longsword in a guard position. Whatever binding Kedar had managed permitted some strength and channeling, but not all the Raw's capabilities. That meant he had a chance to separate the creature from Lieutenant Havven, if he could find and remove the coins where they embedded themselves. Quick enough to help the others confront Kedar, maybe. But keeping the Raw occupied would be enough.

The Aspects are watching, Eyasu.

"I don't wish to harm you," he said. "I would rather help."

"Were you not paying attention, false Requester?" A final crack as the Raw readied himself. "Your kind aren't the champions here."

"I would rather help."

Azure-Seven-Seven snarled as images flashed through Eyasu's mind, faster than he could resist. Ohanna lying facedown in the woods. Aulina in the mortuary with her neck twisted. Vertsa crumbling into the Windroute. The people of Farglade murdering each other, while he watched, helpless.

He chased the visions from his mind as the Raw tore his longsword away. Eyasu drew a knife and slashed, hoping to keep enough pressure on the Raw that he couldn't launch another mental assault. Once he found an opening, he could think about disabling him completely.

Catalyst, I tried another way.

Mavrin grimaced at the pull on his fungus wrap as he helped Deyeri up. She winced lifting her sword, leaving the broken cabler on the ground. When their eyes met, he wanted to offer a reassuring smile, but his mouth only twitched. Deyeri gripped his arm anyway, to steady *him*, and he wondered how he ever accomplished anything without her strength.

Aulina joined them, that faint glow still twinkling along her fingertips, as they approached Kedar. The Voice had gone back to ignoring them, flitting between her machines. On the walls, the shadowy shapes of the Raw picked up speed. Mavrin peered carefully over the edge of the dais and saw Eyasu, feinting and jabbing to keep Azure-Seven-Seven at bay.

"I'll help him," Deyeri said, strain pulling at her voice. "Stop Kedar."

She started down the ramp, thankfully not leaping off the edge like Eyasu had.

As Mavrin and Aulina rushed toward Kedar, every dariss node on her tables exploded with light. Ozone struck his nostrils and crackling filled his ears, broken only by Aulina's gasp of pain beside him. Through his fingers, Mavrin saw sparks fly from cables, meaning there was a salt battery somewhere in that mess, unless Kedar figured out how to generate power from the dariss itself.

Mavrin snapped out his bindcord. It wrapped around Kedar's forearm and he tugged, spinning her around. Kedar's other hand came up faster, clutching a dariss piece no bigger than a smoke pellet. When she pressed it to the bindcord the leather sizzled a handspan in either direction, then disintegrated into dust.

The dariss crackled as Kedar pointed it at him and Aulina. "I'd stop there. This is for all of us."

"How?" Aulina cried. "You're hoping the Aspects kill us."

The Voice blinked at her. "Of course not. I want Them to forgive us. I just don't think They will."

Facing her, Mavrin understood how his audience felt, back when he performed large, dangerous tricks in massive underground theaters. They knew the magician was *supposed* to succeed, that a good magician thought out every way a trick could fail and tried to prevent it. Except there was no way to ensure the outcome until you reached the finale. The key was to commit, and hope.

Kedar must have seen something in his eyes. "I don't believe it. You still want to fight me."

Mavrin shared a look with Aulina. "We don't," he said. He studied those flickering shapes in the dariss, wishing he could speak directly to them. "But I think we have to."

~

With every dodge or strike, Eyasu's limbs grew heavier. Injury and lack of rest didn't affect Azure-Seven-Seven, despite the physical form he occupied. The Raw could tell. His movements became patient, forcing Eyasu to advance, waiting for an opening.

Eyasu feinted, hoping to slash out one of Havven's tendons. The Raw stepped over the attack, spun, and slammed a booted heel into Eyasu's wrist. Even with his bracers, the blow knocked the knife from his grip. He leapt for it, but the Raw grabbed him under one armpit and hefted him into the air. His grip tightened and Eyasu's armor cracked, as pain lanced through his arm.

The Raw dropped him suddenly and spun on one heel. From the ground, he saw Deyeri slash shoulder to waist across Havven's midsection, knocking loose what little of his chest armor remained. Smoke billowed from the wound as Deyeri pressed in again. The Raw recovered in seconds, waving a hand to toss her sword away.

Then he grabbed her by the throat and squeezed.

Despite what Mavrin had said at the island, Eyasu hadn't drawn his Castoff. The entire journey back, part of his mind wondered if Mavrin had been correct all along, and his Aspect-variation was a mistake and a sacrilege. Perhaps the Aspects reforged his Castoff because They wanted him to step onto a different path and *not* use it—that seemed like a worthy test. He had no way to know, until he tried to channel.

As he yanked his Castoff from its pouch, a moment of clarity passed through him. The Aspects placed Their faith in him as much as he did Them. They saw into his soul the moment before he made a Request. He had been taught that particular words mattered so the Aspects understood what you wanted, but he wondered if instead, They needed to hear your words so that you were clear to *yourself*. To confirm whether you would follow what They saw inside you.

Eyasu followed his own faith. The Aspects knew that.

Closing his eyes, he called on the Catalyst as Core and hoped They understood.

The moment Atera took a half-step away, Breck kicked out at the back of her heel. She caught herself with a windrider's nimbleness, right before he cracked his elbow into the side of her head. He threw his leg under her, slowing her fall to the ground.

Then he grabbed her sword and ran for the sanctum.

He needed to fix this. Kedar wanted to ruin everything, but Deyeri and her misfits would only make it worse. Farglade could still be free, from the Unity and the Aspects and anyone else that tried to control them. He'd fought too much, lost too much, to let that slip away.

Two steps from the sanctum, Breck heard fighting still, and knew he had a chance.

His foot hit the base of the ramp, and everything went white.

Chapter Forty

MAVRIN STOOD SOMEWHERE ELSE.

Instead of reaching Kedar's machinery, his hand brushed a material somehow soft and pointed at the same time. When he leapt back, the same material brushed his neck. More chased him as he spun in a circle; slapping it away only helped for a second before it slapped him back. The smell registered next: sharp sweetness instead of stale underground air. And his boots squelched when he stepped. Worried about his eyes getting scratched, he squeezed them closed, trying to push his way through whatever surrounded him, but only made it two steps before his toe caught on something hard and he landed in a sprawl.

Tiny prickles under his chin made him push up from the ground, deciding that cuts across his palms were better than his face. Mavrin ended up in a crouch, arms spread wide around him, staring at the mottled, cylindrical surface of what could only be a tree.

More trees surrounded him, tightly packed with their branches almost touching, which explained why he couldn't escape. Their bark was lighter and rougher than any tree he'd seen before, and the flat, wide shapes sticking from their branches couldn't possibly be leaves; outdoor leaves couldn't grow that large in the Winds. Far more unbelievable, though, was the lush bed of green surrounding his boots, formed from thousands of individual stalks no wider than his fingernail. His stomach flip-flopped as the word came to him.

Grass.

Managing not to yelp, Mavrin hurled his way through the branches. He didn't care which direction he headed; he needed to figure out for sure where he'd been taken, and how.

The trees thinned after only a few steps and he stumbled onto a field, with that same grass rolling away into the distance. Instinctually, he looked at the sky and found it to be several shades lighter than the Lifesphere; it took him a second of bewildered staring to realize the Lifesphere was *gone*, replaced by brighter blue interspersed with mottled, white shapes floating lazily above the trees.

Clouds. He could only stare for a few heartbeats; the sky's glare was too bright. The air smelled different here, too: rot and wet and cold all at once. As Mavrin brought a hand to his brow, looking for the sun, he felt a light breeze brush his fingers, falling away as it rustled the branches nearby.

The not-quite-stillness left behind was so strange.

Where the grass ended hundreds of paces away, coppery sediment filled the gap toward a flat, glasslike surface of pale blue. It covered the horizon, reflecting the sky above. He wondered if it was enough water to get lost in.

A loud, harsh chirp startled him as a half-dozen, brilliantly red shapes burst from the trees, taking to the air. The sight of their wings flapping was finally too much for his comprehension, and he simply stood there, mouth agape, wondering if Kedar struck him before he reached her, and this was his brain hallucinating while he died on the sanctum floor.

"This isn't what I expected." Eyasu limped from the trees.

"If you're my death herald, the Presence has a curious sense of humor."

Eyasu squinted at him, and simply shook his head. Cuts and bruises marred his face, and he was missing one of the shoulder plates on his armor. He studied his Castoff with the same bemused look Mavrin leveled at everything around them.

Somehow, the old artist renderings of the Time Before Unity didn't quite capture where they stood now. The fields were always uniform, like that beadwork panel Mavrin showed Aulina in Vertsa, but this grass was wild and irregular, pockmarked with stalky things sporting fat bulbs and something crimson and fibrous crisscrossing the soil. The clouds weren't lush and puffy; the way they stretched across the sky reminded him of his garnills when they slept.

None of those depictions included the stone pillars dotting the field, either. They varied in height between two and five meters, irregular and hard-edged in a way that never would have survived long on Aelda. Their dark gray shade felt unfamiliar, but the jagged cracks of dariss cutting through each one were unmistakable, along with the crystals periodically jutting into the air.

The others emerged from the trees: Kedar. Aulina. Deyeri. And finally Azure-Seven-Seven. The Raw looked as uncertain as everyone else, but Mavrin still backed away. Or tried to. He felt his legs move, but his position relative to the others and those misshapen pillars didn't change, now that they were together.

Something moved at the edge of Mavrin's senses. It tickled at his hearing, like a whisper imagined in perfect darkness, or the sensation of almost touching someone's hand without making contact. As it left, he felt his attention pulled toward those pillars of stone and saw the unmistakable flicker of shadows moving within the dariss.

"What did you try to do?" Mavrin asked Eyasu.

He didn't answer right away, glancing around the field. "That's what They would like to know." His eyes were wet with tears. "We are with Them."

"Them? You mean . . . the Aspects are *here*?" Deyeri asked, her voice hushed in a way Mavrin had never heard it before.

"Or we're somewhere with Them. It's like when I make a Request, except . . . closer." Eyasu narrowed his eyes, focused on something Mavrin couldn't feel. "They wished to know my intent when I arrived. Now They're focused on something else."

It was Aulina who offered the answer. "Whatever was happening in Farglade, I think it stopped for now." She half-closed her eyes, concentrating. "They're speaking to the Raw. Directly, without a conduit."

Different levels of alarm crossed the faces around him. Deyeri turned wide eyes on Mavrin, but he had no idea what to say. He had accepted the Aspects would find out the truth eventually, no matter what they accomplished in the sanctum, but he hadn't processed what to do when it happened. Nor could he have ever imagined this.

Kedar looked calmest of everyone, as she swallowed and squared her shoulders. "It's here." She nodded. "Their judgment."

"Maybe." Aulina kept glancing out the corner of her eye at the pillars, as though she could hear part of whatever conversation was happening there. "I don't feel any anger from the Raw. At least, not yet."

"Maybe we should be part of that conversation," Deyeri offered.

"And what would you say?" Azure-Seven-Seven looked like he wanted to close on her, but thankfully he couldn't move any more than the others. "Go ahead. Tell them what your kind wants."

Eyasu blinked at him. "I didn't Request for you to be harmed."

"Liar."

Eyasu glared, and Mavrin saw some of the shake leaving him. "What would *you* want the Aspects to hear?"

Azure-Seven-Seven gaped at first, unsure how to respond. "That the scales should be balanced," he spat. He gestured at the illusion as though its existence proved his point. "Whether that means the end of your kind or not."

If that bothered Eyasu, he didn't show it. He looked as steady and focused as Mavrin had seen him since the Waystop. "I don't want you to be harmed. Or any of your kind. Nor the innocents in

Farglade, or my friends." He gestured to the others. "But, like you, I don't know how to achieve that."

"Ask the Aspects to decide." Kedar pointed toward the pillars. "They must know everything now."

"They aren't deciding. I'm not sure how I know that," Aulina added, more under her breath.

"If the Aspects are listening to the Raw, why are we here? Are they going to listen to us, too?" Deyeri asked, but Aulina didn't seem to have an answer.

Hearing that, Mavrin smirked. "They're putting on a show."

When Eyasu frowned at him, Mavrin said, "Remember what I told you about magic? Misdirection. Showmanship. Like petals thrown into the air." He glanced at Aulina, blinking away before he could tell whether she remembered that moment or not. "They're showing us what we lost to dazzle us. Play with our emotions. Manipulate us into something."

Deyeri frowned. "You sure you should be accusing Them . . ."

"Why not?" Mavrin threw his hands up. "We've all been at Their mercy for a long time." Not sure where to look, he fixed his attention on the sky. "You spoke to me earlier, didn't you? You must have the power to solve this. So why don't you?"

At once, the familiar creeping sensation from the island returned, shifting around him. It began at the center of his chest this time, quieting the flip-flopping in his gut before spreading outward toward his extremities. He remembered the soft longing when the Aspects moved Their attention from him, like it had been there ever since and he simply hadn't noticed. That attention had been distant before, but now he felt Their focus on him. And with it, Their expectation.

Aulina sounded wary as she said, "They want to hear from us now."

"Who does?" Deyeri asked.

"The Raw."

Azure-Seven-Seven snorted and crossed his arms, glaring at Kedar. "You told me your Saviors would decide things."

"Did you not want your kind to have a say?" Eyasu asked. "Balance?"

"Balance can be ceded or taken. The issue here is *you*. We trusted your kind too easily," Azure-Seven-Seven spat. He shifted his attention to the pillars. "Humanity destroyed this world. Almost annihilated us."

"Centuries ago," Deyeri said. "None of the people alive today—"

"Are that different from the ones I knew." Matching Mavrin, the Raw looked up at the sky. "Eliminate them. Please."

That last word contained more longing than he would have expected from Azure-Seven-Seven. It only fazed him until he remembered Deyeri's house.

"They won't decide," Aulina repeated, still concentrating. "It's like the Raw aren't putting their fate in our hands. But they want to hear from us."

Eyasu held up a hand. "Perhaps the Aspects don't know what to do, either."

"If the Aspects can't decide," Deyeri said, cocking an eyebrow, "how exactly are we supposed to?"

That's the test, Mavrin thought. Worse, he understood it. The Aspects saved Atera. They stayed at Eyasu's side when his faith was in shambles. He supposed it wasn't too great an ask to offer an opinion on what should happen next. And he couldn't blame the Raw for wanting to look humanity in the face and see what several centuries had wrought—if destroying their world and meeting their Saviors had changed them at all.

"We don't have the means to solve this," he said. He finally looked at Kedar. "Uekel's notes don't include a way to free the Raw outright?"

"Can't exist outside a vessel. Either the dariss, or . . ." She waggled a finger at Azure-Seven-Seven.

Mavrin forced himself to look at the Raw. "I understand why you want your kind released. Where would they go?"

"You are not involved. These Saviors helped you; they can help us."

"They might be regretting the Salvation now." He ignored the intake of breath from Eyasu. "You really think your determination to kill us is convincing Them to help you?"

Azure-Seven-Seven glared and didn't respond.

"The Fracture happened because of us," Mavrin mused, for the Aspects' benefit as much as himself. "The Raw are trapped because of us. We don't have the means to correct that. Yet. We'd need to study."

The cracks of dariss in those scattered pillars pulsed with light. Even without seeing them, he felt scrutinized by every Raw from the sanctum. Possibly every Raw left in existence.

"They don't trust us," Aulina said.

He nodded. "You have no reason to trust us," Mavrin said to them. "Not after the Fracture. And Uekel. And Breck." He didn't look at Kedar again. "None of us are blameless."

Anything else he wanted to say felt wrong. He didn't understand the Raw. He doubted Kedar did either, despite her claims of having listened. The person with the closest tie was Aulina, but he couldn't ask her to convince them of his honesty. Any tactic would seem like how Uekel treated them before. They deserved more than that, but all he had was desperation to survive. And the truth.

"I want to help your kind." He pointed at Eyasu and Deyeri. "So do they. But we don't have the means."

Aulina frowned. "What about later?"

"I suppose we might with time." Mavrin couldn't keep the doubt from his voice.

The Raw didn't answer. Nor did the Aspects. Admittedly, he didn't expect an answer from either. They likely sensed the things he couldn't forget—not only the lives Azure-Seven-Seven took, but the destruction Violet-Twenty wrought, too. He had trouble thinking of them as something other than a monster, despite knowing why they acted the way they did. Even now, part of him was glad they were back in his coins.

He turned to Aulina. "Violet-Twenty said they were lonely."

A new light appeared in the space between them. The swirling maelstrom of energy was about half his height, flickering in and out of space in a kaleidoscope of colors, likely including ones he couldn't see. Violet-Twenty-Four-Ten in their true form, or as close to that as his mind could fathom, brought here by the Aspects.

"Let them rejoin their kind," Mavrin said. "If they want. We can at least do that."

Aulina's shoulders drooped, suddenly calmer. "They'd like that."

The swirling maelstrom broke into a thousand tiny motes, drifting to join the dariss cracks surrounding them. Still trapped, but hopefully no longer lonely. Mavrin watched without interruption, wondering about the conversation that might be happening in those crystals, simply because it was so far from his understanding.

The dariss flashed.

"The Raw want us to try," Aulina said, eyes widening. "They'll watch us try and help them. And if we can't, or won't . . ."

The rest didn't need to be said.

Azure-Seven-Seven flexed in place but couldn't break the Aspects' hold. He called out to the pillars: "We cannot trust them. How can you possibly suggest this?"

Mavrin felt the Aspects' attention already slipping away. That must have been enough of an answer for Them. At least for now.

The illusion of Aelda, perfect in its imperfections, began to fade from sight. No one said a word, seeming lost in their respective thoughts.

Except for Azure-Seven-Seven, fixing Mavrin with a furious glare before light surrounded them again.

Chapter Forty-One

WHEN EYASU RETURNED TO THE SANCTUM, HIS blade was plunging forward, and he swerved to direct it down. The Raw jerked to a halt, staring at the dariss walls around them.

"This isn't balance. How *dare* they do this?"

Whether he meant the Aspects or his fellow Raw, Eyasu never found out. The moment Azure-Seven-Seven raised his hands to strike, they locked in place. Emotions played across his face and he whispered something rapidly, pausing before he whispered something else. Behind him, Deyeri started to rise but Eyasu warned her back.

The Raw's mouth pressed in a firm line as he trembled, fighting against whatever held him. Arcs of light erupted across his stolen body, so bright and sudden that Eyasu staggered back. Azure-Seven-Seven's mouth fell slack as the light grew more intense and the purple leeched from Havven's eyes.

When the last of the purple vanished, he collapsed and didn't move.

Mavrin stumbled sideways when he returned to the dais. Kedar's equipment had stopped thrumming, and the dariss nodes no longer glowed. The deposit around them appeared dormant. Mavrin raised his rapier anyway.

"Still imprisoned," Kedar said, ignoring him. "This wasn't supposed to happen."

"No, it really wasn't."

Something hard and metal struck Mavrin's chin before he could react to Breck's voice. From the ground, he heard a scuffle and a crash from the edge of the dais, and Aulina cry out in surprise. Through the pounding in his skull, he opened his eyes in time to see Breck barreling past, clutching some of Kedar's books under his arm.

By the time Mavrin struggled to his feet, Breck was gone.

Deyeri heard the scuffle and broke into a run, catching sight of Breck disappearing into the tunnel. Ignoring the sharp pain with every breath, she kept after him, hearing Eyasu huff upward to check on the others. Around that first bend in the tunnel, she passed Atera slumped against the wall, stunned but conscious. Breck veered down a side passage further ahead—the same one she and Eyasu found earlier, with the open chasm.

When she caught up, Breck stood near the edge, looking around in confusion.

"They still won't let me see." He spun in a circle, finally spotting Deyeri. "What happened in there, Dey?"

"We made a deal," Deyeri said between gasps. "The right deal. It's done. Please, Woldren. Let things settle." She hesitated, knowing they might need those books, but not wanting him to toss them into the void in whatever mental state this was.

Breck shook his head and tucked the books tighter under his arm. "Not yet. Whatever you decided in there doesn't help us. You don't understand what's at stake."

"What's at stake?" she snapped. Heat rose from her chest,

curling around the barrier she had snapped in place after she learned what he'd done. "What about the cost? How many people are dead because of you?"

"Not by choice! Not my choice . . ."

"Garris was your choice!"

She couldn't hold back the roar, no matter how much she didn't want another argument, or worse. They were past that, now, and she didn't have the strength to keep Breck from taking another step further away from her.

"We should've done this together. Couldn't make you listen, could I?" Breck heaved a sigh, and when he finished, the hard look of the Crossed-General was back on his face. "I'll just have to save everything on my own again."

Even as he walked out into open air, Breck didn't seem to realize what he was doing. Deyeri called out to him, one last time, but it didn't matter. It was only as he started to fall that she saw the shock on his face, before he passed from sight.

Chapter Forty-Two

AFTER SPENDING A DAY BETWEEN THE INFIRMARY, the Watch offices, and the Legislative Council's chambers, Mavrin found it more difficult to rest than he had hoped. Almost twenty-four hours after what happened in the sanctum, rather than toss and turn in nightmares that felt only moments old, he wandered the Standing Keep's grounds, studying the smoothed dirt beneath his boots and opening his collar to the Winds. He steered away from any dariss as a precaution, until someone from the Technical Academy determined whether the Raw under Farglade were as dormant as they appeared to be.

He found Aulina pacing the grounds between the Gannerthen Building and the Windroute, tossing a berrenfruit in her hands. She kept her distance from the crystal enclosure, currently guarded by four Watch. Instead of her Vertsan traveling clothes, she wore the simpler, woolen clothing favored by the Fargladeans, with weights sewn into the seams.

"Are you planning on eating that?" Mavrin asked.

The Winds were strong enough today, or the berrenfruit light enough, to carry it away slightly as Aulina tossed. She caught it deftly and kept walking, repeating the motion.

"They're smaller than average," she said as Mavrin fell into step beside her. "Means they don't bend the branches as much. The cultivators here use individual shields for each tree, so the Winds don't pluck the fruit right off."

"Not quite as sophisticated as your growing dome."

Aulina frowned at the berrenfruit. Its violet flecks were less pronounced than the ones from her family's orchard. "I know a lot about these. Planting them. Storing them. How to encourage a tree to grow sturdier. I'm not sure why, though."

"How much do you . . . ?"

"Your name is Mavrin Leed," she said. "You're a performer. You would have been a Servant or an Interpreter, if you didn't lose your faith. Now you're something else." They reached the Keep's wall and turned around. "Eyasu. Deyeri. And Atera, of course," she added, eyes crinkling for a moment.

Before he could ask about the captain, Aulina said, "We saved this city. Fought the Raw. But not the one that took my life."

Those last three words turned his stomach. He'd been fidgeting while they walked, considering an idea, and hearing Aulina speak confirmed his decision. "May I try something?"

He held out his hand. Three dariss coins sat on his palm, glittering in the Lifesphere's nighttime glow.

Aulina didn't run or slap them away, but peered down in interest. "I carried those. But not in my hands."

"Eyasu can't be sure, but he thinks Violet-Twenty's effect on your memories was accidental. Dariss is a natural conduit, and memories are ephemeral." Mavrin paused, since he doubted anyone understood what memories were. But if they could be taken by force or by accident, it stood to reason they could survive in stasis like a Raw, or the energy stored in a salt battery.

It didn't sound any less wishful when he said it out loud.

They stopped walking and Aulina held out her hand. When she gave him an impatient look, he finally dropped the coins into her palm. And waited.

Nothing changed on Aulina's face. No sudden gasp of realization or widening of the eyes as memories came rushing back. They waited a full minute before her lips formed a firm line and she closed her fist around the coins, shaking her head.

"It was worth a try, at least," she said softly.

When he placed a hand on her shoulder she nodded, letting him draw her into a hug while silent tears rolled down her cheeks. Mavrin blinked away his own, thinking of a little girl in a distant town, expecting to see her sister again.

As Aulina's tears subsided, she returned the hug and gave him a gentle squeeze. "Thank you."

"For what?"

"Trying." She surprised him with a smile. "Besides, most people deserve one hug a day."

Mavrin cleared his throat. "Whoever said that must be very wise."

As he walked away, Aulina called out softly, "Ohanna thought so." She stared out at the Windroute, clutching the coins tightly in one hand and the berrenfruit in the other. "That's her name. The person I taught that to."

"Yes, it is," Mavrin said, and decided to leave it at that for now.

The less Deyeri moved, the easier she could ignore the bruises, cracked ribs, stitches, and other reminders that heroic risks had wretched consequences.

She'd cracked ribs before, and this time didn't feel any worse. When the healers told her to expect a longer recovery, it was because they wanted to make sure she didn't return to complain when there was nothing they could do. But she knew aches and pains would be expected from a supernatural pummeling, not to mention being older every day that passed. Mavrin still gave her a worried look every time she winced or coughed, but she let him because he didn't comment on the other bruises, the ones a healer couldn't easily spot.

She tried to deal with those each morning, on her own.

Losing Breck didn't hurt as much as she expected. She'd lost him gradually, with decisions they both made that meant giving up on each other. What he said about the Raw made her wish she noticed the wrongness of his changes earlier, instead of assuming he'd simply lost himself in power and self-absolution. Especially given that final look as he fell, still burned into her mind, when it was clear he was still Woldren Breck.

Losing Termot hurt far more. Learning what happened helped; Aulina didn't know this, but Termot's daughter Cereil would have been about her age by now. Not having a body to wave the Catalyst's sign over stung. She hoped that if the Presence as Passage did let the dead watch the living, Termot would see her sitting in the Lyarnen Building's recovery room and know it wasn't because of grief or guilt.

She needed something to celebrate.

The surgeons had worked on Havven harder than a Requester. Fungal wraps littered his body in patches and long strips, completely covering his chest, neck, both hands, and more. Eyasu said he spoke briefly after being freed from Azure-Seven-Seven's control, but he hadn't woken since. Once he did, Deyeri would be the one to see how much he remembered and offer the rest, after she explained the extent of his injuries.

He deserved that.

Caspen slept in the next bed over. Her physical injuries would heal, too, but the rest would take more time to ease.

"Commander Renn?" Breck's former assistant, Idriks, stood in the doorway. He seemed to wring his hands constantly, despite being cleared of any involvement with Breck's plans. "The Legislative Council is ready for you."

She gave Havven and Caspen a parting wave on her way out, silently promising to return.

~

"... and then fold the cloth ... no, not like that. Let me show you again."

Mavrin gently coaxed the garnill back onto the indigo cloth. The bird held still as he covered her body and face, carefully layering the fabric to make the seams difficult to spot. He let Eyasu examine his work before he undid the process, setting the cloth and the garnill on the edge of the Gannerthen's fountain monument.

Eyasu hesitantly picked up the corners again.

"Remember that shouting and waving doesn't work for *my* magic. Nuance and careful attention to detail. Otherwise tricks fall apart, or the audience sees through them."

"Your commentary is not helping," Eyasu said as he slowly covered the garnill's body. She hooted encouragement, long neck twisting back and forth.

"I bet you wish you could summon forth some great light to fold this cloth for you."

Eyasu harrumphed, startling the garnill half out of the cloth. She spread her flightless wings in a lazy stretch and settled down again as Eyasu started over. When the last fold covered the garnill's eyes and snout, he raised his hands and backed away, offering Mavrin a smug smile.

A moment later the fabric fell away. The garnill blinked at Eyasu and hooted again.

"We'll try something simpler later," Mavrin said, returning the garnill to her cage. "Unless you'd prefer a rabbit?"

The Standing Keep remained closed to the public and most of the usual functionaries. The grounds and the surrounding city were almost as hushed, except for the steady sound of the Winds rattling the windowpanes and the distant clatter of repairs. Mavrin suspected this was how Farglade felt after the Incursions, and that losing their Lord-Magistrate, senior Voice, and Watch Commander didn't help people's fears.

Other than a handful here and there, ignored by the Watch

as long as peace was kept, no crowds had taken to the streets proclaiming the end of the world. The deathspeakers weren't screaming anyone's life stories at the sky. He suspected most were waiting for an official explanation about what happened, either from the Legislative Council, or the Highest Voices, or maybe the Aspects. Everyone he imagined huddled in their multistory homes looked like his mother.

"You might want to consider a new cloak, my friend."

Mavrin held up the side Azure-Seven-Seven had pierced; his hasty sewing job would need a proper patch later. He'd at least managed to wash out the bloodstain. Several other nicks and tears crisscrossed the violet fabric, and the sleeves and bottom hem had frayed and somehow burnt in one place, though he didn't remember brushing against an open flame.

He imagined stepping onstage in a new cloak and snorted. "Are you planning on trading in that ridiculous armor of yours?"

"Perhaps the one piece," Eyasu said, rubbing his shoulder through his gray linen tunic. "Inscribing the outside would take time."

"Think you'll need it, then?"

Eyasu pursed his lips. "I hope not."

They sat quietly for a while before Mavrin broached the subject. "How long do you think the Aspects will wait?"

"As long as necessary."

"What if 'necessary' means another century? By the . . ." He caught himself, frowning. "If it takes more than ten years to figure out how to help the Raw, I might die first."

"Then you won't need to worry about Their expectations."

"Sounds like a pretty obvious way to dodge Their test."

"Perhaps there is no test."

Mavrin groaned as he stretched out along the monument's outer ring, staring up at a brass spout that seemed prettier with its tiny blue flame than it must have spurting water for no reason. "I haven't slept enough lately for this kind of talk."

It was approaching evening by the time Deyeri joined them. She limped a little, occasionally shifting her posture to put less pressure on her ribs. Mavrin had made a point of not offering her any assistance, hoping his worry didn't show on his features.

"I forgot how much I hate meetings," she grumbled as she sat beside them.

"What is the Council planning to tell people?" Mavrin asked.

"Kedar turned to heresy. Murdered Breck." Deyeri rubbed the back of one of her hands, her voice carefully measured. "They have to be careful about making things public."

They'd told the Council everything about the Raw. Eyasu had been adamant, even after every time someone in authority rebuffed him. Mavrin supposed too many people saw the glowing dariss or Azure-Seven-Seven's damage to ignore the truth. The Council had been debating removing Breck from his position before Kedar activated the sanctum, so they were willing to listen to everything about every secret he kept.

"And Commander Termot? The other Watch?"

Deyeri shrugged. "Killed in the line of duty. Nothing more specific than that. They'll put blame on Kedar, if they can figure out a way to make the charges vague enough."

"Sometimes it's easier for people to suggest we ignore the darkness," Eyasu murmured. "The truth will spread. There's no stopping that now."

"Which means the Highest Voices finding out very soon," Mavrin murmured, "if they haven't heard already."

"You don't sound too worried," Deyeri said.

Mavrin pointed upward and shrugged.

"Where is Kedar now?" Eyasu asked.

"Holding room in the barracks, until they put her on trial."

"Is she allowed visitors?" At Deyeri's confused nod, he added, "The books we recovered won't be her entire collection. We'll need the rest."

As Eyasu collected his longsword and walked away, Mavrin called, “We should find a tavern later.”

Eyasu turned and smiled. “Tomorrow. It would be my pleasure.”

Deyeri stared at the fountain monument, eyes roving over the inscriptions to the previous Lord-Magistrates. Mavrin wondered if it bothered her knowing Breck’s name would be added. Not wanting to interrupt her thoughts, he idly ran his fingers along the garnill cage, until a couple hopped about inside. Deyeri didn’t glance their way.

“Rather, uh, interesting few days,” Mavrin said, and managed not to kick himself. When Deyeri didn’t respond, he added, “I don’t think I said this before, but I’m sorry about Commander Termot.” He considered before adding, “And Breck. I know you were close.”

“History,” Deyeri said. “Woldren wasn’t who I made him out to be.”

Before Mavrin could ask what she meant, she added, “That’s why the Aspects gave us philosophy and alcohol, right? To forget people can be terrible.”

“That sounds like something I used to say.”

“It is, actually,” Deyeri said. “Of course, you usually added ‘love’ at the end.”

Something fluttered in Mavrin’s stomach, unrelated to fatigue or injury. “You told me to never call you that again.”

“I remember.”

She still didn’t look at him, which Mavrin hoped meant she didn’t see his fingers twitching before he got them under control. When he started shaking out his hands and taking a few deep, measured breaths, Deyeri raised an eyebrow.

He squared his shoulders, relaxed them, and said, “May I try something, one more time?”

If crossing her arms caused her any discomfort, Deyeri didn’t show it.

Mavrin cleared his throat and extended a hand. "Hello, Deyeri. It's . . . been a long time."

"Sixteen years." She stared at him expectantly, without taking his hand.

"I found myself in town on other business and . . . got your address from a friend." Mavrin took note of the smile lines around her mouth and the strength she carried herself with, even now. "It's good to see you again."

His voice hitched a little, which bothered him, but didn't seem to bother her.

"My schedule is, well, clear right now. Would you care to go somewhere for a drink?"

Deyeri's eyebrows rose. "You're kidding, right? You look like a drunk takka wrangler who lost a fight with a dirtier drunk takka wrangler."

"I . . . well . . ." Mavrin looked down at his cloak, his rumpled shirt, and his boots, still caked in dirt and dust. "I had a waistcoat before."

When he looked up, Deyeri stood closer.

"You're an odd man, Mavrin Leed," she said. "But I've never gone for drinks with a magician before. Might be fun."

Then she linked her arm with his and led him away.

Chapter Forty-Three

FARGLADE TREATED ITS PRISONERS WELL, EYASU noted. Even someone who would stand trial for killing a magistrate and beloved war hero received a room with a decent bed, a window, and a privacy screen around the washstand and water closet.

Kedar didn't look up as Eyasu placed a stool across from her. Sweat and the metallic odor of blood clung to the room. Someone had brought her clean clothes, a rag and bucket of water, but she hadn't done more than wash her face and hands.

"I examined the tomes Breck left behind," Eyasu said. "I didn't recognize some of the authors. Or all of the languages."

He produced a leather-bound book from inside his satchel, running his hands over its blank cover. Kedar glanced up but didn't respond, even when he opened to the first page and the sketch of a blindfolded human face.

"Tell me what they wrote," Eyasu said. "And if you've hidden away more of the same. If you can, I want you to teach me this language."

"Why?" Kedar's voice was rough, even though he knew the guards kept her drinking water refreshed, too. "Won't do you any good."

He had planned on speaking to her as soon as his wounds were treated. The blessing of the Aspects didn't guarantee they would succeed in helping the Raw; if anything, the chance of failure made the test more significant. Eyasu wanted as much information as possible to help his friends, which meant exploring avenues he hadn't traveled yet. Even further ones than Kedar or Breck had searched.

Eyasu turned to the first page of foreign text. "I'm not here for lies, refusal, or judgment. I'm here to learn. You see your alternative."

Kedar snorted. When she spoke again, it was in a language he didn't understand: clipped and rapid, heavy with vowels.

"What does that mean?"

Her lips twisted. "'You won't learn anything pleasant.'"

But after a while, she took the book from him and started to read.

Eyasu didn't leave the holding cells until well after nightfall. The book he showed Kedar sat at the bottom of his rucksack with his other precious tomes, as well as new notes scribbled on his few sheets of composite. He would need more.

The Watch barracks sat on the edge of the Towers, far enough away from most residential neighborhoods to avoid feeling under observation. He turned down a different street than the one he used to get there, pulling up his hood and cinching his cloak tight against the Winds. Another Longwind was predicted soon, after the Catalyst passed across the valleys south of Farglade. He doubted many people would venture outside even if the Winds were clear.

Despite choosing roads at random, he felt attention on him after only three blocks. Not the familiar sense of the Aspects like when he channeled, but the more mundane feeling of human eyes tracking his movements. He waited until the end of the fourth street before he turned, trying to appear casual to the person tracking his movements.

The Servant of the Hidden stood in the center of the road, with the same stance as in Vertsa. At this distance he could barely make out their shieldmask glimmering in the twilight. The chains wound across their body had been tucked tighter into their off-white robes, to give them better freedom of movement if needed.

Eyasu waited, and finally they stepped to the side, vanishing into an alleyway. He made no move to follow. The Servant's message was clear enough: they weren't here to convince him of anything, this time. That likely meant they wouldn't listen, either.

Leaving Eyasu only one choice, which he had to hope the Catalyst as Core would support.

Mavrin whistled a soft tune as he returned to the Bold and Brazen, an inn across from the Standing Keep usually reserved for Unity dignitaries. Deyeri had secured a suite on the top floor for him and Eyasu until they found something more permanent. It seemed Farglade would be where he settled, for now.

No one paid him any attention as he headed upstairs. As far as the proprietor knew, he was a traveling merchant delayed until he could meet with the Council. Mavrin thought he might offer a performance later, but for now he wanted to focus on the history texts he carted from the Outreach. Deyeri would be busy with government affairs for at least a week, particularly dismantling the Watch from its post-Incursion readiness and preparing for a diplomatic mission from Veristenok. He'd barely seen Eyasu in the two days since their tavern visit, but it was about time they dug into some research together.

"There are some references in here that might—"

He stopped in the doorway to Eyasu's room. It was empty, save for the elegant bed, stone cabinet and enameled heatwell. Not simply empty—bare of any sign of his friend. Feeling strangely numb, Mavrin crossed to his room to set down the books. His garnills stared at him from their cage, and one hooted at a new bag of flavored pellets sitting beside it. That hadn't been there before.

Eyasu's things weren't tucked into one of the closets or behind a piece of furniture. No sign of his rucksack or armor. Slates covered in scrawled notes had been spread on a table in the sitting room, next to pouches of alchemical reagents Eyasu bought to resupply his stocks. None of it remained, other than two books and a note on composite. Mavrin glanced at the copies of Uyekel's *Accounts*, both Eyasu's and the damaged, bloodstained one from Kedar.

He carefully picked up the note.

> *Be well, my oldest friend.*
>
> *May the Catalyst as Core stand at your side until I return.*

He sat on the floor for a long time, staring at Eyasu's handwriting. The Winds pressed against the window, as another Longwind descended on Farglade. Somewhere out there, his friend had gone.

And Mavrin felt alone.

Acknowledgments

I've been thinking about the Acknowledgments page on my debut novel for *so long*, people. Now it's like I'm on stage accepting the award and I need to make sure I don't forget anyone. Yikes.

The obvious first acknowledgment (and a very important one) is to my editor E.D.E. Bell, for seeing something in *Catalyst* and working with me to level it up. She offered this keen insight into things I hadn't considered even after several drafts and challenged me on important preconceptions and blindspots that refined Aelda and the people in it so much. You want an editor like Emily working with you on your debut, plain and simple.

Equally important is Chris Bell for putting together a phenomenal layout and handling the logistics that make a book, you know, a book. That sort of work doesn't get as much shout-out as it should.

I don't even know where to begin on the cover. Just the early sketches made me gasp, and the finished copy made me unbelievably happy. And a gigantic thank you to my friend Sienna Tristen for bringing Aelda to life with a gorgeous map. I got to watch them sketch it in real-time over Discord, and when they showed me the draft, I had this uncanny moment of, *Holy shit, that's my world*. And this after saying to Emily, "Maybe we don't need a map . . ." Aelda took on a new level of realness thanks to Sienna, and I am over the moon.

I wouldn't be where I am as a writer without so many other creatives I'm lucky to know, beginning with the community here in Ottawa. Marie Bilodeau and Matt Moore brought me in first with warmth and openness, at a time where I'd escaped my old life and needed somewhere to belong. That led me to my mentor and friend Derek Künsken, and through him to my (much) older brother Evan May (sorry, couldn't resist, dude) and the hub of creative energy and togetherness that is Can*Con. Without that community, there are so many important people I'd never have met: Cortni Fernandez, Erin Rockfort, Kate Heartfield, Hayden and Liz Trenholm, Katie Bryski, Tyler Goodier, 'Nathan Burgoine, Geoff Gander, Avi Silver, Kelly Robson, Julie and Roger Czerneda, Violette Malan and Paul Musselman, Jay Odjick, Kevin Hearne, Tracy Townsend, Dominik Parisien, Arley Sorg and others. You're all family to me, and I consider it my great honor to know you.

There's so much I could say about the people listed above, and elements of the people I love embedded in this book. But then these acknowledgments would go on forever, and as 2022 readers know, paper is sort of a thing right now.

Thank you so much to *Catalyst*'s beta readers! In various stages, there was feedback from Marie, Suzan Palumbo, my publisher sibling Greg Wilson, Marco Cultrera, Lana Kamarić, Nick Noble, Mark Robinson, and Shireen Faisal. Special gratitude to our consultants who provided key sensitivity insight, and to Shell S. for an exceptional proofread. And a second thanks to Shireen, who's also my assistant, and frees up necessary real estate in my brain while tolerating my terrible sense of humor over email.

No one's playing the outro music over my ramble yet? Good. Special shout-out to some non-writer friends who kept me grounded the last two years, particularly as a teacher in a pandemic: Chris Saman, David Crowe, Laura Hillary, Nancy Watzenboeck, and Shelley Burnside.

I dedicated *Catalyst* to two of my grandparents, but I want to mention them one more time for being awesome. Shout-out into the great beyond to my departed paternal grandparents, Ann and John Crilly, for their advice and acceptance of everything about me. To my brother Josh for committing to strongarm people into buying this book. To my mom, for excitedly asking about everything I'm doing in Writer Land, and more. To my dad, for making his adoration clear by demanding the *first copy* of all my published works, and more.

And finally to Jess, who took the walled-off, terrified hearts of a lonely Time Lord and coaxed them out into the light. Who gives me the space to be me and accepts my idiosyncrasies as a writer. Who fills my life with inside jokes no one else would understand, and which make every day magical and wondrous. Here's to decades more of that and lots of money for Squishmallows.

-- Brandon Crilly, 2022

About the Author

An Ottawa-based teacher by day, Brandon Crilly has more than thirty published short stories to date, involving things like carbon footprint taxes, a bookstore that knows what you need, and selling your soul for a love ballad. He's a conference organizer, Twitch streamer, an award-nominated podcaster, a snake parent, and clearly needs more things to fill his time.

brandoncrilly.com

Printed in the USA
CPSIA information can be obtained
at www.ICGtesting.com
LVHW101604270723
753439LV00003B/491